THE
HIGHWAYMAN
AND
MR. DICKENS

Other books by William J. Palmer

The Detective and Mr. Dickens
The Fiction of John Fowles
The Films of the Seventies: A Social History

THE

HIGHWAYMAN
⟨⟩ AND ⟨⟩
MR. DICKENS

An Account of the Strange Events of the
Medusa Murders

A Secret Victorian
Journal, Attributed
to Wilkie Collins,
Discovered
and Edited by

WILLIAM J. PALMER

St. Martin's Press
New York

Design by Judith Christensen

Library of Congress Cataloging-in-Publication Data

Palmer, William J.
    The highwayman and Mr. Dickens : a secret Victorian journal, attributed to Wilkie Collins / discovered and edited by William J. Palmer.
        p. cm.
    ISBN 0-312-08207-X
    1. Dickens, Charles, 1812–1870—Fiction. 2. Collins, Wilkie, 1824–1889—Fiction. I. Title. II. Title: Highwayman and Mister Dickens.
PS3566.A547H54   1992
813'.54—dc20   92-20754
                                                   CIP

First Edition: September 1992

10 9 8 7 6 5 4 3 2 1

This book is dedicated to Nancy

ACKNOWLEDGMENTS

Special thanks to Professor S. F. D. Hughes.

EDITOR'S NOTE

E ven before the publication of Wilkie Collins' first commonplace book account of the meeting and subsequent adventures of Charles Dickens and Inspector William Field of the Metropolitan Protectives, Bow Street Station (in 1990, under the novelistic title *The Detective and Mr. Dickens*),* which I had the privilege and profit of editing, I wondered could there be any other lost or hitherto suppressed Collins manuscripts, perhaps detailing subsequent meetings or collaborations between Dickens and Inspector Field. Little did I know how soon and in what abundance

---

*That first commonplace book chronicled the meeting and collaboration of Dickens and Field on the bizarre affair of what the Grub Street tabloids of Dickens' and Collins' time termed the Macbeth Murders. That initial commonplace book discovery also introduced a rogue's gallery of denizens of both the Victorian underworld and the upper crust, including Irish Meg Sheehey, Scarlet Bess, Serjeant Rogers, and especially one Tally Ho Thompson, a highwayman turned actor.

those wishfully imagined secret journals would surface out of one hundred years of suppression.*

In January of 1991, two months after the initial publication of the first Collins journal, I received a phone call from Mr. Allerdyce Clive, the Special Collections Curator of the library of the University of North Anglia. "Professor Palmer," his voice crackled from across the ocean, "we received four more boxes of papers as part of the Warrington bequest and I have only now been able to open and begin inventorying them. You are going to be quite interested in what I have found." I knew immediately that he had discovered more Collins papers. I hoped beyond hope that there might be another complete commonplace book continuing the story begun in that first secret journal.

"You've found another Collins manuscript?" I asked.

"No, sir," Mr. Clive answered, and I slumped in my chair. "I've found *five* more full volumes. I think you'd better come and look at them."

It was an incredible literary discovery. I was on the next plane to England.

This memoir, which, consistent with the first, I have titled *The Highwayman and Mr. Dickens*, is the earliest in date of composition of those five commonplace books discovered in the late additions to the Warrington collection. It seems that the original collection, which I had explored during the editing of that first Collins journal, had come from the country home of George Warrington. These new papers, however, had arrived later due to a delay in selling the deceased's London flat, and the neglect in packing and transporting the furnishings and papers therein.

---

*These newly discovered commonplace books were composed between the time of Dickens' funeral in 1870 and Collins' death in 1889. From the internal evidence of Collins' own description of their composition (see his opening Prefatories to this commonplace book), they provided him with a vehicle for memory and the loyal fulfillment of his debt of friendship which he felt he owed his mentor, greatest benefactor, and closest friend, Charles Dickens.

George Warrington's estate bequeathed the papers of his great-grandfather, Sir William Warrington, the renowned Lincoln's Inn solicitor and personal counselor to Wilkie Collins (as well as Queen Victoria), to the University of North Anglia. This new discovery consisted of five full commonplace books, all covered in the best leather, and written in the same crabbed hand with which I became so familiar while editing that first journal. Upon arrival in England, and after the examination and authentication of these manuscripts, I was invited by Mr. Clive and the Regent General of the university to undertake their editing for a wider publication.

This memoir of Dickens, Inspector Field, and himself, written (as was the first) in the style of a novel as befits its author, begins with a brief preface in which Collins testifies as to why he writes these private journals, which were not intended for publication until long after the deaths of the principals. Following that brief statement of motive, this journal launches itself rather indecorously (for a Victorian writer) into its narrative. What this rather sexually charged opening indicates is that, in the interim since writing the first secret journal, Wilkie Collins became much more honest and more uninhibited.*

Once again, however, Dickens is the central focus and driving force of the events of these journal pages. His relationship with Inspector Field is one of those felicitous pairings of history from which myths are born. Whereas the first commonplace book of Wilkie Collins presented a driven, tortured Dickens, this new discovery presents a fiercely loyal Dickens, a man determined to pursue the responsibilities of friendship

---

*By closest estimate, this second commonplace book was begun in October 1870, some five months after Charles Dickens' death and approximately six weeks after the completion of the first commonplace book published under my title, *The Detective and Mr. Dickens*. As the first journal was begun under the impetus of a chance meeting with Field at Dickens' funeral in Westminster Abbey, this second memoir is also begun, as Collins explains in his "Prefatories," under the impetus of another chance meeting, with Forster, Dickens' authorized biographer.

to the furthest limits of personal risk. And always, above it all, looms Field, the master magician of this violent London world.

—William J. Palmer

PREFATORIES

October 25, 1870

I t is staggering how memory, once set in motion, races along at the pace of the night mail. The memory of Charles's ceremonious funeral in the Abbey continues to rest heavy upon my mind, but my meeting with Inspector Field on that sad occasion seems to have propelled not only my memory but also my pen on a breakneck dash, as if whipped by De Quincey's mad coachman. In the weeks following that meeting at the funeral, I managed to fill a complete leather book with the narrative of Dickens's and my first collaboration with Inspector Field. And now, after a needed hiatus during which I took an invigorating walking tour of the Scottish hills, lo, memory draws down on me again, orders "Stand and deliver," and I find myself emptying the contents of my past into another journal that I will never publish and perhaps the world will never see until we all have joined Dickens in a much larger novel written by a much more inventive and ruthless novelist than I.

I must confess, however, that this writing down of Dickens's and my adventures with Field, Rogers, and the rest has proven quite a satisfying diversion, given me a sense that I am, at least, chronicling some unknown biographical facts in the life of a great man. I see no reason to cease the recording of these memoirs, and I see excellent reason to go on. First, I owe it to Charles. He was my patron, my mentor; he made me the novelist I became, staked me to the small corner of recognition and reputation that I ultimately gained. But there is a better reason for continuing.

I encountered Forster—that pretentious boor!—in the foyer of the British Museum this morning. He loftily informed me that he was one hundred pages into a biography of Charles. That dire announcement merely stiffened my resolve to press on with the private memoirs that I have begun.* Immediately upon leaving Forster and the museum, I ducked into Lett's Apothecary and Sundries and impulsively bought myself a fresh leather book. I cannot deny that writing down these memories entertains my bachelor nights, and I truly intend for only my heirs to see this record of our underworld adventures. Nonetheless it gives me solace to know that Forster's crabbed and proper version of Dickens's life will not be the only one extant.

But there lies one other satisfaction, which would be hypo-

*Collins' biographers note this rivalry between Collins and Forster for Dickens' favor both before and after "the Inimitable's" death. Kenneth Robinson in *Wilkie Collins: A Biography* (1951) writes: "The references to Collins in Forster's *Life* are deliberately reduced to a minimum and pay scant justice to the part he played in the last twenty years of Dickens' life. It is difficult to attribute such omission to any other motive than jealousy. Later biographers of Dickens have taken their cue from Forster and are content to deplore instead of trying to explain the undoubted influence of Collins on the other novelist . . . but there is little doubt that in Collins' company he spent some of the happiest periods of his life" (p. 63). Nual Pharr Davis in *The Life of Wilkie Collins* (1956) also writes: "Wilkie had an inner callousness, a cool skepticism toward Victorian proprieties that made him good company for Dickens. . . . the association with Dickens, disposed in his restless mood to long talks and unconventional meetings, was fruitful. Dickens confirmed the still-vague theories Wilkie had begun to form on what fields of experience were the proper subject of art" (pp. 98–99).

critical of me not to acknowledge. These memoirs are not only biographical, but autobiographical as well. When, some five months ago, I first sat down to write about Dickens and Field, I never imagined how much of myself would intrude into their story. Writing about myself as if I were a character in a novel was a strange experience indeed, yet a rather exhilarating and informative one. Writing about Meggy helped me to understand how much force for change that extraordinary woman exerted upon my life. I have always perceived the social and personal irrationality of my obsessive attraction to Irish Meg, but it was not until I wrote my feelings and dealings with her down (more than twenty years later), that I began to understand why I fell in love with her. Her spontaneity and sexuality completely opened up my life; she liberated me from the prisonhouse of my repressive society, and also from the accepted language of my novel-writing art. These journals tell the truth in ways that my fellow Victorian writers, including Dickens, never dared to attempt. Meg instructed me in the ways of love (in fact, addicted me to them), and gave me a new voice that only now have I found the temerity to employ.

Mister Dickens's "faithful bulldog" is how I described myself in that first journal recounting Charles's and my adventures in the world of Inspector Field. And his faithful bulldog I remained for all of his life. If, indeed, these memoirs are any indication, his faithful bulldog I continue even now that he is gone. Inspector Field's dogged Serjeant Rogers is certainly my counterpart, for he has faithfully followed his master through life as I did mine.

Ah, twenty years of memories, of Dickens, of Field, of Rogers, of all the others. These private memoirs are my way of paying my debt to the past, of erecting the only sort of memorial that I, a writer of novels, can dedicate to my lifelong friends.

Perhaps that is why I have become so obsessed with chronicling Dickens's and my adventures on duty with Inspector Field. Perhaps as one approaches the end of one's life, especially a life that has been immersed in fictions, one longs to tell the truth of one's experience in hopes that the future will judge one's existence kindly. Perhaps it is not so important that the truth be told about one Wilkie Collins or one William Field, but generations to come will clutch for the truth about our "Inimitable" and perhaps my memories will help them to understand him.

AN INCONVENIENT KNOCK

January 9, 1852—early evening

Our second adventure on duty with Inspector Field began one evening (not too late, half past eight or so) with an inconvenient knock on the door of my new lodgings in Soho.

I had taken these new rooms for clandestine, even sinister, reasons that I could never discuss anywhere but in this secret journal. Since beginning these journals under the ghostly inspiration of "the Inimitable" on the day of his great funeral in the Abbey, I have found a new freedom of expression never before attempted in my writing, whether journalism, conversational essays, or my fictions. As for my sinister reasons, only my own guilt makes them so.

That timid knock on my new door was indeed inconvenient. When it came, Irish Meg had, only moments before, mounted me and was riding to the finish like some wild-eyed, red-maned prancer in the Ascot Derby. You see, Meggy and all of her attractions were the sum of my dark motives for letting more spacious bohemian lodgings, and we had been together nearly eight months, since the Ashbee affair.*

I had changed lodgings in early September so that she could become my private secretary. The Soho rooms consisted of two flats, a larger set of four rooms including a small kitchen, and a pair of smaller rooms across the hallway that Meg occupied. To public scrutiny, I was not keeping her; she was not living in my household. At first, I was a picture of guilt when, in September, we moved into this utterly transparent (it seemed to my prudish mind) love nest. In Soho, however— as Meg had predicted—no one paid us any attention. The landlord was ecstatic to have a gentleman tenant, and, over time, I grew accustomed to the idea of our licence.

Our domestic arrangements proved more than satisfactory. In return for her bed and board, Meggy had taken to learning secretarial skills. She handled my correspondence by slow dictation and even helped me in some of my researches. She had eagerly given off whoring—well, not completely, as at moments like this when she gloried in playing the whore. She took great pleasure in tweaking my gentleman's discomfiture at her outrageous behaviour and fanning the flames of my ungentlemanly desire. In my earlier memoir, I described Irish Meg Sheehey as "the fire-woman" upon first meeting her as she sat drinking gin before the hearth at Bow Street Station, her red hair blazing in the firelight. Since then, touching her fire had become as obsessive for me as was Ashbee's opium addiction or Dickens's attraction to his childlike Ellen. Irish Meg knew that I wanted her to continue to play the part of the whore for me (even though she had abandoned the role for others), and she played it to perfection. She had divined my voyeuristic appetites that night we were thrown together after

*For those who have not yet read *The Detective and Mr. Dickens*, the first suppressed journal discovered amongst the Collins papers, Lord Henry Ashbee was the gentleman rake, whoremonger, opium addict, pornography collector and author, and member of the notorious defloration society, The Dionysian Circle, who was the principal antagonist of Dickens and Inspector William Field in the events recorded in that first manuscript.

the Queen's performance of our amateur play, *Not So Bad As We Seem,* at Devonshire House. That night, Dickens had dressed her in elegant clothes like an Irish lady to surprise me and to reward her. But after all the festivities were over, and the door of my bachelor rooms closed behind us, Meg slowly shed her royal guise and seized her whore's role once again. She spoke to me coarsely and provocatively as her satiny dress slid down her body to the floor, revealing her secret things. Meg saw in my eyes that night their joy in watching her undress, how they feasted upon her body while the rest of my being stood paralysed in her spell. All novelists must be voyeurs, elst how would they ever find the material of reality out of which to stitch the garment of their fiction?

I swear that Meg was like no other woman of our age. She revelled in exploring the depths of her sexual eccentricity. She insisted that love was to be made either in the flickering light of candles—"the romantick glow o' first love," she called it—or in the livid glow of blazing gaslamps—"wanton fuck-ing," her term. "Myking luv, at's a gift for all the senses," she insisted that seductive night when I asked if she wished me to trim the lamps. "These Victorian 'lye-dees,' these respectable tarts oo' calls themselfes 'wives,' who turns all the lamps off an' won't drop their dresses 'til the whole nyebor'ood, inside an' outsyde, all the way ta the bloomin' river, is black as pitch, they only myke love ta the touch, tykes all the fun out o' bein' a 'ore, which they is no matter what's adornin' their finger.

"But rel love (an' wanton fuckin') is myde ta all the senses," she whispered. "Yew needs to taste an' smell an' touch an' 'ear an' especially see yer lover, look into yer lover's secret places, the seein' . . . 'at's all the fun."

In those first idyllic months of our life together in that Soho retreat, Meggy insisted that our sex was an exploration, a journey into the senses. She was an explorer, like Stanley in Africa. No, rather like Burton and Speke questing for the source of the Nile among the mountains of the moon. Ah, the moon, age-old symbol of imagination! It controls sexuality just as it controls the tides. Irish Meg knew this well. "Yew

7

wish ta watch me strip myself for yew, do yew not?" she would taunt me. "Yew wish ta see me touch and caress myself for yew, do yew not?" It is said that Burton always explored every inch of the bodies of his nubian concubines with a candle before enjoying them. Meggy, too, was an explorer into countries where my fellow Victorians feared to go. Ah, but I romanticise! Yet, as I get older and more realistic, and my age more rigid and utilitarian, that romanticism, whereby the imagination turns our mundane reality into myth, seems so much more real and necessary.

As Meg grew more comfortable in my rooms and in my bed, especially after the move to the Soho establishment, our lovemaking became a show that she would script, stage, and expertly perform. She insisted that I allow her to buy the finest lace, satin, and silk underthings, and she wore only black and red beneath her clothes. She would pose for me in her black silk stockings held up by a thin, lacy belt with pearl buttons, or in her red bone-corset audaciously laced between her overflowing breasts. She delighted in slowly removing her secret things, in unbuttoning, unlacing, sliding her silken underthings off her skin, rolling her stockings slowly up with her legs stretching into the air. With her stockings gartered to her waist, but with no underthings covering her Mount of Venus, she would perform the most extraordinary trick, which I found irresistible. Lying on her back on the bed with her legs tight together showing but a glimpse of her red nether ringlets, she would raise her legs straight up in the air from her waist until her toes pointed directly to the ceiling. As if opening the covers of a book, she would slowly open her legs to the sides and then, somehow, opening her legs even further, she would bend her knees back toward her breasts and wickedly smile. " 'Tis all yers, Mister Collins, sir. Yew paid ta see it." Is it any wonder that I so quickly grew addicted to this book that she opened just for me?

Constantly she mocked my gentleman's reticence in the face of my goatish susceptibility to her temptations. She laughed at how easily seduced I was, how involuntarily the word "love" seemed to leap to my tongue while I delighted in listening to the streams of coarseness that flowed from hers. Even writing about this initiatory period of my life with such uncharacteristic licence from the distance of a full twenty years makes me feel like some dessicated old voyeur spying on the unsuspecting young as they play their fleshly games. But those young were us, long gone, Meg and I forever frozen in a kiss. Writing thus, even for such a brief space in something as harmless as a secret diary, helps me to understand how Henry Ashbee, still heated from his nighttime encounters, could turn straight to his manuscript, his so-called *Memoirs of a Victorian Gentleman*, and record in detail each fevered word, provocative gesture, and wanton movement of his night's conquest. In his twisted way, he was attempting to stave off death (or perhaps impotence). And now, life is indeed ironic, I am imitating him . . . because I long to remember: Meg, my young self, and my first complete addiction to a woman.

"What is it Mister Collins wants?" Irish Meg would beckon from the bed as I stood barelegged in only my shirt at its foot. She lay on her back with her legs apart caressing herself. In the slow divesting of her "secret things" lurked the truth of the alluring possibilities beneath the surface of Victorian life.

"Is this what Mister Collins wants?" she would softly taunt as she continued to caress herself there.

"Does Mister Collins wish to kiss this?" she gently teased, opening herself with her fingers.

Then rolling, suddenly, over on her stomach and pushing up on her elbows to her knees to slowly rotate her full derrière, she would mock my voyeur's hesitance: "Or does Mister Collins want me here tonight?" she would laugh evilly.

Sometimes she would prowl the room like a sleek cat, stop in the firelight or candle glow and touch herself provocatively, offering, beckoning. Her "come hither" look as she stood in her secret things bit into me like a hook. She was a temptress out of myth, but not past myth. She was no whore of Babylon, no Circe or Cleopatra. It was as if she were a mythic figure from the future, some fire goddess from the next century transmigrated into this cold Victorian world to mock its hypocrisy.

It was the race she ran with me, and that race was galloping to its finish when that inconvenient knocking upon my door reined it in.

Odd, is it not? I sat down to recount the events of Dickens's and my second adventure with Inspector Field and now it is almost suppertime and I have only written about myself and Meg (and in ways that even I find shocking). This journal is reading like Sterne's *Tristram Shandy*. It began with a knocking upon my door and yet, a goodly number of pages later, that door still has not been opened.

But that knocking at my door, from twenty years in the past, which precipitated this chain of violent events, still echoes in my imagination as clearly as when it interrupted Meggy and me *in flagrante delicto*.

"Good God, who is that?" I disengaged from our passionate course.

"Wot the bloody 'ell!" Meg rolled off me more than a bit dismayed.

There was a scurrying to make ourselves presentable, and, for safety's sake, Meg stayed behind the bedroom door. I hurried to answer the now more insistent knocking.

When I opened the door, Scarlet Bess burst in as if impelled by demons. Her face bore the desperate look of frightened children and suicides. "Oh Mister Collins, oh pleese"—her hands clawed blindly at my shirt front—" 'ees bin tyken up, sir. 'Ee needs yew, sir. Oh pleese! Oh pleese 'elp me, 'elp 'im."

Her frantic pleas brought Meggy out of the bedroom. "Bess, wot's wrong? Wot is it, luv? Don't cry now. Wot is it?" Meg's voice was like a mother's calming her child, protective and loving. The woman's ability to move from one role to another with such facility and skill never ceased to amaze and amuse me. She was a consummate actress.

Strange that both Dickens and I were so hopelessly captivated by these actresses. I am convinced now that it was the uncertainty of them, the inability to possess a single woman

10

but always being forced into the pursuit of many different women. His beloved Ellen and my Meggy exhibited protean powers, that slippery ability to change shape and elude one's grasp.

Is it not curious that this memoir is embarking very unlike the first? This second memoir seems to be developing as little more than a glorification of my own depravity. But our second adventure on duty with Inspector Field was not at all about myself and Irish Meg. Rather, it was about friendship and loyalty fighting betrayal and murder. That pull of friendship first asserted itself when Scarlet Bess burst into my rooms and Irish Meg so tenderly took her under her wing.

"Wot is it, Bessy?" Meg cajoled.

"Fieldsy 'as 'ad 'im tyken up for mordor, my Tally 'O," Bess sobbed within the protective circle of Meg's arms. "My Tally 'O's no mordoror. 'Ee's innersent. This tyme 'ee's innersent. 'Ee wos with me the 'ole night las' night, I sweer."

"I know. I know," Meg soothed, but her eyes met mine over her charge's shoulders and they were pleading for help. The next voice I heard was my own, though I had no sense of forming words or formulating coherent thoughts.

"Now let us not have any swearing just yet, Bess"—that distant voice inexplicably seemed rather calm and unhurried—"the whole world, especially Inspector Field, knows that you would swear to anything where Thompson is concerned."

"But Mister Collins, sir," she protested. " 'Ee reelly wos with me las' night. 'Ee's innersent, I tells yew."

Our friend Tally Ho Thompson, former highwayman, housebreaker, pickpocket, whatever, was certainly far from "innersent" as she so quaintly put it, but that was my judgement upon his whole personality while Bess was clearly only referring to his hand in the violent events of the last twenty-four hours. "Now calm down and tell us what has happened, Bess," said my voice, which seemed to be functioning independently of my still somewhat rattled self, as I calmly led her to a chair.

11

"It's Fieldsy," Bess insisted, "jus' 'cause they found 'im neer 'er, 'ee thinks 'ee did it . . . an . . . an Fieldsy's 'ad 'im thrown in Newgate."

It had been almost eight months since our first collaboration with Inspector Field, but Dickens and I had not neglected our detective friend. We had visited Bow Street Station a number of times in the course of our evening ambulations, but it had been well over a month since we had last seen Field. Dickens had spent most of the holidays working on the first number of *Bleak House*, frolicking with his family and conducting the typically elaborate Christmas festivities in their home, Tavistock House. The great hall of that new manse was hung so thickly with Christmas greens that Forster remarked in his usual dour way that it looked more like Sherwood Forest than Christ's birthplace. I also had been much involved in my first holiday celebration in my new lodgings . . . with Irish Meg. The last time we had seen Field had been in November when we had accompanied him and Rogers to an inquest in Cook's Court just off Chancery Lane. One night while sitting before the hearth in the bullpen at Bow Street, Field had mentioned that the inquiry into a mysterious death was to be held the next day. Dickens had leapt at the opportunity to attend, which the next morning we did. To me, it had all seemed a horrible waste of time—an obscure scrivener addicted to opium had died of an apparent miscalculation in his dosage—but when the second number of *Bleak House* appeared containing the Nemo section and the subsequent "inkwich," it was all there, word for word, street urchin for street urchin, beadle for beadle, and deceased for deceased.

Out of Bess's hysterical sobbing, Meg managed to extract the sequence of events that had precipitated her knocking upon our door. The murder of a woman had been discovered, and Bess's lover, Tally Ho Thompson, who was acting the role of Poins in the new production of Shakespeare's *Henry IV*, had been taken up for the crime.

It was a splendid production with horses riding on- and

12

offstage, and Thompson had proven just their man. Macready had retired from acting after his last performance in *Macbeth*, but he had stayed on in his position as director of the Covent Garden Theatre, and Thompson (probably due to the association with Dickens) had, from the beginning, been a favourite of Macready. Not only did Tally Ho Thompson act the riding and duelling and fighting parts onstage, not only did he possess a marvellous name to grace the programs, but he took care of the horses as well. He had proven himself invaluable to the company, and the resulting steady employment at good wages had allowed him and Scarlet Bess (who, like Meg, was now off the streets) to take modest accommodations in Seven Dials.

"My Tally 'O could never mordor no poor girl like yew nor me," Bess, on the verge of fainting, wailed. "Yew's got to 'elp us, Mister Collins. Yew an Mister Dickens, yew could talk to 'im, tell 'im my Tally 'O could niver mordor no poor girl."

Meg, cradling the poor girl in her arms, looked up at me, and I realized I had no choice in the matter. Little did I know how much more complicated than Bess's sketchy version the matter truly was. Nor did I realise just how inconvenient that knock on my door was.

DICKENS AND FIELD, TOGETHER AGAIN

January 9, 1852—night

I surprised a hansom lurking in the Soho dark; its proprietor dozing on the box, its four-legged engine breathing smoke in the winter chill. It was greatcoat, heavy woolen scarf, and hold-on-to-your-hat weather. The wind off the river stung our faces. We closed ourselves snugly into the cab, which maneuvered slowly through the grimy narrow Soho streets before it clattered off into the Charing Cross Road.

The awakened cabman, grateful even for a short trip across the West End on such a night, thought nothing of the stout young man in the tiny spectacles clambering into his cab flanked by two statuesque caped women. I am sure he assumed I was some night-stalking gentleman who had commandeered two Soho whores. I am sure that he assumed I needed transport to the scene of my planned trinitarian perversions; or, perhaps, he was resigned to his cab being the site, albeit rather cramped, of my double assignation. Whatever he thought, he must have steeled himself for the worst. He merely grunted from beneath his great black muffler and crooked hat when I tapped on his seat with my stick and shouted up, "Number Sixteen Wellington Street, Strand!"

I was fairly certain that Dickens would be there this blustery night. After the frenetic activity of the Christmas holidays and the welcoming of the New Year, Kate, once again "in her Anti-Malthusian state" as Dickens put it, had taken the children and servants from Tavistock House and withdrawn to Great Malvern to rest under the care of the family physician, Doctor Southwood Smith.* Since the departure of his family from Tavistock House, Dickens had reverted to his familiar bachelor schedule of working long hours in the Wellington Street offices and sleeping on the premises in order to begin the next day at an early hour. The iron bedstead which he had ordered hauled in before he even commenced publication of *Household Words* (and which from the beginning I had speculated to be simply an excuse for not going home to his wife at night) still graced the Wellington Street offices. Besides his usual fierce editing of *Household Words,* he was digging in on the second number of *Bleak House.* He had completed the first number just before the holidays and, even during the hilarity of the New Year's celebrations, had expressed his eagerness to get back to work on his novel. Thus, I expected to find him there, if only he hadn't gone out for one of his insane walks.

Dickens's restless walking of London at night was one of the idiosyncrasies of which few were aware. Since early in our acquaintance I had been privileged to accompany Charles on his night walks into some of the most disreputable pockets of our rapacious and decaying city, and to this day I still do not fully understand why so often of an evening, no matter the weather, he felt compelled to be up and prowling his beloved

---

*Doctor Smith, some ten years later, became famous for concocting a fizzy mixture that when dissolved in water proved indispensable for the release of stomach gas in pregnant women. In the Victorian era, Smith's Seltzer became such an apothecary shop staple that it was used by that population unburdened with child yet afflicted with that state's discomforts.

streets. I had given the psychological motivation underlying his obsessive walks hours of speculation: he had a compulsive need to feed his novelist's memory by observing the city's night life; walking stimulated his imagination in the way that carnality stimulated that of our scurrilous friend Ashbee; the act of sitting and writing all day occasioned a physical restlessness which drove him out into the night streets after dinner; or, perhaps it was a fear of indigestion or insomnia that pushed him to exhaust himself physically each night before retiring. But no matter how much time I invested in thought upon the subject, I still had not the slightest idea what attractions those damp, fog-bound, pestilent, narrow, ill-lit, dangerous streets held for my "inimitable" friend. Perhaps it was simply the risk he craved.

Whatever his motives, Dickens loved his night streets and had, from the beginning of our friendship, honoured me with the standing invitation to accompany him on his headlong treks. "It's good for both the circulation and the imagination, young Wil," he would say before we set out, like intrepid explorers, into the wilds of London. But, once again, I have wandered off into a Shandy-esque digression while our hansom cab is rapidly approaching Wellington Street.

While we were galloping across the town, Scarlet Bess remained in her violently agitated state, despairing under the prospect of her beloved Thompson going to the gallows. Meg consoled her in the corner of the cab as best she could while I agonised over the probability of Dickens still being in. But the wind was up so fierce and the hour was so early that I hoped this night he had forgone the streets for the comfort of the office hearth. My head out the window as we rounded the corner off the Strand and turned up Wellington Street, I saw the gaslamps still ablaze in the second storey. Our cab clattered to a halt and we three tumbled out. "Wait here! You are engaged!" I ordered the cabman even as I was rushing to knock on Dickens's door.

In contrast to the turbulent events of the previous spring when his father and his tiny daughter had died, when *House-*

17

hold Words had been just underway, when he had *Not So Bad As We Seem* in rehearsals for the Queen's Performance, and, of course, when we had first gone on duty with Inspector Field and he had been captivated by young Ellen Ternan, Dickens's life in the fall and winter of 1851 had become regularised. I must admit that I had been quite preoccupied with Irish Meg and thus had not been so frequently with Charles of an evening. Yet I perceived that his life had calmed. For the next twenty years I would observe how that tranquillity always seemed to come upon him when just beginning a new novel (and *Bleak House,* as he had described its general contours to me, promised to be his largest undertaking yet, even more ambitious in its social exploration than had been *Dombey and Son*). Since November he had been writing steadily on it, even while editing *Household Words* with his customary imperiousness, even while installing his family in the new manse. But no matter how domestic or scheduled or intent upon composition Dickens's life became, he still needed to feed his addiction to the night streets.

This night, however, he was still in. "Ah, Wilkie, what a well-timed surprise," he said as he answered my knock. "I was just getting ready to go out for a walk. We haven't had one together in weeks." Only then did he see the two women in my company, which occasioned an "Eh? What's this?"

"Honestly, Charles, I don't really know," was all the satisfaction I could give. "It's all rather a garble so far. And Bess isn't helping by shaking into hysterics every minute or so."

"Oh Mister Dickens, sir, they's tyken up my Tally 'O an' they's goin' to 'ang 'im," she blubbered.

"Please, come in out of the wind." He ushered us in and fastened the door. As we climbed the steps to his office and living quarters, he whispered behind the two women's backs, "What is it, Wilkie? Has he killed someone?" It was then I saw the fire of anticipation blaze up in his eye. I knew in a trice that he was excited at the prospect of some new adventure that might provide some new material or characters for some new novel. Of course, that certainly was not all that he was

18

thinking at the time. The fire in his eye was his sensing that once again we were at the centre of the action of real life, of murder and mystery and the eternal muddle of his night streets. The art of it would come later.

He sat Meg and Bess by the fire, which was burning low, and directed me to a nearby chair. A brandy bottle materialised out of thin air and a clipped "Glasses, Wilkie," propelled me to the cabinet. He poured for the three of us, poked up the fire, then settled, half-standing, half-sitting, on the edge of his capacious desk. He waited while the women sipped.

"Bess, what is it? What has happened?" he finally broke the silence.

The brandy had somewhat restored Scarlet Bess to her senses, but I usurped her turn to speak: "Bess and Meg came to me for help, Charles," I lied. I had not mentioned my arrangement with Irish Meg, our shared domicile, to Dickens, but, nonetheless, I was rather sure that he had guessed at our relationship. Meggy glared at me for this denial. Fear of her speaking out spurred me on: "It seems Thompson has been taken up, though it is all quite confused."

Dickens ignored my nervous intrusion. He moved to one knee in front of Scarlet Bess. "Bess," he quietly prompted (I had seen him act the same reassuring fatherly part with the Ternan girl eight months before), "Bess, tell me what has happened."

" 'Ee's in terrible trouble now, 'ee is, Mister Dickens," she stammered. "With 'is past they'll 'ang 'im sure this time. They think 'ee mordored some poor girl. My Tally 'O'd niver mordor no poor girl, Mister Dickens. Fieldsy's gone an put 'im in Newgate."

"Newgate!" Dickens gasped. It was that word that seemed to drive home the gravity of the situation. "This *is* serious"— he looked to me, then shifted his gaze to Meggy. "Go on, Bess"—he took her firmly by the shoulders as she began, once again, to shake with sobs.

" 'Ee'd jus' niver do sech a thing." Her voice was soft and

19

pleading. "All I knows is 'ee's been tyken up for a mordor an is in Newgate since las' night."

"You told me he was with you all last night." My voice was surprised. "How could he be with you and still be taken?"

She stared blankly at me. Meg glared, fire darting from her eyes to lick at my indiscretion. *You are not helping in this matter at all,* her look warned. I stifled any further impulse toward accusation or truth.

Dickens rose from his position between Bess and the fire, patted her gently on the shoulder, and moved to my side. Silently, with a hand on my elbow, he drew me up out of my chair and across the room into the bay window, well away from the women.

"Charles, what should we do?" I kept my voice down.

"Is this all we know, Wilkie?"

I nodded a silent assent.

"Did Field arrest him?"

"That is what she seems to think," I answered.

For Dickens, there was not a moment's hesitation: "Then, of course Wilkie, we must help him now. God knows he has helped us in the past, and Field as well."

For Dickens, this was not about murder or the reliability of either Tally Ho Thompson or Scarlet Bess, nor was it about guilt or innocence. It was simply about friendship and loyalty between men of the streets, simply about the paying back of old debts. After all, as I look back at it now after twenty years, Tally Ho Thompson had helped Dickens find and save his Ellen. He had helped Dickens, like some swashbuckling Sam Weller or some trick-riding Sancho Panza, play knight-errant.

In mere moments the four of us were crowding back into that hansom cab under the uncomprehending gaze of its drowsy driver and its sloe-eyed horse.

"The Protectives Station in Bow Street. Quickly," Dickens gave the order this time.

We clattered out of Wellington Street and straight up the Strand to Bow. The bells of St. Martin's-in-the-Fields pronounced a doleful ten of the clock and the traffic was thick on both sides as the theatres were just letting out. We weaved our way between coaches and made Bow Street after a respectable interval. No one spoke during this short traverse. As we rolled through the traffic, I observed the return of that same coiled tenseness that had possessed Dickens during that long night eight months ago spent in hot pursuit through the rain and fog of London's streets after the fleeing Ashbee and his young captive, Ellen Ternan. I had observed then Dickens's violent agitation at the thought (and reality) of Miss Ternan in danger, as well as his tenderness when she finally was delivered from that danger. Choosing discretion, however, I had not inquired of her since. I knew that she (under an agreement struck between Dickens and Inspector Field) had never been charged or put on trial for the death of Paroissien the rapist. I also knew that she had been placed, under a fictional name (again by the arrangement of Dickens), in Urania Cottage, Miss Angela Burdett-Coutts's Home for Fallen Women. But that was all I knew of Ellen at that time and Dickens never proffered one word about her. It was only recently, when Field and I talked away that afternoon in the public house under the shadow of the Abbey on the day of "the Inimitable's" state funeral, that I learned how Dickens visited her there every week as if he were John Jarndyce and she were his ward of the court. But again I digress. This second commonplace book feels burdened by the past. Tally Ho Thompson's incarceration had suddenly called in all those past debts. This time Dickens was not off to play St. George, but rather was acting like a biblical father setting out to rescue his prodigal son.

The gaslamps blazed like inquiring eyes on the face of Bow Street Station.

"Stay here," Dickens ordered our seemingly catatonic cabman. "We will need you yet again tonight."

"Not a tuppance 'as 'oi seen yet, guv," the man complained, startling us all with his first words, nay, signs of sentience.

Dickens passed him up a handful of shillings. "You are

21

ours for the night. You will be well paid," he assured the driver who, after clutching the money in his ragged paw, slipped back into his customary doze.

Serjeant Rogers sat in command at the front desk in the act of dispatching two constables on business when the four of us streamed through the front door of the station house. He was his same ruddy, bewhiskered, officious self, a thick block of granite with the disposition of a jealous schoolboy. He didn't like Dickens and me because he considered no one but himself qualified to consult with Inspector Field on any criminal matter. Field was Rogers's private park and he considered us poachers.

"Mister Dickens," he barked, ignoring me, "yee've caught hus hon hay busy night."

"We must see Inspector Field right away"—Dickens faced him down—"about this Thompson affair."

"Yes, huv course, hi hunderstand." Rogers was backing slowly toward the door of the bullpen attempting to placate Charles with repetitious gibberish. "Hi'll tell him, hi'll hask him, hi'll tell him you har here—"

But Dickens was not in the mood for waiting to be announced. As soon as Rogers turned the knob on the bullpen door, Dickens swept swiftly in. The three of us followed. Dickens was addressing Field before Rogers could get out even a word of explanation.

"William, how good to see you. It seems a year rather than but a Christmas month." Dickens charged so quickly across the gaslit room with his hand outstretched for a shake that Field was at first slightly startled and then amused. It was as if the top had been popped off of some magic box and all that identifiably Dickensian energy had been released into the room.

"Dickens, 'ow are yew?" Field took Charles's outstretched hand.

"Concerned is what I am." Dickens was intent upon cutting right to the heart of the matter. "This Thompson affair, a bad

22

business. I feel indebted to the scoundrel." At that, Scarlet Bess, beside me, burst into tears and Irish Meg reached to console her. "Can you tell me what has happened? Why is he in Newgate, of all places?"

"Because Newgate's where we takes the murderers." Field's face went grim, his voice became even, his crook'd forefinger went up to scratch at the side of his right eye.

"But surely . . . I mean, you can't believe . . . surely Thompson couldn't have . . ." Dickens's voice trailed off beneath the firm set and grim determination of Inspector Field's face.

"Nothin' else I *can* bleeve, as things stand." Field directed Dickens to an easy chair by the glowing hearth and motioned for Bess to take the other. Meg sat on the arm of Bess's chair, her hand on her charge's shoulder. Field fetched a straight-backed chair for me. He stood over us, his sharp eye darting from one to the other.

Field chose to deal with Bess first, and quite bluntly: "Bess, I'm sorry, but this time it looks bad for 'im. It's murder 'ee's charged, an' the marks against 'im is strong." At that cruel pronouncement Bess shook with sobs.

Field ignored her display of emotion, figuring rightly that her hysterics were destined to continue yet a while. He turned to Dickens and me: "I realise yew two gentlemuns are drawn ta the romantick aspects o' our friend Thompson—ex-'eyewayman, ex-'ousebreaker, ex-swellmobsman, ex-every sort of criminal game's ta be played—but fact remains that even tho' 'ee's actin' at bein' an actor, 'ee's still got a 'eyewayman's ear an' a 'ousebreaker's foot an' a pickpocket's eye out for the main chance."

"You have mentioned all the things that Tally Ho Thompson has been in times past," Dickens already was pleading the client's case as if he were one of those Old Bailey barristers he so despised, "but you have not mentioned the crime of murder. Really, Field, Thompson has never hurt anyone, never fired a shot in anger, you cannot believe that he could murder some poor young woman."

"Not only does it look as if 'ee murdered that 'un"—Field said as he stared at Dickens—"but 'er mistress as well."

"What!" Dickens was so startled that his voice jumped.

Bess's head jerked out of her wet handkerchief as if tugged at by a rope. She stared wide-eyed at Field in disbelief, shaking her head from side to side in denial even as the tears streamed down her face. *"No!"* her lips formed the word, but its sound died in her throat.

"My God!" I exclaimed.

Field's crook'd forefinger once again scratched at the side of his eye as he stood over us three ambushed auditors.

" 'At's right," he ultimately continued, "we've got two bodies an' we caught Thompson cold leavin' the scene o' the second murder."

Two bodies? I was reading Dickens's mind as our eyes met. *Bess had said nothing about a second corpse.*

"Thompson wos there," Field assured us. "Inside the dead woman's 'ouse. We caught 'im comin' out the garden door."

An awkward silence pooled between Dickens and Field. Charles was thinking hard on this turn.

"You caught him in the act of leaving the house, the scene of the murder?" Charles spoke slowly as if testing the words even as he was saying them.

"We did indeed." Field nodded. He did not, however, seem at all proud of the capture as a sterling piece of detective work. His "we did indeed" was more a cautious admission of fact than a proud acceptance of credit.

"Why were you there?" The question seemed to come to Charles slowly as if fed by some distant ventriloquist. In fact, Dickens was simply thinking through the event aloud. "How did you know to be on the scene at the very moment the crime was committed?"

"I wosn't there when we caught 'im. They called me to the scene soon after. Two street constables caught an' 'eld 'im. Knowin' Thompson I'm surprised two wos enough," Field made a weak attempt at joking.

24

"But why were they there?" Dickens probed again.

"Report o' a disturbance. First they found the dead girl 'alf out o' an alley. Then a street lad pointed out the 'ouse she come from to the two constables just as Thompson wos sneakin' out."

"Can you tell us what happened?" Dickens was no longer interrogating Field, but was asking, quietly, as a friend.

"Per'aps yew should ask Thompson," Field suggested in a voice that intimated he really didn't wish to explore the subject any further. Field was acting strange, not at all like the open ally of whom we had become so fond. For some reason he seemed utterly disinclined to dispense with any information, yet he had quickened with his suggestion that we talk to Thompson.

Dickens caught Field's tone as well and retreated from pressing for more information. "Yes, perhaps we should. Can we see him?" I think both of us sensed at that very moment that this case was proving much more delicate and complicated than Scarlet Bess had led us to believe.

To our great surprise, Field's face broke into a small grin at Dickens's request: "Yes, yew can see 'im . . . tonight if yew wish . . . summat irregular, but I can write yew an authority."

Dickens looked at me and I at him in further surprise. There was an instability in Field's demeanour. At one moment he was aloof and defensive and at the next he was grinning in easy accommodation. Something strange was going on which neither Dickens nor I quite understood.

Field summoned Rogers from the front of the station and within moments the document of passage was in Dickens's hand. Strangely, after handing Charles the piece of paper, Field stuck out his hand for a farewell shake and detained Dickens's hand with his other. "Dickens, gauge Thompson's story well. I want ta know what yew think on it," I overheard his charge.

He has got us working for him once again. That shadow of an insight fluttered across my mind but was summarily dispelled as Field shook my hand with a gruff "Good evenin', Mister Collins," and placed a consoling arm around Bess's shoulder muttering, "Chin up, Bess, 'ee's not 'ung yet."

In swift moments, Field's letter of passage in hand, we shook our cabman awake, entered our hansom, and were underway toward Newgate.

NEWGATE

January 9, 1852—midnight

D espite his predilection to doze, our cabman nonetheless flogged his four-legged partner down the near-
deserted Strand into the more-deserted Fleet Street.
Dashing across Ludgate Circus, he careened into Old Bailey
which dead-ended into the sullen, black walls of Newgate
Prison. We clattered up to the looming iron gate. A small
door cowered in its right corner. A tiny grated window peeked
suspiciously out near the top of the door. The sound of our
wheels on the paving stones drew a pair of black-browed eyes
to the window grate as our cab reined in. To those hooded
eyes staring out of that tiny window Dickens addressed himself.

In Dickens's wake, we looked quickly around, and then at
each other. The great stone walls, blackened with the soot and
grime of the city, or perhaps by the fire during the riots of
'eighty,* rose above us. The outer walls of a prison, window-

*In 1780, during the Catholic Riots, also called the Gordon Riots because
they were planned and incited by the radical fanatic Lord George Gordon,

27

less, are frightening in their bleakness, their impenetrable gloom, their rejection of hope. The look of panic upon Meg's face sent a shudder through me. This was one of the places where Meg had always feared she would end. *"Eyther Newgate or the river, 'at's where I'm bound . . . if I don't quit the streets,"* her voice echoed in my mind out of a not-so-distant past. A look of utter terror at the prospect of entering such a villain-ous place sparked in Meg's eyes and flared in the spasmodic tightening around her mouth as she looked up at those dead walls.

Upon looking up at the grim walls, Scarlet Bess erupted into renewed fits of sobbing. I left Meg to console her and caught up with Dickens at the turnkey's grate. He was just passing our letter of passage through to a hand that I as-sumed was attached to those dark-browed eyes which had greeted our arrival. As the gaoler examined the document, Dickens looked back over his shoulder at me. That unmistak-able fire of excitement blazed in his eyes. I realised that he was having a smashing time spending this cold raw night in this squalid narrow street knocking on this grimy, wretched door. *Newgate Prison,* I envisioned Dickens thinking, *what better place to find entertainment of a winter's evening, eh Wilkie?*

If indeed that was what the almost demonically happy look upon Dickens's face meant, I for one could not share his enthusiasm. It was as if the smell, the damp, the taint of that prison was floating down over me, polluting my very skin, closing around my throat like some paralysing drug. If New-gate Prison excited Dickens, it threatened me, made me want to wash its taint off my hands and face.

"Seems hin horder," came the turnkey's evaluation of our

Newgate was stormed (much as was the Bastille in Paris in 1789), set afire, and all of its prisoners let loose by the rioters. Dickens examined this historic episode in detail in his novel *Barnaby Rudge* (1841). Dickens' familiarity with that place most probably explains why he was not as strongly moved by the experience of Newgate as were Collins and Irish Meg. It was not the first time that Dickens had been there, at least in imagination.

letter of passage. With iron grinding, his small entrance door in that great iron gate set in those high gloomy walls stretching out down those two narrow, dark streets, swung open. "Henny paper signed with Hinspector Field of the Protectives' mark his hevidence heenough for me," the man added as Dickens and I stepped through. We had to wait a moment for Meg and Bess to follow and, all the while, the turnkey was looking us up and down as if taking our likeness for the walls of the National Portrait Gallery. "Tall smooth-faced specimin with stick hackompanied by short thick specimin with hundersized spectacles," our host muttered, unheeding that we heard his accurate though not very flattering description. *He wants to remember us,* I thought, but I was not, at that late hour in that intimidating place, thinking clearly enough to deduce why.

Helping Bess through that prison door, that look of panic again flashed in Meg's face. But she was there in the name of friendship, pursuant to her strange sisterhood of the streets with Bess. She had decided to see it through no matter how frightening. Once marshalled inside the prison gate, the black-browed turnkey committed us to the custody of a brother gaoler of bloated body, shaggy mane, and dogged mien who proceeded to march us across a cold, dull yard. In the corner of that space, chilling in the dim moonlight, stood a high gallows. That gallows tree in the prison courtyard actually signalled an advance in English culture. Condemned prisoners of Newgate used to be carted to Tyburn Hill for their rendezvous with Jack Ketch. In the last year, however, hangings had ceased being public spectacles and had been moved inside the prison walls.* All of our eyes measured that

---

*This change in execution procedures was occasioned by the outcry against public hanging immediately following the executions of Sylvia Manning and her husband in November of 1849. Dickens' own eloquent letter to the *Times* describing the obscene spectacle was instrumental in stirring up the public outcry against those barbaric displays. Coincidentally, it was at the public hanging of Mrs. Manning that Dickens was first introduced to Inspector Field.

perverted cross as we passed through the yard. Our dogged Serjeant of the Door stopped abruptly to open yet another door in the opposite wall. As a consequence of his sudden stopping, all four of us, marching in a column, suddenly piled comically up upon one another's heels. Our shaggy dog of a gaoler simply shook his jowls at our clumsy antics and led us on into the maw of the prison proper.

The corridors were narrow, mouldy, and dark. They were also old and draughty, windy as the halls of Parliament. Prison sounds—doors clashing, locks turning, moans of de-spair—seemed to blow through those corridors like an ill wind. We descended yet another mildewed staircase into the bowels of this wretched lock. At intervals, along the narrow corridors, the closed doors of the inmate chambers emitted muffled sounds that could have been talking, snoring, cough-ing, moaning, howling, cursing, choking, or any combination of disgusting possibilities. At eye-level on each door gaped a grated hole through which a gaoler could observe or shine a bull's-eye upon the inhabitants of the cell. "These har the private rooms," our doglike guide informed us. "Your man haint bought one of hem yet." The more private prison ac-commodations went to those able to pay just as did digs in London's posher neighbourhoods. That being the case, I prepared to greet Thompson in the Newgate equivalent of Dickens's Tom-All-Alone's, the pestilent neighbourhood soon to be introduced in the first number of *Bleak House*.

"The public dens har hon the bottom," our guide growled as we started down yet one more greasy pile of stone steps.

That last stairwell opened into a long, dirt-floored, low-ceilinged, column-supported cellar that stretched dimly out of our sight. This low expanse of pillared catacombs was peopled with muttering piles of clothing stretched out in all manner of heedless repose, some sleeping, some smoking, some motionless as if long dead. The sounds were not loud nor threatening but were incessant and troubling like the sounds of wards in Bedlam.

"One Thompson, key number one-nine-three-four," the

30

gaoler who had led us down into this hellhole barked, causing that sea of ragged mounds to shift and curse and sink back into their twisted repose.

"Over 'ere, mates!" came an immediate and surprisingly cheerful shout. It was Tally Ho Thompson's voice no doubt, but we could not divine its source in the dimness of that rambling catacomb.

"Ho'ver cheer." Our dogged guide went on point like a Hertfordshire hunter.

"Over 'ere!" Thompson called out once again. The sound of his mocking voice hung in the dull air directly before us. We moved past the filthy columns which held up the grimy ceiling, all written upon with past inmates' indecipherable messages, both desperate and obscene, and we climbed over muffled mounds of snoring prisoners until we came upon Thompson sitting with his back to one of the pillars blithely smoking at the butt of a cigar. He looked like a raconteur preparing to hold forth in a public house.

Taller and longer in the leg than ninety-five percent of his countrymen—the English being renowned as a short and wiry race—Thompson's over-six-foot frame stretched out across the dirt floor defining an area which none of the other inmates of that gloomy corner of that gloomy chamber seemed inclined to violate. In his height and long-leggedness, in his barefaced, clear-eyed openness, he looked remarkably like a younger version of Charles Dickens. Were it not for Dickens's much more formal carriage and quietly elegant dress, one would be hard-pressed to tell them apart.

Hung precariously upon the stone column, which Tally Ho Thompson had claimed as his domicile, was a dirty oil lamp. We learned later that it burned all day and all night (if those distinctions actually held meaning in Newgate) except when the often forgetful gaolers failed to replenish its slow fuel. It cast a dim light on the proceedings for a radius of one column in each direction.

"Welcome ta Newgate, mates." That maddening grin, which seemed to mock the seriousness of any situation to which Thompson was attached, danced across his face. "We're a bit short on chairs 'ere, but the dirt is clean, as dirt goes, an' I'm certainly 'appy ta see yew."

At that, poor Scarlet Bess fell sobbing upon his chest. Thompson was truly a wonder. It was as if he were addicted to seizing the attention and moving to the centre of any situation, no matter how serious or threatening.

"Aw Bessy, I sure 'opes yew 'aven't been doin' this ever since yew 'eard they'd cast me in 'ere, because if yew keeps it up yew're goin' ta dry up like a Portland prune." We all laughed nervously at that, except for Irish Meg, who glared angrily at Thompson as if to say: *If yew'd stayed out of trouble we wouldn't 'ave to be in this pestilent 'ole.* Bess even seemed to calm a bit. She looked into his face before she started snuffling into his collar once again.

The rest of us ranged ourselves cross-legged on the floor around Thompson's column. The light from the dingy lamp flickered over his bailiwick. Meg gently pulled Bess away from her man, whispering "They've got to talk this out, Bess," and "Yew're doin' 'im no good carryin' on like this." Scarlet Bess looked as if she were in a daze, her wet eyes wide and blank, her face stretched tight with worry.

"Yes, we must talk this out," Dickens began.

"Mister Dickens, Mister Collins, I am sincerely beholdin' ta yew for comin'. When I asked Fieldsy ta tell Bess wot 'ad 'appened, I thought she might come ta yew."

"She did and we are here," Charles went on, "but she doesn't seem to know a thing, nor do we. What has happened, and why are you here?"

Thompson grinned his maddening grin: "Ta tell the God's truth, sirs, I'm embarrassed ta be 'ere. I can't remember the last time I did anything so stoopid. When I wos just a young-ster learnin' the ins an' outs o' Shooter's 'ill, I once looked back ta see if the sheriffs wos gainin' an' my 'orse ran me right into an over'angin' limb. Knocked me flat on my back in the 'eyeroad while friend 'orse gallops merrily off. I was sharp enough ta roll off inta the ditch 'fore the sheriffs saw wot 'ad

32

'appened an' they rode right by, but I've niver looked back since, an' I ain't about ta start now. In other words, gennulmen, I been smiled at, mounted up, run right inta a tree pretty as yew pleese, an' it's all me own bloody fault. In other words, gennulmen, I've been done, tied up with a bow an' prettily done, delivered to Fieldsy an' 'is bulls like a bloody birthday favour." Thompson ended this expansive gallop with a shrug and another mocking grin.

Dickens wanted more, however, than Tally Ho Thompson's rhetorical flights: "Thompson, you must tell us exactly what happened so that we can consult with Inspector Field. It is the only way we can get you out of this dreadful place."

"Wot 'appened?" Thompson grinned wryly. "Mister Dickens, I'm not sure I exactly know wot 'appened."

"Just tell us what you think happened, step by step," I prompted, feeling that I ought to enter this colloquy at some point to let the others know that I was still on the premises.

"I've got me suspicions that it all began last October when Mister Macready 'ired me ta act Poins an' look after the 'orses for the new Shakespeare show, Prince Hal yew know. To open o'er the Christmas 'olidays. It wos soon after that Mister Macready interduces me ta Doctor Palmer's wife. This doctor is one o' the new members o' the Covent Garden Theatre board o' patrons. 'Ee 'as come up ta London ta take over a built-up practise; old doctor ups an' dies o' sudden 'eart conditions an' young doctor comes up ta take o'er 'is practise, that sort o' turnabout. Because the doctor rides 'orses, wife wants ta take riding lessons on the Outer Circle an' Rotten Row.* The doctor 'ad bought the lady a 'orse which they boarded at the 'Eyde Park stables an' I got 'er up on it a few times, me ridin' a nag she rented so as ta accompany 'er. But after the Shakespeare gets underway in December I didna 'ear from 'er again. Then, right after New Year, one o' the actors,

*The Outer Circle is the bridle- and footpath that rings Regent's Park. Rotten Row is the straight bridlepath on the southernmost end of Hyde Park.

named of Dunn, Dick Dunn, corners me about a recovery problem . . ."

"Recovery problem?" I was glad that Dickens asked because I had no idea to what Thompson was referring.

"Yes," Thompson went on without so much as a reining in, " 'ee wonted me ta recover some brilliants, a necklace an' earrings o' silver 'ee'd given a married 'ooman. 'Ee said 'ee even 'ad the keys ta 'er 'ouse, but 'ee couldn't get near it or she'd call the constables an' 'ee wos afraid ta tell 'er 'usband who was a powerful man for fear for 'is life or 'is liveli'ood or both."

"A 'orsy tart, I might 'ave predicted that," Irish Meg could not hold her sharp tongue. Luckily, Bess did not hear her.

Thompson ignored her and galloped on: "So 'ee comes ta me to git the trinkets back an 'ee offers twelve pounds for the job which is more than I make on the stage in two months," that last directed at Irish Meg. "I takes 'alf in good faith an' 'ee gives me the key ta the back door an' the number, Thirty-five Cadogan Place, an' tells me ta wait for a night when 'ee knows they'll be out o' the 'ouse. Meanwhile, I go by the sight o' the crack for a look-see. 'Eye 'ouse with back garden, fronts on the Sloane Street greensward. Looks simple enough, an' las' night, when 'ee gives me the go, I'm over there watchin' the 'ouse by nine o' the clock after Poins 'as left the stage in Act Two with three full acts ta go. Yew see, if blame looked my way, I could always say I was still at the theatre since I planned ta return with the sparklers before the play wos ended an' I planned to go drinkin' with a crowd after the theatre wos empty. Anyway, all looks well, so I go through the garden an', smooth as a racehorse's rump, the door opens ta the key an' I'm in. I go ta the ladies' bedroom up the main staircase ta the right an' strike a glim. That's when the crack goes dicey. Little did I know I wos alreddy a gleem in the eyes o' the bailiffs."

"What do you mean?" Dickens asked.

"I knew I wos done as soon as I struck the light. The room wos alreddy picked over an' a dead 'ooman wos right in the middle o' the floor. I knew from one look I'd been conied. I niver even looked at the 'ooman's face. I turned tail out o' there as fast as I might, but I wosn't fast enough. I swear, I niver touched a thing in that room. I niver laid a 'and on 'er. But Fieldsy's constables caught me comin' out the garden door. Poins never took 'is curtain call last night."

"You were only in the house a matter of minutes, yet the Protectives were waiting when you came out. Extraordinary timing!" Dickens was talking more to himself than to Thompson or the rest of us.

At that moment, merely adding to the grotesquerie of the whole situation, a whiskery tramp, decidedly drunk, wearing what looked like a composite of three different but equally ragged coats, with a hat stove in on one side so that its top jutted precariously at a right angle from its brim, stumbled into our charmed little circle. Staggering, the man made an extremely rude noise, causing all of us to gasp. Thompson, without a moment's hesitation, catapulted to his feet and, clasping the ragged inmate by the scruff of his neck and the tail of one of his coats, flung him off into the darkness amidst the grinding and gnashing of teeth where the rude emission of his drunken body would no longer offend.

"Ah, but it gits diceyer," Thompson continued on, almost laughing at the absurdity of the whole proposition. "When Fieldsy gits there, 'ee goes inta the 'ouse, then comes back out, then goes off a pacin' back an' forth an' scratchin' 'is eye with 'is finger like 'ee duz. 'Ee can't seem ta figure wot 'as 'appened so 'ee comes up ta me all tossed up an' wants ta know, 'wot the devil are yew doin' 'ere?' I tells 'im the truth. I'm there ta steal some sparklers for a client. Now, 'ee stomps off an' scratches 'is eye some more, then 'ee comes back an' asks me right out, 'did I know 'er?' 'No, I didna even git a look at 'er. She wos dead when I walked in an' lit the lucifer,' says I. That's when Fieldsy 'it me with the worst news o' all. That's when 'ee dropped the noose right down around me neck."

"How is that?" Dickens prompted.

" 'Ee asked me if I knew a Missus Annie Palmer, the doctor's wife that I'd gone ridin' with for 'ire. I'd always met 'er

35

at the stables in 'Eyde Park. I'd niver been ta the doctor's 'ouse. 'Ee told me she wos the dead 'ooman!"

As he finished, Thompson's voice rose ever so slightly as if, more than twenty-four hours later, he was still stunned by the situation he found himself in. He had told the whole story as if it were a dream, as if he had been some detached observer floating above the reality of the rifled room, the dead woman, and the constables.

"I couldn't believe it wos she, so young an' pretty," Thompson went on. At that, Scarlet Bess let out a howl of pain. Meg folded her in her arms and glared over her shoulder at Thompson.

"But all the while Fieldsy wos lookin' at me," Thompson continued over Bess's protest, "an' I knew 'ee knew that I knew 'er. I knew 'ee'd caught me off guard when 'ee said 'er name. So now 'ee sends 'is constables away, all exceptin' Rogers, an' I'm chained to the iron fence around the garden, an' 'ee comes in close an', real quietlike, 'ee says 'you know 'er, don't ye, Thompson?' an' I nods, an' 'ee turns ta Rogers shakin' 'is 'ead an' says, 'I don't like this. It smells worse than week-old finnan-haddie.' With that, 'ee yells for 'em ta push me off ta Newgate without so much as a fare-thee-well. I 'ad ta yell at the top o' me lungs out o' the conveyance wagon for someone ta tell Bess."

Irish Meg succinctly put a complexion on the situation: "It stinks as bad as Smithfield Market if yew ask me."

I, of course, was more suspicious than she, yet I felt I knew Thompson somewhat and, I must admit, I could not envision him a murderer. His story seemed plausible; the absolutely propitious arrival of the Protectives seemed suspicious. The whole affair did, indeed, give off the smell of an elaborate hoax.

"What can we do to help put this right?" Dickens asked.

"Wot I needs is someone ta talk ta Fieldsy for me. 'Ee's the one can put it right. 'Ee's the one can find 'oo killed that poor girl. Since I'm presently indisposed, could yew, Mister Dickens? I needs a go-between. Could yew intercede an' git Fieldsy

ta 'elp me? 'Ee's the only one can find the real murderer."
Thompson was actually fighting to mask his desperation.

Dickens looked at me and I at him. I felt I knew what he was thinking. After our adventure with Ashbee and Field's preferential treatment of Charles's Miss Ternan, we had anticipated Inspector Field coming to us for help on one of his cases. We did not expect to go to him, hat in hand, to intercede for our highwayman-turned-actor friend. No doubt Dickens was suspicious, as he rightly should be, of our highwayman friend. It was something of a sticky wicket.

"Oh pleese, Mister Dickens, 'elp my Aloysius." Scarlet Bess had thrown herself at Dickens's feet and was pawing at his ankles in supplication.

"Aloysius?" Dickens looked at me.

"Aloysius?" I looked at Dickens.

Near bursting with laughter—neither of us had ever heard Tally Ho Thompson addressed by his Christian name before—we turned together and gaped at him.

" 'Ooman's distraught!" Tally Ho Thompson was visibly disconcerted. " 'Ooman doesn't know wot she's sayin'," he blustered. " 'Ooman's hysterickal, mad, not makin' sense, can't be trusted 'ere. Gents, gents"—placating now—"let's just forget wot she's blurted 'ere an' git back to Fieldsy. I needs 'is 'elp."

Dickens and I could not suppress our amusement at Tally Ho Thompson's obvious embarrassment. God, the man stood accused of murder and what shook his composure was the inadvertent revelation of his Christian name.

"Aloysius, is it?" Irish Meg could not resist. "Now 'at's a bit o' information Fieldsy would really like to get aholt of."

Thompson glared at her.

Bess, utterly unaware of what she had done, subsided in a pile of petticoats at Dickens's feet. Irish Meg bent to calm her.

"We can certainly go to Inspector Field on your behalf," Dickens promised, "but what shall we tell him?"

"Tell 'im ta find Dickie Dunn. 'Ee's the one 'oo put me up

ta it. I'll wager 'ee knows somethin'. 'Ee's got ta be the one 'oo set the sheriffs on me. 'Ee gave me the keys ta the 'ouse."

"I'll do it." Dickens shook Thompson's hand to calm him. It was really quite unusual to see our highwayman friend so agitated.

"Can I offer you a loan of some money, Thompson?" I had contributed almost nothing in the course of this intimate colloquy, so I felt such an offer to be the least I could do. Before Thompson could even answer, I looked to Irish Meg who winked her approval.

"A few quid would git me a room 'n per'aps some cigars." Thompson leapt at my offer.

"Yes, by all means, here." Dickens placed a half crown in his hand, utterly ignoring the fact that I had made the offer and should have been the one to disburse the loan. "We have to get you out of this dungeon and into a private room aboveground." I added another half crown to Thompson's war chest.

At that, Thompson shook our hands heartily all around and Dickens, Meg, and I withdrew to the foot of the stairwell to allow Bess and her Aloysius (I honestly must grin every time I write that comical name) some moments to themselves. When Thompson delivered Bess to us some minutes later, she was visibly calmed, her fortitude strengthened. She was apologetic for the spectacle she had been making of herself to such good friends.

In a gruff gesture of thanks, Tally Ho Thompson clapped Dickens and myself on the back. Meg could not resist hooting, "Good night, Aloysius," down the stairwell as we retreated. Her jibe echoed hollowly in the thick prison air.

We climbed the stone steps up out of that pestilent catacomb and felt the air freshen and the weight of guilt lessen with every ascending step. When we reached the courtyard, the dark gallows seemed almost beckoning as we hurried across its grim shadow in the faint moonlight. Much to our amazement, when we reached the turnkey's booth, Inspector Field and his faithful bloodhound Rogers were waiting to take us into custody.

38

CHEATIN' GALLOWS JACK

January 10, 1852—one A.M.

I nspector Field and Serjeant Rogers loitered in the shadows of the turnkey's lock as we crossed the gloomy courtyard.

"Newgate's no place for 'onest men this time o' night," Field said as he stepped out of the shadows to intercept us. "Nor wimmin neither," he added as an afterthought.

His appearance startled us all, excepting perhaps Charles, who sharply answered: "From what we've seen of it tonight, it's no fit place for any man."

"They puts themselfes 'ere," Field reflected. "We picks 'em up an' delivers 'em to this door. It's they who sets their course." Field wore his exceedingly sharp hat and carried his exceedingly dangerous stick and, when he jabbed his ferocious forefinger at the inner depths of the prison to punctuate his metaphor, there was no mistaking the professional detective, the nemesis of London's night streets for whom we had gone on duty eight months before.

"Why 'ave you thrown my Tally 'O inta this 'orrible place?"

39

Bess was cowed and hanging back with Meggy, and there was a quaver in her voice as she spoke, but she knew she must make this weak attempt to stand up for her beleaguered man.

Field ignored her.

"What is it?" Dickens moved close. "Why are you here?"

"We must talk," Field's voice dropped to a nearly inaudible whisper—so that the turnkeys would not hear, I presumed—"but not 'ere," he added in a conspiratorial murmur. "Can yew, an' all o' yer party, retire to the Lord Gordon? I've instructed 'em already . . . ta snug a room for us."

"Of course," Dickens, speaking for all yet consulting none, asserted. As his eyes met mine for my expected nod of silent assent, I once again caught that fire of restless anticipation, which only the promise of experience out of the ordinary lit in them. It was as if Dickens needed the constant reassurance that he was real, that the world of his novels truly existed, that his existence meant something. In other words, the fire that Inspector Field and the night streets kindled in Dickens was a cleansing fire, which burned away the isolation and unreality of his novel-writing life, gave him flight from his fictions and, ultimately, passage back into them. Inspector Field ushered Dickens out of art into life and Dickens, turnabout, transformed that life into art. "We've got a cab waiting," Dickens whispered back. "We will follow you."

The turnkey, jumping to Field's terse order of "Open up," passed us through the lock without challenge. But then Field did a strange thing. Holding me back until after Dickens had passed out of the prison walls, he whispered, again conspiratorially, "Wilkie, make some excuse to talk to the turnkey, show yerself to 'im, go," and he gave me a sharp push to the shoulder with his forefinger.

I knew not what to say. "Yes, ah, sir, ah, turnkey," I stammered. "We, ah I mean, have provided Thompson, the inmate we visited, with some coin. Can you, however it is done here, can you see that he gets a room, a better place, whatever is the custom." I seemed to be making little sense. The man stared wide-eyed as I babbled. Field hovered over my shoulder in the darkness. "You will be suitably rewarded when we return if all goes well," I finished lamely. Field tapped me once again with his controlling forefinger as a signal that it was quite enough. The black-browed man in the small booth nodded vacantly as I fled. The small episode fluttered me.

Inspector Field's hulking black post chaise, like a chariot from hell with its caped coachman shivering on the box and its black stage horse pawing the paving stones and snorting smoke, waited in the shadows against the high wall of Newgate. Our hansom loitered nearby.

"We must not talk 'ere," Field whispered once again. "The less we're seen together 'ere the better," he added mysteriously.

Our cabman, his crooked top hat protruding crazily from the huddle of blankets in which he had buried himself, dozed on the box. Field struck the side of the cab smartly with his fiercely knobbed stick, sending our cabman straight up in a flutter of blankets and a mutter of curses. "The Lord Gordon Arms in King's Abbey off Bow," Field commanded with an upward jab of his murderous stick.

"Careful with 'at bloody oar, guv," the cabman squawked, his crabbed hand catching his crooked hat, which had tipped off his scrawny head. The man continued with a string of curses muttered under his breath, a litany that sounded suspiciously like "Faggin' West End swells struttin' 'ores bloddy pleece wit loud sticks bangin' box bloody 'ell," or something near, as the four of us climbed into the cab and Field closed us in tight. Our cabman, whose name I later discovered to be Sleepy Rob Colby, seemed to suffer from a strange malady that sent him into a peaceful doze whenever he was not directly engaged with something or someone. Oddly enough, as this case unfolded, Sleepy Rob attached himself to our entourage as personal cabman. Uncannily, we found him waiting (and nodding off) outside our Soho flat whenever we found ourselves in need of transport. One more sharp rap on the door with Field's stick sent us careening off down the street, our vehicle moving as erratically as the contours of our cabman's cockeyed hat.

Once inside the cab, huddled close for warmth, our knees touching, I, and I'll wager the others as well, felt an immense relief at wiping the dust of Newgate from my hands and feet. Speeding along High Holborn toward Bow Street, we all were occupied with our own thoughts. Once I felt Meg's hand squeezing my leg, but when I looked up out of my own reverie she simply smiled as if acknowledgement with my eyes was all she needed.

As for Dickens, he kept his own counsel. That fire, however, never left his eyes. It burned like the bright tip of a cigar in the darkness. It was the visible flame of what Dickens, just before Christmas, had named to me an "intolerable restlessness" smouldering beneath the surface of his seemingly ordered life. Seeing that fire flash in Dickens's countenance I once again felt as if I were a character in one of his novels, as if he were pulling me along by the sheer force of his restless imagination. Soon I realised that Dickens was rehearsing his lines, as a good actor does, in preparation for the imminent confrontation with Inspector Field. His eyes flamed in anticipation of once again taking centre stage. Some men prefer to remain backstage, but others, like Dickens, must come out from behind the curtain to make the audience think and feel and laugh and cry, must persuade them, touch them, move them. Field was like a playwright whom Dickens realised delivered him exciting parts to play in the theatre of the real.

We pulled up in front of the Lord Gordon with a clatter of hooves and wheels and a rattle of reins. Field's sinister black post chaise was directly behind and, directing our coach to wait while Field sent his back to the livery for the night, we all got down and went into the public house together.

I had not been back to the Lord Gordon* since the Ashbee

*This public house, to which Inspector Field had introduced Dickens and Collins during their previous collaboration as described in that first com-

42

affair, but it was obvious that Dickens had become as much of a regular there as were Field and Rogers. Miss Katie Tillotson, the ruddy publican, was sitting at the tap of the clean, well-lit house. She greeted Field and Rogers and Dickens jovially by name while nodding amiably to the rest of us. Field ordered spiced gins all around and Dickens added a request for "two plates of that excellent toasted cheese."

"And please send a mug of spiced gin out to our cabman," I added. To my unconsidered afterthought, Dickens nodded his approval.

That business done, Miss Katie pointed us down a hallway and we retired to a private rear chamber where a vacant-eyed boy of about sixteen blessed with large ears and a slack jaw was already busy blowing up the fire with a fat ancient bellows. In mere moments he had it blazing like Dante's Inferno. Soon thereafter, Miss Katie and the dull-faced boy returned with our mugs of gin and Dickens's plates of toasted cheese. Thankful to be out of the cold, we sipped greedily from our steaming mugs. That hot gin, spiced with lemon and nutmeg, tasted so hearty, warmed so deep, that I, at that moment, could understand how one could become as addicted to it as to opium or the sexual lure of a woman. Sure that all was secure, Miss Katie retired with her idiot boy in tow. It was a combative Dickens who finally broke the silence.

"Surely, Field, you can't really think that Thompson killed those women," Dickens began his defense.

Field stared levelly at Charles for a moment then, inexplicably, grinned.

"What?" Dickens raised his eyebrows at his antagonist. "What is it?" Dickens asked, darting a glance over his shoulder to see if someone was standing behind him prompting Field's eccentric behavior.

"Nothin', it's nothin'," Field mumbled as he buried his face in his mug of gin.

monplace book, was named after Lord George Gordon, the anti-Catholic fanatic who led the mobs in the popularly called Gordon Riots of 1780.

43

"I say, it really is impossible for me to believe that Thompson could have murdered those two women," Dickens caught him up again.

"I don't bleeve it for a minute," Field answered rather matter-of-factly.

"Well, whatever the appearances—" Dickens was charging right on with his defense of Thompson when what Field had said suddenly registered upon his consciousness. "What did you—"

A strange mischievous grin danced across Field's face as he cut Dickens off. "Thompson fancies wimmin too much ta ever kill one." Field chuckled. "That's why we're goin' to cheat Gallows Jack. I know Thompson didn't kill those wimmin. I know there's more goin' on 'ere than meets the eye. That's precisely why I wants yew ta 'elp Thompson escape."

INSPECTOR FIELD
CHANGES HIS COLOURS,
OR,
INSPECTOR FIELD,
PLAYWRIGHT

January 10, 1852—toward dawn

I t goes without saying that we were all perfectly stunned, mouths agape, at Field's announcement.

"Escape!" Dickens gasped.

" 'Tis true? Do yew mean it?" Scarlet Bess jumped up.

Meggy looked at me and I at her. Both of us felt that this evening, spent in the company of these demented people, was taking yet another predictable amble into the bizarre. She shook her head discreetly in minor disgust, and I agreed wholeheartedly with her silent sentiment. *They interrupted us in our warm bed and dragged us all over London in the cold raw hours of the night for this?*

I was gratified that Dickens had been as much in the dark as I in recognising Field for the playwright of this whole Newgate Prison–George Barnwell scenario.* But once Dick-

---

*George Lillo's *The London Merchant* (1731), popularly known as *George Barnwell* after its young protagonist, was one of the first of the Newgate plays of crime and punishment, and, perhaps, the play most oft-mentioned

ens knew, a change came over his demeanour, and Field's face too relaxed into a gloating grin, accompanied by that knowing flick of his forefinger to the side of his eye. Dickens knew that he had been gulled and, I am sure, was already plotting his revenge. And, I am equally sure that Field was thinking: *Yes, Dickens old man, this 'as all been but a game ta draw yew in.*

Field sat in his chair sipping his hot gin with his exceedingly sharp hat still on his head and his exceedingly sharp eyes darting from one of us to the next. For a moment he seemed amused, but then, with a sharp tap of his forefinger on the oaken table, he commanded our attention.

"I've known that Tally 'O Thompson didn't kill those wimmin from the very beginnin'," he began, and Scarlet Bess broke down in tears once again. I glanced at Meggy but, instead of tending to Bess as she had been doing the whole evening, she was glaring at Field, the colour starting to rise at her cheekbones, the fire of anger kindling in her eyes.

"What? Then why have you dragged us all over London, sent us into that infernal dungeon, in pursuit of this ridiculous charade? Why have you cast Thompson into Newgate at all if you have known him innocent all along?" Dickens protested.

"Because I need both 'im an' yew"—and Field made a horizontal sweep with his controlling forefinger to include all of us—" 'im in Newgate an' yew visitin' 'im in Newgate."

"I don't understand." Dickens was no longer combative. His voice took swift passage from puzzlement to curiosity to quickening interest.

"Nor I," my voice was more brusque. Field's coyness certainly did seem an impertinent imposition upon our goodwill.

"I knew within moments after I came upon the scene o' the murders that Thompson wosn't our man," Inspector Field

or alluded to in the novels of Charles Dickens. The play was acted every year on the London stage throughout the nineteenth century.

began his narrative. "Oh, 'ee told us 'ee 'adn't done 'em right off, but nobody bleeves a criminal. Wouldn't look right at all if I took Thompson's word for it right there in front o' all me men, now would it, Serjeant Rogers?"

"Hoh no sir, not hatall sir." Rogers was wearing his martinet smirk that said, *Haven't yew been had, yew smart gentlemen huv the writer class,* which so annoyed me.

"But I needed time ta piece together wot 'ad 'appened," Field went on, "an' 'avin' Thompson in prison fit me purposes ev'ry which way. With 'im in Newgate, yew see, the real killer feels secure, thinks 'ee 'as gotten away, tossed us all up. With 'im in Newgate, we can 'ave the time for the chemists ta work on the corpses, per'aps find out 'ow they died. I knew that Thompson didn't kill either o' the wimmin. 'Ee's not a killer. A 'eyewayman, a burglar, a pickpocket, yes! But 'ee's not a killer. 'Ee's too smart an' too nimble ta ever git caught close ta a crime like this. I 'ad 'im taken up ta give me time, ta 'elp me plant a false trail. I knew our friend Thompson could bear up for a few days. I knew our friend Thompson 'ad been gulled, set up ta take the blame for these murders, so wotever I did wos in Thompson's best intrest."

The fire blazed in the Lord Gordon's hearth. The fire of curiosity and anticipation blazed in Dickens's eyes. Yet another fire, one of anger, rose to a blaze in Irish Meg's commanding countenance. My own face must have been ashen in bewilderment. I had been perfectly happy at home that evening in Meggy's arms before being dragged out into the company of these mad people and this smirking policeman. Of all the fires burning in that cosy chamber, Irish Meg's was the first to burst out and singe the eyebrows of our facetious friend Field.

"Yew, yew, yew," she was stammering with rage, but she managed to rein in her voice and her anger. "Yew think yew can do anything you bloody well please," she accused him with a sharp jab of her own ferocious forefinger, "with anyone's life. These two 'ad a good life"—she rubbed her hand along Bess's hunched back as Bess, sitting, bent sobbing into her shawl—" 'til yew stepped in!"

" 'Ee put their good life in danger 'imself," Field spit at Meggy. He was in no mood to endure accusations from one who so recently had been but a common street whore. " 'Ee put it in danger by takin' up burglary once again, 'ee did."

Field glared at Meggy, but she did not retreat, cowed, as she might have eight months before. She was still the same fire-woman of the night streets, but stoked with a new confidence acquired with her step up in social class and her newly attained respectability as a gentleman's mistress.

" 'Ee wos doin' it for a friend," Meggy spat back. In the face of her animated resistance Field calmed. A small grin of amusement commandeered his countenance. His quiet reply utterly disarmed Meg.

" 'Ee did it for the money first, an' because 'ee wos bored an' wanted ta keep 'is 'and in 'is old game," Field said softly, almost coaxingly, "but I don't care about aw that, 'tis not important. Right now I need Thompson an' I need 'im out 'o Newgate just as las' night I needed 'im in Newgate."

"Yew bastard," Irish Meg shot one last weak spark futilely at Field, to which he simply replied with a raised eyebrow and a tightening of the mouth that said: *That will be quite enough of this for now, Meggy!*

His look forced Meg to subside into a sullen silence that I tried to show her I shared by reaching out to touch her hand. Violently, she pulled her hand away and glared angrily at me. *What had I done? Or not done?* That woman was the central confusion of my life. As I look back upon it now, it was, at that time, an immature tendency of mine to rush headlong into every confusing experience that presented itself. My excuse was that I was but following Dickens's rule that it was necessary for a novelist to live life in all its variations in order to qualify to write about it. I owe that to Dickens. That novelist's rubric of risk liberated me from the crabbed, hypocritical, guilt-plagued and podsnappered Victorian life sentence of so many of Dickens's and my contemporaries. Remembering

48

Meg's fiery outburst at Field that night in the Lord Gordon's snug makes me laugh now as I write. In the time that we were together, Meg acquired a nickname, of the sort that lovers append to each other, which only I called her, one of those private things we alone shared. She was my "Lucifer Box," volatile, ready to ignite at any moment at the slightest possible friction. Of course, between the two of us, her nickname carried a more private designation, for it marked her most secret fire.

Having subdued Irish Meg temporarily, Field turned back to Dickens and myself, but before he could continue, Dickens's curiosity took its turn to blaze.

"You said you knew from the very beginning that Thompson was not your murderer?" Dickens pressed. "How?"

"Some instinct per'aps. Don't rightly know, but as I got down from the coach an' saw Thompson manacled to the fence, 'im lookin' straight inta me face, not blinkin', I knew. Yew gets so yew kin see it in their eyes an' it wosn't in Thompson's. Murder niver 'as been 'is style. 'Ee's always been speed an' skill an' gone before the crime's been even found. If 'ee'd stayed on 'is 'orse up on Shooter's 'Ill they might 'ave written ballads an' broadsides 'bout Tally 'O Thompson rather than Dangerous Dick Turpin."*

This speech was very unlike Inspector Field, and Dickens subsequently remarked upon it. Field was never one to rely solely upon something as ephemeral as a spontaneous instinct, a feeling. Hard facts, evidence, were the tender in which he dealt.

---

*Dick Turpin (1706–1739) was a legendary highwayman who robbed stages and plagued individual travelers all over England for twenty years in the early eighteenth century. Noted for his equestrian skills, the speed of his hit-and-run tactics, his charming way with the lady passengers he robbed, and his anger toward any gentleman who raised a voice or a hand against him or any member of his gang, he was immortalized in the Victorian popular press and mythicized in the ballads, broadsides, and penny dreadfuls of the day.

"That was it?" Dickens, incredulous, pressed him. "An instinct that he was not the one?"

"No, not atall, o' course not," Field scoffed. "I said that wos wot struck me as I got out o' the coach at the scene. Once in the 'ouse, on the premises by the dead 'ooman's side, I knew, quick enough, that Thompson wosn't our man atall."

"How?" Charles pursued.

"There were other signs in the 'ouse. They all points away from Thompson. Two freshly washed champagne stems on the kitchen sideboard. Someone else wos there that night, a friend, a lover, a 'usband. 'Ooman don't drink champagne with a burglar. But wot wosn't there, wot 'adn't been done wos wot proved with certainty it 'ad been no burglary. Some dresser drawers were open, an' a table overturned, but no picture on any wall, no silver in any cabinet, no plate in any closet, nothin' of any substance seemed to 'ave been disturbed. 'Err jewellery o'erflowed 'er jewellery box on 'er dressin' table. There was no marks of strangulation on the body, no blows ta the 'ead, no blood on the rug. Nothin' that shouted 'Burglar caught in the act' wos on the premises. But the main of it wos exactly the first thing that yew pointed out earlier this evenin'." Field chuckled as if this were afternoon tea and tapped Dickens congenially on the forearm as that latter leaned in to him across the public house table.

Our steaming drinks forgotten, the blazing fire unheeded, we were all captivated by Field's deductive reasoning.

"And what was that?" Dickens spurred the spellbinder.

"I always said 'ee'd wear well in my line, make a fine detective," Field teased, mischievously complimenting Dickens with a scratch of his crook'd forefinger to the side of his eye.

"For God's sake," Dickens exclaimed. His impatience brought an arrogant glint into Field's eye that declared: *The gentleman amateur must always wait while the professional man builds his case.*

"Thompson niver would o' got caught doin' an easy crack like that," Field said. "Somebody sent for the constables at jus' the right time so's they'd surprise 'im in the act." Then

Field's eyes went hard and the jut of his jaw went serious. He tapped once sharply with his ferocious forefinger on the oak of the table and said: "It wos all a game an' I don't fancy bein' cat an' moused. If any games are ta be played, I'm the one's ta do the playin', I'm the one's ta place the pawns."

There was an awkward silence as none of us seemed inclined to chip at this stony wall that Field had erected around his sense of himself as the master of the London night.

"Tell hem habout the maidservant." Rogers, prompting his superior, firmly rescued us from that pool of spreading silence.

"Yes, of course." Inspector Field stalked out of his hard reverie. "The whole affair keeps gettin' more 'n' more complicated than anyone wos led ta believe when Thompson so neatly tumbled inta our laps. A servant girl attached ta the household, her keys gone, is found dead on a stoop six flats from where Thompson 'as been taken. Maid an' mistress 'ave both suffered the same death."

"What?" Dickens was taken aback. "How do you know that?"

"Because there's no marks o' violence on the corpses." Inspector Field had a precise order for dispensing his revelations and, no matter how hard Dickens or anybody else might press, that order was to be observed. "The whole affair is suspicious from the first alarum. Both wimmin died with the same twisted look on their faces, as if their 'earts stopped an' their faces froze right in the midst o' a scream o' 'orror."

"Has soon has we saw the housemaid's corpse," Rogers affirmed his master's declaration, "Hinspector Field looks hat me han Hi looks hat him han we both know with ha certainty. 'My Gawd,' says Hi, 'their faces his the same.' An' 'orrible!' says he."

"Indeed, both wimmin seemed ta 'ave died the same death. A 'death rictus' the Protectives' surgeon names it. We're still waitin' on the surgeon's report. Seems these murders are more tangled than our usual garden-variety Soho stabbin's an' Bloomsbury bludgeonin's an' Sloane Square stranglin's."

51

"Looked like they wos frightened to death," Serjeant Rogers added brightly.

"My God," said my own voice this time. Perhaps I was feeling neglected at having listened so long without interjecting anything unconsidered, which in those years seemed my stock in trade. "My God, what sort of a Medusa monster can be so horrible that it can stop women's hearts in the very middle of a scream?"

Dickens looked at me as if I belonged in an asylum for the incurably literal.

Field chuckled, but politely, behind his hand.

That arrogant little martinet Rogers laughed openly at my extravagance.

"I don't think we've got a Medusa killer stalking the streets." Inspector Field turned my alarum into an ironic joke. "I'm bettin' it wos the champagne."

"Wot?" Evidently even smug Serjeant Rogers hadn't been privy to this speculation on Field's part. Now it was my turn to smirk at his momentary (and undisguised) discomfiture.

"What do you mean?" Dickens inquired, capturing all of our incredulity and delivering it to Field tied in an adamant red ribbon.

"There's more yet," Inspector Field went on. "One o' our constables finds an empty champagne bottle in the dustbin outside the mews door o' the murder 'ouse. ' 'Ow did it get out there so soon,' I asks, 'if the champagne wos drunk jus' that night in the two stems we found in the kitchin?' There's no sign of any other kitchin dust in the bin an' the kitchin box that the 'ousemaids empty into the outside dustbin is 'alf full."

Field stopped for a maddening sip at his burnt gin.

"And?" Now it was Charles who couldn't restrain his curiosity.

"I think the servant girl pinched a 'alf empty bottle an' drank the dregs as she wos leavin' the 'ouse. That's wot I'm bettin' on. The two wimmin was poisoned, but only one by plan," Field finished.

All of us around that public house table, Serjeant Rogers included, stared at our convener, aghast.

"Poisoned!" I gasped.

"My Tally 'O ud niver poison no one," poor Bess sniveled. Marooned in her distraught state, very little of what Field had been saying had penetrated her watery upset.

"We know that, Bess." Field reached across the table and touched her on the shoulder, at which she jumped as if scalded. But the softness of Field's voice and the gentle lightness of his touch—my God, the very fact of his reaching out to touch someone at all not in the act of taking them into custody—was a startling deviation from his typical mode of operation.

"It's all right, Bess girl," Field cozened her in a voice as thick and smooth as Devon cream. She accepted his gentleness suspiciously, but he patted her twice more and assured her, "The sooner we spring your Tally 'O from the Gate, the better."

Turning back to us from that brief and highly irregular interlude of choreographed compassion, Field tipped his gin cup and waited for more reasoned reactions.

"Poisoned!" I repeated myself, having assumed the mantle of the company's undaunted stater and restater of the obvious. "Gad zooks, what a horrible death."

"Are you certain?" Dickens's more controlled voice reasserted the sway of rationality and logic that my blathering interjections had undermined. "Have you any other evidence besides the two wineglasses and the discarded bottle?"

"No. None at all," Field readily admitted, clearly disappointing Serjeant Rogers, who thrived on basking in the glow of his master's ratiocinative powers. "Yet poison is a certainty that I 'old without condition ta be the case. I jus' know it!" he finished with passion, punctuating his certainty with a hard tap of his forefinger to the solid oak of our table.

"If yew knows all this so strong," Bess shrieked, "then why'd'jew cast my Tally 'O in gaol? Why 'ave yew left 'im in that awful place?"

53

The softness was still in Field's voice, but it was clear that his patience was being strained. Never had we ever seen him allow one of his creatures of the streets to speak out against his omniscience, to challenge his judgement and authority, yet he was allowing Bess, in her distraught state, to question him. There was a reason he was indulging Bess in such a way, I was sure of it. "We will 'ave 'im out of there soon, I promise." Field once again patted her arm reassuringly, almost paternal in his concern. It was so unlike him.

"In fact, I need Thompson out o' the keep as soon as possible." With a quick snap of his head, a high sign, he motioned for Dickens and me to follow him. He rose, and with a quick silent sweep of his forefinger motioned for Serjeant Rogers to stay with the two women. This order slashed a quick look of pain and resentment across Rogers's incredibly uncomplicated face. Irish Meg, busy attending to her hysterical charge, saw none of these eloquent silent gestures. Like obedient pull toys Charles and I followed Field down the corridor into the tap.

It was not crowded. Only one local character and what, from her dress, looked to be his whore sat drinking gin against the far wall near the hearth. We took up station at the wooden bar and Miss Katie Tillotson replenished our glasses with smoking gin.

"I need Thompson out o' there soon," Inspector Field in an even voice confided. "I need 'im out an' I need ta 'ave power o'er 'im, ta control 'im when we git 'im out. Scarlet Bess will 'ave to do us for that, I'm afeerd." And suddenly I knew why he had been so solicitous toward her back there in the drinking chamber. He never did anything without reason. "I want 'im ta work once again for me," Field went on, "jus' as 'ee did in the Ashbee affair."

Field was inviting us in as co-conspirators, but neither Dickens nor I knew why.

"What can we do to help?" Dickens offered, as usual volunteering our services in dangerous undertakings without once even considering consulting me. "Wilkie and I are at your service."

That light was in Dickens's eye once again, that eagerness in his voice, which signalled his readiness to take risks, to sally out into Field's tangled underworld and do battle with the monsters who inhabited its labyrinthine ways. That light of the novelist burning to live out the fantasies of his fiction most certainly was once again smouldering in his eyes. *We are off*, that light flashed out, *upon a new adventure*, and I knew that somewhere in back of it lay some tiny reassurance for one skeptical Wilkie Collins that said, *Never fear Wilkie, follow along with us and we'll make a novelist of you yet.*

"Yes, of course, what can we do to help," to my utter disbelief I heard myself offering aloud.

"As I said." Field spoke in a low voice even though Miss Katie sat smoking her pipe at the far end of the tap. "I need 'im out, but the crime is too great for me ta simply release 'im inta my own Protectives' custody. An' if I did, all o' London would know 'ee was under my power an' 'is usefulness for my purposes would be gone. But if 'ee escapes, 'ee's out there on 'is own, dangerous, a threat ta everybody, an' 'at's jus' 'ow I want 'im ta be. An' 'at's why I wants yew two ta 'elp 'im escape."

"But why us?" Dickens was a veritable fount of questions this night. "Why not two of your constables, men unknown to the turnkeys at Newgate? Why us, two gentleman amateurs?" The gleam in Dickens's eye told me that he was toying with Field. He didn't believe for one moment that two Bow Street constables could effect the release of Tally Ho Thompson from Newgate any more efficiently than could Dickens and Collins, Detectives.

"Yew two are perfect for a Queen's shoppin' list o' reasons." Field had that same game-playing twinkle in his eye that was flashing from Dickens's mischievous orbs. "But one o' the best is the Fleet Street appetite for the sensational crime."

"What!" Dickens was puzzled. "There's already been a

55

double murder, how much more sensationalistic can the crime be?"

"I want Thompson's escape ta be a ripper, a screamer in big 'eads on every front page an' broadside in London. It won't be if 'ee jus' escapes on 'is own. The gaolers at Newgate are notorious for coverin' up escapes until they are news no more, or until they've sent their own blood'ounds an' bounty 'unters out ta catch the rabbit an' either skin 'im or bring 'im back for roastin'."

"So?" One could not help but sense that Dickens was a bit impatient with the extravagance of Field's quaint metaphoricism.

"So, if the famous Mister Dickens is connected ta the escape o' an accused murderer, suddenly all the front pages, sesame or such-like, swings open ta us. The connection o' one Mister Charles Dickens, novelist, ta this escape will be grist for ev'ry paper mill on Fleet Street an' Grub Street."

The man was truly a marvel. He missed nothing and he thought of everything. There were more angles to his intelligence than there were pretenders to the French throne or titled murderers in Italian opera. Field was one of those rare specimens who always seemed to know exactly where he was going and never wavered from that path. As long as I have known the man, going on twenty-three years now, I have never ceased to be amazed at the talent he had for plotting, for moving his characters (like Thackeray with his puppets in *Vanity Fair*) from room to room and house to house and county to county. If, as Field often said of Dickens, the novelist would "wear well in my line," then the opposite certainly might be true. The detective, if by some miracle he could write, would make a captivating novelist.

Leaning conspiratorially close to the two of us and lowering his voice even further, though Miss Katie had not moved one inch from her smoking perch at the opposite end of the tap, Field whispered: "The play's the thing, gentlemun. Now 'ere's me plan."

THE ESCAPE

January 12, 1852—evening

hree days passed before Inspector Field tipped us the
wink for putting his plan into motion. The cue for
mounting this melodrama in his Newgate Theatre of
the Real materialised in the form of Serjeant Rogers, who
stepped down from the Bow Street Station's black post chaise
just after the dinner hour and knocked upon my door with an
irritable sharpness that brought Irish Meg into her doorway
across the hallway. When I opened my door, Rogers was staring at Meggy and, turning to me, offered a smug look of
prudish disapproval. *So the gentleman his keepin' his whore.*
Rogers's look censured me on the spot. Thank God Meg
couldn't see his face or she might have clawed out his eyes.
Always as officious as Queen Victoria's butler, Rogers
snapped back to the matter at hand and delivered his message
in a curt, clicking style.

"Tonight his the night, Hinspector Field has hinstructed
me to hinform you. You har to hire public conveyhance, fetch
Mister Dickens, hand proceed with hour plan hat Newgate.

Hi've halready marked the cabman Mister Dickens put on halert t' other night. He han his horse har waitin' hacross the street."

Serjeant Rogers delivered this speech as if each word were a deliberate insult to his professionalism. From the beginning, he had never been comfortable with Dickens and me, the gentleman amateurs, intruding upon his bailiwick, drawing the attention of Inspector Field away from the contemplation of Rogers's own superior merits as a detective. Like a jealous wife, he wanted Field all to himself. He reminded me of that pretentious boor Forster.*

His missive delivered, Rogers could not help but nod, step back, and cast yet one more stony look of disapproval at Meggy and me before turning on his heel and descending the stair.

"Bloody little weasel," Meg hissed after him (though he was gone and couldn't have heard) as she crossed to my doorway. "Wot is it?" she asked as I drew her in out of the hallway.

She knew that something was wrong. Her arms were around my neck and her body clinging to mine in a frightened way (most unlike her) even as I swung the door closed.

"Tonight is the night for Newgate." I tried to calm her. "I must go." She kissed me with the desperate passion of a woman sending her man off to war in the Low Countries.

In short minutes I was beavered, gloved, greatcoated, and muffled in two heavy wool scarves according to Field's directions. As I made these common preparations for going out, Meggy, unable to sit, flitted about the room like a disoriented bird.

"Well . . . I am off," I declared cheerfully, trying to break her panic, ease her skittish mind.

She rushed into my arms and crushed my lips with her kiss

---

*John Forster was Dickens' closest and oldest friend, solicitor, confidant, and ultimately biographer as well as Wilkie Collins' fiercest competitor for Dickens' favor.

as if I were a condemned man being carted off to the gallows or the guillotine.

"Pleese tyke great care, Wilkie," she breathed against my lips. "Newgate's a 'orrible plice. None cares yoo're gentlemuns there. They kills people for their shoes."

I could feel her breasts heaving against my chest. She startled me. There were few things that Irish Meg feared, but there was fear in her voice, in her clinging arms, in her desperate kiss. I broke away from her, shaken, and fled, tossing an unconvincing "don't worry" (or something garbled to that effect) back over my shoulder as I bolted for the stairs. For these people of the London streets, Newgate, the word, the idea, was a portrait of hell.

Sleepy Rob was dozing in the box parked against the kerbstone when I burst out of the building. I startled his horse, but Rob reacted at the speed of mud. His eyes rolled up out of their cradle in his elbow and he addressed my arrival with all of the animation of a slug: "Wheeeerrre tooooo, guvv?"

"Wellington Street, you know the place!" I shouted up while jumping in. I wanted to make good my escape before Irish Meg might appear for yet another desperate farewell. With surprising alacrity, probably more attributable to the heightened sentience of the horse than the driver, we were off.

Charles, who, obviously, had also been alerted by Rogers, was waiting on the doorstep at the *Household Words* offices. He, too, was bundled to the ears in greatcoat and scarves. While I had on my sporty short Oxonian beaver, he was topped by a full Tilbury hat. It was a raw January night. The streets were as empty as the Prince Regent's head. The cold wind whipping off the river had driven the whole population of London indoors.

Before climbing in, Charles greeted Sleepy Rob with a sharp tap of his stick to the box. "You remember your instructions from two nights past?" Dickens addressed him as if giving an order rather than asking a question. The sluggish cabman must have nodded, or given some other slow indication of assent, because Dickens grunted, "Good, you shall be well paid."

"It *is* a howler tonight, Wilkie," he offered by way of greeting as he settled himself across from me and wound a mouldy cab blanket around his ankles. We two were a curious sight. Two gentlemen, muffled up in greatcoats and scarves like Turkish dervishes, our top hats pulled down over our ears and foreheads, huddling from the cold in a hansom cab, clattering across London in the dark of the moon on the rawest evening of the year.

Nine o' the clock sounded from the black steeple of St. Dunstan's as we trundled out of the Strand and into Fleet Street. Because there was no moon, it was as dark as the depths of Loch Ness. I remember looking out of the window as Sleepy Rob flogged us toward Newgate and remarking to Dickens on the blackness of the night. "It is as if we've descended into hell," I said.

"No, Wilkie, we are not there yet," Charles somberly disagreed, "but we soon will be."

At first I thought his answer strange, but thinking back upon it now, I understand it well. I do not believe he meant Newgate alone. Perhaps he was contemplating what Newgate held in store for us that night, yet I do not feel that was his sole concern either. He had that particular sort of rapt look as we rumbled toward Newgate shut in against the swirling wind and driving sleet that signalled his novelist's preoccupation with larger issues.

"I hate prisons, Wilkie." He suddenly broke the silence of our rolling closet and startled me out of my own contemplative attempt to read his mind. "I fear this is going to be a long, dark night."

It already is, I was tempted to retort, but I held my tongue and he, as suddenly as he had spoken, subsided into his meditative mood.

As I look back upon our ride across West London that bitter night, I feel I know what it was that so wrapped Dickens in thought. He, for some reason, mayhap some fright or fascination of his childhood, had always been fascinated by prisons. In his first full novel, he had cast Mister Pickwick into the Fleet, thus precipitating the only dark interlude in that otherwise sunny and hilarious book. In his second, *Oliver Twist*, he had actually dragged his readers into the condemned man's cell to witness the guilty madness of Fagin, the corrupter of youth.

Large tracts of *Barnaby Rudge* employ Newgate as their setting. It would certainly not be untoward to inquire why all his life Dickens would display such a morbid fascination for prisons, why the image and portent of the prison would cast its shadow over almost every one of his novels to come. He had put Pickwick, and Fagin, and poor brain-battered Barnaby in prison, but until this night had he ever been there, really been there, himself? Perhaps that was what he was thinking, perhaps not.

Sleepy Rob reined in, Dickens and I turned out, and, muffled against the wind and sleet, presented ourselves to the turnkey on the Newgate lock.

Sleepy Rob had his directions. Three nights before, after leaving Field and Rogers at the Lord Gordon Arms, Dickens had, essentially, put our somnolent friend on a retainer. I had overheard Dickens engage Sleepy Rob. "You have done well for us tonight," Dickens complimented the doltish cabman. "I will need you again. Here is coin to insure that for the next fortnight you shall, in the evenings, always be available to us, Mister Collins and myself. Your post will be directly outside Mister Collins' door. You will drive us where we wish to go and wait for us while our business proceeds." Sleepy Rob looked at him with the incomprehension of idiocy and slowly nodded his head in the affirmative as he took Dickens's money.

As had been the case three nights before, we carried authority to enter Newgate to visit from Inspector Field. Greeted by a pair of yellowing eyes, we duly passed this document through the tiny grille. The turnkey admitted us without hesitation; our names and Inspector Field's signature were on the document. After a cursory inspection—the man reached out

61

and adjusted my scarf so that he could better see my face, and, reaching up to the much taller Dickens, did the same, giving him but the slightest of glances—the turnkey scuttled quickly back into his cubicle out of the wind and sleet that pelted down upon the gallow's courtyard. I was forced to follow into the tiny guardhouse.

"We don't know where to go," I protested. "The prisoner has obtained a room."

"At's number one 'undred an' five, north corridor," the turnkey offered, clearly harbouring no intention whatsoever of leaving the shelter of his lock and confronting the bitter winter night in order to guide us to our destination within the labyrinth of the prison proper.

"And how might we find one hundred and five, north corridor?" The man was stretching my patience, but Field had specifically ordered that it would be in the plan's best interest if I gave the turnkey on the gate ample opportunity to become familiar with my face, voice, mannerisms, and temper. It was, indeed, all part of the plan.

The reluctant turnkey, hugging himself as a way of keeping all the warmth of his closet in custody, gave me directions— enter the door immediately across the gallows yard, follow the corridor to the second intersecting passageway and turn north—and then repeated, as if to add insult to disinterest, " 'At's one 'undred an' five, north corridor, guv."

Without thanking him, I stalked out, collected Dickens from the black shelter of the wall, and, at the helm, beat across the gallows yard against the buffeting wind. Unhooking the heavy rope fastener of the door, I followed as Dickens cast himself into the darkness within.

"One hundred and five, north corridor?" I spoke into a void of blackness.

"Wait, Wilkie," Dickens ghostly voice was soft and coming from somewhere to the left. "I can't see a blessed thing." Where we stood in the throat of that corridor there were not even shadows, for there was no light whatsoever to feed them. It was black as pitch and silent as a cloister. The only sound was a quick rustle, not unlike the sweep of a tiny broom, as a rat skittered along the facing of the stone wall.

In short moments, our eyes grew somewhat accustomed to the black, but there was no way that we could see any numbers upon any cell doors. We could hardly see the dark outlines of the doors themselves. We felt our way along the mouldy walls until we found the second intersection of hallways, and took what we hoped was our turn to the north, though, God knows, in that abyss of blackness how anyone could maintain a sense of direction. After making that turn, small snatches of flickering light seemed to escape from beneath and around some of the doors only to be consumed by the darkness of the gaol corridor.

"We'll never find it in this light," Dickens muttered, more to himself than to me. "We must find a guide."

A blind Virgil to lead us further down into these depths, that wry thought taunted my already over-anxious mind. If I hadn't thought it a hundred times already since our first being included in the machinations of Inspector Field, I had certainly been thinking it adamantly since the first moment of our entry into that infernal dark hole: *We are gentlemen, not policemen! We should not be doing this. By all that's holy, we should not be Here!* But I knew that my secret thoughts and misgivings would make no impression whatsoever upon Charles, even if I was able to muster the courage to express them. "Oh Wilkie, where is your sense of adventure?" he would surely say with a heedless laugh.

A brief thought of Meggy darted across my mind. Back in our Soho flats she would be waiting, pacing like a caged cat, fretting about my safety. It was somehow comforting to think that she was thinking of me.

We felt our way along the corridor until we found a chamber door that showed some promise. A dim light emanated from the chinks at its sides and bottom. Somewhat more aggressive murmurings seemed to be hissing from within. Charles's sharp knock on that door, unannounced to me, caught me utterly by surprise, straightened me up in alarum, made the very hair on my head tingle with the sudden threat. When the door quickly opened, momentarily blinding us with a flood of dim lamplight, I had even more reason for alarum.

Immediately, that door was filled with a veritable mountain of a man, covered with hair from the top of his head to the neighbourhood of his knees. Coursing through my body was the instantaneous horror that savages in the American wilderness must experience when suddenly confronted by one of their great grizzly bears. But this apparition was man, not bear. The resemblance stood in his matted hair, his tangled beard, and the raggedness of his torn and tattered wool coat and leggings.

"Ooze at?" the thing growled out the door of its den. "Wot yew want?"

"We need your assistance, my good man." I could tell by the moment's hesitation and the slight waver of uncertainty in his voice that even the generally fearless (or heedless) Dickens was somewhat taken aback by this creature confronting us in the doorway.

" 'Moy gude mon,' moy bloody *arse!* Yew fagging quimsby," the grizzly in the doorway snarled, assuming what seemed to me a stance of imminent attack. But Charles did not turn tail and run as I so wanted to, and, for some reason, his temerity prevented me from fleeing as well.

"We need help in finding number one hundred and five, north corridor," Dickens, speaking quickly and sharply, momentarily subdued the brute. "We will pay," Charles hastily added. That stipulation proved the saving grace.

At the mention of coin, that hairy devil in the doorway stepped backward into the light, which revealed his face breaking into an avaricious grin. His mouth opened in that instinctive reflex of approval, and showed him to be an utterly toothless bear indeed, and somehow, despite his intimidating size, no longer the threat he had initially seemed.

" 'Oww much?" he cajoled through that toothless grin.

But before Dickens could answer, a much more intelligible

voice from within cut off our combative colloquy with Ursa Major.

"Bring 'em in, Jemmy," that laughing voice ordered, "they're mates o' mine."

The thing backed further out of the doorway and, in the exaggerated mimicking of a minuet dancer's bow (made even more incongruous by its sudden appearance in a place such as this), and with a disgusting widening of that toothless grin, beckoned us to enter.

I must admit that I had no inclination to dive into that particular Newgate chamber of potential horrors; quite the contrary, my inclination was to flee. Dickens, however, without the slightest hesitation, swept right into the room, actually clapping that toothless, hairy creature on the shoulder in passing. I, of course, had no choice but to follow. When I think back upon it, upon all of those years of our friendship of the night streets, the one recurring memory that pushes itself to the front of my consciousness is of being forced to enter the most infernal dens of that dark city against both my better judgement and my will simply because Dickens, that madman, went first and I had no choice—as a man, as a friend, as a would-be novelist—but to follow.

Perhaps Charles had recognised that laughing voice, and perhaps that recognition had contributed to his intrepidity, but I, in my trepidation and disorientation, certainly had not. Thus, when I finally and unwillingly followed Charles into that room, you can imagine my astonishment to come face-to-face with the very object of our quest sitting at a rough table with guttering candles on its corners playing at cards. It was, indeed, none other than Tally Ho Thompson himself, in the flesh, smirking at the looks of anxiety and relief on our faces and tipping a wink to his cohorts at the discomfiture of the two swells who had come stumbling in search of him. They were playing at a game of "sharps," and seemed disinclined to divert their attention from their cards for formal introductions, so Dickens and I simply nodded genially all around.

With grizzly Jem reclaiming his seat at the makeshift card table, the game was enthusiastically resumed, giving Dickens and myself a brief interlude in which to study the inmates of this jolly cell. Next to Jem sat an extremely high forehead sloping into an extremely long nose overhanging an extremely sparse mustache. He looked a comical rat. "Yewrr draw Shylock," hulking Jem addressed this creature as the game progressed. I do not think that was the man's given Christian name, but rather a racial epithet, yet, since he was called by no other over the course of the game, it must have been acceptable to him and all. Across the table from the bear and the rat sat the giraffe. This creature was addressed as Rory as the game became heated. He had flat and dull red hair, listless vacant eyes, an emaciated torso and limbs, and the longest, thinnest neck of anyone ever placed upon this earth. Finally, across the table from these others with his back against the stone cell wall sat Tally Ho Thompson himself like some sort of jolly zookeeper holding court amidst his creatures.

There was something courtly, gentlemanlike, about Thompson, even in these squalid surroundings. I have always marvelled at his protean ability to shift shape and adjust temper according to his surroundings while never losing that maddening grin of amusement no matter how threatening the neighbourhood or intimidating the circumstances. Armed with his ironic grin, which intimated that he did not really care about anything—whether he won or lost, succeeded or failed, loved or lusted, lived or died—Thompson floated through life as if it were the world's task to buoy him up and carry him along and deposit him at his destination without his being in any way responsible for the transaction. Thompson was a man who exerted startling control over his world without exerting the slightest effort toward that end.

Tipping us a laughing wink, Thompson played the decisive card upon his animal friends and declared "Sharps to yew, mates!" even as he was bending forward to collect his meager winnings. The other three looked at him with the dull incomprehension of their subspecies and threw down their cards in what looked to be a well-practised disgust. Offering a teasing excuse—"These gents 'ave come all the way from Swellstown just ta see me, mates"—and a seductive challenge—"Ye'll git yer chance ta win it back afore the night 'as blown itself out"—Thompson sprang to his feet and slid lithely out from behind the table.

"So ye want to see one hundred an' five, north corridor, do ye?" he addressed us with that mischievous grin dancing around the corner of his mouth. "Well, it sure ain't my idee o' suitable bachelor digs. It's Rats' Castle damp an' church steeple cold an' 'Ampstead 'Eeath quiet an' dark. Thank God for the rats, they raise the quality o' the neighbour'ood." With that pronouncement, he led us out of their gaming room, along the dark corridor some indeterminate distance, and into a black cistern of musty smells and rustling sounds.

He groped his way across the barely six feet of chamber— honestly, the cell was little bigger than a grave—and fumbled into dim light a candle guttered into a tiny hollow in the windowless stone wall. As the candlelight quickly dispersed across the cell to where Dickens and I stood in the doorway, it revealed the most squalid, rotting, smoke-stained, water-marked, and polluted of accommodations. The air in one hundred and five, north corridor, seemed heavy enough and close enough to suffocate us. The walls were blackened with soot, and covered with obscene, desperate, perhaps insane tracings, garbled words and mad pictures all run into each other like wall drawings in some caveman's Bedlam. The floor was bare except for a dingy, unmade bed manacled into the darkest corner of that narrow closet. Thompson had no chair to offer us, no table to seat us around, no fire to warm us. He simply stood there beside that guttering candle with that maddening grin crooked on his face like a crack in a mirror.

It utterly baffled me, how in the most squalid or threatening or oppressive of circumstances, Tally Ho Thompson never lost his equilibrium, always was able to muster up that insane cheerfulness and unconcern, which seemed to trumpet to the

67

world, "It's all the same ta me, mates; oy've seen worse an' will agin an' this ain't so bad." The grin was his way of disarming others, deceiving them into thinking that he was just another bumpkin who would be an easy mark.

"Well, mates"—Thompson grinned—"it ain't Buckingham Palace, but it ain't got dirt walls an' floors neither." Was his reference to the grave or to some highwayman's cave? I could not decode his meaning.

At his signal we entered, if taking two small steps to the centre of the room can be deemed an entrance. I closed the heavy wooden door reluctantly behind us, wondering if there was enough air accumulated within to service all three of us. We needed our privacy, however, and the swinging to of the heavy door of that pestilent cistern was a necessary evil.

"To what do I owe the pleasure, gents?" Thompson knew something was up as soon as the door swung closed. "We're a bit glum an' intent this evenin' are we not?" he teased.

"You are leaving Newgate tonight," Dickens whispered urgently, though, God knows, one could shout at the top of one's lungs in that tiny cell in that black labyrinth and not a soul would pay any heed. "Inspector Field needs you free, on the outside, in order to proceed in the solving of this murder case."

"Fieldsy needs me agin, I knew it." Thompson was positively gleeful. "I wos gimcracked right inta the middle o' these murders like a puppet on a string an' I'm the one ta wrap that string around the puppetmaster's neck."

I observed the infectiousness of Thompson's animation upon Dickens. In the flickering light, that look of renewed excitement flowed back into Dickens's eyes. *Now we are in the middle of a new adventure!* Dickens's whole carriage and mien seemed to shout. Suddenly that squalid, suffocating room was infused with purpose and anticipation.

"Wot's the plan?" Thompson's conspiratorial glee was even drawing me into the spirit of the moment.

"You and I are to change places. We are near the same height. You will leave with Wilkie in the identity of Charles

Dickens and in the morning I will protest that you forced the change upon me," Dickens delivered his explanation as if giving an after-dinner speech at the London Tavern.

"Yew're gointa spend the night in Newgate so's I kin bolt?" Thompson was momentarily taken aback at the prospect. You see, it was a question of rank. Thompson was having a moment of trouble understanding why a gentleman like Dickens would give up home and hearth of a winter night to help a ne'er-do-well like him escape from Newgate. Thompson finally fought his way out of this quandary: "If Fieldsy set yew ta it, then it must be up ta snuff," Thompson acquiesced to the plan. " 'Ow do we mount up?"

"We have come muffled in greatcoats and scarves to hide our identities. We must change boots and you must wear my gloves," Dickens explained as he sat down on the small bed to remove his boots. "It is a brutal night outside. We are depending upon the turnkey to be not overscrupulous."

I watched as Dickens removed his hat and pulled off his boots while Tally Ho Thompson did the same. Thompson handed his boots—much higher and rougher then Dickens's and decidedly of the horse-riding kind—over to his understudy. I had uttered nary a word since entering Thompson's dark den, but, as Dickens bent to pull on Thompson's boots, I saw my opportunity to tug upon Thompson's shoulder and move my lips to his ear. I had been well-schooled by Inspector Field on what to say and do at this juncture. This was my private part of the plan which Dickens neither knew about nor must overhear.

As Thompson straightened up at my tug on his shoulder, I whispered into his ear, "You must hit him with this as you did the footman in Ashbee's house the night we broke into his secret library.* Be most careful. You must only stun him yet leave a mark. It is for appearances. He is one of the greatest

*This event was described in Collins' first discovered journal that I as editor retitled for publication as *The Detective and Mr. Dickens* (St. Martin's Press, 1990).

69

minds in England. I hope you realise how much is entrusted to your expertise." The black gutta-percha equaliser slid like a snake out of my hand into his.

"Turn him so that I am behind," Thompson, understanding immediately, murmured back.

"Your feet are bigger than mine," Dickens remarked as he stood up, interrupting our private colloquy.

"Mind those boots, guv." Thompson chuckled. "They fits the stirrups like a glove. I'd hate to lose 'em."

Charles was removing his scarves and greatcoat and handing them to Thompson when I spoke: "Look here, Charles"— my voice was quavering despite the fact that I had known for three days what I must do—"the hieroglyphs on this wall must contain the material of ten novels. I'll wager there are Pickwicks and Fagins and Barnwells galore represented in these divers hands."

Charles, momentarily distracted, took two steps across that pinched cell in the dim candlelight to peruse the shadowy wall toward which I pointed. As he straightened to comment upon my observation, Thompson, who had moved as silently as a cat behind Dickens, tapped him at the back of the ear. In the flickering light Charles's eyes suddenly went wide, then vacant. He collapsed face first into my arms, his dead weight almost knocking me to the floor.

We carried him to the bed and laid him amongst the ragged blankets. Guilt flooded into my consciousness. *My God, what have I done,* I thought. His eyes were closed and he lay deathly still. *Oh Lord, he's dead.* Panic gripped me like a huge tentacle pulling me beneath the surface.

"You haven't hurt him, have you?" I was still whispering like a felon. "We haven't hurt him, have we?" I took my share of the responsibility.

Thompson was standing there grinning in that maddening way of his. " 'Ee'll be fine. Not ta worry a tot. 'Ee'll 'ave a small robin's egg back o' 'is ear come mornin' but 'ee'll still be able ta write those novels as easy as a jumper clearin' a 'edge.

70

Or"—and his mocking grin widened—"would yew like ta be writin' 'em for 'im?"

I was tempted to go for the man's throat, but we had more pressing business at hand.

In Dickens's greatcoat with the scarves wrapped high around his chin and Dickens's top hat perched high upon his head, Thompson could easily pass for Charles. Thompson was clean-shaven of face, though somewhat stubbly after four days in Newgate, and Charles had just recently begun to affect a square little goatee, like some Russian czar or Gypsy busker (quite ridiculous-looking, I thought), but the scarves covering Thompson's chin concealed this one defect in the disguise. Thompson looked to me for approval. I nodded emphatically. We solicited one more examination of Dickens's condition on the ragged bed—breathing steady, sleeping soundly—then stepped out into the black corridor.

As we groped our way along the walls of that dark labyrinth, Thompson in the lead, a position that I would assume as soon as we reached the prison yard, I remembered what Inspector Field had said three nights before in the snug of the Lord Gordon Arms: " 'Ee's an actor, for gawd's sake! 'Ee art ta be able ta mimic anyone, 'specially they're same size as 'ee." *He's not an actor,* I thought, my nerves starting to fray like a piece of old worsted, *he's a highwayman and pickpocket temporarily walking around onstage. This is not going to work.*

When we reached the door to the gallows yard, I stopped Thompson with a hand to his shoulder. "Let me go first," I ordered. "The turnkey has seen and marked me. If we are stopped, I am prepared to bribe the lock. If that does not work, you must be prepared for violence. Field and Rogers will be waiting outside down the street." With those curt and rehearsed directions delivered, I pulled on the rope latch of the door and plunged out into the driving sleet of the Newgate gallows yard. I glanced quickly back over my shoulder. Tally Ho Thompson was, indeed, following jauntily behind.

Dickens is the lucky one, I thought, *sleeping peacefully while I must face this terrible uncertainty.* I had complete confidence in

71

Field's plan, in Thompson's disguise, in the inattention of the turnkey, in the abetting bitterness of the weather, yet my heart was racing in fear of discovery. Some people perhaps, like Thompson, are simply bred to be felons, but I, incontrovertibly, was not one of that breed. I was terrified of being caught, horrified at the spectre of embarrassment, frightened that I would prove myself a complete fool in carrying out this task of derring-do that had been assigned to me, and I vowed to never again allow Dickens to draw me into any of his mad schemes of this ilk. In the future, I would assert myself more forcefully against his presumptuous will.

We crossed the courtyard bent low against the driving sleet and approached the turnkey's cubicle. The man, muffled as tightly as we against the winter cold, poked his head out quickly from his hovel and measured us in the most cursory and weather-avoiding way. He did not ask us to step in and unwind our mufti of collars and scarves so that he could peruse our identification. He did not ask to see again the document of passage that I had supplied upon entering, and that I had ready to hand in my greatcoat pocket. As we stood before him, he seemed to immediately decide that the two gentlemen, who but thirty minutes before had entered the prison on Inspector Field's authority, were still the same heights and shapes (or near), were still bundled tightly against the winter wind, were still above suspicion. With little more than this cursory glance, the keeper of the lock turned back into his shelter to fetch his huge ring of keys from their peg on the wall. Then, hugging the prison wall to avoid the cut of the sleeting wind, he moved to open the door for our embarkation.

It has worked, I thought, *we're out. Field is, indeed, a genius.*

The turnkey worked his key on its huge ring at the small door inset in the high iron gate. I stood, with Thompson in Dickens's guise directly behind, waiting for the key to turn and the door to open, and our passage out of that infernal place to be signalled.

The key turned, the lock surrendered, and that muffled

clown worked at the door's large black iron hasp. With a sudden pull, that small door sprang open, giving passage to a bitter blast of wind from the street that blew me backward into my partner in crime. Perhaps because my Oxonian was not a full top hat, perhaps because it was tight-fitting and pulled down almost to my ears, I was able to keep it on when that lash of wind rushed in upon us. But perhaps because Dickens's Tilbury was higher and wider, and did not tightly fit the contours of Thompson's head, my partner in gaol-break was not so lucky.

Dickens's hat went pinwheeling off of Thompson's head and across the prison yard like a flushed grouse scurrying for cover. It rolled on its brim over the smooth stones and came to rest hard against the base of the gallows tree. Thompson hesitated but one brief moment, in which time he darted first a brief glance at the open door through which the wind was rushing and then a glance at me straightening and staring wide-eyed at him, and then he did an inexplicable thing.

He ran after the hat!

He ran back into the prison yard to retrieve that bloody hat!

Good God, I thought, *his hair is much darker than Charles's and he is beardless. Now we are done!* Inspector Field's plan had worked so well, each step ticking off like a piece of precision clockwork, and now the hazard of the elements, some vengeful Aeolian banshee, had stepped in to ruin it all. "Victims of the ill-judged execution of a well-judged plan," I think Samuel Johnson once said. That was certainly what we were at that moment.*

He chased that spinning hat across the prison yard and retrieved it from the grasp of the gallows. He returned, walking naturally, not hurrying the slightest, probably doing it so casually just to plague me (who wanted only to get through that open door and away from this infernal den before the world gave way beneath my anxiety), walking toward me and

*This was quoted by James Boswell in his compendious life of Dr. Johnson, a staple of every reputable Victorian library.

73

the uncomprehending turnkey. As he strolled so nonchalantly, Thompson pulled the recalcitrant hat down around his ears and wrapped the woollen scarf tighter around his chin. I swear, though I could not see his mouth beneath the mufti, that the man was grinning the whole way, mocking me with his heedless unconcern, his actor's ease at being onstage. In a sense, that whole little melodrama, which had entwined me in a web of such excruciating suspense, was but an actor's choice. Instead of bolting for the open door immediately upon the opportunity presenting itself, Thompson instead chose to remain in character, maintaining his role as Dickens rather than assuming the role of an escaping murderer. He reacted with an actor's instinct and his audience of one bought it utterly.

"She's a mean wind off the river this night, gennulmuns." The turnkey was already turning tail to flee back into the shelter of his tiny box even as he ushered us out through that small wind-lashed door. " 'Old onto yoore 'ats," he tossed a final bit of sage (though rather obvious) advice back over his shoulder as he clanged the door closed behind us.

Then we were, miraculously, in the street. I breathed a towering sigh of relief. Thompson, I am sure, beneath his scarves, was grinning madly like some fearless idiot incapable of even recognising a threat when it jumps up and tweaks his nose.

As I look back upon it now from the safe vantage of twenty years, trying to capture the tension of the scene in my words, I am almost moved to laughter. Strange how the haze of memory, of "recollection in tranquillity," can brush a comical cast over what seemed at that time a life and death situation. As I remember Thompson scurrying across the yard to retrieve that hat, pressed against the face of the gallows like a newly severed head just dropped from under the guillotine's blade, it all strikes me as more comical than threatening, actually absurd. Perhaps comedy always lurks in the underbrush of life and one must attain a certain perspective upon

74

it, flush it into flight, before one can perceive its laughing face.

As I and my charge stood there in the dark street outside Newgate with the wind howling all around and the sleet pelting down like devil's spit, I felt as if I had just walked some pirates' plank or run an Indian gauntlet in the American Wild West . . . and survived. Sleepy Rob's hansom cab clattered up out of the darkness in the most natural way. The two of us stepped into it with the ease of practise, and it rolled off down the street away from that dreadful prison as if it were but another smooth-turning part in some ingenious machine. Which, of course, it was. And, the grand machinist, the master of these machinations, awaited us.

Sleepy Rob's cab took us straight to Inspector Field. He was sitting in the sinister black post chaise with THE METROPOLITAN PROTECTIVES, BOW STREET STATION rendered in a circular medallion on its side door, parked only minutes away in the privacy of Shoe Lane. Field and Rogers stepped down from that vulture of a coach as we pulled up. Thompson and myself climbed out of our cab even as Inspector Field rushed up to me, grasped my hand, and began pumping it as if he expected that vigorous motion to produce a flow of water from a well. As Field shook my hand, I had a sense of him turning me toward him while I simultaneously had a vague sense of Serjeant Rogers accosting Tally Ho Thompson in a similar way behind my back. Then suddenly, persisting in holding my hand tightly in one of his, Field, for some inexplicable reason, as if possessed by some mischievous impulse, reached up and knocked off my hat. As I looked at Field in surprise, my knees suddenly buckled and all went black in my head. It was a rather quick sensation of sinking underwater before all sentience left and I drowned in the black void of unconsciousness.

I learned later that just as I had set up Dickens for Thompson's facile trick for the rendering of unconsciousness, so had Field's brisk handshake maneuvered me into position while Rogers gave Thompson the high sign to hit me with the very equalizer with which I had supplied him earlier in the evening.

I awoke more than two hours later in the back of Rob's cab surrounded by constables in a completely different area of London with my hands bound up by my own cravat and my ankles tied together by my own braces. Rob was also sporting a rather ostentatious bulging under his left eye, which he swore was administered by the tall man in the tall hat and the grey scarves whom he had acquired at Number Sixteen, Wellington Street, Strand, earlier in the evening and conveyed to Newgate Prison. I, of course, affirmed his halting story as best I could in my befogged state of recovering consciousness. A constable had found Sleepy Rob's four-legged business partner grazing unconcerned in the middle of the way on the Chelsea Embankment miles from Newgate and well out of Inspector Field's Bow Street bailiwick.

Both myself and Sleepy Rob gave sketchy narratives of what had happened since my entering the cab outside Newgate with the tall man in the tall hat whom I steadfastly asserted was Charles Dickens. The constables wrote down our muddled statements, taking me for a gentleman badly confused by a tap on the head and Sleepy Rob as the slow-moving, slow-witted imbecile whom he gave consistent evidence to the world of being. No report of Tally Ho Thompson's escape had yet surfaced in the flow of police communications by the time we were released at almost five in the morning.

I had a splitting headache and Sleepy Rob was utterly noncommittal. He didn't seem to mind at all the large brown mouse swelling beneath his left eye. He retrieved his business partner from the hitching post in the alley behind Chelsea Town Hall, packed me into his cab, and delivered me to my Soho rooms. Irish Meg was waiting up for me in the parlor, sitting with her legs tucked up beneath her on the love seat, with her face streaked with tears of worry. As I opened the door, she leapt up and ran into my arms, crushing me in her embrace as if holding on to the last spar in a shipwreck, pulling my face down to her kiss in desperate need. She kissed me long and passionately, and then she buried her face in my chest and held me fast in the circle of her arms for a long moment.

Suddenly, however, she stepped back from me. The old fire once again blazed up in her eyes, that anger and defiance I knew so well. Without the slightest warning or the least provocation, she slapped me hard across the face. "If yew ever put me through somethin' like this again, Mister Wilkie Collins," she hissed, "I swear I'll 'ave yew done!"

A NIGHT IN NEWGATE

January 12–13, 1852

Dickens's night in Newgate was not one of induced and dreamless sleep as was mine in the back of Sleepy Rob's cab.

"They came to me in the night, these familiars, these devils sent from some other world. They danced around me like furies sent to plague my imagination. They were familiar familiars, indeed, yet changed and mixed, distorted and confused. They were grotesque, but not deformed. They were indeed frightening, yet in no way maimed or twisted or threatening. They were, perhaps, so unsettling because they seemed to follow no plots, move in no foreseen direction, exist for no reason but to plague me with past guilts, past sins, past omissions, and new spectres of threat. Perhaps they were a warning for the future.

"These phantasms swirled around me, sometimes flying in the air, sometimes dancing and jumping and howling around that tiny cell, striking sparks off the touching of their feet, flames bursting out in their hair, circling with grotesque grins and maniacal laughter, pointing crook'd forefingers at me as if I were the sacrificial victim at the center of some strange satanic rite.

"That tall and ragged Jew, that twisted dwarf, that hanged man, that lecherous nobleman, those fiery rioters, the dying children, the starving workers, the drunken husbands, the shrewish wives, the cursing rich and the weeping poor, the murderers, the monsters, the lawyers.

"All were there to plague me, as if a magical casement had suddenly opened in that solid stone wall and they had all flooded in to drown me in their palpable presences. In a profane chorus they cursed me for creating them, and not heeding them, and killing them off at my whim. They screeched demands of me. As they danced and howled around me, they were ghastly devils, mythic monsters, real people begging for new life. As they swirled and jumped and flew around me, I had the power in but the blink of my eye to shift their shape, control their destinies even as they spun in the midst of this demonic dance. At once they were both daimons and demons, angels and devils, human beings and phantasms insubstantial as air. And yet they all were grey as death no matter how animated in their dance or fiery in their demeanor or gay in their finery. They were all dead, ghosts, and it was as if they held me solely accountable. I felt like Odysseus in the underworld facing the despair of his fellow comrades from the field of Troy.

"But this dance of my furies, my devilish familiars, was but a general phantasmagoria, a prelude to my real horror. Soon I was cast into a terrible dream. My real nightmare began.

"I was in a closed room, at first it was that cell in Newgate, but then it was this newspaper office, but then again it was my study in the Devonshire Terrace house. I was being held prisoner in that protean room which kept changing yet was always so familiar. I tried to leave the room. There was a polished brass knob on the door. I turned it, pulled at it, tried with both hands to open the door, but the knob simply froze and the door would not open. I braced my feet against the door and pulled on that mocking shiny knob, but the door would not open. And then the voices began.

" 'Play with me, Daddy dear. Do you have to go?' a child's voice, not sad, laughing but coaxing. My baby Dora?* 'Charles, how nice of you to come, I haven't seen you for awhile,' my own dad's voice, I think,† not censuring, only making conversation, filling dead air with meaningless babble as he always did. But the next was different. 'Help me, someone help me!' it screamed, terror quivering in all its registers. And I pulled harder at the knob and the door 'til my arms ached with the effort and a burning pain seared between my shoulder blades. It was *her* voice, Wilkie, not screaming for me, but screaming for help, for someone, anyone, to save her from that rapist, from those men.‡ And there was nothing I could do. I was helpless, Wilkie, locked in my room, trying to get out, but locked in behind that heavy immovable door, at the mercy of that cold, polished brass knob.

"I stepped back and stared at that brass knob, then fell to one knee to see if I was right. My face was staring back at me out of that polished piece of brasswork. I was my own gaoler. That brass knob mirrored my own restless unease with this locked-in life I lead. That is what that dream meant. Unable to open that door, imprisoned, whether in a gaol like Newgate as I was last night, or within my own mind, it makes no difference, a prison is a frightening place, Wilkie. The horror

*His youngest child, Dora, had died of a strange seizure on April 14, 1851, some ten months earlier. The night of her death is described in Collins' first secret journal.

†His father, William Dickens, had died in March, 1851, barely three weeks before the death of little Dora Annie. Dickens, after these two family deaths following one upon the other, had fallen temporarily into a morbid state and had remarked to Collins: "Death seems closing all around me."

‡Collins' first secret journal also told of the rape, by an assailant subsequently murdered, and the abduction, by Lord Henry Ashbee, of a young actress named Ellen Ternan who, at the time of the events of this second secret journal, was residing in Urania Cottage, a Home for Fallen Women sponsored by Miss Angela Burdett-Coutts, a close friend of Dickens, where she was recovering from her ordeal.

81

was in the realising that I was in that prison and that I was the gaoler as well; my whole life was a prison keeping me from the important things beckoning on the other side of the locked door.

"I tell you, Wilkie, when I awoke from that nightmare I thought for a moment that I actually was in the condemned cell; I was going mad myself as Fagin did before I executed his grim sentence. I felt as if I truly knew what it was like to have that dreadful scaffold looming over my whole existence."

Dickens, tired and haggard, had a wild and troubled look in his eye as he related all of this strange dreaming to me. He had only two hours before been released from Newgate. Upon awaking from his menacing dreams in that cold dark cell, he had rushed to the door and, to his great relief, it had opened effortlessly to his touch. Stumbling in Tally Ho Thompson's riding boots, he rushed to the lock and set up a clamour of protest that he was none other than Mister Charles Dickens, the famous author, and that he had been knocked on the head while visiting a prisoner the night before.

The turnkeys, indeed, had a great laugh at that. They thought Dickens more fun and entertainment than a one-man band in Piccadilly. In short, they did not believe his story at all at first. They sent him back to his cell to stew. He must have felt he was in a waking nightmare. But then Forster, who is, after all, Charles's solicitor, had arrived at the prison, summoned no doubt by Inspector Field, with an order from the Queen's Bench for Dickens's release. At the same time, somehow, mysteriously, the Grub Street hacks, as well as reputable reporters of the Fleet Street persuasion, began to arrive at the Newgate lock.

Forster found Dickens with a small bump behind his ear (which Forster wisely insisted the turnkeys on duty examine carefully), but otherwise unhurt. Yet Forster remarked to me later that he had been concerned for Charles that gloomy winter morning as they rode in a hansom away from Newgate.

"He had a troubled look about him," Forster confided, in

a patronising way of course, as if I were some child allowed to sit at the table with the grown-ups. "He seemed shaken and scared."

Forster, with Dickens in tow, had fought through the crowd of newspaper reporters outside Newgate and had, at Charles's request, transported him to the *Household Words* offices in Wellington Street.

"As I walked out in the morning in the company of Forster and a constable, sent by Field no doubt, past that terrible scaffold of death," Dickens pressed this frightening confidence upon me, "I felt utterly guilty, fit to be hanged. I felt, I swear Wilkie, as if I had just spent the night before my own execution upon that perverse tree."

Once safe at Wellington Street, Charles, evidently, had assured Forster that all was well and had sent him away. Immediately thereafter, however, Charles must have sent for me because his messenger arrived at my lodgings a bit after eleven as I was yet nursing my headache. Dickens's message was urgent. He *must* talk to me. Come quickly.

I, of course, wondered if some hitch had been thrown into Inspector Field's plan. I hurried to dress and was relieved to find Sleepy Rob dozing on the box of his hansom at the kerbstone before my door. When we arrived at Wellington Street, the sharks had already gathered and were building toward their feeding frenzy. The Grub Streeters ringed the door to Number Sixteen and I had to push my way through them to enter. Wills, Dickens's faithful office Cerberus, was guarding the door and let me in, though not without trouble in keeping the hungry reporters out. All the way there I had speculated upon the reason for the urgency of the summons, but upon arriving it soon became evident that Dickens simply wanted to talk, to narrate his strange dreams, to give voice to his troubling thoughts.

"It was as if the dream had come to me from somewhere else, some other world or time, perhaps the future, the twentieth century. Who knows?" He smiled and shrugged. But that smile was but a brief interlude in his morbid mood.

83

"It was a frustrating dream. A door one is unable to open, a prison one is unable to escape, voices one is unable to silence, a gaoler who is oneself. I'm telling you all of this because I think it is some sort of message from the future and is important, but I don't know why, and I want to understand it. What do you think, Wilkie?"

I stared at him wide-eyed as if he had just asked me to murder his wife or empty his dustbins or polish his boots. I didn't have the remotest idea of how to reply, and my inventive faculties were severely hindered by the throbbing headache with which I was still afflicted. "About the closed door and the brass doorknob?" I stuttered stupidly.

He nodded, waiting.

I could feel the beads of perspiration starting to push out of my forehead as if fleeing the pounding of my headache. I knew I was about to say something incredibly ridiculous and inappropriate, but I knew I had to say something—after all, Charles was depending upon me. I cast around for anything to fill the awkward silence beginning to gape between us.

I couldn't control what I was saying, but my head hurt so badly that I was distracted. I said the first thing that came to mind. "It reminds me of Scrooge's door knocker in *A Christmas Carol*," I blurted out, and then immediately wanted to strangle myself for saying something so stupid. "The brass doorknob does, I mean. Sort of alike they are, don't you think?" I waited for Dickens to strike me for being such a dolt or laugh at my moronic answer or hiss at me in anger for saying such an inconsequential thing. To my consternation, he did none of those.

"Good Lord, Wilkie, that's brilliant!" he exclaimed. "You are right. It is like Scrooge's dreams, fashioned from the material of my own mind."

I stared at him, flabbergasted. He wasn't mocking me. He was serious . . . or he was in a worse condition than I had imagined.

"Alone in that prison cell, Wilkie, I honestly felt utterly abandoned, a shipwrecked man washed up on some barren

84

isle, a Robinson Crusoe, only worse, lost, no man Friday for company, no prospect for human contact. Imprisoned in that dream, it was as if there was a whole other world existing parallel to this one, within my mind. A world beneath the surface of this world that we know and write about, an inner world that we don't write enough about."

Dickens never ceased to amaze me. In the age of Victoria, introspection was not a proper investment. Self-knowledge was in no way redeemable as coin of the realm. The idea of a man attempting to understand some other, inner self would be received with the same hostility that Strauss encountered in his attempts to find a historical Jesus. Our age was simply neither inclined nor equipped to delve beneath the surface of its own closely regulated life. It felt comfortable with the surface appearance that it worked so hard to cultivate. It felt vastly uncomfortable with the ugly realities that lurked beneath that smug surface.

As Dickens talked, I remembered the terrible self-accusation and guilt he expressed that night ten months before as we kept vigil over little Dora Annie's deathbed. The man was always very hard on himself, and tended to shoulder the blame for all sorts of things over which he had little control. That tendency toward self-doubt and self-blame was certainly one of Dickens's self-made prisons, his "mind-forged manacles" as William Blake, that madman, might have called it. It was as if this fevered introspection brought about by his dream was an addiction that had locked him in its grip. "I have not been able to get it out of my mind all morning, Wilkie, but you have helped me to understand it."

Those were Dickens's own words as he confided them to me that gloomy morning after his night in Newgate. I have recorded them as best I can remember them. Strange, the images of his tormented Newgate dreams remain vivid to me today as if he had only confided them within the last few hours. In fact, since I began these commonplace books I have many times felt his presence upon my text, as though he were here in the room with me even as I write of these secret things

85

lurking beneath the surface of our society, our official biographies. I have no ambition to be his Boswell, yet, perhaps, that is, indeed, the role that I now play. Good God, so often as I write I feel that he is feeding my memory from the vast store of his capacious imagination.

But more than anything else that gloomy morning after Tally Ho Thompson's escape from Newgate, I remember the great satisfaction I felt in the fact that Dickens had sent that overbearing and petulant prig Forster away and had summoned me to be the receptacle of his secret confidences. Indeed, that alone made all of my feelings of inadequacy and confusion worthwhile.

Dickens had visibly calmed. That fevered, troubled look around his eyes had almost been exorcised. One pressing problem, however, yet remained. The Grub Streeters were still clamouring at his door. I feared that he was going to once again saddle me with the responsibility of dealing with them. Wills poked his timid head up out of the stairwell like a bald kitten peeking from a basket. "They show no signs of leaving, Charles," he announced in despair as though he had failed in some dangerous mission.

"I'll attend to them straightaway," Dickens assured him in his old eager voice devoid of all the indecision and self-doubt of the previous half-hour. Wills gratefully retired as if being lowered out of sight on a dumbwaiter.

"What are you going to tell them, Charles?" I asked as he hitched up his braces and buttoned his vest and snapped on his collar and adjusted his foppish cravat like a knight preparing for a latter-day joust.

"I mean to do exactly what any good novelist ought"— Dickens grinned Tally Ho Thompson's larcenous grin—"tell a good story, create a fiction."

"IN THE THICK OF IT ONCE AGAIN"

January 14, 1852—late morning

After confiding the substance of his nightmares to me that morning after his night in Newgate, and after dealing labouriously with the clamouring press, we decided that our respective headaches deserved attention and that we ought to retire to our respective beds. But as we waited in the bay window overlooking the street for the loitering press to disperse, Charles honored me with one last morbid confidence.

"I fear, Wilkie," his voice was tired and sad, "that the landscape of my imagination nowadays claims for its central landmark a bleak and abandoned house on a gloomy, haunted moor where the hunted flee the pursuit of the city. The city is always with us. We are imprisoned within it. Yet this deathly house lurks insistently in the landscape of my dreams. Shrouded in fog, it draws me to its dark secrets. I hate that bleak house, Wilkie. I hate it because I cannot capture it in words. One tries to write about both worlds, but it is nigh impossible. One world, our Victorian surface, the city, all of its ills, is too available to us, while that other world of our inner selves seems hardly available at all."

On that enigmatic note, I left him nursing his headache and foundering in the melancholy for which I had no ready antidote. If I were composing a novel rather than writing down the truth in this secret journal, there would be no meditative narrative upon Dickens's dreams. But this is not a novel, and the rules of plotting and pacing do not here apply. Charles was visibly shaken by his dreams. The interior action of his soul was at that time every bit as important as were the stunts Inspector Field was putting us through. I happily accompanied Charles upon his ferocious night walks, and I always went reluctantly along with his adventuring in the company of Inspector Field, but I could think of no way whereby I could become a companion of his troubling interior journeys.

The next morning I awoke to a languid knocking upon my door. It was Sleepy Rob, evidently dispatched by a fully recovered Dickens, with an armload of newspapers and broadsides. The headlines all trumpeted the escape of a suspected murderer from Newgate Prison at the expense of England's most revered novelist. One penny dreadful blared:

NOVEL ESCAPE!

Another cryptically dabbled in Miltonic allusion:

MURDERER UNBOUND; DICKENS FOUND

Doggerel from one broadside wagged its wit:

Murderer fled;
Knocked on head,
Dickens awakes in
Newgate bed.

One runninghead drew an immediate chuckle when it caught my attention:

ACTOR IMPERSONATES "THE INIMITABLE"

But I did not find myself laughing at what followed this head-line:

> Even Dickens's rather dull visiting companion to Newgate, one Wilkie Collins, an aspiring writer and protégé of "the Inimitable," did not recognise the impersonation which was, evidently, accomplished while said Collins's back was turned. For his inattention, Collins also was rewarded with a knock on the head in a hansom cab after the escape was accomplished.

Needless to say, Inspector Field had fully succeeded in garnering the sensationalistic coverage of his case that he desired. In that sense, Dickens's and my escape charade had been unquestionably successful. When I had consented to be a part of Inspector Field's plan, however, I had never envisioned being made a fool of in the popular prints.

Accompanying the papers delivered by Sleepy Rob was a brief letter from Dickens:

> We are the talk of London, Wilkie. It seems that Inspector Field has pulled this one off. No word from him as yet. Has promised to summon us. It seems we are in the thick of it once again!

Dickens's excitement and anticipation of some new nighttime adventure veritably leapt from the terse note. *He loves this intrigue more than all else,* I could not help but think. *More than our reputations. More than our very heads!*

After Sleepy Rob left, Irish Meg joined me for the perusal of our notoriety. She was impressed at how full the papers were of our names. My embarrassment at having been made to look the fool and then knocked on the head seemed not even an issue to her. "Yew've become a reg'lar item, yew 'ave, I'd sye." Meg had that mischievous twinkle in her eye. "Pretty soon, yew'll be a famous man jus' like Mister Dickens." Her face was all alight with the joy and the joke of it. "I'll jus' bet"—she pursed her lips in delight—"I could sell the secrets o' yer sleepin' 'abits ta one o' these for a pritty penny."

She was wrapped in a cotton robe, and as she turned to flee I caught its tail in my lunging hand. The robe slid off her back as easily as cutting a page in a new book. She wore only red lace bloomers beneath. As I stood with her robe in my hand, she turned slowly to me, her hands cupped over her breasts. The eloquent dialogue of our eyes dictated our movements. I flung away the robe. She opened her hands and dropped them to her sides, revealing, inviting.

I was in her arms in a breath. Her hands moved to my face, pulled me to her mouth. Our tongues engaged in a dialogue that predated words. I could read the imagery in her touch, her kiss. There was a wildness about her as if those words, my name in those newspapers, had inflamed her, fed her need to reassert her possession of me. Her leg wrapped around the back of my knee. Her naked body pressed against me.

I could read her control over me in her eyes, in her lips, in the heat of her skin. She was like a book one simply cannot put down, its pace and passion carrying you away. I was helpless in Irish Meg's arms. There was a terrible irony to it. She was acutely aware of her power over me, utterly confident in her ability to control and possess me in the labyrinth of her sexual world. And yet, naked in her arms, slowly removing those wisps of red lace from her opening body, I have never felt so free, so unbound from my imprisoning Victorian world.

There are different sorts of prisons. Lord Byron wrote of this irony in his poem about Chillon. I realise now, looking back upon those days when we feared nothing, that Dickens and I were constantly shaking the bars of our cells trying to somehow escape all the restrictions and hypocrisies of the age of Victoria. And yet, our sexual possession was a prison as well. His beloved Ellen, my Meg, they were the pages of our passion to be free, and yet they made us prisoners of their fire.

We write volumes with our bodies just as we weave webs with our words, and we are all caught within this mad twisting dance of freedom and imprisonment. Like Empedocles longing for his volcano, I tore free from the crabbed prudery of our age and threw myself into Meg's sexual fire where I was once again imprisoned in the sweet bondage of her arms, her legs, her seductive voice.

I had planned on joining Dickens at the *Household Words* offices that morning to discuss the newspaper hullabaloo and, under the auspices of working upon the next number of the magazine, to wait for Inspector Field's summons back into "the thick of it once again." All of those fine intentions, however, were forgotten in a trice for the sweet imprisonment of Meg's more enticing diversions. Those days were so carefree between us, so unthinking and abandoned. Love blazed up so easily. A smile, a touch, and we would be in each other's arms. We fed the fire, bathed languidly in the flames. I am not sure that either of us ever understood the intricacies of our attractions to each other. We would spend whole afternoons in bed, slowly caressing, exploring every secret place, reading the eloquent chronicles of our freedom and imprisonment written in the feel and the smell and the taste of our passion. I wish Meg understood my attraction to her as a repudiation of my world. In moments of helplessness under her naked spell, I often told her that it was in bed with her that I felt most alive. But I also know that she was fully capable of exploiting my weakness for her, and she frequently did, glorying in her power over my darker half. And yet, there was no more willing victim in the age of Victoria than I.

THE SHOOTING GALLERY

(January 17, 1852—mid-afternoon)

T hree days had passed. Dickens was regaining his good humour, throwing off that fit of melancholy occasioned by his nightmarish sojourn in Newgate. He was, however, having greater difficulty conquering a messy head ailment and barking cough contracted in that damp prison chamber. When I arrived at the *Household Words* offices at mid-afternoon, Dickens was treating his head congestion with a steaming cup of English tea doctored with a strong dosage of Tollamore Dew. "I do not know if it helps against these sniffles and sneezes, Wilkie"—he grinned—"but a toddy like this warms me all the way down and I do not pay near as much heed to the discomfort."

"The Irish make it so that you do not care."

"Exactly." He laughed.

We speculated briefly upon the murder case, which was uppermost in our minds. Tally Ho Thompson had disappeared as if tumbled into a hole. Even Scarlet Bess had no word as to his whereabouts. Through Irish Meg, she had been plaguing me daily for news of her beau. Both Dickens and I were certain that Field had sequestered Thompson in a safe place but we had not a clue as to where.

We worked about the office for the next two hours or so—I was preparing an article on the need for more lighthouses off the Devon coast as indicated by *Lloyd's List*'s shipwreck statistics of the previous two years. Dickens popped his head in about six, a large white handkerchief dabbing at his inflamed nose, and proffered a familiar invitation: "Wilkie, will you dine with me? And then perhaps a walk? Good heated exercise is what I need to rid me of this stuffed head." I, as always, assented. Dickens, just as promptly, sent a street porter to The Bride and Weasel in St. Martin's Lane for chops, clamshell potatoes, and ale.

We were just finishing, having laid out the delicacies upon Dickens's desk in the bay window, when a loud knocking on the below-stairs door fractured our well-fed camaraderie. The door opened, to our surprise, upon Field himself. Our usual agent of summons, Serjeant Rogers, stood one step off his master's shoulder like some oversized parrot awaiting permission to speak.

"We've not far ta go," Field announced without preface or explanation. " 'At's why I came ta yew meself, didn't send Rogers ta fetch yew. 'Ee's only in Leicester Square, 'ee is. We kin walk. Well, 'ow is it then? Are we game, gents?"

I stared, popeyed with confusion I am sure.

Dickens was all questions and enthusiasm.

"Who is in Leicester Square?"

"Why Thompson, of course."

"Why have you come for us?"

"I want yew in on this interview. If yew're game, I think yew can 'elp me on this case. It involves yer class 'o people."

"My God, Field," I finally jettisoned my surprise and broke up their colloquy, "haven't we helped you enough? I mean, really, helping him escape from Newgate, our names all over the papers . . ." I sputtered.

"Oh, don't mind Wilkie." Dickens darted a silencing look

94

in my direction. "I am quite curious to hear Thompson's side of the story and quite eager, indeed, to continue on with this case.

"And besides, Wilkie"—Dickens turned back to me with that mischievous twinkle in his eye—"the 'Medusa Murders' has a nice ring, does it not? Who knows, someday perhaps *you* will write a murder mystery."

It was the old Dickens argument, resorted to every time he wished me to risk life and limb in the pursuit of one of his ill-conceived schemes. A novelist must throw himself into life as if it were a volcano, must partake of every experience which offers in order to write about it later. According to Dickens, a novelist must be fearless, willing to risk all for art's sake. I must admit that I was much more than skeptical as to the efficacy of his theory. Nonetheless, as Dickens was well aware, that novelist argument always worked with me. Clearly, I desired to be a writer more than I desired to be a conventional Victorian gentleman. Dickens was a master at exploiting that weakness in my character.

Each new turn in my narrative steps off with Dickens and me being summoned into the fray by Inspector Field, usually with Serjeant Rogers serving as his messenger. Thus summoned, we invariably follow along, caught in the pull of the plot. More interesting, perhaps, might be some accounting of the procedures that Field and his minions had exercised in order to reach our point of summons and precipitate the next break in the case, and carry forward the plot. I have written it before and must again: If Dickens is indeed a realistic novelist, then Field is a novelist of the real, in control of the plots of real life in the London streets. In the three days following the escape of Thompson from Newgate, Field and his constables had ascertained the whereabouts of one Dick Dunn, play actor; had received the surgeon's report on the corpses of the two dead women; and had attended the funeral of Missus Palmer, the doctor's wife, where they had unsuccessfully attempted to interview the grieving husband. As we prepared to accompany Field and Rogers on this foray into

Leicester Square, we knew nothing about those preparations that had attended our summons back into Field's plot.

We stepped out of the Wellington Street offices into a regular "pea souper" as those too few lightkeepers on the Devon coast might call it. It was that typical London fog that spread itself over the city like thick frosting on a Bavarian cake. It coats you, fills up your pores, cuts off your air. We struck out into that suffocating fog like Livingstone into Africa. Nonetheless, Field actually seemed to know his way, and, as he had said, Leicester Square was not far. We tramped one direction and then another and then turned another way until I felt as if I had been soundly spun in a fogbound game of blindman's buff. Suddenly, however, we emerged out of the darkness of residential streets into the eerie gaslit haloes of a commercial oasis in that desert of fog.

In those days, much different than it is now, the vicinity of Leicester Square was a twisted labyrinth of gaming dens, houses of low repute and ill fame, tattoo establishments, drinking rooms, pawnshops and billiard parlors frequented by street sharpers, more discreet swindlers of the money-lending sort, practitioners of the fencing of property sort, and mercenary soldiers of the murder-your-husband-or-wife-or-rich-uncle-for-ten-sovereigns sort.

"Over 'ere 'tis," Field's voice floated out of the fog. I had simply been following close to the odd glimpse and the steady sound of his heels on the paving stones as we marched. "Down this alley 'ere, I'd say."

Amidst all of those shady dives of the disreputable sort and those gaslit houses of the gaming sort, Field led us to a doorway sporting a sign under a gaslit halo: CAPTAIN HAWKINS SHOOTING GALLERY. It looked to be a run-down warehouse of the low-rent sort.

There was no indication whether that gallery was open or closed to sharpshooting business. Inspector Field assaulted the door with three knocks, then scratched the side of his eye with his crook'd forefinger as he waited for his answer. None was forthcoming. When the door did not open, Field did nothing, displaying more patience than a lawyer on a Chancery case. His exceedingly sharp forefinger continued to scratch at the side of his exceedingly sharp eye. As the wait lengthened and Field showed no inclination toward further communication between his knuckles and that door, I realised that those three hard knocks must have been a pre-arranged code.

At long last, the door swung to and we were escorted in by a twisted apparition out of some pirate chronicle of Captain Cook's voyages to the South Seas or Phillip Quarl or some like book. The man who bade us enter was less a man than a meeting place for spare parts. He stood upon one wooden leg with a smooth leather knee. He leaned upon one wooden crutch with a bright fabric armpiece curved nicely to fit the contour of his hunched shoulder. One eye was covered with a dark patch and one hand was shrouded in a dark glove. His back was humped like a Greenland Sea whale and his shoulders sloped like a decrepit stile. He was altogether one of the more pieced-together specimens of hurried surgery that any of us had ever encountered. I could not help but wonder how his body had come to such a state. But by far the most unsightly appendage to his mangled body was a dirty-green parrot, which appeared to be growing like a second head out of his canted right shoulder. The parrot, as if it too had been surgically connected to that miracle's body, never teetered even as this agglomeration of artificial limbs lurched around the premises.

"Welcome to Cap'n 'Awkins' Shootin' Gowry, Mince Lane," that worthy greeted us, shooting a hilarious gap-toothed grin in our direction. It was, however, somewhat difficult to distinguish which of those two heads, his or the parrot's, was doing the talking. "I knows yew an yew"—he rolled his heads at Field and Rogers as we filed into the dark hallway—"but 'oo is these two ducks?" He cocked his heads at us and grinned like poor Yorick's skull squared.

"Fock theer beerds, bloody poms!" his other head chirped gleefully. This wonder immediately ducked his occupied shoulder and took a swipe at his profane parrot with his gloved hand, but missed.

"Don' mind 'im, lads," he apologised with the gaps in his teeth spreading into a fractured grin. "Bad infloonces shipboard when larnin' the langwidge. Niver bin able ta cure 'im o' it."

"Fock yoor eyes, bloody knockers!" his second head protested that patronising apology for its social shortcomings.

This startling two-headed wonder ushered us into a large, long room with a high ceiling inadequately lit by a dingy skylight overhead. Four gaslamps illuminated the room. Two illuminated a long, narrow table holding an assortment of pistols and military muskets, which bisected the front half of the room; two more, at the far end of the room, lit up a number of objects lined up on a shelf (such as balls, bottles, playing cards, and paper circles) and effigies (such as birds, rabbits, lions, tigers, and bears) all made of paper and mounted upon sticks rising out of the floor.

Waiting at the gun table were two men. One, a tall, broad-shouldered brute with an utterly bald head, either naturally so or meticulously shaved for intimidating effect, was quite frightening to look at. The other was Tally Ho Thompson, grinning his maddening grin of unconcern. No matter what his surroundings or circumstances, Thompson never seemed to care enough or be threatened to the point of not grinning. As soon as I saw him, my hand instinctively went to my fob to check upon the continuing presence of my watch.

The bullet-headed brute stepped forward with his hand outstretched in the most friendly manner as we approached. My inclination, if I were being totally honest, was to shrink back, but Dickens took the frightening man's hand and I stood ready to do likewise.

"George 'Awkins 'ere," he introduced himself in the most jovial of voices, rather quiet actually, not at all fitting his Thuggee appearance and intimidating size. "Yee've met Serjeant Moody I takes it." He nodded to that twisted agglomeration of parts who had escorted us in. "Bert, we calls 'im. Short for Philbert, but 'ee 'ates the Phil. Wee're jus two ol' sojers keepin' on." He was certainly hospitable enough despite his murderous appearance. As I took in the bluntness of his head, however, the broadness of his shoulders, the deepness of his chest, the thickness of his wrists, and the muscular tightness of his frame, I felt utterly convinced that I never wished to have that man angry at me.

Thompson, likewise, was upon us immediately with out-stretched hands. "Mates! Me mates!" He took one each of our hands and stood as if looking for something to say, but unable to take himself seriously enough to say it. "Sorry 'bout those taps behind the eers," he finally said, " 'ad to do it, realism an' all, yew know." We sensed his sincerity. He truly wanted to thank us for abetting his escape but simply could not find the proper words.

"All for realism, eh? We certainly know how that works, do we not, Wilkie?" Dickens laughed and clapped Thompson on the shoulder.

"Bert, bring the gin bottle," the hulking Hawkins ordered in an almost tender voice.

"Aye Cap'n." The little pieced-together man sidled off to obey.

"The streets are almost clear, Thompson," Inspector Field announced. "They're losin' interest in lookin' for yew. Yer beerd an' mustache are still a bit on the ragged side, eh?"

Thompson laughed at that and rubbed his scraggly chin. "Another week or so"—he grinned—"an' Scarlet Bess will scream rape when I sneak inta 'er room."

"There'll be none o' that for a while," Field cautioned, "but we must begin puttin' the fear inta the principals afore we lose the purpose o' the play."

"I'm a'ready for that." The eagerness spilled over in Thompson's voice.

Broken Bert returned with mugs of steaming gin.

"Fock yoor bellies, bloody jack tars!" the parrot (whose name I learned later was Walter) shrieked.

"Musn't mind him," Captain Hawkins apologised in that

99

soft, accommodating voice that was so poorly matched to his huge intimidating body. "Grew up on a bad ship."

"What do we do now?" Dickens was just tossing his question into the centre of the assembled group, but then he turned on Inspector Field. "And why was it so necessary to get Thompson out of Newgate?"

"Friend Thompson's task"—Field's forefinger crook'd across the corner of his eye—"is ta put the fear o' God inta our murderer or murderers or whoever is spreadin' this epidemic o' Medusa death. Meantimes, I try ta find out 'ow those two wimmin died."

"We'll start with Dickie Dunn." Thompson's grin went a bit tight. "I'll shake evrythin' 'ee knows out o' 'im an' then I'll wring 'is scrawny little neck. Arter all, 'ee almos' got my neck stretched, didn'n 'ee?"

"Yew'll do no sech thing." Field yanked on the chain of his eager bulldog. "Yew'll face down yer actor friend, but yew won't beat 'im. 'Is job is ta take the message ta Palmer, the good doctor. We want 'em ta know that yew are out an' on the case an' it an't o'er yet. Remember Thompson, there's a bounty on yer 'ead. Queen's Bench offers ten pounds for 'elp in the capture o' any escaped convicts. That oughta stir up all yer ol' mates in Rats' Castle."

Thompson grinned wistfully at Field. Did I detect a trace of bitterness around the corners of his grin? *You fool,* I thought, *his grin is always the same and yet you try to read it as if it were one of Dickens's new novels!* For some reason, since the heightening of my association with both Dickens and Inspector Field, I had become much more inquisitive as to the inner feelings and motives of the people I observed. Pity I couldn't find a way to get that type of reality, those secret things going on beneath the surface often so contradictory to what we say or do, down on paper.

"In the old days, among the 'eyewaymen,'" that wistfulness had transferred itself from Thompson's grin to Thompson's voice, "we 'ad the cutter's law. It wos a rule o' trust an' loyalty. The cutter's law don' work in the city. 'Ere they'll sell yew off for a glass o' gin," he opined, drinking off his own glass of hot gin.

"Aye, those were good days," Captain Hawkins agreed in his soft schoolmaster's voice. I gathered that at some point he too had ridden the dark byways of Shooter's Hill and Hampstead Heath.

"Those days are gone for good," Field mocked their nostalgia, "an' so is yer sacred cutter's law. In case yew've forgotten, yew work for me, an' I'm the law now, 'ere in London. But the time may come when I'll need yew again ta ply yer trade on the heath." Then, as if talking to himself in an aside, "Gawd knows, soon enough the heath will be part o' London any'ow." He paused to digest that thought, then pointed his terrible forefinger at Thompson as a way of punctuating his next: "An' don' forget one other"—he was clearly sending Thompson a message of warning—"yew can be back in Newgate in the snap o' my fingers. Yew know 'tis true."

No one spoke. Thompson, finally, laughed his heedless laugh and, making a deep actor's bow to Inspector Field, said mockingly: "Gawd knows this 'uns eternally grateful for yer springin' me from Newgate an'," he added ironically, "Gawd knows I'll probly be payin' off that debt eternally as well."

At that, Field could not fight off his own little inscrutable grin. He and Tally Ho Thompson seemed quite clear on the terms of their agreement. Both also seemed quite clear on their adversarial duty to either exploit or violate that agreement. I got the distinct feeling that Thompson did not plan to be long under Inspector Field's thumb.

"I needs ta see Bess," Thompson added, almost as an afterthought. "She needs ta see me in the flesh, or she could muck us all up with 'er 'istericks."

"I'll 'ave Meg bring 'er ta yew," Field said, begrudgingly.

Dickens, no longer able to contain his curiosity, pressed on. "Why was it so urgent to get Thompson out of Newgate?" he asked point-blank.

"Yeah, guv, wot's the game a'tter all?" Thompson chimed in. "Yew didn't play res'rection man an' dig me outa thet

101

tomb jus' ta sit 'ere in Cap'n 'Awkins's an' tidy up me pistol shot."

"Fear, 'at's the game." Field warmed to the conspiratorial enthusiasm of the company. "I want the others in this case, an' there aren't menny, only yer friend Dunn 'oo put yew up ta the crack, an' the woman's 'usband, the doctor. I want 'em afraid o' yew, Thompson. I want 'em ta know the case an't closed."

"But does not Thompson's escape draw attention away from the case?" Dickens was totally caught up in the formulation of strategy now, a novelist editing his own text, poking holes in his own plot.

"Not a'tall," Field demurred. "Thompson's so convenient arrest drew 'tention away from the case. We know 'ee didn't kill those wimmin, but nobody else knows thet, an' as long as they've got the suspected murderer in prison, nobody cares. Meanwhile, the real murderer is off as free as a kite on a 'eye wind. But as soon as the suspected murderer is out o' keep, then the real murderer is worryin' agin, 'cause 'ee knows 'ee's goin' ta be come after. There, yew see, Thompson is my bulldog. I set 'im upon my principals in the case, 'ave 'im growl at 'em 'til they break cover. In their fear, mates, they 'and me the evidence I need."

"All fine and well"—Dickens still was intent upon playing devil's advocate—"but what if the police get to Thompson before he gets to the real murderer? They might kill him in the act of taking him."

"I *am* the police." Field seemed bored with all this speculation. "Bleeve me, the Protectives will git no closer ta this case than I allow 'em. Nobody will try ta take 'im without consultin' me."

Thompson rolled his eyes comically at that. He seemed less than comfortable with Field's assurances of protection. He seemed quite aware of being caught between two worlds and welcome in neither. Field had contrived to press him into a position in which both the murderer and the Protectives

102

wanted him and were not overly scrupulous about how they got him, whether dead or alive.

" 'Tis a pretty spot yew've got me in, Guv." Thompson's irrepressible grin taunted Inspector Field. " 'Oo do *yew* think is gointa try ta kill me first?"

"I'd be careful o' Scarlet Bess, 'twas me." Field played off his taunt. "Most murders is domestick."

The company could not help but laugh at Field's ready wit. One had to get up quite early to best him.

"She does 'ave a temper," Thompson conceded, clapping Captain Hawkins a good one on the back.

" 'At she does," that worthy, who had evidently had experience of the lady, agreed.

"But really," Dickens turned the conversation back to strategy, "who is to be feared and observed in this case?"

"So far there are only two principals 'ere," Field answered. "We've got yer actor friend"—he nodded toward Thompson—" 'oo put yew up ta the crack the night yew got pinched, an' we've got the woman's 'usband. 'Ee's my choice, 'ee is. But I've already been wrong in this case."

"About what?" In chorus Dickens and I voiced the startled concern that Field's unexpected declaration had occasioned in the entire company.

"The police surgeon's report." Field did not seem overly concerned. "It told us little. 'Ee found no sign o' the common poisons in the corpses or in the champagne bottle, can't rightly say wether wimmin were poisoned or no. Bodies all point to poison, but no sign o' poison yet."

"Yet?" Dickens pursued.

"They've given blood ta a chemist"—Field was laconic at best—"but 'opes are not 'eye." His eyes moved from one to the other of us, from Dickens to myself to Serjeant Rogers to Tally Ho Thompson to Captain Hawkins, finally coming to rest on poor broken Bert. "That is why we must put pressure on those 'as done the murders," Field went on. "Our only 'ope is their givin' themselfs away."

103

"Themselfs?" Thompson missed little. "Yew think there's more than one?"

"Don't think. Don't know. Could be. Can't tell," Field again seemed thinking aloud and succeeded in further bewildering all of us.

"Fock yer brains, bloody sots," Bert's second head parodied Field's earnestness.

There was nothing for us to do but laugh at the bird's profane yet somehow apposite editorials.

"If only the Medusa murderer would poison that infernal bird," Thompson chided poor broken Bert, whose gapped teeth immediately took on a pained and protective look.

"Wot we must do now"—Field drew all our attentions back from the parrot to these birds of quite different feather—"is begin again, start all over. That is why we're 'ere, Thompson, ta 'ear yer story cleen, ta find wot we missed afore."

At Captain Hawkins's order, broken Bert replenished our mugs of gin. Assorted stools and distressed chairs appeared out of the dim corners of the Shooting Gallery until we all sat in a ragged circle under the guns.

"Tell it from the beginnin'," Field ordered Thompson. "I'll stop yew if I see fit."

" 'Ee 'ired me ta teach 'is wife ta ride," Thompson began. " 'Ee's a 'orseman, the man said, an' 'ee wanted 'is wife ta learn."

"Wait. The 'man' yew say. Wot man?" Field interrupted straight off.

"I thought you said that Macready introduced you to Palmer?" Dickens, editor that he was, interjected his query directly upon Inspector Field's heels.

"No. 'At's not the way 'twas." Thompson shook his head, now amused by this standing upon minimal detail. " 'Ee sent 'is assistant, 'is laboratory man or wotever, a foreigner 'ee wos, ta put the arm on me for the job."

"Yew mean to say yew've nivver met this Doctor Palmer?" Rogers, this time, asserted his presence.

"Never met the bloke." Thompson shrugged. "Seckertary

104

'ired me, sent me money over each time by street porter. I've only met the dead wife, never the live 'usband."

"Then yew kin stop growin' those silly whiskers." Field winked at Rogers. "No fear of the good doctor reckernizin' yew then."

"None indeed." Rogers agreed like the toadying little martinet that I always viewed him to be. Both Dickens and I were quite puzzled at the two policemen's interest in Thompson's not having met the murdered woman's husband. Evidently, Inspector Field already had some scenario percolating in his "novelist of the real" mind that hitherto had required Thompson to play his part in whiskers.

"Sorry. Go on." Field chose not to enlighten us just yet.

"Not much to it 'til last week." Thompson seemed a bit tentative as if expecting to be interrupted at every word. "As directed, I'd meet 'er at the stables at 'Eyde Park. 'Ee'd given 'er a 'orse, small brown gelding, looked a good lady's jumper, looked fast too, but too low ta the course for me. She'd 'ire me a nag. Those skins wosn't much ta speak of. An we'd ride. Don't think she liked it much. Animal seemed ta fright 'er a bit."

"Wot wos she like?" Field asked. "Did yew talk as yew rode? Wos she 'appy, sad, for'ard, shy, ever mention 'er 'usband?"

"Shaky woman. Learnin' ta ride 'cause 'er 'usband told 'er to. No pet name for 'im, no Bill nor Willy, always William this or William that, once said 'If I learn ta ride p'raps I'll see 'im more.' Gave the idee 'usband wos off ridin' a bit."

"She ever show any intrest in yew?" Field's questioning got more touchy. "In more than a mistress ta servant line, I mean."

"I wos 'er ridin' teacher, no servant." Thompson bristled at Field's characterisation, which produced a short chuckle from that worthy. " 'Andsome woman"—Thompson took a short pause to either stimulate his memory or speculate on the possibility or merely bedevil Field and Rogers with a touch of suspense—"but she made no advances in a gay way." He

105

grinned as if he couldn't believe she could resist such a specimen as himself.

"Quite." Field abandoned this line of questioning. "Wot next then?"

" 'At's it. We rode, three times I think, until that twit Dickie Dunn come ta me with 'is recovery scheme."

"Did 'ee say 'oo the 'ooman wos?" Field's forefinger worked contemplatively at the side of his eye.

"Not a word. Said 'ee'd been havin' it off with a gentleman's maid an' wanted some sparklers 'ee'd given 'er retrieved." It was at this point that Tally Ho Thompson evidenced slight discomfort, embarrassment I should say, at being so easily duped. " 'Twas the price made me do it," he protested. "Said 'ee'd stand me twelve guineas, 'alf on the table right then. I 'ad rent to pay for me an' Bess. 'Twas more than I'd make in three months o' 'orse ridin' onstage."

"It wos monumental stoopid!" Field showed him no sympathy. "But that is by the by now. Wot else?"

"Yew know the rest. I cruised the 'ouse an' made the crack. When I got in an' saw I'd been done, I bolted. I didn't even reckernise the dead woman. 'Er face wos all twisted an' I wos too busy leavin'."

"Quite so. I'm not surprised." Field seemed quite philosophical about the whole affair.

Thompson relaxed somewhat. The strain of story-telling drove him to his gin.

Captain Hawkins nodded solemnly as if he wished to console Thompson for such ill luck.

Dickens and I waited for Field to digest the narrative and give us further direction.

"Fock her head, bloody arse!" broken Bert's profane appendage broke the delicate surface of our contemplation and sent ripples of laughter out of all of us at Thompson's expense. His strained grin emitted an inclination to twist off the head of that disgusting bird.

" 'Ow did yew git in the 'ouse?" Field was not finished.

" 'Ee gave me the servin' girl's key. Said she'd given 'im it so 'ee could git ta 'er at night after the 'ouse 'ad retired."

"Quite," Serjeant Rogers parroted his master.

For a long moment silence pooled over the gathering of auditors in the Shooting Gallery. All seemed cogitating upon the details of Thompson's narrative. In reality, we were all trying to see into Inspector Field's mind. He was the detective genius. *What clues are important to him?* we speculated. *Are the maid's keys the key? Why is Field so pleased that Thompson and the dead woman's doctor-husband have never met?*

"If we are, indeed, ta make an 'onest man o' yew, Thompson"—Field chuckled, breaking our speculative silence—"which I'm not convinced anyone could ever do, mind yew, we must do three things."

"Yes, three." Rogers nodded sagely, as if fully possessed of the full details of Field's plan, which I sincerely doubted.

"First," Field began, "we must find out 'ow the two wimmin were killed. The police surgeon's report offers not a clue. Per'aps the chemist's analysis will supply the answers. If not, we must somehow find out ourselves. I personally feel that the two wimmin were killed by some sort o' exotic poison." He paused and we all looked at each other expectantly, but no one had anything to add.

"Next," Field went on, "we must beerd and grass* yer traitorous mate Dick Dunn. 'Ee probly wos not the arkiteckt o' this elaborate entrapment o' Thompson, but rather the creature o' a more powerful mind, yet we must force 'im ta spill the identity o' 'is master."

Thompson's grin broadened and we could all sense the anticipation building in his tall and wiry body. Field also smiled at Thompson's instinctive reaction.

"Yes, lad." Field leaned in and tapped him on the knee with his fatherly forefinger. "That worthy will be yer assignment. Any way yew wish, I want yew to scare the bejabbers out

*A boxing term meaning "to knock one's opponent to the ground" in the parlance of the Victorian sporting scene.

o' 'im so as 'ee'll run straight ta 'is master. But"—and he raised his cautionary forefinger in the air in front of Thompson's face—"I don' want yew confrontin' Dunn alone. I not only need witnesses, but I want yew backed up. The man may be dangerous."

"I kin be summat dangerous meself." Thompson bristled.

"Oh psaw!" Inspector Field smiled benignly. "We all know yew are no more than a sticky-fingered, playactin' tabby cat," Field jibed him, causing all of the rest of us to laugh. Bert and his obscene bird virtually howled in unison.

"And lastly"—Field tempered that momentary hilarity—"we must somehow obtain an interview with Doctor Palmer, even violate his mourning if we must." As he placed this third step in the investigation before the group, his eyes shifted ever so slightly beneath his dark brows toward Dickens and myself. That subtle signal assured me that we were still very much on duty for Inspector Field.

"I want ta go back into that 'ouse." Thompson smacked the Shooting Gallery table with a sharp whack, causing every rifle to rattle down its length. Fortunately, none seemed to be loaded, thus none discharged by accident. "There is a secret there, I'm sure on it."

Field's crook'd forefinger leapt nervously to the corner of his eye as if questioning himself. *Could the lad be right? Could I 'ave missed something?* Slowly he nodded, as if in agreement with Tally Ho Thompson's impulsive statement.

It was almost eight when that jolly group dispersed from Captain Hawkins's Shooting Gallery in Leicester Square, but each of us had a full evening of possibilities to contemplate. I, for one, took my speculations home to Irish Meg's bed.

A SAVAGE CONSULTANT

January 17, 1852—late evening

No sooner had the gaslight in my sleeping room been trimmed, sending dancing shadows over the lavender walls; no sooner had our teacups, which moments before had steamed with a fine chubwat and hot gin, been set aside on the small secretary beside the bed; no sooner had Meg's secret things (black lace this night) slid silkily to the floor; no sooner had she enfolded me in her arms and murmured her first words of perverse suggestion than there came an insistent knocking upon the outer door.

I sat bolt upright in the bed.

Meg collapsed in frustration upon the pillows.

" 'Oo the fock is 'at?" she growled in her rough idiom.

I, of course, knew immediately who it must be. It could only be Dickens or Field, or both, come to collect me pursuant to some new twist in the murder case. Or, I suppose, it could have been that toady, Sergeant Rogers, sent by the other two to fetch me. Or, perhaps (the possibilities do tend to multiply when recollected in tranquillity, do they not?) it might have been Scarlet Bess come once again in search of information and consolation about that rogue Thompson. My first instinct proved correct. It was Dickens that I saw through the small peephole in my outer door. He was muffled in his greatcoat and scarf, and was banging excitedly upon the wooden panels with his stick.

As I opened the door, I could not help but think how I must consign myself to a life of coitus interruptus as long as I cultivated the acquaintance and patronage of this madman of the night streets. I must admit, however, that upon seeing Dickens upon my doorstep all of my lascivious thoughts of Irish Meg were ushered rather unceremoniously into the back of my mind. Despite all, I must admit that I was instantly excited to see him, and knew instinctively that I was about to witness some break in Inspector Field's case.

"Charles, what is it?" I searched his face for signs that he might suspect or perceive the presence of Irish Meg in my bed on the other side of the flimsy sleeping-room door (though I am sure that he knew of our living arrangements). I tried to hide my embarrassment behind a guise of surprise and concern (I was not up to mustering "enthusiasm") at his sudden appearance so late of the evening upon my doorstep. "What has happened?" I gasped somewhat melodramatically.

"Wilkie, Wilkie, calm down," he reassured me. "Nothing is wrong. I have simply had the most revolutionary idea and have already set its wheels in motion. I knew that you would wish to accompany me. You must get dressed. Quickly! I've got our cab waiting. I've dismissed mine. I spotted your faithful cabman dozing at the kerbstone and knocked him up. I think we can solve one of our mysteries yet tonight. So . . . what are you waiting for?"

His words galloped forth and leapt over one another as fast as steeplechasers at Epsom. I must admit, I was caught up in his headlong rush. I stared at him aghast. Standing there in my robe with my hair all mussed and my ankles bare, I must have presented quite a sight, something out of *Tom Jones* perhaps. For his part, he hadn't the slightest idea that he was asking me to forgo Meg, who was naked, willing, and already warmed in my bed.

Much to my chagrin, he pushed his way right into my parlor and stood, tapping the head of his stick against the palm of his grey-gloved hand, as if to say, *Good God, Wilkie, get moving will you! I haven't all night!* It was all I could do to station myself between him and the sleeping-room door, behind which Irish Meg was surely eavesdropping. I envisioned a need to prevent him from rushing right into my sleeping room and collecting my clothes like some demented valet de chambre intent upon dressing me up and getting me out as quickly as possible. I finally subdued him into one of my tattered Queen Anne chairs and begged him to sit still for the few moments it would take me to dress. I felt like Parson Square.

I slid around the door into my sleeping chamber hoping against hope that Meg would choose to uphold the proprieties and not put up a squawk over Dickens's presumptious intrusion. My finger was to my lips in that age-old gesture of silence as I skulked into the room. Meg's mouth, as I had expected, was twisted into a mocking scowl. I knew it was folly to expect a woman as volatile as Irish Meg to obey my silent signal. The best I could hope for was that she would choose whispered discretion over a fishwife's snarling anger.

"Wot the 'ell is it this time?" she snarled in a laboured whisper, against her better inclinations I am sure.

"He wants me to accompany him upon another of his nighttime excursions. I cannot say no," I replied lamely. I was more begging permission than offering up a decision. "If I say no, he will know that you are in here." That last was the worst thing I could have said.

"So wot if 'ee does!" she scoffed at my cowardice. "Is it sech a stain on yer bloody shield for 'im ta know I'm in yer rooms? Bloody 'ell, I lives 'ere!" Thank God she was still whispering!

"No, no, that is not it, not it at all," I struggled to placate her. "Something important has happened in this murder case. He expects me to accompany him. He includes me in all

111

of these night adventures, you know." I smiled weakly, but she only scowled the more. "I must go. I will explain it all to you when I return."

"Yew won't find me 'ere in yer bed when yew return, yew bloody ponce. Yew kin tell yer story ta yer bloody pillow!" And with that she threw her charmingly naked self upon the bed and sat like a sulking buddha, legs crossed beneath her, arms crossed over her breasts, an angry scowl blazing upon her countenance.

I dressed hurriedly and fled. Dickens leapt up the moment I rejoined him in the sitting room, and in short seconds we were out the door and into Sleepy Rob's waiting cab.

"The Africa Hotel, Trafalgar Square!" Dickens shouted up, and with a crack and a clatter we were off.

"What is this all about, Charles? Where are we going at this hour?" As I settled into the cushions of the cab and pulled the musty blanket around my legs against the chill, I felt I deserved some explanation in light of what I was giving up to accompany him on this nighttime excursion.

"It is about genius, Wilkie." His eyes blazed with excitement. "It is about solving the mystery of how those two poor creatures were murdered. It is about meeting one of the most extraordinary and knowledgeable young men in the Empire. But above all, it is about soliciting his help in understanding what you have so melodramatically christened these 'Medusa Murders.' "

"Who is this extraordinary personage?" There was more than a slight note of skepticism in my voice. I do not know whether Dickens was holding back his name under the instinctive impulse of the novelist to build suspense or simply for the purpose of aggravating my curiosity.

Dickens was, however, not yet ready to reveal the identity of his mystery man. "The idea came to me as I was walking back to the *Household Words* office from the Shooting Gallery after you had hailed your cab in Leicester Square." His eyes were bright and his voice was lively and eager as it always was when talking about himself and the workings of his own devious

112

novelist's mind. "It came to me just like, like"—he groped a moment—"like a header of a revelation, you know, Saint Paul, that sort of thumper. I rushed to The Explorers Club on lower Regent Street and inquired if he was there." He was utterly caught up in his story as the cab rolled into the Strand and proceeded toward Trafalgar Square. "As luck would have it, he was, indeed, there."

Your usual good luck and my ill, I could not help but think.

"Because I am not a member, I could not enter to seek him out, but the porter, enamoured of a half crown which I dangled before his eyes, assented to reconnoitre the club for me. My man was just finishing his after-dinner brandy in the Honoured Guest's lounge. The porter, now positively aflame for that seductive half crown"—Dickens, in metaphorical jollity, was becoming transported with the telling of his story— "carried a note and my card to the Honoured Guest requesting a private audience within the hour concerning matters interesting and mysterious. The note evidently piqued his curiosity because the gentleman in question, whom I had met only once before at a public gathering of the Geographical Society, returned in person to the foyer to make the arrangements. He is waiting for us in his lodgings at the Africa Hotel this very moment."

"For God's sake, Charles, who is he?" I blurted out, my patience at his building an artificial suspense having reached the end of its tether.

"Why, Burton, of course." But before I had a chance to demonstrate my ignorance, Dickens bounded on. "I was simply walking along Leicester Square recasting in my mind the exchanges of our Shooting Gallery conversations when Field's words 'exotic poison' shot like an arrow into my mind. Those words immediately conjured up Burton. Perhaps he can help us."

"Burton?" I had not a clue as to who this 'genius' was.

"An extraordinary man." Dickens was positively glowing with admiration. "Has been all around the world, Wilkie. An

113

adventurer. Has gone places you and I would not even think of going if we knew they existed in the first place." He laughed. "But not just an adventurer, not just some bearish soldier of Empire. No, he is an educated man, a scientist and a great reader and a fine and evocative writer. He is, indeed, a prodigy is Dick Burton, a genius I feel, destined to be a great man."*

Dickens never ceased to amaze me. It was astounding the people he knew, his ability to track them down in the middle of a raw London evening, and be immediately welcomed to their home and hearth. I wonder if he ever spoke of me, his literary protégé, in the terms he used that evening to describe Burton. Sleepy Rob circled Lord Nelson's monument and reined in before the high oaken doors of the Africa Hotel.

*Charles Dickens' evaluation of the potential of Richard Francis Burton was destined to come true. At the time when Dickens first met him in the summer of 1851, Burton was but twenty-nine years old and had already served six years with the East India Company in Bengal. His greatest talent was as a linguist. He was reputed able to learn any language in the shortest space of time. Upon quitting the East India Company in 1848, he returned to England by way of a two and one-half year, around-the-world journey that included stops in Borneo, Australia, the South Pacific islands, Brazil, and the islands of the West Indies. At the time of the events of this memoir, Burton was attempting to convince the World Geographical Society of his potential as an explorer, and was attempting to raise the necessary funds for an expedition to Central Africa to search for the fabled source of the Nile. At the time of this conversation with Dickens and Collins, Burton was, perhaps, somewhat frustrated at the World Geographical Society's refusal to fund him due to their commitment to the Stanley expeditions. Burton ultimately proved his mettle as an explorer in 1853 when, in disguise, he made a forbidden journey to Mecca and Medina. In 1858, finally gaining the support of the World Geographical Society, and in the company of John Canning Speke, he mounted his African expedition in search of the source of the Nile. True to Dickens' prediction, Burton—linguist, scientist, geographer, adventurer, writer—became one of the Renaissance men of the Victorian age. He was knighted by Queen Victoria in 1876. His books, recounting his journeys to Mecca, to Africa, to Utah in America, and to Brazil, were classics of the literature of his time. His translation of *The Book of The Thousand Nights and a Night (The Arabian Nights Entertainment)* was perhaps his most elegant contribution to Western literature. As in Collins' case, Dickens had this knack for recognising fine writers before they ever wrote their masterworks.

114

"But how can this Burton chap help us on this case?" I asked as we disembarked from the cab.

"He is a young man," Dickens warmed to his subject, "whose age belies his intelligence, knowledge, and experience. He has an encyclopaedic memory, a mind that is a veritable storehouse of information. If anyone knows of 'exotic poisons,' it will be Dick Burton.

"It is my hope," Dickens continued as we passed quickly through the outer foyer of the hotel—bamboo chairs and settees cushioned with black plush pillows, tribal masks and fans, and feathered ceremonial headdresses decorating the walls—and mounted the stairs, "that in the course of his journeys or in his extensive reading Burton will have encountered deaths similar in their horror to those of the two poor women."

His long legs taking the black marble stairs two at a time, with my shorter ones double-stepping to stay abreast, we rapidly ascended to the third storey, the top, and, at the end of the corridor, beneath the slope of the roof, found the number that Dickens had been given.

I was gasping from the climb when Dickens tapped lightly twice upon the door with his stick (not at all in the brutal manner in which he had saluted my door). I was still breathing in gulps when the door slowly opened.

The room was spacious but dim. No gas was lit. The small fire in the hearth and two candles, sitting in holders upon a desk covered with open books on the far side of the room, provided the only light. The ceiling sloped with the contour of the roof so that in its inner half a man could stand to his full height, but in its outer half, where the aforementioned desk and a small daybed covered with an eye-catching white fur pelt were located, a man could reside only in a sitting position. Burton had opened the door from within and had stepped back to the centre of the room. The candles glowed behind him giving a yellowish tint to everything. To his side, the fire flared then fell, sending long shadows up across the sloping ceiling.

115

Even in that dim light, the first thing I noticed about Burton was the deep fire burning in his eyes. As we stepped in and he stood looking at us, sizing us up, his eyes seemed to blaze with an intensity, an openness, a curiosity perhaps. *Who are these specimens?* his eyes might have been asking. *Of what tribe are they? What language might they speak?* Have you ever seen the flash of a cat's eyes when caught in a light after dark? It was that sort of bright intensity that beamed from Burton's eyes. Though not overly tall (Dickens stood half a head above him), nor excessively broad of shoulder, nor thick of neck or arms, he was, nonetheless, somehow an imposing figure. His hair, which dipped into his collar, was as black as ebony as was his mustache, which turned down at the corners of his mouth giving him a rather fierce Turk-like countenance. Even when he smiled, which he did immediately upon our entrance, that mustache gave him a frightening barbaric look. As he stood before us, I sensed a muscular tiger's body, lithe and trim, yet coiled tight with a power and grace that could erupt into violent motion at the slightest alarum.

"Mister Dickens." He stepped forward with his hand outstretched. "This is, indeed, a great honour for me. As you know, I aspire to be a writer, and to actually have the greatest writer in England in my poor room is . . . well . . . I can't tell you . . ." and he gave up the attempt, overcome by the intensity of his writerly emotion.

Charles took his hand warmly. "It is all my honour, indeed," he assured Burton. "Those of us who know you rest in the complete certainty that quite soon all the honour shall fall to you both for your exploits and your writings."

Visibly moved by Dickens's high praise, perhaps because he was not a man used to that sort of encouragement, Burton was momentarily speechless, but then, remembering himself, he stretched out his hand to me: "I am Richard Francis Burton. I don't believe we've—"

"I *am* sorry." Dickens pounced upon the introduction. "This is my colleague and also a fellow writer, Wilkie Collins. He, too, shall soon garner the honours of the literary world."

116

His interruption of my sexual interlude with Meg, his insistence that I dress and follow him out into the raw London night, his coy withholding of the object of our expedition's pursuit in the cab—all was forgiven when he rewarded me with that morsel of praise. *He does think I can be a writer,* I must have beamed the affirmation of it. *The honours of the literary world, indeed.* Nothing Meg could have offered me that evening could have tempted me more than that snippet of praise from Dickens.

Pulling a worn armchair of indeterminate lineage and design out of the shadows of a corner, and turning his straight-backed wooden desk chair around, Burton begged us both to sit. Graciously placing our coats and hats atop a large steamer chest and satisfied that we were settled comfortably, he poured us each a cup of brandy, snifters evidently not being included among his household furnishings. That done, Burton sat with his legs crossed beneath him on the white fur skin covering his bed. He looked like a savage at a jungle fire.

Dickens offered him, then me, a cigar. He took it eagerly. One received the impression that, despite his dining at the Explorers Club, Burton led a rather Spartan existence devoid of the usual amenities—such as cigars—common to the life of a London gentleman. He literally lunged to his desk for a vesta and, after fastidiously lighting our cigars before his own, drew the smoke deep into his chest.

"Mister Dickens"—he smiled his fierce smile from his savage posture perched on the skin of that wild animal—"such a fine cigar places me utterly at your service. You said earlier in the evening that you had some questions to put to me. Fire at will."

"It is about a murder, two murders really, right here in the West End," Dickens began, and Burton's black brows raised in a disarmingly innocent display of shock at the barbarity of civilisation. "We and Inspector Field of the Metropolitan Protectives believe that the two women were poisoned, but the police surgeon has not been able to provide us with a clue to the cause of such a horrible death. There are no traces of the usual poisons, such as arsenic, in the bodies."

"Horrible? How were they horrible?" Burton seized upon one of Charles's words. "I mean, in what ways were the deaths horrible?" Burton was hooked, his eyes burning for information.

"It was the horrible twisted looks upon their faces as they died," I interjected, not wanting to sit there in silence like some pull toy that Dickens dragged around after him.

"What do you mean?" Burton pressed.

Dickens echoed Field's description of the two corpses as best he could and tried to lighten the mood a bit by ending, "And Wilkie here, due to the looks on the dead women's faces, christened them the 'Medusa Murders.' "

"It was as if they were turned to stone in an instant," I defended myself against Dickens's irony.

"Faces twisted . . . as if turned to stone." The smoke from Burton's cigar languidly trailed out of the corner of his mouth as he held counsel with himself. "A grotesque death rictus," he murmured as if remembering faraway places. After one more puff at his cigar, he straightened his shoulders, which had been hunched over in thought, his head rose up, and a single word exploded like a dart from an African native's blowpipe: "Curare!"

"What?" Dickens and I exclaimed in unison.

"Curare," he repeated, "is really a portmanteau term for a whole group of vegetation-derived poisons. Your corpses sound like curare to me."

"What is it? Where does it come from? How is it used to kill?" Dickens's questions tumbled out like Jill after Jack.

"Curare is any of a variety of different substances"—one could sense the schoolmaster in Burton emerging—"extracted from the saps of jungle plants. It is used by the Indians of the Amazon of Brazil and the pygmies of Africa as an arrow and spear poison for hunting and warfare."

"How does it work?" Dickens asked.

"I have only seen one instance of its effect upon human

118

beings. It was when we came upon the immediate aftermath of a battle between two native tribes on an excursion into the Amazon jungle of Brazil out of the port of Janeiro. We heard the skirmish ahead in a clearing, wild whoops and screams of either hatred or agony, so we fired our muskets into the air to scare whoever it was off and they all ran. They left behind three dead men. Warriors, from the looks of their paint. Those men looked as if they had been stopped in their tracks, brought up short and frozen in mid-air. Curare poisons seem to induce an instant paralysis by somehow interfering with nerve impulses to the human muscles. In a substantial dosage, it can induce a most sudden death."

"Good God!" I gasped.

"Like turning a person to stone." Dickens looked at us, the myth of Medusa surfacing in each of our minds.

"That must be it . . . curare." Dickens was merely speculating aloud, not addressing either of us in particular. "But there were no knife wounds or puncture wounds of any sort upon the victims. Is that the only method of administering the poison?"

"Not a'tall," Burton was quick to answer. "Jungle natives dip their arrows and axes and spear blades in it in order to more efficiently kill their enemies, but it is a liquid and could be dissolved in another liquid or in food, or it could be injected. The puncture hole of a single hypodermic needle, between the toes, say, could be easily overlooked in a surgeon's inquest."

"By George, Wilkie"—Dickens slapped me on the knee in his exuberance—"I think we have found at least one of Field's answers." I think it gave Dickens great pleasure to demonstrate that the amateur detective could out-detect the professional. He and Inspector Field were great friends, but, for Dickens, Field was also a fancied rival. All of life was a game for Dickens. For Field, life was a job, and Dickens was not a rival at all, but rather an extremely valuable tool to be used in the performance of his tasks. In detecting, that was, with-

119

out question, the difference between the professional and the amateur.

"We cannot thank you enough." Dickens rose and extended his hand to Burton. Our sitting idol leapt to his feet and warmly shook Dickens's hand. It was a signal that our conversation had come to an end. Burton seemed genuinely chagrined. I too rose, but my curiosity salted my parting handshake.

"Might I inquire," I asked, "what sort of an animal skin that is which so magnificently adorns your bed?"

"It is a white tiger." Burton beamed at my interest. "Shot him in India in 'forty-six. Damn few of them to be had."

"What are your prospects now?" Dickens asked as we folded ourselves into our coats and wrapped ourselves in our scarves. "If there is anything that I can do to help, please do not hesitate to call upon me."

Burton smiled again, his fierce mustache making it look like a scowl. "Whitehall wants me to spy for them in foreign lands, go on the tick of Empire," he said, and made a comic shrugging face. "Travel the world as a traitor to everyone I meet. Can you imagine?"

Dickens laughed awkwardly with him for a moment, but then Burton took his hand in one final shake of farewell and, with those irresistible eyes of his burning into both of us, almost pleaded: "They think it is all so simple, that human beings can just give themselves up that way. I could no more betray some poor trusting pygmy of the African mountains than I could betray my own mum. Whitehall, my God, they tried to tell me that theirs was an honourable profession," and he laughed a hollow laugh.

"If I can be of service," Dickens reiterated as we took our leave. Burton nodded, somewhat embarrassed, I think. I do know for a fact, however, that only six months later Dickens did, indeed, answer a private subscription to the tune of fifty pounds to help finance a very secretive expedition that Burton wished to undertake. Three years later the world would read of that expedition, of the daring adventure of the first

Westerner ever to enter the ancient forbidden city of Mecca. Dickens always knew, somehow, what horses to back. Burton was, indeed, one of the singular young men of our age. Though I only met him in person that once while on duty for Inspector Field, I followed his amazing exploits for more than thirty years thereafter.

Dickens and I had a scene at the kerb in front of the Africa Hotel. He wished to race straight off to Bow Street to present our little trophy of information to Inspector Field, but I insisted that it must wait until morning. It was already half after one on my new repeater, and the night was as cold and unforgiving as a Christian wife. I, of course, still had faint hopes of securing Irish Meg's understanding and good offices. Thus I demanded that Dickens transport me directly to my lodgings in Soho. He reluctantly agreed, but in turn extorted my promise to be at the *Household Words* offices no later than ten the following morning, so that we could share our triumph with Inspector Field. Needless to say, Irish Meg was not waiting up for me when I arrived at our flat.

THE DUEL, OR, INSPECTOR FIELD, PLAYWRIGHT

January 18, 1852—midday

"We got ta ketch 'im unawares," Inspector Field declared with conviction and a sharp tap with his demonstrative forefinger to the top of Captain Hawkins's gun table.

We were once again assembled—Dickens, myself, Field, Rogers, Hawkins, and Moody—at Tally Ho Thompson's hiding place, the Shooting Gallery in Leicester Square. That morning, immediately upon Field's arrival at the *Household Words* offices to collect us, Dickens had apprised him of the poisonous intelligence we had ourselves collected from Burton the night before. Field was stunned; who knows, perhaps even a bit jealous of Dickens's initiative and easy success in the detecting line.

"Curare, extraordinary! Never 'eard o' it," Field pronounced. "Dickens, yew are a reg'lar barnacle, yew are. Once yew take 'old, 'tis 'ard to pry yew loose." His enthusiasm for Dickens's discovery was building slowly, but then with a quick lunge of his crook'd forefinger to the side of his eye, he gave in to it and, clapping Dickens heartily upon the shoulder, said: "Well done, I say! We might never 'ave found that partickler poison. Knowin' t'will come in 'andy on this case, I'll wager."

Now, at the Shooting Gallery, Thompson, our footpad friend, became the centre of Field's attentions while the rest of us and our fugitive's hosts, Captain Hawkins and his one-armed, one-eyed, humpbacked, parrot-plagued lieutenant, Serjeant Moody, looked on. As for me, I was curious as to what Field's next move would be and to what use he planned to put his pawn Thompson. Certainly, no one was more eager for this intelligence than Tally Ho Thompson himself. His restless pacing of the room clearly showed him to be champing for action and the opportunity to clear up the dark cloud hanging over his name. For a man whose life included stints as a highwayman, housebreaker, pickpocket, sneak thief, and actor, Thompson had this peculiar sense of honour that disregarded the incriminating evidence of his belonging to such a litany of unsavoury and dishonourable professions. Somewhere, in the sheltered cave of his own mind, Thompson actually believed that he was an honest man.

" 'Ow do yew propose ketchin' 'im unawares?" Thompson questioned Field's opening foray. " 'Ee knows I'm on the weasel from Newgate. 'Ee knows I'll come after 'im."

"Ah, but 'ee 'as no place ta go ta git away." Field indulged in a tiny grin at the prospect of having his prey right where he wanted him. " 'Ee 'asn't the money ta flee ta the Continent. 'Ee can't afford ta pack in 'is job an' 'ide out 'til all blows over. 'Ee is too well known ta 'ide 'is identity. No, our Mister Dick Dunn 'as been under our surveillance since the day after the murders, an' 'ee 'asn't so much as twitched in the followin' o' 'is reg'lar routine."

"T'will be the dark alleys 'ee fears." Thompson got into the spirit of Field's working out this scenario for confrontation. " 'Ee'll look for me ta surprise 'im in the dark, when 'ee's alone, comin' 'ome after the play or the public 'ouse."

124

" 'At's why we must take 'im unawares, in the bright day-light." Field slammed his forefinger down upon the unsus-pecting gun table once again. "When 'ee thinks 'ee's safe. Where do yew think 'ee is right now, Thompson?"

"Should be at the theatre by now. Fight rehearsal is each performance day at noon."

"Precisely! Macready's fight master rehearses his actors every day at this time. Except today. Today, 'ee 'as contrived, at my biddin', ta release all the cast 'ceptin' our friend Dick Dunn. Yew know, don't yew, that since yew 'ave been out o' the play Dunn 'as moved up from fifth business* into yer part? 'Ee makes a sullen, slinking Poins. 'Ee 'as been told that 'ee must polish 'is swordplay. An' that, my boy, is 'ow yew are goin' ta take 'im unawares."

With that, we bid farewell to Captain Hawkins and Serjeant Moody. Field packed us all into his black post chaise for the short dart to Macready's Covent Garden Theatre. As we rode through the narrow twisted streets muffled against the raw January wind, Field rehearsed Thompson in the subtleties of the scene that had been scripted. In the course of that short trip crosstown, however, Field did say one thing that, to me, certainly seemed worth noting and remembering, whether one is in the detecting or the novel-writing line. "Detection is one-'alf dramatisation," he said, more to Dickens and me than to Thompson and Rogers. "Yew must create a scenario in which yer murderer or thief or scoundrel of whatever sort will betray himself. It is like puttin' on a play. Yew put yer characters in place an see 'ow they act ta each other." Later, Dickens and I decided that Field's "detection is dramatisa-tion" speech belonged right up there with his "simply ob-serve" speech of the Ashbee affair.†

Covent Garden Theatre, like any other theatre at midday, evidenced no signs of life as we reined in at the stage door.

---

*A stage term for those actors who play all the nameless supporting parts.
†See pages 157–58 of Collins' first secret commonplace book.

This was the carriage yard where, on performance nights, the coachmen waited, tending to their horses, for the rich gentlemen and their ladies to emerge from the play. On the other side of the theatre, in a wide alley lit by gaslamps, there would be hansom cabs queued for hire, waiting on the whims of those theatre patrons who did not indulge themselves in the extravagance of their own private coach.

Upon Field's order, we disembarked and approached the stage door. At a single knock from Field's murderous stick, old Spilka opened that wooden door, and, at an age-old signal from Field, straightened forefinger to the lips, ushered us silently in. Old Spilka evidently had been schooled by Field because he scrupulously observed that signalled silence as he led us through the darkened backstage area. There was light and some indeterminate sound onstage that was audible as we groped our way through the darkness.

With the touch of his hand, Field stopped us, bid us wait, and led Tally Ho Thompson away into the shadows. When Field returned, he was alone. Old Spilka, at Field's bidding, next led us off in yet another direction and ushered us through a backstage door, which opened into the far side aisle of the darkened theatre. This aisle was beneath the overhang of the balcony. Thus, we were drowned in the deepest shadows of any section of the stalls. We took seats in this black pool of shadow and waited for the curtain to go up. We did not have to wait long.

On the lighted stage, Macready's fencing master was giving instructions to a tall but rather slight of stature, swarthy, black-haired Irishman who was halfheartedly attempting to ape the fencing master's feints and parries. Both men were wielding tipped foils for the obvious purpose of safety. Thompson, in that maddening way of his for appearing and disappearing out of and into thin air, materialised out of a cleft in the curtain at centre stage, and stepped forth in his shirt sleeves with a fencing foil in hand. Upon Thompson's sudden entrance, the fencing master, clearly by prearrange-

126

ment, faded off into the wings. Dunn did not perceive Thompson's entrance at first, but as he watched the fencing master withdraw without explanation, he quickly realised that all was not right. Then, turning his head, he found Thompson facing him, rapier in hand, at centre stage. Inspector Field's little drama had begun.

Thompson's first hostile act, even as he stood there with that maddening, utterly confident, totally heedless grin on his face, was to slowly reach out with his free hand and forcefully push the protective wooden button off of the tip of his sword. That tiny button landed on the floor and comically rolled right up against Dick Dunn's foot.

"Jaysus, Meery, un Joseph," Dunn gasped with an intake of breath that stood him up on his toes.

"Yer goin' ta git a fencin' re'earsal the likes o' wot yee've never 'ad before," Thompson spat at him. With a quick thrust, he pointed his rapier directly at Dunn's face and began to rotate it in a slow, hypnotic circle. Simultaneously, Thompson, with smooth, sliding, sideways steps, began to slowly circle Dunn, cutting off any of his adversary's avenues of escape.

"I'm goin' ta carve yew like a Christmas bird," Thompson volunteered for Dunn's amusement and great chagrin, "if yew don't heave to an' fight."

Dunn seemed mesmerized, like a man caught in the gaze of a swaying cobra, by the naked point of Thompson's sword rotating before his face. With a quick flick of his wrist, Thompson brought Dunn out of his reverie and drew blood from just beneath the frightened actor's left eye. "I could 'ave taken yer 'ole eye, mate." Thompson continued to grin evilly. "Yew needs ta react more quickly."

With that, Thompson stepped back a step and made a fencing-room salute—sword drawn up to his face pointing skyward. This anticipatory pause allowed his shaken adversary to collect himself. "We are done with this playactin' as o' right now," Thompson announced with murderous intent, causing

127

a truly frightened Dick Dunn to jump backward and assume the familiar posture of defence. Thompson stepped forth, his rapier once again extended toward Dunn's eyes, and moved in with those tiny tapping steps observed only in the fencing room or on the ballet stage. Their blades flashed in the stage light. Thompson thrust. Dunn successfully, if clumsily, parried. Thompson crowded in upon his foe, then gracefully retreated. The foils twirled at one another and the blades clashed.

Thrust and parry, thrust and parry, across the stage and back, circling each other at cautious speed as if dancing some sort of deadly ballet. Amazing how convincing actors can be when they are not acting, or at least do not think they are acting. As I watched this set-to, I was impressed by the threatening grace of it, the swordsmen's moves as they stalked each other. Is it not a pity that the ancient tradition of the duel has gone the way of the Industrial Revolution, flashing swords replaced by pistol and ball, ten boring paces, and a puff of smoke?

Thompson was much the better swordsman and quite the quicker upon his feet, but Dick Dunn managed to put up a dogged defence. With a feint and a sidewise move of lightning delivery, Thompson slashed his adversary's shirt right across the chest without drawing so much as a dash of blood from the skin beneath.

"He is playing with him," Dickens whispered, touching my shoulder in the dark. "Thompson is a remarkable specimen, is he not, Wilkie?"

Dickens said it lightly, but the admiration rang clear in his voice. That admiration on Dickens's part, I am convinced even today almost twenty years later, was one of the reasons we had so precipitously catapulted ourselves into the centre of this adventure. Dickens had led me here out of his novelist's ravenousness for adventuresome experience certainly, out of his gratitude for Thompson's aid in rescuing his beloved Ellen from the perils of the Ashbee affair definitely, but also, quite obviously, out of his admiration of and friendship for Tally Ho Thompson, whom, I am convinced, he looked upon as a true gentleman without portfolio.

On the stage, Tally Ho Thompson warmed to his task. He was now hard on the offensive. Moving in fast and engaging Dunn's blade, he executed a classic fencing move. With a cobra-quick double twirl of his wrist he spun the sword from Dunn's grasp and sent it clattering across the stage. He held his adversary at bay, disarmed, once again slowly rotating the naked point of his sword within inches of Dunn's terrified eyes.

"He is a marvel!" Dickens exclaimed in the dark, giving me an enthusiastic clap on the shoulder.

"Only if 'ee plays out the script," Field tempered Dickens's premature celebration.

Thompson backed his helpless victim up against the stage curtain and laid his blade tenderly to the man's chest just over the heart. Dick Dunn's eyes went wild with fear. No playacting there!

" 'Oo put yew up ta it, Dickie?" Thompson demanded in a voice somehow both cajoling and murderous. " 'Oo paid yew ta lure me in an' peach me?"

"I don' know, Gawd's truth, I don' know," Dunn begged for his life. " 'Ee paid me forty pound. But I never saw 'is face."

"Not good enough, not good enough, Dickie bird"—and with another series of deft flicks, Thompson slashed Dunn's shirt to tatters.

"Oh Gawd no, don' cut me." Dunn fell to his knees pleading. "Hit's the truth. I never saw 'im."

"That's it, yew lying little weasel." Frustration and anger quavered murderously in Thompson's voice. The blade pressed against Dunn's chest.

" 'Ee met me in the streets, at night, in the dark, in fog," the kneeling man's voice raced desperately. " 'Ee always wore a dark 'ood, like some monk's dress. I never saw 'is face, but I 'eard 'is voice. 'Ee's a foreigner, 'ee wos. Wos no English-

129

man's nor Irishman's voice. A Spainiard mayhaps, but not a Spainiard neither. 'Ee met me in the dark in 'at 'ood an' paid me forty pounds, an' tol me wot ta do. 'Ee said 'ee'd 'ave me fired, turned out in the streets if I didn't. Don' cut me! I never saw 'is face, I swear it."

Tears of terror were running down the snivelling weasel's face. His body was shuddering on the verge of collapse.

Abruptly Thompson pulled back the point of his sword, turned, and walked to the foot of the stage as if he were Hamlet about to deliver some tortured soliloquy. Then he shrugged with both hands, his right still holding the sword, to the darkened stalls. Inspector Field led us up out of the darkness onto the stage.

"We're done," Thompson complained to Field. "I think 'ee's tellin' the truth. Now we don't know 'oo put 'im up ta it."

"Patience, lad," Field was almost fatherly in his consolation to Thompson, "every bit o' news 'elps. We'll find this 'ooded man if, indeed"—and he cast a baleful glance accompanied by a violent scratch of his crook'd forefinger to the side of his eye at the snivelling Dunn, who was still kneeling hopelessly on the floor of the stage—"there really is a 'ooded man."

Evidently Field was less disposed to believe a practised actor than was Tally Ho Thompson.

"Mind you, Mister Dick Dunn," Field growled, "my men will be watchin' yer every twitch. Don't vary yer routine one quid, or I shall 'ave yew in Newgate quicker'n yew kin say John Barsad.* Git 'im out o' 'ere, Serjeant Rogers."

Rogers, not at all pleased at having been dispatched upon what he surely considered a trivial errand, dragged the shaken actor from the proscenium.

---

*After researching the newspapers and broadsides of the day, I have been unable to unearth the source of or explain the allusion to this name. The fact that the name "John Barsad" appears later, appended to a character in *A Tale of Two Cities*, intimates that it was a recognizable name and allusion for its time, but has since lost its meaning and dropped out of use.

A contemplative Inspector Field sat down on the front edge of the bare stage. We all, Dickens, myself, and Thompson, reluctantly joined him there, sitting shoulder to shoulder, our legs dangling into the shallow pit that served as a moat between the stalls and the stage, the real world and that of make-believe.

"We've ridden the course an' lost the race, 'aven't we?" Thompson was glum.

"Not a'tall," Field reassured him. "In fact, we 'ave learned quite a bit."

"Such as?" Dickens prompted.

"Well, if Dunn is telling the truth o' it, then our man speaks with a Spanish accent an' is some'ow connected ta the Covent Garden Theatre."

"Wot?" Thompson exclaimed. He jostled me roughly by accident as he turned in surprise toward Field.

"I beg your pardon?" Dickens pressed.

" 'Ee threatened ta 'ave Dunn fired, didn't 'ee? Turned out on the streets 'ee said. Therefore, our 'ooded man must know that Dunn, like t'other o' the fifth-business actors, lets a room belowstairs in the theatre. See, Mister Dickens, I too am doin' my 'omework." Field clearly took pleasure in surprising both Dickens and Thompson with this information.

"The fact o' it is," Field trotted on upon his little ratiocinative excursion, "that our 'ooded friend seems ta think 'ee 'as the power ta git 'im evicted. Now 'oo could do that? A blackmailer? Not likely. Dunn 'as no money ta squeeze, an' only a limited usefulness. A powerful man in the theatre? Not likely again. Since the scandal of Paroissien,* Macready 'as 'ired only persons o' impeccable character; that is, if those sorts are even ta be found in the actin' profession, an' certainly excludin' Thompson." Field pronounced this last with a mischievous pursing of his lips to subdue a grin. "But a man o' some other sort o' power then? Quite likely, in this case. Doctor

*In Collins' first commonplace book, Paroissien was the sinister stage manager of Macready's farewell production of *Macbeth*.

131

William Palmer, the murdered woman's 'usband? 'Ee's a patron o' Covent Garden Theatre we 'ave found out, a new member o' less than a year o' Mister Macready's governin' board, right in there with Miss Burdett-Coutts an' the Duke o' Devonshire.''

Needless to say, all of us sitting on that empty stage were astounded by Field's new information. Rogers had returned just in time to share in his master's triumph. "I'd like ta see the look on Mister Dick Dunn's face when this Doctor Palmer's name is mentioned," Rogers crowed.

"No. 'Tis much too soon for that," Field cut him off. "We don't want ta spook our Doctor Palmer jus' yet. If Dunn is 'is creeture, t'will come out nat'ral in the course o' things.''

"Does not his hooded man seem a bit melodramatic?" Dickens's skepticism went in the face of Dunn's obvious upset under Thompson's blade. Dickens's skepticism also embraced the highly unlikely possibility that Dick Dunn was one of the more convincing actors in England.

Field pondered that a moment.

"Dickie Dunn is diff'rent, ye know," Tally Ho Thompson interrupted Field's reverie. "They says 'ee goes with wimmin an' *men*. That's just wot I've 'eard."

"Hello! Now there's a reason for blackmail." Field seized upon it. "Per'aps the 'ooded man story wos a lie, or 'alf a lie, just a desperate ruse ta 'ide the identity o' some'un Dunn fears even more than Thompson's sword."

"And yet the man was crying and trembling in fear," I reminded them. "Those are not easy emotions to counterfeit."

"No, an actor kin do those things." Thompson's voice was regretful. "I never should 'ave let 'im up. I should 'ave sliced off 'is ear. We must git 'im back up 'ere an' go at 'im again."

"In time," Field said, as he tried to calm his excited highwayman, "all in good time. Let 'im recover from this shock. Let 'im think 'ee 'as gotten away with it. We will talk ta 'im when needs be. 'Oo I wants ta talk ta now is the 'usband, this Doctor Palmer. Wot time is it anyways?"

I reached for my gold repeater hanging on its gold fob in my vest coat pocket, but it was gone.

"Two o' the clock." Serjeant Rogers beat me to the honours as I searched all of my pockets for the missing timepiece. In my bewildered turning of my pockets inside-out, I failed to note the look of amusement that crept up out of Field's shirt collar and took his face into custody.

"Thompson?" Field finally prompted, even as I still wondered where I had misplaced my ticker.

Everyone turned to Tally Ho Thompson.

Sheepishly he fished my shiny gold repeater out of his trousers pocket. "Gots ta keep me 'and in, mate," he, utterly unremorseful, shrugged to the others and apologised to me, the injured party. "I'd a given it back ta 'im, Guv," he pled his case with Inspector Field. "Can't blame me, wos jus' sittin' right out there beggin' ta be lifted," he justified himself with another shrug to the assembled company as he handed it back to me.

Everyone laughed heartily at this little diversion. Everyone but me, that is. I was sick of being the repeated butt of Thompson's slick-fingered jokes. Serjeant Rogers laughed greatly to excess.

"Palmer's surgery is at Bart's." Field was on his feet. "Per'aps we can still catch 'im there this afternoon."

Dickens's face was positively animated at the prospect. *Now we're getting somewhere,* I could see him thinking, *beard the lion in his den.*

As we exited the theatre by the stage door, Inspector Field stopped Dickens and myself, drew us back inside for a brief conferral: "This case smacks o' that last we worked together, don't it gents?"

Dickens did not answer. Perhaps, like me, he was not quick enough to follow Field's flow of thought. Field sensed this from our silence and elaborated: "Nothin' is 'arder for me ta stomach than a swell 'oo thinks 'ee kin git away with murder jus' because 'ee's a swell. Rich men seems ta think they're exempt from the laws just because that 'as always been the case. But 'at don't mean it always will be the case. Or that 'tis the case right now, even though our friend Ashbee an' all 'is fancy solicitors 'ave proved so far it 'tis."*

*That previous case, as described by Collins in his first commonplace book, came to an unsatisfying disposition. The rich antagonist, one Lord Henry Ashbee, was never brought to trial for his crimes. This misfiring of justice, however, was less due to Ashbee's clever solicitors than to Dickens' and Field's unwillingness to press a prosecution, which would surely have incriminated the young actress, Miss Ellen Ternan.

A "SPAINIARD" AT BART'S

January 18, 1852—late afternoon

Bart's, as it always has been familiarly known, or Saint Bartholomew's Hospital, as it is formally designated, is an island marooned in the encompassing shadow of Newgate, a shadow that seems to loom darkly over my entire memoir. The black Bow Street Station post-chaise, which ferried the five of us from Covent Garden Theatre to Bart's by way of High Holborn, glided to anchor at the Newgate Street entrance to the hospital.

In the coach on the dash crosstown, Inspector Field relayed to Dickens and me full instructions as to how to conduct ourselves at Doctor William Palmer's surgery. Field desired ours to be a private inquiry. Palmer, Field presumed, would surely have read of Dickens's and my connection to the escape of Tally Ho Thompson, and thus would be somewhat suspicious of our visit. Field was gambling, however, that Palmer would not be nearly as threatened by our coincidental visit as he might be if Thompson in the flesh accosted him. We gathered that Field was keeping Thompson in reserve, in the manner of a general holding back his cavalry for some fortuitous moment when he meant to spring him on the "swell," Palmer. Field also theorised that we could not be sure that Palmer had never observed Tally Ho Thompson from afar, either onstage or by some other spying arrangement, and thus he did not wish Palmer to recognise Thompson right off and become skittish. Pursuant to all that speculation, when we arrived at Bart's, Inspector Field immediately dismissed Thompson in Serjeant Rogers's custody, sending them in the post chaise back to Captain Hawkins's Shooting Gallery. Rogers took the news like a man ordered transported to the colonies of Australia. The bitter resentment that opined *Why do these writer swells get to stay on the case while I am sent off to baby-sit?* bloomed in his face like a huge weed in a rock garden.

As the carriage trotted off with its unwilling passengers, leaving us standing on the narrow stone steps of Bart's, Field bestowed upon us our final instructions.

"I'm not goin' in with yew, gents," he informed us. "At this point, 'tis still ta our advantage ta not declare that 'ee is under official suspicion. But yew two kin still let 'im know that someone is interested in 'im." What followed was a somewhat shortened version of Field's aforementioned "simply observe" speech, which he seemed to dust off for our instruction whenever he conscripted us to go on duty for him. His plan was for us to confront Doctor Palmer, inquire as to whether he knew Tally Ho Thompson or Dick Dunn, and observe his reactions. It all seemed simple enough, and we left Inspector Field waiting in Bart's outer doorway as we entered the hospital.

An Indian gentleman with one leg leaned precariously against the wall of the foyer. This teetering sahib directed us to an officious mountain of a woman with a wart on her nose stationed behind a low counter at the foot of the hospital stairs. This overstuffed mountain of pretension in turn ordered us to climb three flights of said stairs whose ascent delivered us to the outer holding area of Doctor William

136

Palmer's surgery. On a low bench against the wall sat an assortment of what appeared to be paying patients, persons of both sexes, holding their hats, babies, bundles, or purses upon their laps as they waited to be admitted to the doctor by a thin, sallow, sharp-faced woman dressed in an official-looking jumper of white cotton, and guarding a single wooden door leading into the inner sanctum of the hospital. With Dickens in the lead, we approached her congenially. She answered our greetings with the hostile scowl of an abandoned soldier guarding the last outpost of Empire.

"Doctor Palmer?" she answered our inquiry with a patronising amazement. "Good Lord no, oh no sirs, 'ee only visits the surgery on Weds'day morns. 'Ee calls on the most o' 'is patients in their 'omes, 'ee does."

"Well then, who are these people waiting for? Who is in charge of the surgery?" Dickens pressed a somewhat perplexed inquiry, although why he was perplexed, or why either Field or we expected to find a doctor of Palmer's stature in his surgery in the first place, merely evidenced the naïveté on our part and, at that time, toward the Hippocratic dedication of the medical profession. Now, twenty years later, it is taken for granted that few doctors ever really attend their surgeries or are available when needed, certainly not a physician of the wealth and stature of a Doctor Palmer.

"Doctor Vasconcellas administers to the surgery patients." She made a sour face even as she spoke, as if either that name gave her indigestion or speaking to us did.

"I realise that we do not have an appointment," Charles's voice dripped sugar as a hopeful antidote to the sour aspect of this guardian of the gate, "but it is most important that we speak to Doctor, ah, ah . . . ?"

"Vasconcellas," the hag reminded him with relish, though there was still almost an instinctual shudder of distaste in her voice as she spoke the name.

"Yes, Doctor Vasconcellas it is. I am sorry. I am Charles Dickens"—he handed her his card—"and this is Mister Wilkie

Collins. It is not a medical matter, and will take only a minute or two."

At the famous name, immediately reiterated and confirmed by the prized card, that pinch-faced Cerberus metamorphosed into the most accommodating of humanitarian practitioners. "Oh Mister Dickens, sir, I 'ave read all of yer stories"—not much of a recommendation for his readership I could not help but think—"especially that of Little Nell, poor thing," the woman gushed with a sincerity and tenderness that belied the sour hostility of her previous address. "I will tell the doctor yew are 'ere. I am sure 'ee will be able to see yew soon." With that, she scurried backward through that lone door like a mouse ducking into its hole.

Within moments, she emerged from that inner sanctum, and, without speaking, not wanting the waiting patients to hear, we presumed, she signalled for us to follow her down a dingy corridor and through another lone door where she deposited us in a shabby office furnished with a heavily scarred desk, two straight-backed wooden chairs, and a desk chair with its padding spilling out of a split seam. An oil lamp complemented the dim light struggling through a single filthy casement above the desk. It did not at all seem the office of a wealthy society physician. Perhaps it was merely his assistant's workroom?

When the woman had left, after gushing some more sentiment having to do with "poor little Paul Dombey and the tragedy of Little Em'ly at the 'ands o' that scoundrel on the boat," I turned to Dickens quite puzzled: "What are we doing?" I asked. "Palmer is not here. What good does it do seeing his assistant?"

"I don't know," Dickens admitted. "I have no idea. I just thought we might learn something that Field could use. I hate to go away empty-handed."

"But what do we say to this man?"

"I shall think of something," Dickens was assuring me when the door opened.

The man who entered was short and wiry of stature, dark of

brow, high and sharp of cheekbone, black of mustache and actively nervous about the eyes. His cheekbones and the deep copper of his skin signalled his Latin heritage, but if there was any doubt in either Dickens's or my mind it was dispelled as soon as he began to speak. "Gentlemen," he pronounced it slowly in the manner of one speaking a strange word with an illogical inflection in a newly learned language, "I Doctor Rodrigo Vasconcellas, Doctor Palmer's assist. How do I help you?" The man's voice was soft and passive even as he struggled with the unfamiliar words. Despite his wiry stature, which intimated a fit and muscled body beneath his morning coat, his delicate hands moved nervously as he spoke, and his eyes never stopped darting from one of us to the other.

"Doctor Vasconcellas"—Dickens stretched out his hand. The man's delicate gesturing hand swept up and was rather cruelly engulfed by Dickens's paw—"I am Charles Dickens."

"Ah yes, I been told. A great author I been told."

Dickens bowed at this recognition, then charged on: "I had hoped to talk with Doctor William Palmer, but I am sure that you can answer my questions."

"I weel try." This Doctor Rodrigo Whatever was quite accommodating. He sat down at the desk and crossed his legs at the knees waiting for Charles to continue. I had not said a word, because, to tell the truth, I had not a single clue as to where this unscripted conversation was going.

"Missus Dickens, my wife," Charles began, "is presently, and has been for some three years, under the care of Doctor Southwood Smith of Great Malvern. I am sure he is a fine doctor"—Dickens said this in a way that intimated quite the opposite—"the Queen places great confidence in him"— again Dickens said it in a way that questioned the Queen's sanity—"but Missus Dickens is not getting any better and Great Malvern is not getting any closer." He chuckled at his little joke. "Therefore, I am seriously considering placing her in the care of a London physician. Your Doctor Palmer's name was brought immediately to my attention." With that little canter over the fantastical ground, Dickens momentarily

139

reined in to allow Doctor Rodrigo of the Spanish accent some time to ruminate. "I would very much like to discuss this with Doctor Palmer," Dickens went on, before Doctor Rodrigo had opportunity to reply. "Could you possibly arrange an appointment for me to meet and talk with him? At his convenience, of course."

"*Sí.* Yes, *señor.* I would be, how you say, pondered and incited to set down such a meeting." The man was smiling idiotically as he spoke. I hesitate to speculate whether it was nervousness with us or with the language that made him so jumpy.

"Thank you very much." Dickens bowed politely. "If I might ask," his voice took on a low conspiratorial tone, the voice of a whore about to stab a customer, "where are you from, doctor? South America, I presume, but what country and city? I am, you see," and he carried the conspiracy right over into the whispered jocularity of his apologetic explanation, "an amateur linguist," and he nodded to me while Doctor Rodrigo nodded knowingly to him as if he understood what Dickens was saying, "and though your English is excellent, you speak with a slight accent and I am fascinated by the geographics of accented speech."

"Whot? I beg . . . who?" The man was clearly bucked off by Dickens's large words like "geographics."

"I am sorry," Dickens said, oozing conciliation, "where are you from in South America?"

"I am from Brazeel," the man confessed. "Sam Powlow." It sounded like an bandit's name. "A coastal ceety, menny peeple, few buildeengs." For some inexplicable reason the man shrugged both hands at us as if to say *sorry, nothing I can do about it.*

"Ah Brazil." Dickens leaned in toward him from the edge of that wooden chair. "That is in the heart of the Amazon jungle, is it not?"

"Well," the man was hesitant, not wishing to offend. "No, *señor,* my country not jungle all. Sam Powlow old Portuguese feesheen veellage. Jungle ees center of Brazil."

140

"Quite. Quite so." Dickens was starting his retreat, rising from his chair, extending his hand, edging toward the door. *He has gotten what he wants,* I thought, *whatever in the name of all that's holy, that is.*

"When will Doctor Palmer be in?" Dickens fired one more dart as we retreated through the doorway.

"Hee ees never een," Doctor Vasconcellas fired back, clearly perturbed and unaware of indiscretion. "One finds heem more easily at hees riding club than heere."

With that eyebrow-raiser as a fare-thee-well, we took our leave of the good doctor. As we came out of St. Bart's, one of those strange and fortuitous metamorphoses that infrequently bless a London winter occurred. The sun came out. It made us blink, and warmed our blood, and put an entirely different aspect upon the day. Inspector Field was waiting expectantly on the stone steps, his face gruffly upturned to our approach so that it quite comically formed an eloquent match with the upturned snouts of the stone lions between which he loitered.

"Well?" Field opened his interrogation.

"Palmer was not there." Dickens killed Field's hope aborning.

"Palmer's never there. Spends more time at his riding club than in his surgery it seems," I added, echoing our put-upon Doctor Vasconcellas.

Field sputtered with anger as if the planets were lining up against him in this case: "Bloody 'ell!" he cursed, not quite under his breath. "I'll talk ta that toff if I 'ave ta ride ta the 'ounds with 'im."

"We did have an interview with his assistant," Dickens interrupted Field's little fit of pique.

"I wondered wot wos takin' yew two so long," Field interrupted right back, " 'specially if friend Palmer wosn't even in."

"But that is not all," Dickens wrested back the floor. "Assistant is Brazilian, a Portuguese, almost a Spaniard, one Rodrigo Vasconcellas."

141

"Says yew!" A glorious grin, like the sun that had only moments before, like some heavenly alchemist, transmuted that grey day into gold, bloomed in Field's face and resurrected his hopes. "A Spainiard in a 'ooded cloak. 'Tis wot our actor friend said."

"And this Spaniard is a doctor as well," Dickens added. "And he lives on the edge of the Amazon jungle. And curare is known and used by the Indians in that jungle."

Dickens had utterly caught me by surprise by his aggressive journey down this trail of deduction. I think he caught Field by surprise as well. Dickens clearly meant to keep centre stage in this case and uppermost in Field's mind the information gleaned from Burton concerning the probable cause of those poor women's deaths. It was a subtle sort of gloating upon Dickens's part, as if he were reminding our professional detective colleague, *you are right, I Would wear well in your line.*

"Dickens, my friend, yew are a genius." Field, in his enthusiasm, did not hesitate in giving credit where due. " 'Ee must be our man," Field was absolutely twitching in his certainty, his crook'd forefinger jigging at the side of his eye as if tapping out a tune. "Now all we needs is 'why?' Why would 'ee kill 'is master's wife?"

"Perhaps he is not the killer." Much to my own surprise, it was my voice entering this animated colloquy. "He certainly did not seem like a murderer when he spoke to us just now. Somehow he seemed too, I do not know, too, well, gentle . . . to do something like that, I mean."

"Appearances can be deceivin'," Field scoffed at my naïveté. "The politest o' men kin murder yew just as dead as the gamest Rats' Castle strong-armer."

"He *is* different, that is for certain." Dickens supported my contention with a slightly raised eyebrow that left me utterly puzzled as to its meaning.

"Collins, old mate." Field's enthusiasm for this turn in the case had not ebbed a whit. "That is yet another 'ard possibility. Assistant at direction o' 'usband 'ires Dunn who 'ires Thompson, provides poison, is the man in the middle 'oo

142

keeps Doctor William Palmer completely out o' 'arm's way. But why would any bloke do that? No, 'tis too farfetched. People don' do others' murders unless . . . unless . . ."

"Unless?" Dickens coaxed.

I caught myself raising up on my toes on those stone steps as I strained for Field's answer. Even the lions seemed to be listening.

"Unless someone 'as such a 'old on 'em they can't break it any other way," but Field's voice displayed little confidence in this possibility.

"Blackmail?" Dickens asked.

"Yes, certainly possible." But Field's mind was off hunting other game. "The next step is ta let Dickie Dunn identify this Spaniard's voice. T'would never serve as evidence in the dock, but at least we would be certain 'at we 'ad the right man." He was actually talking aloud to himself, talking out his tactics. "We ought ta do 'at next, but 'tis too soon. If we wait, per'aps our Brazilian friend will think on all o' this, will wonder if we are on ta 'im. Per'aps if we keep away jus' a bit 'ee will don 'is 'ood once again an' we kin ketch 'im wearin' it."

It was a rather long soliloquy for Field's taste, but evidently necessary for his plotting of strategy. Dickens and I bore up well under it.

"There is one other thing I noticed about our Doctor Vasconcellas." Dickens most certainly had taken Field's latest rendition of the "simply observe" speech to heart.

"An' wot might that be?" Field was once again on the alert.

Dickens hesitated. Either something unseemly or of great gravity or of which he was rather uncertain was bothering him, and he was weighing whether to open this new Pandora's Box for our discussion. He must have decided that the box contained a relevant wind because he unleashed it upon us.

"Did it not appear to you, Wilkie, as it appeared to me, that Doctor Vasconcellas . . ."—that hesitance surfaced once again—"that he appears to be, though as Inspector Field has already noted 'looks can certainly be quite deceiving,' ahem . . . I mean . . . appears to be, well, ahem"—slight cough

143

behind his hand once again, his eyes moving from Field's face to mine and back to Field's—"a man of somewhat exotic tastes and, perhaps . . . one can never say for certain . . . of somewhat unconventional life-style."

I stared at Dickens, utterly uncomprehending.

"Are yew sayin' wot I think yer sayin'?" Field pressed.

"A man of sexual difference, I mean." Charles nodded.

"You think he is a Sodomite?" The two of them flinched at the unconsidered loudness of my reaction and cast quick glances over their shoulders to see if anyone had heard. Only the lions bore witness to my amazement.

"Wot brings yew ta that?" Field was a bit open-mouthed himself at Dickens's making such an unusual charge.

"It is his hands, I think," Charles spoke slowly, strongly aware of the defamatory gravity of this new terrain that he was exploring, "they never stop moving, and his voice, I do not know really, it is merely an impression, he seemed so feminine in his sensibilities, his movements. There is simply something very different in his manner, his mode of speech. Really, Field, you must meet him to understand."

" 'Tis a grave charge." Field was talking aloud to himself once again, and we could see his mind racing with the possibilities that Doctor Rodrigo Vasconcellas's "otherness" might open in this case. He pondered another moment, and then dismissed the whole discussion. "But one we cannot make."

"I meant to make no charge," Dickens protested. "I was merely expressing a perception, an observation of the man."

"I too 'ave observed 'im, I think." Field ran his memory over this ground once more. " 'Ee wos the one fawnin' o'er Palmer at the funeral. 'Is assistant I think I saw on one o' the constable's reports. 'Ee wos there, but 'at's no evidence o' anything."

"Perhaps so." Dickens gave it one last poke. "But he *is* different. I am sure of it."

Field shrugged. The lions frowned. The sun disappeared behind a cloud.

A London sun in January is like a chameleon. It tends to

mime the colouration of its surroundings, the personality of the season. Standing there upon Bart's steps discussing that case, we had been granted a short respite from the grey dreariness of London winter. Our momentary sun was, however, obliterated with such force that it was as if some giant's foot had trampled upon it or some malignant goddess had turned it to stone. The gloom of that dislocated world closed around us as we stuffed ourselves into a random hansom for the ride back to the Shooting Gallery.

When one rides with a hansom cabman on a regular basis as we had been riding lately with Sleepy Rob, one becomes accustomed to his style of driving. Sleepy Rob was slow and sure and, for all his exterior appearance of unconcern, attended to his business (or else he had an uncommon sharp horse!). This strange cabman was quite the opposite. He was jerky with the reins and inattentive to the winter holes that sometimes gaped between the paving stones. If hansoms are, in truth, "the gondolas of London" as, I believe, our friend Disraeli, who fancies himself a novelist, calls them, they certainly do not float through the city as their namesakes do on their Venetian roadways. We bounced and jolted toward Leicester Square.

Inspector Field, Dickens, and I had received a number of jolts in the course of this day. Little did we know that there were still more to come. By the time we reached Captain Hawkins's Shooting Gallery, all three of us had been forced to remove our hats to keep them from being crushed against the ceiling of the cab.

THE UNKINDEST JOLT
OF ALL

January 18, 1852—evening

P ursuant to Inspector Field's three goals as articulated in
the Shooting Gallery the previous day, we had progressed quite handsomely. First, we had isolated curare
as a quite probable cause of the two women's deaths. Second,
we had confronted the actor Dick Dunn and extorted a confession of his complicity. As for Field's third wish, however, an
interview with Doctor Palmer, we were no closer to that desired goal than we had ever been.

"Wot do we know about 'im?" Field posed the hypothetical
question to the assembled company, including Captain Hawkins, Serjeant Moody, and that worthy's indecorous bird. He
had already narrated for Thompson and Rogers the particulars of our afternoon's interview with Doctor Rodrigo Vasconcellas. He had focused that narration upon friend Rodrigo's
"Spanishness" and likely knowledge of Amazonian poisons,
but he did not mention Dickens's speculation upon the man's
sexual preference. "We know 'ee's rich"—Field turned his
attention to Doctor Palmer—" 'ee rarely goes to 'is surgery,

'ee is o' the 'orsey sort, an 'ee'd recently married a young wife 'oo is now dead. Wot else, Rogers?"

Serjeant Rogers, always ready to shine as an exemplar of efficiency and preparation, extracted a small, square note-book from an inner pocket of his greatcoat and commenced to read.

"I have dispatched three constables hupon Palmer, sir. Hallmost hall huv their reports har complete. Hee hinherited his wealth. Left nearly seventy thousand pound when father died hin forty-two hin Staffordshire. Came hup to London to study med'sin hat Bart's hin forty-three. Licensed has hay physician hin forty-hate." Rogers took a breath. He was reading these facts from his notebook as if they were Blue Book statistics on textile exports or colliery accidents. Perhaps that is why he took his pause, because, when he went on, his statistics gave way to more personal information, became a bit more gossipy. "Word has hit that he lost hall seventy thousand pound got from his father's death withhin two years hupon comin' hup to London. Horse-race bettin', they say. Hestablishes medical practice hat Bart's hin forty-nine. Marries young hairess, name huv Hannie Brooks hin fifty. She his hour deeceeased." At which point, having brought us nearly up to the present, that smirking little martinet took pause. I could see it in his face. He was milking the moment. He stood smug as an oyster in the certainty that he had some pearl of information to disgorge of which none of us yet had any knowledge, not even Inspector Field.

Also seeing it in his face, and perhaps resigned to the man's little games from having been subjected to them much longer than we, Field slowly and sarcastically nudged Rogers into dispensing his valuable information: "Yew seem to 'ave more ta tell us Serjeant, might we bother yew ta proceed."

"This just came hin this hafternoon, sir," Rogers resumed excitedly. "This his the capper, Hi'd say."

"Dammit man, git on with it." Field's impatience triumphed in its battle with his tongue.

"Constable O'Jordan hinterviewed han hagent hat Lloyd's

148

this hafternoon hoo says that huone month hafter they wos married, Palmer took hout hay life hinsurance policy hon the missus. Twenty thousand pound he stands ta gain pending the houtcome huv hour hinvestigation. Constable halso hinterviews Palmer's solicitor. Hasks how much Doctor will hinherit from wife's hestate. Solicitor raises highbrows, but won't hanswer. Client privilege yoo know, but O'Jordan thinks hits hay pile," and, with that, Rogers, dripping with self-importance, snapped shut his notebook as if to say *and there you have it! My police procedures have solved this case!*

"Good," Field, perhaps still a bit perturbed at Rogers's dramatising of his gathered information, the drawing out of his moment, spoke it dryly, unenthusiastically, "all circumstantial, but quite good nonetheless. So . . ."—he turned back to the rest of us—"as I expected, Doctor William Palmer stands ta profit 'andsomely from 'is wife's death. No doubt, when interviewed 'ee will 'ave a brigade o' witnesses ta 'is whereabouts the night o' 'er murder. An' then there are the Spaniard an' Thompson ta reckon with, but 'tis the man 'oo gits the money 'oo's the one"—and he slammed his decisive forefinger down upon the gun table—"I'd stake me life on it!"

"So wot do we do now?" Tally Ho Thompson, less than comfortable at Field's still including him as one of the suspected murderers in the case, exhibited his impatience.

"Nothin'." Field squelched him.

All of us, including Dickens, were struck dumb. So much progress had been made, so much information gathered in the course of this one day, that Field's placidity, his unconcern, was received with unanimous consternation. The case seemed to be gaining a momentum that could possibly carry it straight through to its destination, and suddenly Field wanted to pull on the brake.

"Wot do we do now?" There was a mischievous glint in Field's eye as he scratched at it with his crook'd forefinger. "Is that dinner I smell, Cap'n 'Awkins?"

"It is indeed, sir"—Hawkins's open face bloomed with

149

pleasure at the prospect of entertaining such an august company—"and a better yule niver git in any regimental mess in Her Majesty's Empire!"

With that, we gathered our ragtag collection of chairs around the gun table, and Captain Hawkins and Serjeant Moody set our places. It was a savoury hunter's stew prepared over the Shooting Gallery's stone hearth on a cast-iron cooking hook of the sort that soldiers in the field would drive into the ground over an open fire. Dished out of its open pot into pewter bowls by Serjeant Moody, who used an iron ladle also of a military cut, the stew steamed on the table before us, encircled us in a mesmerising aroma that killed our conversation and sent us leaping for our spoons. That enticing smell, composed of stewed beef hearts, potatoes (skins still on, of course), and a magical mixture of spices, danced and swirled around us with the seductive power of a Salome at her dance or a Scheherazade at her tale. As befits the truly impromptu character of any hunter's stew (which is a cook's metaphor for the originality of the creative act), all of its ingredients had, most likely, been bought in Covent Garden Market that very day. They all found expression in a strong beef gravy with pieces of onion swimming about amidst the essences of nutmeg, clove, and a touch of ginger, and beans, carrots, and heavy cauliflowers drowning in the seething boil, all well-peppered, with islands of soldiers' drop biscuits floating on the top. That stew, exuding the richness of the West Indies, was complimented by mugs of strong coffee, the most common military potable next to rum, and penny loaves of coarse English bread.

No dish depends solely upon the delicious culinary chemistry of its ingredients, but rather upon the generous creative spirit of its maker and the receptivity of spirit of its devourers. No one could deny the fine spirits of Captain Hawkins and his faithful squire, and we did, indeed, unhesitating, devour that imposing hunter's stew in the high spirits of his openhearted hospitality. We were a close company drawn into a tight circle of comradeship around that savoury pot and those smoking mugs. As we ate, broken Bert bustled around us in his crabbed and stilted way, refilling our cups and bowls while his evil parrot squawked out a running commentary upon our cannibal rapaciousness: "Fagging rips, bloody hogs, fagging bloody glutton sots." Whether he really pronounced those things that clearly or we just imagined that those were the words formed by that evil bird's chorus of gutteral sounds I am not certain even to this day. I do remember clearly, however, that in later years whenever Captain Hawkins's name came up in conversation between Dickens and I or Inspector Field, Charles always played the same chord: "Most generous man in London," he would declare, "would take anyone off the streets and give them a home!"

We consumed our banquet and closed out the evening with cigars magically produced out of some capacious pocket hidden beneath Charles's flash waistcoat.* Our chairs pulled up to the Shooting Gallery's flaming hearth, our stomachs glorying in their heavy tribute, the soft smoke of our cigars wrapping itself around our tongues, we were a contented lot. By ten of the clock, we had tucked Tally Ho Thompson in under the protection of Captain Hawkins and Serjeant Moody; Field was in the act of dispatching Serjeant Rogers to the Bow Street Station to collect the intelligence of the evening; and Dickens and I were attempting to flag a hansom cab when Field suddenly stopped us in mid-wave.

"Mister Dickens, Mister Collins, might you join me in the Lord Gordon for a Dog's Nose† or a mulled wine?" It sounded more on the order of an order than an invitation. "I needs ta talk ta yew in private, I do."

Rogers glared, hesitated, but one heavy-browed look from Field sent him off in the direction of Bow Street. The three of

---

*In the parlance of Victorian England, a "flash waistcoat" was a vest matched to a suit, which, however, was lined in a brightly colored silk that would "flash" in the eyes of the beholder when the waistcoat was unbuttoned.
†The English equivalent of an American "boilermaker," a shot of straight gin followed by a pint of bitter.

us remaining crowded into a passing hansom and were settled in Miss Katie's snuggery within ten minutes. We decided upon some of Barclay's Best,* neither Dickens nor myself wanting, after such a long day and heavy meal, to risk the headachey dangers of a Dog's Nose of gin. We watched at the bar as Miss Katie drew it from the pull marked with an anchor out of her shiny new beer engine, which possessed no less than five pulls like shipboard belaying pins. Settled at one of her oak tables with our mugs of porter, Dickens, his enthusiasm ever unflagged, pressed our host: "What is it, Field? What have you in store for us now?"

"There is really nothin' more we kin do right now," Field assured Dickens with a nod to me as an afterthought, "except, of course, lay the groundwork for our next move."

"What do you mean 'nothing more to do'?" Dickens was terrified by the prospect of perhaps having to spend an evening at home reading a book by the fire rather than running about in the wind and the rain, or in prisons and pestilent slums risking life and limb trying to track down murderers.

"I wants all o' this, our findin' Dick Dunn, yer interview with Doctor Vasconcellas, I wants it all ta sink in upon our principals for a day or so. I wants 'em ta worry an' fret a bit. Or mebbe feel they are safe. I want ta wait, ta let things settle. 'Oo knows, mebbe one o' 'em'll git nervous an' tip 'is 'and," and, with a scratch of his crook'd forefinger to the side of his eye, he gave us a quick wink. Little did we know as we talked that such was not to be our luxury, that events were even then in the making which would put such a leisurely stalking of our Medusa murderer quite out of the question.

"So . . . what *is* our next move?" I think I brought a bit more rationality and patience to the posing of my question than Dickens had thus far been able to muster in posing any of his.

"I wants yew two ta go back on duty for Inspector Field, spies once again."

*"Barclay's Best" was a dark, sweet porter made by the Barclay Brewery whose commercial sign was an anchor.

"Capital!" Dickens exclaimed with an unbridled glee, which I did not share. All he could see was the adventure, while all I could see was the hardship and danger. I think Dickens was in love with the very ideas of housebreaking and spying and deceiving and chasing around after murderers. It had almost gotten him killed once,* but that did not seem to deter him in the least.

"In spite o' the incriminatin' evidence 'round Dick Dunn an' the Spainiard at Bart's, I still think that our Doctor Palmer is at the 'eart o' this. We must talk ta 'im."

"We?" I glanced from Field to Dickens, then back to Field.

"Yew two move in this swell's circles. Yew kin find out where 'ee is, ask Macready per'aps, or find out 'oo 'ee 'angs with, wot racin' club 'ee frequents, that's wot the Spainiard said, wosn't it?" He took a brief pause simply to mark the predictable enthusiasm in Dickens's face, then sped on. "If we find out where 'ee 'is, then yew can visit 'im for me, as yew did Ashbee, make 'is acquaintance, measure the man." It was quite a speech for Inspector Field, but it had its calculated effect. Dickens was ready to head out into the field right then and there.

It was at that moment that Serjeant Rogers rushed in.

"A runner has come," he announced, then paused. No one likes to bear bad news.

"Wot is it, man?" Patience was never one of Inspector Field's virtues.

"Dick Dunn's been found dead . . . hand Tally Ho Thompson has flown!"

---

*In Collins' first memoir, Lord Henry Ashbee had actually discharged a pistol at Dickens at close range, but the charge had failed and Dickens escaped with nothing more than a bruised throat.

THE SCENE OF THE CRIME

January 18, 1852—nearing midnight

T he runner's message to Bow Street that Serjeant Rogers relayed to us at the Lord Gordon Arms was from a surveillance constable. It requested Inspector Field's immediate presence at the Covent Garden Theatre.

"There is only one thing could be worse than the death o' our major witness," Field complained as we four strode toward Covent Garden through the murky fog that had lowered itself over the streets during our brief sojourn in the public house. He paused a moment for the effect he knew such a pronouncement would produce, then continued with a touch of bitter resignation, "If Thompson, our only other witness, though an unsound one, 'ad anything ta do with it!"

Constable Timko was waiting for us outside the stage door at Covent Garden. Poor Dick Dunn was waiting for us within, on his back in the centre of the bare gaslit stage, his eyes white and wide, staring up at a hanging flat of Falstaff and Prince Hal's tavern haunt, with a fencing foil, perhaps the very one that either he or Thompson had used that very afternoon, quivering up out of his heart.

"Wot 'appened 'ere, Timko?" Inspector Field was grim.

"We don't know 'ow 'ee got in, sir," the wary constable, knowing that he had severely bungled his duty of surveillance, answered in a voice burdened with the heavy weight of contrition, "but we saw 'im run out," the last added in hope that it might provide some reason for absolution.

"Yew saw 'oo run out?" Field asked the question because he knew he must, but it was clear that he already knew and dreaded the answer.

"Tally 'O Thompson, Sir . . . the escaped murderer, Sir," the dim constable answered brightly. " 'Twas 'im all right, Sir. Both me an' Hutter is sure on it. I carries the flyer right 'ere in my inside uniform pocket, Sir."

"Well, 'at's jus' aces," Field scowled at the poor writhing man. He must, however, have been impatient to get on with his investigation of the crime scene because, despite the sarcasm in his voice, he chose to forgo any immediate public humiliation or professional punishment or even disgusted tongue-lashing of his inept constable. "Did yew note the time that Thompson run out?" Field's forefinger quivered slightly next to his eye as if he were having trouble preventing it from poking out at the stammering Constable Timko.

"Uh, no . . . no Sir . . . we, Hutter an' me, Sir . . . we didn't think ta mark the tie, Sir. But it wos after the play wos ended an' the theatre closed."

Field turned his back quickly on the constable and walked two steps away, muttering into his hand something that sounded like "bluddydimwittedfool!" Turning back to his underling, he ordered Timko, in a clipped voice, to guard the street door. He punctuated that order with a sharp jab of his ferocious forefinger.

When the constable was gone, it took Field but a breath to reach out and grasp control, which his anger at the constable's ineptitude had momentarily loosed. He moved to Rogers's side and looked down at Dunn's corpse. The sword stuck up out of the red circle of blood on his chest like an

156

arrow from a bull's-eye. Dickens and I ranged ourselves on the opposite side of the body, also looking down.

"Our witness ta wotever 'tis we're inta is dead." Field was addressing everyone and no one, perhaps wishing that the corpse would respond, "An' that idiot Thompson seems intent upon buildin' a better case against 'imself!"

"I cannot believe that Thompson killed this man," Dickens took up Field's reverie.

"Nor I," the Inspector averred.

Rogers looked at me and I at him. It was clear that neither he nor I shared the certainty of our colleagues. He rolled his eyes. It was all I could do to suppress a grin. The man did have his moments I must admit.

"If he did not kill the two women in the first place, then there is no reason for him to kill Dunn now," Dickens pursued. " 'Tis not his style."

I glanced at Rogers to see if he, too, was fighting off the shaken certainty in Thompson's innocence that was assaulting me.

"In fact"—Field knocked a final nail into his conviction— "Thompson needed Dickie Dunn alive. 'Ee wos the only one could prove that Thompson got lured ta the murder scene. No, Thompson could not kill Dickie Dunn, but 'ee could try ta scare the rest o' the truth out o' the little weasel. Only problem was, little Dickie wos dead when Tally 'O got 'ere ta work on 'im."

"So Thompson finds the body, takes a fright, and flees," Dickens took up Field's hypothetical narrative.

"At's it," Field concurs. "If Thompson could sneak in 'ere past Timko an' 'Utter, someone else could as well."

"With those two hon duty, the whole cast huv the play might huv come in here han rehearsed han those two would huv missed hit," Rogers commented with sincere disdain. His effect, however, was to make all of us laugh. His comment broke the tension of the moment, but we all quickly realised that we were standing there laughing over a corpse. With that

157

grim reminder staring up at us, we quickly regained our death decorum.

Field and Rogers bent to examine the body. They fretted over it for long minutes, but found nothing out of the ordinary to argue against the rather clear facts that someone had walked up close to the unarmed man and stuck that fencing foil through his heart. As they worked at the body, Dickens stood strangely silent above them. He was looking around the stage, into the darkened wings, up at the chaos of flats hanging ready to be lowered into place for each change of scene.

"What is it, Charles?" I, finally, observing his pensive stillness for long moments, moved to his side and asked.

"It is nothing, Wilkie. No, it is this death that has once again raised its pitiful face. This poor man. He did not know that in the next moment he would be dead. Look around. Look up there, Wilkie. That must have been what he saw at the last instant of his life."

My eyes followed Dickens's gaze upward. Hanging directly above the corpse was a painted background flat of the back wall of the Boar's Head Tavern where Falstaff and Poins and the other highwaymen of Shakespeare's play drank and caroused and plotted and gamed with Prince Hal.* The flat, in that magical three-dimensional style of theatre artists, recreated a sloping, raftered ceiling, a dirty wooden back wall, and a small section of oaken bar (probably to be connected to a real bar to be placed against it). Standing against the dingy wall to one side was an ancient clock.

My eyes, in concert with Dickens's prompt, looked down into Dick Dunn's dead eyes, then jolted back to the painted panel hanging above. When I looked back at Charles, he, too, was looking intently up.

"It is as if in death he is looking up at that clock," Dickens said in a near whisper.

*The reference is to Shakespeare's *Henry IV, Part I*, the play being performed at the time of these murders by Macready's Covent Garden Theatre Company, and in which first Thompson, and then Dunn, played the role of Poins.

My eyes careened from Dickens's eyes to Dunn's to the face of that painted clock upon that painted wall silent in suspension above us. The hands of that clock, frozen in time, stood together as one, straight up, midnight. Dickens stood as if paralysed, his gaze riveted upon the expressive face of that clock. I realized that he was doing it again, moving into the dimension of that dying man, feeling what he was feeling, his panic, his despair, seeing what his eyes were seeing in their final moments of sight. If I were prone to believe in melodramatic omens, that ominous image of time run out would have been one. Yet, that painted theatre flat held no particular meaning, carried no symbolic message of time or threat, was in no way a warning. Strange how our minds imbue the furnishings of our world with meaning. The ghostly fancy of my thoughts danced over that scene: *Perhaps the revelers in the Boar's Head of two centuries gone were the gaping witnesses to the murder of this hapless latter-day Poins. If only they could direct Field to the murderer, bear witness in the dock.*

The haunted quality of that empty stage, of Dickens staring as if in a trance up at that stopped clock, of those two men bending over that still, dark form, of those wide, dead eyes staring up, sent a shudder of dread through my whole being. All I could feel was an overpowering need to close those empty eyes, break that sinister time-stopped spell.

Field and Rogers rose from the body, finished with their ministrations.

Without even thinking, I bent to one knee and, with my right hand, closed those terrible, empty eyes.

"There is nothin' more for us 'ere," Field broke our morbid silence, and I shuddered once again as if hearing those ghostly tipplers of the Boar's Head Tavern laughing at the grim joke time had played on their drinking companion Poins.

As we left the theatre, the fog was draped like a dingy yellow curtain over the West End. And Tally Ho Thompson, shape-shifting actor that he was, had disappeared behind it.

159

"STIR THE GENTLEMAN UP!"

January 23, 1852—late morning

F our days passed uneventfully. Waiting to be summoned
by Inspector Field, Dickens and I finished mounds of
work at the *Household Words* office. We were certain that
all manner of detective machinations were underway during
that period of maddening and interminable calm. We, we
presumed and resented, were simply not privy to them.
Doubtless, we reasoned, Field felt the mundane workaday
advancement of his procedures too pedestrian for our attention.

Yet, as day piled up upon day and no summons back into
the case arrived, Dickens became first morose, then nervous,
and finally combative. One moment he would be sitting working at his desk and the next he would be up and pacing like
one of Burton's tigers in a cage. In the evenings, he would beg
me to eat pub dinners in the office on the chance that Field's
summons would come. On two of the four nights, I acquiesced. I spent long evenings in speculative conversation
upon the case with an increasingly impatient Dickens. On the

other two nights, I offered lame excuses and fled Wellington Street for the more seductive offices of Irish Meg.

Yet, I felt regret those nights at leaving Charles alone to brood over the case. There was something about it that fascinated him, which drew him like a moth to a flame. He insisted that it was the offices of friendship owed to Thompson that compelled us to work on our highwayman's behalf. But, observing Dickens's growing obsession, I came to believe that there was more to it than those bonds of friendship. The second night of waiting, I had the temerity and meanness to play devil's advocate, to raise doubts about Thompson that no one else seemed willing to raise.

"How do you know he did not kill Dick Dunn?" I astounded Dickens. I truly think that he had never considered the possibility. One of the things that always amazed and drew me to Dickens was his innocence and hope in human nature. He walked his London world with an almost total lack of cynicism remarkable in a man of forty years of his experience and human insight. I found his naïveté incredible, at times laughable. "For that matter, how do we know he did not kill those two women? He could have been having a love affair with the wife, his riding pupil." I was beginning to amaze myself with the lasciviousness of my dirty little mind, but I pressed this gambit: "How do you know? Good God, Charles! Thompson was a highwayman, a housebreaker, a thief. How can you know he is not guilty?"

"I just know," Dickens answered, taking it all very seriously. "He is our friend, our charge. We must believe in him and help him. Thompson would never do something like that no matter how desperate he got. Murder is not his style"—Dickens smiled—"and style is everything."

"Style?"

"Most certainly. How you live your life. The way you order your world. The way you choose to look. How you write. Everyone has his own style, and Thompson's is not murderous."

It all sounded like gibberish to me, but I will be the first to

162

admit that I was often incapable of keeping pace with the fierce stridings of Dickens's mind. He plunged into ideas and motives as aggressively as he plunged into the streets of London on his fierce night walks. He was, indeed, a restless chimera of a man. Perhaps these journals, these "recollections in tranquillity" as our poet laureate Mister Wordsworth wrote, are my attempts to understand him. Whatever was my reaction, however, Dickens steadfastly insisted upon Thompson's innocence and relentlessly kept up to the responsibilities of his friendship. But I still doubted whether it was all that simple, whether Dickens fully understood the motives of his own mind.

I feel that it was more than friendship that fueled Dickens's fascination with this case. My theory, which I almost hesitate to present, may seem rather farfetched, but it is the best explanation I can concoct for the terrible restlessness and nervous agitation that Dickens displayed during those four days and nights of waiting. I think that what so drew Dickens to this case was the possibility that a gentleman had actually poisoned his own wife. Dickens was fascinated by this act of spouse murder. I certainly do not imply that Dickens wished his wife dead, or, heaven forbid, ever contemplated killing her, but their marriage at that time was not a source of joy for either of them. Kate's persistent illness served to keep them apart—she in the country for her treatments, he in the city with his work—for long periods of time. In a sense, it was as if Dickens had simply outdistanced Kate, left her behind as he plunged forward in his career and his fame as one of England's great men. And then, of course, there was his guardianship—for, at that time, that was all it was—of the Ternan girl.

Forgive me, it was just a feeling, a groundless theory, not really worth considering. But, to use Dickens's own words, every man has his style, and Dickens's was ungodly hard to grasp. He was, if anything, protean, always changing in his life and mind and writing. Might it be possible that Charles Dickens could be a great man, and a loving husband and father, and a good friend, and a murderer? During those four days of waiting, Dickens would sit at his desk by the bow window overlooking Wellington Street, working most of the time on the second number of his new novel, which bore the ominous title *Tom-All-Alone's: The Ruined House that Got into Chancery and Never Got Out.** It was due to go on sale in serial gatherings in February or March. I was writing my article for *Household Words* on the lighthouses (or the lack thereof) on the Devon coast, which would lead off the next issue. At intervals that afternoon, when restlessness would overtake him, he would burst into my office with some new speculation upon the poisonings case.

"Evidently, the body told them nothing, Dunn's corpse I mean," he would say, his words, like an idea fired from a pistol, preceeding him through the door to my working closet, "or they would have come for us by now." Or, "There has been no word from Thompson," he would say, "he must be in deep hiding and they have not found him yet else they would have sent for us, don't you think, Wilkie?" He needed my reassurance, on an almost hourly basis, that Inspector Field had not forgotten us. I placated him, and sent him back to his writing. That, after all, was my role as a Victorian version of the court jester, acolyte to the great man.

But the one thing, I think, which troubled him the most was the failure of Inspector Field to set in motion the plan for interviewing the hitherto invisible Doctor Palmer. His whole mien gave evidence that his impatience and restlessness stemmed from his intense desire to meet this man. I think Charles was utterly fascinated by the criminal potential of the man, perhaps he saw the elusive doctor as the next great villainous character in his gallery of corrupt and evil gentlemen that hitherto included Sir Mulberry Hawke, Tigg Montague, and Steerforth the seducer. He even, descending into depths of morbidity, started referring to Palmer as "Doctor Death."

*This, of course, was one of the early working titles of *Bleak House.*

With Thompson nowhere to be found, Palmer not interviewed, Dickens unravelling before my very face, the open
eyes of the dead man staring at the stopped-at-midnight
hands of the Boar's Head Tavern clock—is it any wonder that
I fled this madhouse of unanswered questions and unresolved
desires so gratefully to Irish Meg? Yet, though she offered the
enticing diversions of her bed, she offered little else in the way
of consolation. My plight was that of a man trapped between
two powerful magnets. Meg pulled in exactly the opposite
direction of Dickens. She openly mocked our absorption with
Inspector Field's murder case.

On the third of those four nights of waiting, I had begged
off Dickens's company by complaining of a headache. As I
was muffling myself up to leave for home, Dickens offhandedly observed that I was getting to be quite a "domesticated
animal." *He does not know how right he is,* I thought. Then he
joked that Thompson had been getting so with Scarlet Bess,
"but certainly seems to have thrown that over." And then he
showed me out with the question: "Do you really think
Thompson might have been having an affair with the dead
wife, Wilkie?" Little things disturbed me during that time.
Dickens said it as a joke, but for some reason I took it to heart.
In the hansom on the way home, I was sure that Dickens knew
all about Meggie. Thoughts of marrying her raced in my
mind. *But I can't marry her,* I thought, *I am a gentleman.
Thompson has not married his Bess. But he is no gentleman. Or is
he? Perhaps Dickens was right. Perhaps who you are is simply a
matter of style. But a gentleman marry a woman of the streets?*

Meg was, indeed, waiting when I returned to my rooms. She
was wearing a white blouse and a serviceable, almost nunlike,
blue jumper, but I could see at her ankles that she had black
stockings on beneath. Her arms snaked around my neck as I
came in the door. She kissed me long and hard without the
formality of a greeting. It was a desperate sort of kiss, excited
to see me but wary of my motives for spending so much time
away from her. "I'm glad yer 'ome, Wilkie." *Very domesticated,*
I thought, *wifely. Good God!* "Yew've given all yer time ta '*im*

the last few days." She spoke that "him" as if it were a pronoun for Satan.

I kissed her hard once again as a means of evasion, to close her mouth and not have to open mine, though both of our mouths were open, our tongues coupling.

"Yew wants me right now, don't'choo, luv?" There was a hard triumph in her voice as she realised that her control over me was firm.

Kissing her hard yet again, I answered with my hands, moving them to her waist and pulling upward upon the skirt of her prim housewifely jumper until it bunched at her hips and I could get my impatient hands beneath it. My fingers ran over the tops of her stockings where the garters hooked and moved up to the warm mounds of her arse. As my hands finally touched her bare skin below, our lips fought each other off and, moving down her by flexing my knees slightly, my hands kneading her arse and pressing her hard against me, I buried my head in the sanctuary of her breasts. "Oh yes I want you . . . right now I want you," I begged.

She moved herself firmly against me, up and around, in control, arousing me with the slow movement of her hips as if she were a Greek or Indian dancer. Her hands caressed the back of my head, moved down to the valley between my shoulder blades, pressed my face hard against her breasts. "Yew wants ta fuck me right now, do yew?" her voice was harsh and guttural. "Yew wants ta fuck me, but yew don't wants ta pay, issat it, sir?" She was teasing me, I think, though her voice still had that hard-edged, domineering quality about it.

"I will pay," I begged, submission in my voice, playing her game, whatever that was, kissing at the fabric over her breasts, running one hand greedily down over the top of her thigh and up between her legs in the back to caress the tight moist silk gathered there.

Her hands moved slowly over the back of my head as her hips pressed hard against my chest. Moving her hands down over my ears to my shoulders, she pushed me to my knees and stepped quietly back, disengaging us. I knelt before her like some avid supplicant in the temple of a pagan goddess. With one fluid motion, she pushed the straps of her jumper from her shoulders and let the shapeless dress slide down into a pile on the floor around her feet. Stepping out of that circle of nunnish restraint, and with a single motion stripping that white blouse over her head, she stood before me in only her red-and-black secret things.

"Yew stays on yer knees a moment yew do," she ordered, as, turning her back to me and bending at the waist, she pulled down those red silk pantaloons, which I had felt bunched between her legs. This stripping away of the final veil revealed the full, white globes of her glorious arse. She paused, slightly bent over, letting me look as she knew I loved to do, becoming less harsh and more playful now, less angry and more loving, yet still adamant in her control as she turned back to face me. "Yew must kiss me 'ere ta pay for wot yew wants." She moved up close before me, taking a legs apart and hips outthrust stance of challenge and intimidation as I knelt before her.

Like a border around a Turner painting, her black secret things set off the fiery red blaze adorning her mound of Venus. Into that unholy fire, I buried my face.

What ensued there on the floor of my parlour, not even knowing if the door to the corridor was closed behind, was the fiercest, most savage dance of love that Irish Meg had ever enticed me into.

How quaint, is it not, that I should phrase this indecorous description in that way, "enticed me into"? Not only does my language come up short grammatically, but it breaks down in terms of truth as well. My appetite for Meg's charms needed little enticement. I became, with little resistance, her slave at the mere unveiling of her secret things and secret places. Is that not what these games of love and literature and detecting are all about, the discovery of the secrets of others and the entering of them?

She mounted and rode above me there on our Soho parlour rug like some African queen rising above the throngs of the everyday on the shoulders of her bearers. She rallied me to her service, my fire-queen, and collapsed in ecstasy upon me as our flames consumed us both. Metaphors notwithstanding, we made savage love on the parlour floor. It was magnificent. It burned off from my mind any thoughts but those of my deep and secret need for Meg, a need that liberated a second secret self that lurked beneath the false façade of my existence as a proper Victorian gentleman. We lay for long minutes, she atop me like a warm quilt, in the sweet aftermath of our lovemaking.

She was the one who broke the spell. She rolled off with a muffled ribbon of a laugh.

"What is it?" I inquired, still struggling to catch my breath.

Lying upon her side and propping her chin upon her elbow and hand, she considered. This was no prelude to playful pillow talk. Good God, we were naked in the middle of the parlour floor.

"Yew men are such a muddle." She was too studied to be spontaneous. This was a speech that she had rehearsed to deliver after making love. I am quite sure, however, that she did not envision delivering it in the middle of the parlour floor.

"What do you mean?" I really did not desire this colloquy. A sudden and intense exhaustion was overtaking me, beckoning me to a warm bed and sleep, preferably wrapped in Irish Meg's arms.

"Yew 'ave been gone the better part o' a week chasin' around after Mister Dickens and Fieldsy. 'Tis the middle o' winter. Yew men are sech children, little boys lookin' for adventure."

"Meggy," I tried to argue, "there have been three murders and Thompson stands accused of all." But she was in no mood to listen or to interrupt the rehearsed script of her speech.

"Really?" She laughed hollowly, that rehearsed as well. "I 'ave spent all me grown years tryin' ta escape the streets an' yew an' yer Mister Dickens rush to seek out their filth an'

168

death. 'Tis as if yew must follow 'im anywhere 'ee leads." Did I catch a hint of jealousy in her voice?

"The streets are the landscape of his imagination. They bring life to his novels. I believe him when he tells me that," I tried to defend Charles, and then myself, "and if I can be a great novelist like him, I must find my landscape as well."

"Why not make me the landscape o' yer imagination?" Meg teased, half-serious, as she rolled over atop me once again and kissed me about the eyes. "Don't scowl, Wilkie, loike some wounded bear. Yew git so 'ard 'it when I don't agree with yer childish ways. I could really love yew, Wilkie, but yew won't let me. Yew are too much the gentleman an' the wantin' ta be novelist . . . too much like 'im. Life 'as ta be somethin' yew kin put in a book, can't be somethin' yew jus' injoy."

She didn't deliver her speech with malice, rather with a pensive sort of regret, as if she wanted me to be something more, or perhaps less, than I was. It certainly was a dilemma living with that woman. She tended to look so deeply into things.

At any rate, caught between the powerful pulls of Dickens on one hand and Irish Meg on the other, four days of waiting passed. On the morning of the fifth day after the discovery of Dunn's corpse and the disappearance of Tally Ho Thompson, Dickens and I were working upon the final layout of the upcoming *Household Words* issue when we were interrupted by an insistent banging upon the downstairs door. Wills, Dickens's ever-vigilant office Cerberus, jumped up immediately and we could hear him clicking across the wooden floor below to answer the door. The harsh banging, which did not cease until Wills flung open the door with a heated "Good Gawd man, stop that pounding," drew Dickens and myself to the head of the stairs. We found ourselves looking straight down upon Serjeant Rogers bursting in out of the thin cold sunlight of Wellington Street. Before Rogers said his first word, Dickens looked at me and I at him, and we knew right off that he had come to summon us back into the fray.

169

"Look sharp, gents." Serjeant Rogers glowered up the stairwell. "Hinspector has sent me for yew huonce hagain."

"Do you know where Thompson is?" I shouted down.

"Have you located Palmer?" Dickens shouted down.

"Hin the cab," Rogers growled back up at us, "git yer coats hand hats!"

Rogers had evidently been dispatched to Wellington Street on foot because he had commandeered Sleepy Rob's cab for our conveyance, that worthy having fallen into his morning doze at the kerbstone after delivering me to the *Household Words* office earlier. Galloping north out of the Strand into Bloomsbury, then continuing north past Regents Park through King's Cross and onto the Hampstead Highroad, Serjeant Rogers dispensed little information. Yes, Doctor William Palmer had been located and they hoped to obtain an interview. Yes, they knew where Thompson was. "We have, hi means Hinspector Field has, known where he his for two days he has," Rogers gloated as the cab emerged from Saint John's Wood and careened off the highroad at the base of Downshire Hill to begin its climb toward Jack Straw's Castle at the top of the heath. It was certainly a familiar locale for Dickens. His perpetually indigent friend, Leigh Hunt,* had lived for years in a small rented cottage just off the heath. "We've been keepin' hour heyes hon him," Rogers officiously assured us, "Thompson that his, for two days now."

"And you have not taken him up?" Dickens asked, somewhat surprised.

Rogers shook his head a solemn "no" as our cab came up onto the top of the heath and rolled into a flat, open space used as an outer coachyard for the large and elegant inn, Jack Straw's Castle, the view from whose upper rooms commanded the wide, wooded expanse of Hampstead Heath below.

Pulled up to the edge of the hill that descended to the

---

*There is almost universal agreement among critics that the minor poet and professional debtor Leigh Hunt was Dickens' life-model for the character Skimpole in *Bleak House.*

heath at the far end of that flat meadow, perched like a black vulture waiting for its dinner to go still below, was the sinister black Bow Street Station post chaise. Two constables, one holding the reins of a grazing horse, sat on the box. Inspector Field, alone, occupied the uncovered carriage. He stood up to greet our arrival and gestured for us to join him in the open carriage. The thin, cold sunshine made the day brighter than most of its January brethren, but we could see our own horse's breath in the frigid air. Back to our left across that open expanse of brown hilltop meadow, the grey, red-shuttered bulk of Jack Straw's Castle rose up to its gabled rooftop overlookin the turning where the Heath Road curved down into the pine trees and the gorse. Out to our right over the edge of the bluff, o'erspread like a Constable view,* stretched the wide brownish green expanse of the Hampstead Heath.

"Good afternoon, gentlemun," Field greeted us as we joined him in his carriage. "Yew'll be glad ta 'ear that our slippery Doctor Palmer 'as resurfaced an' is jus' down there." He pointed down in the general direction of a somewhat far-off break or clearing in the forested expanse of this end of the heath. "O'er there, neer the ponds, that's 'is ridin' club, it 'tis, an' 'ee's there amusin' 'imself right now."

As we registered our appropriate silent surprise at this intelligence with perfectly predictable raisings of the eyebrows and shruggings of the shoulders, Field unceremoniously extracted a monocular, vulgarly known as a "spyglass," from one of the capacious inner pockets of his greatcoat. "That is the 'Ampstead 'Ounds Ridin' Club." Field extended the monocular to its full length and handed it to Dickens. " 'Ee's the swell in the red coat an' small black ridin' 'at."

Dickens put the monocular to his eye and scanned the heath until he settled upon what I presumed to be the club in the clearing that Field had pointed out. "Yes, there he is!"

*This is a particularly apposite simile for Collins to use because Constable lived in Hampstead and did most of his landscape painting from vantage points like this one above the heath.

Dickens exclaimed excitedly. After spying for long moments, Dickens, remembering himself, passed the monocular to me.

As I put it to my eye, the trees of the heath seemed to leap right up to the end of my nose. With little difficulty, I found the clearing and the riding club, which Inspector Field had designated. It consisted of two white wooden buildings, one clearly a barn for horses, while the other was a more residential building with a porch and curtains that probably housed the clubrooms and dining areas. Appended to these buildings was a quantity of white fencing in the form of two horse-training rings and a chute into the forest that must have been the beginning and end of the club's bridle path. Looking through the monocular, my eye moved along the fences until it came to rest upon a group of three men standing by a gate behind which two magnificent Arabians were being hot-walked in a training ring. Only one of the three men seemed dressed for riding; he was in the aforementioned red coat and his back was to our vantage point.

"The one on the right in the red ridin' coat"—Field bent toward us, pointing vaguely out over the heath—"that's 'im."

Tall, thick in the shoulders and neck, he looked a powerful and dangerous man. Suddenly, as if he could feel someone spying upon him, he turned and seemed to look right up at me. Inadvertently, I ducked down in the carriage, afraid, I guess, that he had seen me, or had, at least, caught a glint of sunlight off the spyglass. Both Dickens and Field smiled at my quick ducking reflex. "He can't see yew way hup here." Rogers shook his head in disbelief.

"He looked as if he was looking right at me." I grinned sheepishly, handing the monocular back to Inspector Field. In that one brief second when our eyes met, however, the countenance of Doctor Palmer made a lasting imprint upon my sensibilities. The only adjective I can raise to describe that face is "Satanic." The dark black hair over dark black eye-brows over a dark black mustache and a tight black goatee presented a glowering image of an angry devil looking for revenge.

172

"That's 'im"—Field gave the monocular back to Dickens—"swarthy divvil ain't 'ee?"

Dickens nodded and studied the man some more through the glass. With my naked eye I could mark that dash of red in the distance, assume that our Doctor Palmer, after his suspicious look around, had resumed his conversation with his riding-club friends.

"I wants yew an' Mister Collins ta go down there an' talk ta 'im," Field thrust directly to the heart of his reasons for summoning us.

Dickens's shoulders tensed momentarily at the excitement of that charge.

"I don't care wot yew tell 'im," Field continued, "use the ploy about wantin' ta change doctors for yer wife, say the Spaniard at the 'ospital sent you out 'ere, tell 'im yer writin' a novel about doctors, like yew told Ashbee that time. Tell 'im anythin'."

"To what purpose?" Dickens, too, was more than capable of the sort of directness for which Field was renowned.

"I need some sense o' the man." Field's forefinger tapped slowly for emphasis upon the upholstered inner wall of the carriage door. "I think yew 'ave found out 'ow it wos done with the curare, an' I think we knows why it wos done, for the insurance, but we still 'ave no means o' provin' 'ee done the deed. That's why I needs yew now."

"Why us?" I started to protest, for Field evidenced no hesitation whatsoever to chucking us right into the lion's den. Dickens silenced my small cough of protest with a withering look.

"I needs ta know more about Palmer an' 'is wife. 'Ee runs in some o' yer same circles."

Here it comes, I thought, *the "simply observe" speech he has used upon us before.*

"This time I don't want yew ta simply observe our man. I wants yew ta stir the gentleman up, make 'im break cover if yew can. Be glad ta make 'is acquaintance, be friendly enough, but keep goin' back ta the murders. Yew know, 'terrible thing,' that sort o' rot. Remind 'im o' Thompson, 'wos our friend, turned on us,' take thet line mayhaps. 'Ow yew would love ta find Thompson, thet sort o' chatter. Just see if yew can draw 'im out." Field finished and sat down as if that long speech had taken all the wind out of him.

The whole time, as Field spoke, Dickens had remained standing in the carriage with the spyglass to his eye held unwavering on the tableau of those three men talking against that white fence below in the distance.

"I know slightly one of Palmer's companions down there," Dickens informed us, bringing Field back up to his fcet as if yanked upon by an invisible rein, "a young doctor I interviewed about a year ago for a *Household Words* article, name of Jekyll." Dickens paused for a moment, thinking. "Yes, Jekyll, I'm sure on it. Surprised he would be in the company of one like Palmer," Dickens now was thinking aloud. "Did not seem the horsey type to me."

"Wait 'til yew see 'oo rides in off the course next." Field chuckled; he, too, was quite capable of springing surprises.

We all gaped at Field, who milked the moment ruthlessly.

"And who might that be?" Dickens was clearly amused at Field's suspenseful antics. There was a subtle camaraderie between the two of them, as if they were both novelists or playwrights orchestrating their scenes and timing their dialogue for its most powerful impact upon the assembled audience.

Field took the monocular out of Dickens's hands and put it to his eye. He scanned the heath and woods around the Hampstead Hounds Riding Club for a long moment. "In just a moment yew'll see." Field lowered the glass.

"Who?" Dickens was no longer amused by Field's coy drawing out of his little game of "button, button."

"There"—Field handed back the spyglass to Charles and pointed toward some amorphous movement in the distance—"put yer glass on thet 'un."

Dickens looked through the monocular, focused it clearly, stepped back and exclaimed: "No!"

My curiosity piqued, watching Field's and Dickens's eyes meet, their mouths begin to break into simultaneous smiles, I grabbed the glass out of Dickens's hand and raised it to my eye. What I saw, riding out of the woods and into the club on a lathered red horse, dressed up like a Regency gentleman as pretty as you please, was the last person I expected to see.

"My God," I exclaimed, "it is Tally Ho Thompson!"

THE HORSEY SET

January 23, 1852—early afternoon

"Intrestin', eh?" Field ironically understated our surprise at spotting Thompson dressed thus and in such company. The smug look upon Serjeant Rogers's face especially irritated me. It announced that he knew Thompson was on the premises all along and had coyly withheld that information from Dickens and me. "Both o' our men seem ta 'ave surfaced out 'ere on the 'eath, an' Thompson is playin' quite a new role than 'is usual stage brigands." Field chuckled merrily on as I watched Thompson dismount in the cold January sunlight through the monocular. Consigning his lathered horse to a waiting groom, he joined the group of conversing men by the training-ring fence. He looked as at ease in this gentlemen's group as a young lord at court. Sensing Dickens's impatience, I passed the glass to him and he took up the surveillance.

"Talkin' ta Palmer an' t'other swells as pretty as yew please, I'll wager," Inspector Field provided the commentary even though Dickens possessed the glass. "Struck up 'is acquaintance this mornin', 'ee did. Gawd only knows wot Thompson's game is, wot 'ee told these toffs ta gain their ear."

"What is he up to?" Dickens, remembering his manners, handed the monocular back to Field who, without looking through it, passed it on to Rogers, who greedily stole his first look.

"No tellin'." Field shrugged. "Gettin' close ta 'is prey, I'd say. Figures this Doctor Palmer is the one 'oo can clear these murders off 'is tick. Probly took thet idea from me. Plans ta stay close ta 'im in 'opes o' makin' 'im break cover."

"Han mebbe he just wants ta git him halone han beat hit hout huv him." Rogers, handing the monocular back to Field, smirked.

"Are you going to take him up? Thompson, I mean?" Dickens asked.

"I think not," Field hesitated not a whit in answering. "Let's jus' wait an see wot our Tally 'O 'as in mind." That hard glint of the gamester engrossed by his game was in Field's eye as his crook'd forefinger came up for its customary punctuating scratch.

Dickens cast a quick glance at me as Field raised the monocular to his eye to devote his attention to Palmer, Thompson, and the horsemen's convention below.

I returned his look accompanied by a slight, expressive shrug of my mouth and shoulders, my indecisive sign that I had not yet really caught up with the game that was being played before us, around us, and with us. But it was in that quick exchange of looks that I realised that both Dickens and I were entertaining the same thoughts. *Field Wants Thompson out there on his own,* my line of reasoning went, *wants him out there stirring everything up, distracting our good doctor, a loose cannon careening around on the stage of this murderous drama of Field's scripting. That is why we helped Thompson escape from Newgate,* I suddenly realised. *Field knew how he would use him all the time.*

"There 'ee goes," Field provided a running commentary, holding the spyglass tight to his eye. "Packin' it in for now is our Tally 'O. Smart o' 'im, I'd say. Not movin' in too fast. 'Ee's learned somethin' from our association, 'ee 'as." Field chuckled at his private little joke.

With our naked eyes, and sighting over Field's shoulder along the line of the monocular which he kept aimed at the horizon like a rifle, we could see Thompson's tiny figure walk to a waiting carriage, climb in, and trot away down the Spaniard's Road toward the Vale of Health.

"Now 'tis yer turn ta put in yer appearance." Field turned to Dickens and me. "Remember, 'eavy'anded this time. Stir 'im up. Broad strokes."

Glancing at Charles, I could see that tensing of anticipation ripple through his being. " 'What larks,' eh Wilkie?" he said, and laughed with that open enthusiasm of his, quoting one of his own characters.* In a mere moment, we were in Sleepy Rob's cab and heading down over the hill to the riding club.

Ten minutes later, when we disembarked at the front gate to the Hampstead Hounds, Palmer's red coat was still loitering near the training ring in conversation with the other members of his horsey set. Dickens presented his card to the club servant stationed on the front porch. The man, duly impressed, extended to us a free run of the club and grounds after Dickens gave him some concocted story (accompanied by a half crown) about trying to find an old friend who was in residence. Those amenities of club-crashing attended to, we turned the corner of the building and set out in pursuit of our prey.

Without the slightest hesitation, Dickens, with me in tow,

---

*Collins, in writing this memoir in 1870, must be misremembering here. "What larks" is a line delivered by Joe Gargery, the blacksmith in *Great Expectations,* written in 1860–61, more than eight years after the exchange that Collins is reporting here as having occurred in 1852. Dickens could not quote a character he had not yet created. This could be faulty memory or an embellishment on Collins' part, or, "what larks" could possibly have been a favorite expression of Dickens' regular vocabulary that didn't appear in a novel until *Great Expectations,* but which was in common use by him long before.

strode up to Palmer and the two men with whom the doctor was conversing. I wouldn't have been the least surprised if Dickens had opened the conversation with "Doctor Palmer, how nice to meet you, did you poison your wife yesternight?" That is how boldly he walked up and intruded upon them. But he did not address Palmer at all. Rather, he stuck out his hand to a younger blond-headed man of less than thirty years who made one of that trio conversing at the riding-ring rail.

"Doctor Jekyll." Dickens beamed. "How nice to see you again."

I learned later that Dickens had interviewed this young man more than a year earlier for a *Household Words* article about the training and admission procedures to the medical profession.

"Why Mister Dickens, I say," and the attentions of the other two leapt up at the dropping of that famous name.

"This is my colleague, Wilkie Collins." Dickens had utterly usurped any conversation the three might have been carrying on. "Doctor Henry Jekyll, Wilkie."

I shook hands with young Jekyll who was then not that much younger than myself and a medical student. He has in the intervening years become quite a renowned physician as well as a medical researcher into methods of chemically pacifying the violent criminal mind.* After we shook hands, there was a brief awkward pause as young Jekyll recovered himself from the surprise of being recognised and greeted by such an eminent man. Dickens and I waited expectantly. Finally, recover he did, and stepping back and drawing himself up a bit, he did the expected thing.

*Little could Collins know, writing in 1870, just how far this Dr. Henry Jekyll's researches into the criminal mind actually had taken him. The world did not know the macabre results of those researches until the story was published by Robert Louis Stevenson after the discovery of the Solicitor George Utterson's secret journal following Dr. Jekyll's mysterious disappearance in 1883. Stevenson hypothesized the reasons for that disappearance in that famous factual speculation upon the case titled *The Strange Case of Dr. Jekyll and Mr. Hyde* (1886).

180

"Doctor Palmer, Mister Guiliano," he began the introduction which Dickens had so audaciously choreographed, "Mister Charles Dickens and Mister Wilkie Collins."

At the mention of Palmer's name, Dickens fairly jumped skyward, then stepped forward, hand outstretched, gushing: "Doctor Palmer, what an extraordinary coincidence"—and he took the man's hand—"not five days ago I spoke with your assistant, Doctor Rodrigo, ah, ah . . ."

"Vasconcellas." The red-coated doctor supplied the remedy to Dickens's affected confusion.

"Yes, of course," Dickens said soberly, "he apprised me of the recent terrible loss of your wife. My deepest sympathy."

At that Palmer was startled. His face darkened and he stepped back to recover himself before bowing his head silently to Dickens in acknowledgement. Up close, Palmer was even more forbidding than his dark visage, seen through the monocular from the top of the heath, had predicted. Only a bit shorter, yet quite thicker, than Dickens, the two of them side by side presented a severe contrast.

Dickens, with his ready smile, presented a bright open appearance. Palmer, to the contrary, looked as closed as a pirate's keep. His glowering black-browed, black-bearded visage had a murderous look about it. Deep furrows under his eyes, yellowish as if diseased, gave his face a wolflike cast. He was, in physique, a younger man than Dickens, about thirty-five years of age I surmised, but he looked older, more world-worn. Yet he was also an imposing man in his dark, brooding way. He reminded me of the villains of Mister Godwin's or Mister Walpole's gothick novels.* One could see how a woman like his dead young wife could be attracted to him. But perhaps I am being too melodramatic in my description. Field would surely laugh at the idea that murder can be

---

*Here, Collins is probably referring to the character Falkland in William Godwin's *Caleb Williams* (1794) and the character Prince Manfred in Horace Walpole's *The Castle of Otranto* (1764).

written upon a man's face. But, if it could, it was written here.

"Mister Dickens"—Palmer recovered himself politely enough—"it is, indeed, a pleasure to meet you. I have, of course, as has everyone in England, read a number of your stories." At that, it was Charles's turn to bow politely. "What brought you to consult with Rodrigo?"

"It was about *my own wife.*" Dickens's slightly inflected allusion once again to the man's murdered wife startled even me in its crudeness. I noticed a slight tightening of Palmer's black brow, a flinch as if from a feinted blow. "She has been ill for more than a year and has been taking treatments from Doctor Smith in Great Malvern, but she is not recovering as expected. I am seriously considering bringing her back into town and placing her in another doctor's care. Your name was given the highest recommendation to me by Macready of Covent Garden."

Palmer made a slight bow of the head to this compliment, but, not giving him leeway to reply, Dickens sailed right on: "Strangely, it seems that Mister Collins and myself were involved rather distantly in the sad affair of your wife's murder." Like a vulture at carrion, Dickens kept pecking mercilessly at the poor woman's death.

"Oh? How is that?" Palmer's voice was guarded, but I could see the rage building in the tightness over his cheekbones and behind his eyes.

"The housebreaker who murdered her, victimized us as well," Dickens answered, as if it were a comical story being told in a men's club. He was playing to the hilt the role of a tasteless, overtalkative buffoon. His vulgar persistence was stoking an impotent rage in Palmer.

"About *your* wife," Palmer abruptly changed the subject, "I would be glad to consult with her. When you bring her up to London, please do not hesitate to contact me. Here is my card," and he handed it over to Dickens, preparatory to fleeing our company and ending this conversation.

Dickens took it and turned it over in his hand: "Ah,

182

M.R.C.S.,"* he said, stalling, groping for some way to carry on this tactless conversation about the man's murdered wife, "ah, but you can help me in a much more immediate way."

"Oh? Just what is it that brings you out here to the heath in winter, Mister Dickens?" Palmer, on the lean to escape, yet held back by Dickens's mindless persistence, looked as if he wanted to go for Charles's throat.

"I am out here poking around in search of detail—the lingo, you know—that necessary authenticity for a riding-to-the-hounds scene I shall soon be writing for my new novel. I am looking for some advice from some real horsemen. Would you gentlemen help me?"

"I would certainly like to," Palmer huffed, still fuming at Dickens's rude audacity, "but I must be back—"

"That was the reason Mister Collins and I were interviewing that man Thompson in Newgate the night he knocked us on the head and made good his escape," Dickens cut off Palmer's escape with this gabby ramble. Palmer glowered all the more. "Ex-highwayman—reputed a miracle with horses, Macready put me on to the fellow—was Covent Garden's horse-riding man. Oh, excuse me, you know all of this," Dickens rambled on as if his head were as empty as Mister Dick's,† "after all, you did hire the fellow to give your poor wife riding lessons, did you not?"

Once again, Palmer was caught utterly off balance and that wolfish rage again began to well up behind his eyes. "Yes, perhaps, but—now listen here Dickens, I don't know what your—"

"But that is why we are here today, you see," Dickens cut the man off once again, blithely ignoring the obvious rage that made our black-bearded friend look as if he were about to spontaneously combust. The other two men, young Jekyll

---

*This designation upon Palmer's calling card means "Member Royal College of Surgeons."

†An empty-headed character in Dickens' last completed novel prior to these events, *David Copperfield* (1849).

and the Italian, stood there as aghast as I at the lunacy of this conversation. "This Thompson made good his escape before I could get anything out of him. So now I must find someone else to help me with my scene." Dickens threw his hands comically up in the air at the inconvenience of it all.

Doctor Palmer stared at Dickens a long moment as if he hoped that Charles would disintegrate in a fireball before his hateful gaze. "Well it will not be me," Palmer growled and, without another word, stomped off toward the refuge from lunatic nonmembers of the club's inner sanctum.

"Well that's odd." Dickens watched him go, still smiling stupidly. Then, never missing a beat, Charles turned back to the others and, as if nothing had happened, asked, "Perhaps you two would help me with this?"

Young Jekyll and the Italian looked at each other at a loss. Both were, I think, rather stunned at the vulgarity of Dickens's insistence on dredging up the unhappiness of the murder of Palmer's wife to the man's face. Needless to say, I, too, was astonished at what Dickens had just done, and relieved that he had lived through it.

The Italian mumbled some "excusa, excusa" in pidgin palaver and left the three of us standing there by the fence rail. Dickens, continuing to smile stupidly, looked as if he could not be happier if the Lord Mayor of London had just dedicated a building in his honour.

Young Jekyll, still basking in the attention Dickens had bestowed, seemed reluctant to abandon Charles to the farriers and liverymen going about their chores in the barn and ring.

"How do you know Doctor Palmer?" Dickens asked cheerily.

"And who is that Italian gentleman?" I chimed in.

"Oh"—Jekyll was eager to accommodate—"for the last year I have been an assistant to Doctor Palmer's chemical researches. He learned that my father taught me to ride at a young age and he brings me out here sometimes to ride with him. In fact, I think that is why he gave me my place working with him."

"And the other?" Dickens prompted.

"Guiliano?" Jekyll chuckled. "He is a tout at Ascot, a book-maker who toadies to his gentleman clients. He knows his horses, though."

"Is it not a rather cold time of year to be out here riding horses?" I asked. The late-afternoon wind had come up and sent a shiver straight through me.

"Oh no, not at all"—Jekyll, still eager to please, seemed most innocent and forthcoming—"not for true horsemen. They ride to the hounds here on the heath right into December, and when Ascot and Epsom are not in session, private horsemen match race their horses across the heath."

"And wager heavily upon them, I'll bet," Dickens was thinking aloud again.

"Oh, that they do." Jekyll laughed. "The horsemen fancy themselves jockeys. They race, and then drink in the club-room and lie about their heroics on the racecourse. Naturally, the money changes hands freely. Why, only this afternoon, a new member, an Irish gentleman, challenged Doctor Palmer to a race for money. They will set the course and do it some fine day soon, I'll wager."

At that, both Dickens and myself could hardly suppress our laughter. We glanced quickly at each other in acknowledge-ment of the success of Tally Ho Thompson's little game.

"Palmer is a betting man then?" Dickens pressed.

"He lives for it," Jekyll confided.

"He seems not overly mournful at the death of his wife," Dickens remarked wryly.

"Yes," Jekyll answered quietly, suddenly subdued, begin-ning, I think, to wonder, "it would seem so. It is less than a fortnight since his wife's terrible death."

"And who might this new club member he is going to race be?" I was just being mischievous for we both knew it was Thompson.

"I do not really know much about him," Jekyll was growing

185

more measured and suspicious in his answers, but Dickens certainly showed no sign of caring, "an Irish lord visiting from Cork, I believe."

"Is that so?" Dickens reflected.

I almost laughed aloud. Dickens frowned at my self-indulgence. Actor and stage manager that he was, I think he felt I was stepping out of character, and his damning look made it clear that such an actor's gaffe would not be tolerated in one of his productions.

"I know we have been very inquisitive about your colleague"—Dickens set out right away to allay young Jekyll's suspicions—"but he seems such a singular fellow that he has truly captured my curiosity." At that, Dickens moved in close to young Jekyll, quite personal, conspiratorial. "He seems an interesting psychological case, especially to me, a novelist. Gambling in the wake of his wife's murder? Tell me, Jekyll . . . seriously . . . what do you think of Doctor Palmer?"

The young man caught the spirit of Dickens's seeming to confide in him. He thought a long moment before answering. "I think that he is a man who tends to excess," Jekyll spoke slowly, ominously. "For that reason, he seems at times a bit unstable, almost as if he were two different persons."

"Well." Dickens laughed and clapped young Jekyll lightly on the shoulder, "he probably would not appreciate our making so free with the working of his excessive mind, now would he?" and Dickens winked at the young man by way of a broad hint. "Goodness Wilkie, that wind certainly has come up. I think we've got plenty of information from our friend Jekyll here about the workings of private riding clubs." He beamed at our informant. "Shall we flee back into the warmth of the city?"

Before I could even voice my assent, Dickens was shaking Jekyll's hand heartily and beating his retreat toward our cab parked in the road at the front gate. We left Jekyll standing there alone by the ring, puzzled I am sure.

Once in the cab with Sleepy Rob clucking to his business partner, I turned to Dickens with genuine amazement: "Good

God, Charles, what a performance. If that does not flush him out, nothing will. I am surprised he stood for it."

"Perhaps we should hire tasters for our food and drink." Dickens chuckled. "He was, indeed, scowling fit to kill." Then more seriously, "A bit heavy-handed to be sure, Wilkie, but it was what Field asked us to do. I, too, am surprised at the man's control. He is hiding something, I am sure of it."

I marvelled at Dickens's understatement. The man had stalked off as if looking for a butcher's knife with which to cut us up and bake us in a pie.

At the top of the hill, with his exceedingly sharp hat pulled down over his exceedingly sharp ears against that exceedingly sharp winter wind, Inspector Field waited patiently for his report. Dickens gave it with all of the novelist's expected embellishments. I cut in once to recount the particulars of Thompson's elaborate masquerade, which, for some reason, truly tickled me.

"Is not this dangerous?" Dickens asked as he finished his narrative. "Palmer could drive up that road and see us here."

"We will be signalled if 'ee leeves the club," Field assured us. "I 'ave a man in there." He was truly amazing. He seemed always one step ahead of the rest of the world. "Wot yer friend Jekyll told us squares with some o' the incidentals my men 'ave gathered about Palmer." Field was delighted. " 'Ee's our man, I know it!"

"What incidentals?" Dickens pressed. On this case, unlike the last, the Ashbee affair, Inspector Field seemed constantly holding his cards closer to his vest and out of view of the rest of the table.

"Since comin' up ta London in 'forty-two, Palmer 'as gotten involved with a fast crowd. Gamblers, rakes, drug fanciers, the 'Ounds Club down there is a refuge for such sorts, the very rich and very loose. 'Ee wos usin' 'is wife's money ta support this life. Killin' 'er for the insurance would 'elp 'im carry it on. Seems 'ee loved 'is 'orses more than 'er. Yer Jekyll 'as put aw thet in stark for us."

"So what do we do now?" That fire of anticipation was back

187

in Dickens's eye, that excitement for nighttime adventure ringing in his voice.

"Equally intrestin' about yer little visit down there is Thompson's game," Field answered. " 'Tis startin' ta git dark. Might jus' be a good time ta look in on our slippery highwayman friend. 'Ee ought ta be jus' settlin' in ta the cosy o' 'is 'ideout, eh Rogers?"

"Right, sir," that worthy said, smirking, possessed of knowledge to which we hated amateurs were not privy.

"Are yew gentlemen still on duty for Inspector Field?" Our master grinned archly, turning back to us.

Dickens, answering for me, leapt eagerly to the invitation.

"Then let us go." Field grinned ominously. "I'll wager they 'aven't frequented a den this low in a while, eh Rogers?"

THE SPANIARD'S INN

January 23, 1852—night

hile Jack Straw's Castle at the top of Hampstead Heath was a respectable inn and public house, at the bottom of the heath, set back from the road opposite the Vale of Health and sheltered by an overhanging grove of trees, lurked a house of an entirely different colour. This was the Spaniard's Inn. Named after an infamous pirate and highwayman of the seventeenth century whose Christian name had long since given way to his nationality, its sign, bearing the effigy of a grinning Spanish pirate, complete with a drooping mustache, an ominous eye-patch, and an ugly scimitar, hung askew, one of its chains having broken at the dark entrance to what seemed but another country cowpath. In the two intervening centuries up to 1852, the time of this memoir, the notorious reputation of the Spaniard's Inn had not been raised one whit. It remained in wide renown as the refuge and playground of all manner of ruffians, cutthroats, and criminals. It was the country estate of the habitants of the Rats' Castles of the city, a place to cool off and dig in and hole up when the heat of the Peelers got too intense. The Spaniard's Inn was the sewer into which all of the scum of the city ultimately drained when it had nowhere else to go.

Inspector Field had instructed Sleepy Rob to wait at the top of the hill so that we might have proper conveyance home when the evening's adventure was over. Thus, the four of us, the two professional detectives and the two amateurs, descended into the heath-side woods in the Bow Street post chaise. At Field's command, the driver reined in an appropriate distance from the Spaniard Inn's sign. The January moon was well committed toward full and the usual fog had not yet shown its face, so we were able to observe the bulk and contours of the building from this distance. It was, indeed, a sullen, shadowy place. Set back from the road in a thick grove of ancient oaks and chestnut trees, it looked a moody, brooding, bleak house. A narrow, rutted carriage path drew a half-circle from the Heath Road to the inn's hitching rail and front porch and then out again through the trees and back to the selfsame road. A cart, a carriage, a coach, or a horseman might enter from either side of the wood, which formed a barrier between the inn and the road, but not undetected. A sentry posted upon the porch of the inn commanded a clear view in both directions up the turnaround. Field advised us that such a sentry, usually smoking and drinking from a jug on the porch, was always set, and could signal to the inner occupants of the inn by merely knocking upon the shutter in a centuries-old cutter's code.

"We're not goin' ta surprise nobody 'ere tanight," Field assured us. "As soon as we enter the lane, the word'll be passed. Let's jus' 'ope they're too drunk ta know 'oo we be right off." Giving his directions to the driver, he turned back to us: "We'll go in fast, yew two stay behind me. These're not gentullmun we're dealin' with 'ere. These won't stand on propriety, or 'esitate ta strike out if stirred."

He ended his directions with a knowing nod to Rogers and a tap on the box with his murderous, knobbed stick. At that,

190

the driver snapped his reins and we turned into the dark tunnel of trees leading to the Spaniard's Inn.

It slumbered ghostly before us as we rumbled up through the overhanging foliage, its high slate roof broken by seven dilapidated gables. A long sprawling building of three storeys, the length of its front was belted with a pillared porch up three steps from the rutted lane through which we were careening. Low, broken-down stables extended into the woods from its backside like the useless legs of a cripple. The main building's south end, out of which rose a high smoking chimney, was built of stone while the other half of the building, which looked of a more recent vintage (sometime in the previous one hundred years) was built of wood of a common clapboard design. On the porch, sitting on an ancient high-backed settle just to the side of the high double door, with a jug between his knees, sat a solitary man who gaped at us wide-eyed as we galloped up.

Field, not waiting for the carriage to stop, leapt out, landed at a run, and charged up onto the porch. The startled man with the jug and a corncob pipe, whom I presume was the afore-described sentry, had evidently been surprised by our rapid approach. He was just beginning to knock on the shutter behind his settle when Field, with one swift blow, broke all of his knuckles under the knob of that murderous stick. The man howled in pain, his whiskey jug rolled all the way across the porch and down the steps, and he fell to his knees moaning.

Field never paused to even consider the man's agony, but bulled his way through the double doors into the public tap of the Spaniard's Inn. He strode across that high-raftered room at double military march time straight to the tap with Dickens and me right behind. Charles was as startled, I am sure, at Field's sudden speed and violence as was I. Serjeant Rogers, inexplicably, had disappeared. As we remaining three crossed the room, I remembered seeing, blurred in my excited vision, country folk, sitting at tables over pints of ale to our left and right, gaping in mute inquiry. We must have been

191

quite an exotic sight: a burly bull of a man wielding an ugly knobbed stick followed by two well-dressed gentlemen wearing looks of startled apprehension.

"Don't touch it!" Field growled, raising his stick to a large hairy potbellied sloth of a barman, who was reaching for the rope of a cast-iron bell hanging on the wall over the tap. The bloated barman froze in mid-reach as Field vaulted over the bar and jabbed the knob of his stick deep into the man's protruding belly. "Yer not tippin' yer friends, yer not." Field's face was right up against the man's grizzled jowls.

Meanwhile, Dickens had turned, placing his back against the bar, to face the room (and me still stumbling across it). His instinctive intention, I am sure, was to protect Field's back during the interrogation of the barman. *Where in God's name is Rogers?* I thought. As I reached Dickens's side, I, too, turned to measure the threat from the rest of the room. No one at the trestle tables along the walls showed any inclination toward moving upon us. These tapsters seemed simple country folk, small groups of men and women in floppy hats and coarse farming smocks come to the dim pub in the forest to drink off the fatigue of their day's work. They gaped, their pints in their hands, as if we were some freaks from a travelling carnival come to invade their quiet haven. Four strapping bumpkins occupying a table in the chimney corner stared, but showed no sign of vaulting to their publican's rescue.

"Where is it?" Field prodded at the barman's belly with the knob of his stick.

"Where's wot, guv?" the oaf tried to counterfeit guilelessness.

"Don't give me *wot.*" Field slapped him across the side of the head with that exceedingly sharp hat. "The cosy, man! Where's the door ta cosy where the reg'lars o' the 'ouse drink?"

Field slapped him again with that exceedingly sharp hat and prodded him again with that murderous stick.

Dickens and I gaped at the tapsters and they gawked at us.

192

My head swivelled from them to Field to the curious bump-kins in the chimney corner and back to Field.

"O'er there." The barman pointed to a door under the steps which rose up to the rooms on the second floor. "O'er there and down 'tis," he said, his voice surly. Field must not have liked the man's tone because he snapped his stick up and tapped the man hard enough on the breastbone for his breath to whoosh out and his hands to cross his heart as he doubled over.

"Now," Field instructed in a brutal Yorkshire schoolmas-ter's voice, "yer goin'ta escort us down there with nary a sound, arn'cha lad," and placing his hat back on his head, then grabbing the publican by the scruff of the neck with his free hand, he steered him toward the door under the stair. Dickens and I followed like leery cubs being led into a strange den.

Above-ground, in the public tap, the Spaniard's Inn looked a respectable-enough public house where one might order up a jugged hare or a steak-and-kidney pie to go with one's pint of bitter on a night like this with the January wind howl-ing dismally in the naked trees outside. Below-ground, how-ever, the Spaniard's Inn catered to a quite different clientele. Even before we started down into the darkness, I could sense the difference, the danger. Descending those cellar stairs, the very air, heavy with cigar and pipe smoke, closed upon our throats like a strangler's hands. At the bottom of the stone steps, a dim corridor moved to our right toward flickering firelight. The pungent odours of fowl cooking, human sweat, and horses assailed our noses. Traversing that dusky corridor, we turned a short corner and blundered into the midst of the Spaniard's underground tap.

It was a low, heavy-beamed room; its wooden ceiling black-ened by two hundred years of heath fires and pipe smoke. The ruddy glow of a well-stoked fire lit the room in a shimmering gold. The settles and tables were gathered for warmth around that glowing hearth in the chimney corner.

The tapsters of this other barroom of the Spaniard's Inn

were quite a different gallery of rogues than had stared at us in the public room above. Around the tables, glowering into their pints, or reclining on the settles sipping their hot gins, congregated the most grotesque band of cutthroats and their red-lipped whores that Dick Turpin ever suffered to ride the roads of England. As we turned the corner and entered right into their midst, I noted how heavily armed the men who immediately confronted us were, and how unarmed we were (Dickens and I, that is). When we turned the corner and disturbed the tranquillity of this den of thieves, the five men, sitting at the tables pulled up to the hearth, spontaneously leapt to their feet, and faced us down. Each wore a pistol in his belt and had a knife strapped to his leg. In the brief seconds upon our entering the room, these coves had measured us, decided we were the bulls, and reached for their weapons.

Inspector Field, however, never gave them the opportunity to draw their pistols or unsheath their blades. Without the slightest hesitation upon entering that smoky warren, Field threw our hostage, the slow-witted fat publican, at the five cutthroats who had risen against us. With a mighty shove, Field launched him like a beer barrel into their midst causing all manner of confusion. That momentary distraction allowed Field to wade in and deal out the first heavy strokes with his vicious knobbed stick. He put two of these rogues out of action immediately with a sharp ringing knock to the nearest knee and a powerful upward cut of the knob of his stick directly under a second thug's chin. The first man collapsed as if felled by an axe. The second flew head over heels backward into the midst of the three women toasting themselves in the chimney corner. With those two knocked to the grimy floor howling in pain, Field turned quickly to the others and waded in with his oak-knobbed equaliser.

Dickens, hesitating not a moment, rushed to Field's aid and closed with one of the ruffians in a hand-to-hand grapple. The cutthroat was thick and hairy and squat. When Dickens rushed upon him, he caught our "Inimitable" in a bear hug and attempted to squeeze the life out of him. It was then that I observed Dickens do an extremely ungentlemanly thing. Thrusting his knee sharply up between his antagonist's legs, he drove it hard into the man's most vulnerable appendages. The pain of it forced the man to unhand Dickens and doubled the oaf over, at which juncture Dickens stepped back and, taking careful aim, kicked the already staggered man full in the face. Wearing his heavy travelling boots, which he had deemed appropriate for our little daytrip to the country, Dickens's kick catapulted its victim backward. The man recoiled as if slammed with a sledge and, landing flat on his back, lay quite still.

I, too, attempted to wade in to fight at Field's side, but before I could successfully enter the fray and honourably engage the declared male enemy, I was attacked from the flanks by two doughty camp followers. The viragos descended upon me like vengeful lionesses, teeth bared and claws out. The first went straight for my eyes. The other kicked out at my sexual quarter. I was lucky to evade their onslaught, though I later discovered that I sustained a red welt the length of my cheek from a claw extended for blinding. I slipped the slashing nails of the woman rushing upon me high, and clasped in a headlock the whore attempting to dismember me below. Just as I was wrestling this unmanning attacker under control, the other wench re-entered the fray by leaping upon my back, wrapping her legs around my waist, and proceeding to pummell me about the ears.

In the meanwhile, on another front, Inspector Field was choking an additional large ruffian into unconsciousness. Having gotten somehow behind the man, Field had pressed the shaft of his stick against the man's windpipe and was pulling back hard as the man's knees and feet kicked out in an earthbound version of Jack Ketch's dance.* Dickens was keeping the remaining cove busy by snapping the man's head back once, twice, thrice, with lightning-quick jabs to the vicin-

*"Jack Ketch" is the generic English term for the hangman.

195

ity of the man's nose. All was happening so fast that it formed a spinning tapestry of motion into which all of us were embroidered.

But I had not time to dwell upon the other battles swirling around me. The two women, one on my back, one's head locked under my right arm, were prodding and pounding me this way and that as if I were a bull being baited. The woman on my back was scoring heavily with her fists to my ears and forehead. The woman down below was clawing frantically at my thighs.

Suddenly, my jockey flew off as if yanked from her saddle by a rope.

"Leeve 'im be, yew drunken 'ore!" a strangely familiar voice screamed to my rear.

Again miraculously, a small white hand grasped the hair of the clawing woman under my arm and dragged her away from me.

"Leeve 'im be or I'll tear yer eyes out, bitch!" that same commanding voice ordered from a dark corner of that swirling tapestry.

It was Irish Meg's voice. I knew it now that I had a moment's respite from the battle. She gave this second woman a good push onto a settle by the hearth and growled *"Stay!"* as one would to an over-frisky house dog. Then she turned back to me and a huge laughing grin bloomed in her face. " 'Ello, luv," she said as she laughed, "yew niver were verry good with wimmin."

Field and Dickens were standing back to back in the centre of the room taking stock. Five men lay strewn about. One, knocked head over heels against the grimy wall by Field's stick, was attempting to right himself, but his legs didn't work. He was a handsome man, though there were some rather evident flaws in his beauty: most of his front teeth were missing, and one eye was swollen shut and turning blue due to its correspondence with the knob of Field's stick. Another cutthroat was trying to rise from the hearthstones. He was uncommonly red in the face due to the blood streaming out of

196

a cut in his forehead. The other three lay still upon the floor, but from a closer perusal of their faces could be described as every bit as ugly and unkempt as these others. One of them, incredibly thin with bulging eyes and mottled skin, looked like a snake who had just been trod upon. What none of them could be described as being or looking like was Tally Ho Thompson. He was not among this fallen phalanx of hairy, filthy, deformed, grotesque, toothless, earless, mindless, heavily armed men that Field's stick had laid so low. The blokes' women kept to the settles in the chimney corner, held at bay both by the inert condition of their beaus and the fierce gaze of Irish Meg standing with her hands upon her hips in the middle of the low room.

"Meggy," I exclaimed, "what on earth are you doing here?"

"Ask Fieldsy," she said and grinned. " 'Ee's the one wot pulls our strings."

Field was busy asking the toothless snake and the bloated sloth the whereabouts of Thompson.

"Meggy, good God, you shouldn't be here"—I found myself leaning to her and whispering in a secretive way, which even at the time I remember thinking to be utterly absurd. "It is dangerous. This is a terrible place."

"I've been in a lot worse." She laughed at my whispered concern. "Yew remember I used ta live in places like this afore I became yer private 'ore." Thank heavens she was still whispering when she said that. Then she found her regular hard, ironic voice: "Wot's a swell like yew doin' in a den like this?" she taunted.

"Meggy," I was still whispering, "I thought you were content to stay at home with me, off the streets, out of places like this."

"Yew see, luv, wimmin can do stoopid things out o' friendship too. Can't we now?"

"Where is 'ee?" Inspector Field, growling like an enraged bulldog, scuttled our private colloquy. "Where is 'ee, dammit Meg?"

I saw the old terror of Field pulse back into Meggy's eyes.

197

"Upstairs. In a room. 'Ee an' Bess are upstairs," she stammered. Field exerted this strange hold over her, a frightening control that I knew I could never gain nor would ever wish to.

"Show us," Field ordered.

Despite her terror at the power he held over her, Meg spoke up to him: "This an't a good time ta be disturbin' 'em," she stalled.

"Not a good time!" Unable to resist, I leaned in to her and murmured under my breath in hopes that neither Field nor Dickens could hear, but knowing that they probably would. "It is not as if anyone picks good times to disturb *us*, now is it?"

Meg couldn't help but smile. Dickens seemed amused. Field just stared. I realised that I had revealed much more of our intimacy than I had intended.

In a softer voice, almost cajoling, Field lunged once more at his main concern: "Where is 'ee, Meggy? Tell me or I'll 'ave ta beat it out o' one o' these poor coves. I 'ave ta talk ta 'im. Show me where."

Meg acquiesced.

We locked that band of ruffians into that cellar den. Who knows, they probably simply returned to their drinking and whoring and the nursing of their Field-inflicted bruises.

In a line behind Irish Meg, we ascended to the public tap and then climbed the steps farther to the top of the house.

Meg stopped as we reached the top of the stairs. " 'Ee's up 'ere, in one o' these. I don' know which," and I sensed that for some reason she was still stalling.

Once again, following Field's reckless lead, Dickens and I found ourselves at the head of yet another dim corridor ready to plunge once again into heaven knows what unforeseen dangers. I knew that Field must, and Dickens, as always, certainly would, plunge ahead into this new challenge and adventure. I, however, was not so eager. "How did you know that Thompson would be here?" I now was stalling, and Field knew it. It irritated him.

"We've 'ad Meggy an' Bess under watch ever since 'ee

198

'ooked it the night Dunn died," Field hissed. "For Gawd's sake, man, be quiet."

He moved stealthily to the first door on the dim corridor and listened. The door was badly hung, crooked on its frame. No light seeped from beneath it, but muffled indeterminate sounds did. Out of another of the numberless inner pockets of his capacious greatcoat Field produced a bull's-eye. Stepping back away from the door so as to shield the light, he struck a lucifer and lit the lamp.

"Dickens, Collins, follow me in quick. Meg, pull fast the door behind us so the sound don't carry," he ordered in a whisper.

Moving back to the threshold, he tried the outer latch. It gave to his touch. Pushing silently and slowly on the door, he found it offered no resistance, was not barred. Those guttural sounds from the darkness within continued unabated. With a sudden move, Field sprung through the door, uncovering his bull's-eye to illuminate the room. Dickens and I followed on his heels, pulled along by Field's blind confidence in his own powers. As soon as all three of us cleared the threshold, the door swung sharply shut behind. Meg had done her part.

What we had broken in upon was startling, grotesque, comic, and indeed, eye-catching. It was truly fuel for the voyeur who lurks within every novelist. The room was small and dominated by a curtainless canopy bed in its centre. That bed, when Field shined his bull's-eye upon it, looked to be occupied by a huge writhing octopus. That many-tentacled monster struggling in the dark turned out to be two naked whores and a starkers red-bearded ruffian having their ways with one another all at once. The blonde who was riding the face of the red-bearded man on his back on the bed looked up into the bull's-eye and shouted "Wot the fock his this!" in surprise. For some comic reason, she reminded me of twisted Phil Moody's foul-mouthed parrot. The red-haired whore riding his hips—her curls cascading around her face and streaming down her back, then flaming up in the bull's-eye's light like those of a malevolent Medusa—simply stared uncom-

199

prehendingly and quickened the pace of her ride to the finish. The moaning sounds we had heard from outside that ill-hung door were coming from deep within her expressive chest. In the harsh light of the bull's-eye, the women's breasts moved voluptuously like dunes shimmering in a Mediterranean sun.

Plunging us into darkness once again by thrusting the bull's-eye under his coat, Field backed up quickly toward the door, extending his arms to his sides and thus pushing Dickens and myself forcefully in his path. He made no apology to that six-armed, six-legged octopus as we fled. He only muttered "Damn!" in the hallway once the door was again closed behind us. To our knowledge, those three indulging themselves acrobatically in that first room barely noticed our intrusion and simply went on about their romantic business.

"Wot?" Meg queried when we backed out.

"Wrong room, uh, very confused, uh, tangled up in there," Dickens stammered. Field was already moving on burglar's feet down the corridor to the next waiting door.

Candlelight flickered out from beneath this door, accompanied by a familiar splashing sound. Not hesitating, not even considering a knock, Field flung the door open and confronted a fat burgher, or perhaps schoolmaster, sitting in the middle of the room on a chamberpot. A body formed a bulbous lump beneath the comforters of the bed, but did not poke its head out when we entered. This was turning into one of those comical nighttime misadventures out of Mister Fielding's *Joseph Andrews* or Charles's own *Pickwick Papers*.

Field pulled the door shut in frustration and glared at Meggy as if to say: *Yew know where 'ee bloody is, don't yew? Why must we go through all o' this clumsy 'ousebreakin'?*

Meggy set her lips and said not a word.

Never one to give up, more stubborn than a Spanish Inquisitor, Field stalked in disgust to the next closed door. He put his ear to the wood. Neither light nor sound emanated from the room. His bull's-eye at the ready, Field tried the door. It did not give. Just the slightest ripple of a mad glee washed across Field's face and suddenly I knew exactly what

200

he was going to do. I think, perhaps, that he enjoyed breaking down doors and charging into the unknown more than all of the other, less forceful, more intellectual aspects of his profession. He stepped back three steps and hit the door running with his shoulder. He splintered it around the latch where the bar, undoubtedly, was in place on the inside. Stepping back once more, he kicked it in with the heavy heel of his boot. It took two more small kicks to clear the splintered debris from the doorway so that we could enter the darkened room.

Needless to say, all this thrashing around certainly had alerted anyone who was inside that room (or the whole inn, for that matter) to our intrusive presence. When Inspector Field shined his bull's-eye through that splintered portal, Scarlet Bess was sitting up stark naked in the bed like a hapless doe caught in the shine of a poacher's lantern, and Thompson, also as starkers as the day he was born to be hanged, was on his bare feet in the middle of the room pulling on his shirt and reaching for his breeches.

"Thompson! 'Alt!" Field shouted, shining the light on our highwayman's struggle to enter his clothes.

Field's order actually gave Tally Ho Thompson pause. He straightened, turned to us (still quite bare from the waist down—Meg told me later that she got more than a glimpse of the scene and that she fully understood why Scarlet Bess and all the others were so drawn to that rogue), and grinned his maddening grin right into the harsh light of Field's bull's-eye. Then, without hesitating for as much as a parting salute, his breeches in his hand, he dove out of the open window into the darkness below.

Scarlet Bess screamed.

Dickens stared, aghast.

Field rushed to the window.

"My God, he has committed suicide!" I exclaimed.

That open window was, after all, three storeys above the Caen Wood. It was only natural on my part to assume that he had fallen to his death. The more I think about it in retrospect, however, the sight of that white arse disappearing

201

out of that open window strongly reminds me of one of Mister Hogarth's comical etchings from *Marriage à la Mode: Cuckolded Husband Surprising His Wife and Her Lover Who Is Forced to Flee Alfresco.*

"Roof is flat outside 'ere," Field, whose head and trunk were half out the window, shouted back over his shoulder. " 'Ee's 'ooked it inta a tree."

None of us were immediately able to divine what that meant, but before we could bother Inspector Field for an interpretation, he was through the window and scrambling along the roof shouting something unintelligible into the pit of forest darkness below.

Dickens, of course, without the slightest hesitation—in all of our years together I never figured out whether Charles was just naturally intrepid or utterly foolhardy—climbed right through the window behind Field and negotiated the roofline to the edge where Field stood peering into the moonlit abyss. I had given up trying to keep up with the two of them. They never thought before they leapt. They never harboured the least doubt about their capabilities. In other words, whether novelist or detective, they were both daft.

When I caught up, they were both peering down into the skeletal tangle of branches of a venerable chestnut tree all messy with frozen hanging Spanish moss. It seems, Field filled us in later, that Thompson had run across the roof and launched himself into the web of branches of this tree, by which lattice he had descended to the ground and, we presumed, made good his escape. It was a risky business for sure, but Field did not seem the least surprised by Thompson's acrobatic ingenuity. "Damn, the man's a marvel." Field laughed. "Come on," he commanded us all. We followed him at a run back through the window, past the more modest, though still bedded, Scarlet Bess, through the corridor into which at the clangour all the occupants of the other rooms in various states of deshabille had emptied, down the stairs, and out into the stableyard of The Spaniard's Inn. That is where the next surprise of an evening replete with surprises awaited.

Rounding the south corner of the inn from the stable-yard where the forest virtually runs right up against the side of the building, a comic tableau spread out before us in the filtered moonlight beneath an ancient chestnut tree.

Dancing gleefully round a trussed-up bundle on the ground in a pugilistic imitation of the Wembley Whip* was Serjeant Rogers. The bundle, it turned out, was Tally Ho Thompson, inextricably tangled in a cord net of the Sandwich Islands fishing sort.

"Hit worked perfect," Rogers gushed to Field as we came up to him. "Hevry Constable should hev huone."

"I see. Good work, Rogers." Field clapped him on the shoulder. "I see our sprightly friend 'asn't 'ad the opportunity ta put 'is pants on yet." Field chuckled. "All tangled up in yerself, are ye?" he taunted Tally Ho Thompson, who had given up his struggle with Rogers's net and lay there on the ground like a piece of cargo waiting to be lowered into the hold of a ship.

It seems that Rogers, who with foresight had been dispatched by Field to guard the back of the inn, had heard, from his post below, the commotion emanating from the selfsame open casement out of which Thompson had escaped. Hearing the sounds of Thompson's flight across the rooftop, he had been waiting at the bottom when Thompson swung himself down out of that handy chestnut tree. As Thompson paused in his flight to pull on his trousers, Rogers had run at him and cast his net, which he had taken to carrying folded small in a pocket of his greatcoat since having confiscated it from a drunken tar in a waterside pub some months before. The constables had been called, Rogers told us later, because that sailor had taken to amusing himself

*The Wembley Whip, it seems, according to numerous accounts of his pugilistic victories and exhibitions in periodicals as diverse as *The London Times* (1846–54) and Captain Marryatt's sporting stories in *Punch,* was a much more famous boxer than either Chelsea Smalls or the Tewksbury Duck (mentioned in Collins' first memoir).

203

with netting whores and refusing to release them until he was allowed liberties with their persons.

"Seems yew've netted a big 'un," Field joked, all at Thompson's expense. "We could 'ave it stuffed an 'ung on the wall o' the Bow Street Station."

"And ye shall be fishers of men," Dickens struck a biblical stance over the trussed-up Thompson.

Not to be outdone, I taunted him as well: "Perhaps 'tis a mermaid's gotten tangled in our nets?"

"Hit's Thompson, hit his." Rogers was fair dancing with glee. "Han my net wrapped him hup like ha hobbled herring."

Thompson never said a word. I am sure that he was amused. He was such a good-natured fellow and treasured a joke every bit as much if not more than the next man. I am sure he was lying there all trussed up in that net with that maddening grin on his face already plotting his escape once liberated from this tangle. Inspector Field took no chances. Sending Rogers to enlist two of those strapping bumpkins from the public room, he had Thompson carried back into the Spaniard's Inn, down a labyrinth of corridors on the first storey to a secluded cozy in the back of the house most probably used for gambling. With the door locked, the fire lit, the bumpkins dismissed, and Thompson unencumbered, we all sat down around a circular oaken table covered with a green felt to play out this hand, though, as he made abundantly clear right away, Field felt that he held all of the cards.

" 'Ow long 'ave yew known where I wos?" Thompson opened the colloquy.

"Since day afore last," Field answered readily, "when one o' my constables watchin' Palmer spotted yew. I figured yew'd be lookin' for 'im."

"This is passin' stoopid," Thompson said it almost offhandedly as if they were discussing handkerchiefs and riding boots rather than murder and poison. "I 'aven't done anythin'. I wants ta git Palmer jus' like yew do."

"No need for yew ta be runnin' away then, is there now?

That wos stoopid!" Field thumped his expressive forefinger upon the oaken table for emphasis. "I don't want yew back in Newgate anyhow."

Thompson's head snapped up and he looked Field full in the face as if trying to read the detective's dark designs.

Field grinned evilly back at him as if to say, *Yew are my creature, an' must play out my 'and.*

In an instant, Tally Ho Thompson understood, regained his heedless equanimity. That maddening grin bloomed in his face and, with a tight little laugh, he thumped the table with the knuckles of his right hand as if to say, *Go ahead, Fieldsy, shuffle the cards an' deal me in.*

Those two, the detective and the highwayman, hunter and hunted, communicated more in a grin, a look, a thump on the table, than most men reveal in testimony under oath or interrogation under torture. They could read each other like clear writ texts. Their bargain struck, they proceeded to put their heads together and formulate a plan.

SHOE LANE IN THE SNOW

January 25–28, 1852

The best-laid plans sometimes become snowbound. The morning after our nocturnal adventure at the Spaniard's Inn, the great snowstorm of 'fifty-two struck. It effectively imprisoned all of London and her environs for three days. One could move around only on foot, and only for short distances at that, due to the depth of the drifted snow and the rather extreme cold. London's streets became like white canals, a snowbound Venice of the North, except that no snow gondolas seemed available for transporting people to and fro.

Against my better judgement, on the second day of the city's icy imprisonment, and leaving Irish Meg in our warm bed, I set out for the Wellington Street offices. For almost two days Meg had busied herself at convincing me (by the applications of her considerable charms and acrobatic talents) that she had gone to the Spaniard's Inn without consulting me purely out of motives of friendship, and not at all out of boredom with me or our life, or urges to infidelity and longings for her old ways, or even desire for public house gin. Actually, I did not press her hard for explanations upon why she had gone there. It had seemed obvious enough. Scarlet Bess had asked Meg to accompany her there, and Meg had acquiesced. In the almost four months that Irish Meg and I had been sharing our living arrangements, I had come to realise what an aggressively independent woman she truly was. Life for her was a constant competition for control: of one's own destiny, of the desires of others, of the knowledge she was constantly collecting from the books I procured for her and which she read voraciously. She developed various strategies by which she maintained her control. She had, doubtless, come to exert a powerful control over me and my habits.

Nonetheless, snowstorm or no, and despite Meg's inducements against, I felt compelled to visit Dickens, drawn to him (and whatever news of the case he might possess) like a gossip drawn into back-fence conversation with the other neighbourhood crones. Labouriously I traversed the snowbound streets between Soho and the Strand in order to look in upon Charles. I knew, in his restlessness, that he would be straining to escape this imprisonment by the weather. How right I was in my assumption!

Dickens opened the office door like a shipwrecked sailor spying a full-masted ship bearing down upon his desert isle. "Wilkie, I am so glad that you have come." He ushered me solicitously in out of the cold. "I have not heard from Field and I am about ready to call upon him in Bow Street."

He was alone there in the *Household Words* offices. Wills was snowbound in the suburbs, and Dickens had received word that Kate and the children were all snug at Great Malvern. He had decided not to chance the journey through the snowdrifts by coach to be with them. He told me that he wrote to her: "This shall all melt in a day or so, and we shall all sit down together to a nice shepherd's pie." How he expected to get his letter delivered, however, I had no idea.

It was good that I had come. He was as nervous as a caged

208

tiger. The writing of his new novel, titled that day, I think, *Tom-All-Alone's*, was not a strong enough inducement to keep him at bay. After observing him for little more than an hour, I feared he was on the verge of rushing out into the streets and collaring some poor passerby. After accusing that unsuspecting innocent of engineering the Medusa Murders, he seemed fully capable, out of sheer restlessness, of hanging his victim from a lamppost. In truth, he was literally unable to sit at his desk longer than ten minutes at a time.

I assured him that no one else was out in the city of London, that we were not missing out on any of the action of the case. Nonetheless, he would stand in the bay window looking out at the white wasteland of the city with the forward tilt of his body signalling how he longed to be out chasing after murderers and metaphors with his detective colleague. I managed to calm him down that day, but two more days passed before the storm truly abated and another day yet before I thought it sane to attempt to slog my way back to the Strand to look in upon him.

The sun was out and the snow already beginning to melt as I stepped out into the Charing Cross Road for the walk into the West End. Coaches and hansom cabs were not yet able to negotiate the streets and highroads, but at the rate the snow was melting they would be splashing through the mud as soon as most of the water ran off into the river. Dickens, as harried as he had been two days before, again met me at the office door and, this time, would not allow me to convince him of the ill-advisedness of going out in the slush to Bow Street. He never even gave me time to remove my muffler and gloves before he too was greatcoated and top-hatted and we were setting off in quest of Inspector Field.

Little did we know that at that very moment, as we were stepping out into the snow and slush, Inspector Field was gathering his greatcoat, placing his exceedingly sharp hat upon his exceedingly blunt head, taking up his murderous knobbed stick, and dispatching Serjeant Rogers to search us out and summon us back into the world of the detective. As we turned into Bow Street out of King's Alley, we almost ran up against Serjeant Rogers trudging along with his head down muttering incoherently for the enlightenment of his boots. When he saw that it was both Dickens and me, together and right there, his face lit up as if he had just witnessed a Christian miracle. "Mister Dickens, Mister Collins, hi wos jus' sent for ye." He was ecstatic. "He wants ye ta come ta Shoe Lane. Somethin's hup hat the doctor's house."

"Palmer?" Dickens asked the obvious. "But his house is in Chelsea?"

"No. T'other," Rogers cryptically answered.

"What? Not Palmer? What other?" Both Dickens and I were stumped.

"Spaniard doctor name o' Rodrigo." Rogers, who had never met the aforementioned, dispensed the name like any other meaningless bit of information.

"Aha!" Dickens looked at me and I nodded knowingly back. I must admit, however, that I hadn't the slightest clue to what his "aha!" meant.

"We'll take the Strand, then Fleet Street, they're clear." Rogers waved for us to follow and, at Dickens's prompting, briefed us upon the situation as we went.

It seems a surveillance constable had followed Doctor Rodrigo Vasconcellas home from Bart's to his third-storey rooms in Shoe Lane the evening before. Posted in a narrow mews across the street, the constable waited for the good doctor to turn off his gaslamps and retire. The Metropolitan Protectives have a defined set of procedures for surveillance and a constable cannot leave his post until he is sure his subject has retired for the night. This particular constable, watching Doctor Vasconcellas's third-storey window, never reported in.

"We sent relief to his post this mornin' "—Rogers seemed puzzled—"han the constable reports him that Doctor Rodrigo niver went hout han niver turned down his gas hall night."

"Why, what do you make of that?" Dickens asked the obvious.

"Don't make nothin' hov hit," Rogers rejoined, "but Hinspector thinks somethin' his wrong hand worth lookin' hinto."

"I should say so," I said, as we tramped through the snow toward Shoe Lane.

Doctor Vasconcellas's rooms were located at the top of a high, gloomy box of a wooden tenement house. It was a sunny day and in the bright glare off the melting snow, we could not really tell from below whether or not the gaslamps were still lit in those rooms. Field's constable popped out of his mews to greet us upon arrival, but reported absolutely no movement on the part of his subject.

"Passin' strange 'tis." Field's crook'd forefinger scratched at the side of his eye as he stood in the middle of that melting street looking up at that unresponsive window. "Let's 'ave a look," he decided, preparatory to vaulting up the icy stone steps and into the gloomy building. The rest of us, of course, followed like the dancing tail of a crazy kite. Field, Dickens, and Tally Ho Thompson had put their heads together and carefully laid their plans for trapping Doctor Palmer and solving the case of the Medusa Murders, but what happened next simply had not been accounted for in that plan.

We climbed the wooden steps to the top of that dark house and found Doctor Vasconcellas's door. Field knocked politely.

No answer.

Field knocked again, and when total silence continued his sole answer, that violent gleam sparkled in his eyes. I swear the man truly loved kicking in doors, and he was measuring this one in gleeful preparation.

Stepping back only one step, Field raised his heavy boot and gave the door one sharp kick over the latch with his heel. The wood barely splintered, but the door sprang open as if mounted on the face of a Swiss cuckoo clock. It was a delicate little bit of boot surgery.

Field stuck his head in the door, and then, stepping back and frantically extracting a clasp knife from one of the inner pockets of his capacious greatcoat, he sprang the blade and rushed into the dimly gaslit room with Rogers close behind.

When Dickens and I reached the door, Field was up upon a chair cutting down the body, which dropped limply into Rogers's waiting arms. He lowered it to the floor. It was Doctor Vasconcellas, staring up at us with wide eyes and a twisted look of agony frozen upon his face.

DOCTOR RODRIGO'S
ILL-KEPT SECRET

January 28, 1852—late afternoon

The hanged man's lodgings were a jumble. Neither I nor Field nor any of the others was immediately able to determine whether that chaos of medical books, scientific journals, and blue books strewn thither and hither amongst dirty shirts and stockings and all manner of soiled apparel, boots, shoes, and eating utensils was simply the ordinary housekeeping arrangement of our Doctor Vasconcellas, or the result of a violent struggle. The bittersweet smell of opium smoke still hung in the air. The rope from whence Field had cut the dead man down had been looped over an exposed ceiling beam and secured to the leg of a heavy chest on the far side of the room. Beneath that ceiling beam had been pushed, cutting a swath through the clutter of the room, a heavy oaken desk. Field later speculated that Rodrigo had either climbed up or been dragged up upon that desk, gotten the noose placed around his neck and jumped or was pushed off. A long-throated clay pipe, its bowl stained with that black oily residue of opium, lay abandoned on the floor beside a low divan of Oriental design. The pipe's bowl was cold, and thus Field was not readily able to determine if the man had smoked the opium just prior to taking his own life the night before or if this was but a discarded pipe from a previous session with the drug. A note in English on white writing paper rested beneath a flowered paperweight in the desk from which, it was speculated, the suicide jumped. That was the text of the poor dead man's lodgings that Inspector Field was, I am sure, preparing to read.

For the longest time, Field bent over the corpse looking hard into its empty eyes.

The corpse stared back wide-eyed, that silent scream contorting its face.

Field's right hand ran over the rope burns upon the corpse's neck. Their feel, evidently, caused him to scratch once, twice, speculatively, at the side of his eye.

Straightening up from his kneeling position, Field moved to the pipe, felt its bowl, examined its ashes. Returning it to exactly where he had found it, he next moved to the suicide note upon the desk. It was printed in block letters, not written in script. It was also unsigned. Taking it up, Field read aloud to the rest of us.

> I KILLED HER. HE MOURNS HER DEATH,
> AND REJECTS MY LOVE. WITHOUT HIM, I
> CAN NOT LIVE.

"My God!" Dickens exclaimed as Field finished reading. "He has committed suicide out of unrequited Sodomite love for Palmer. That is it. That *is* what it means, does it not?"

"This is no suicide," Field scoffed, handing the note over to Serjeant Rogers. " 'Ee didn't 'ang 'imself."

"What?" Now it was Dickens's turn to be perplexed. As for me, I was so utterly confused by all of it that my head was spinning and I felt as if I needed to sit down.

"Oh, 'ee 'ad plenty o' reason ta commit suicide." Field chuckled slyly at Dickens's consternation.

"But he did not commit suicide?" I expressed in my tone of voice both my skepticism at Field's chosen stance and my support for Dickens, whom Field's surprising declaration had momentarily unsteadied.

"No indeed, Mister Collins, 'ee did not." I could sense Field smugly poking fun at my imperception.

"Now just how do you know that?" I was quietly petulant, though trying my best to keep sarcasm out of my voice. Nothing seemed to bother Dickens. In fact, he seemed rather amused at this exchange between Field and me.

"Yes, enlighten us please, Inspector Field," Dickens chided him good-humouredly. "I can promise you that we shall prove a rapt audience for your instruction in the fine art of detectiving."

Field glanced at Dickens as if to say: *Aha! So the gentlemen are ready to listen to the facts, are they?* But he did not say it. Instead, he dwelt directly upon the ill-kept secrets of that text written in the signs there before us in Doctor Vasconcellas's room.

"One cannot speckalate as ta whether Doctor Rodrigo's twisted love for Doctor Palmer wos ever answered," Field began, "but one can speckalate that 'ee wos bein' blackmailed a'cause o' it."

"By whom?" Now Dickens was truly interested.

"Probly by Palmer, 'oo, it seems, wos the object o' that love. Per'aps by Dunn, 'oo 'ee may 'ave killed in order ta silence 'im, either consarnin' the murder o' the two wimmin or 'ee an' Dunn's sexual tendencies."

"What!" Again, it was Dickens's turn to be taken utterly by surprise by Field's pronouncement.

"We searched Dunn's room hin the cellar hov the theatre," Serjeant Rogers took this opportunity both to explain and to gloat that he was possessed of information to which Dickens and I were not privy, "hand his trunk wos full o' wimmin's dresses."

"Both men were Sodomites, it seems," Inspector Field took up the speculative narrative once again. "Perhaps both were

215

bein' blackmailed. In fact, if Palmer wos responsible for all this, they probly were bein' blackmailed by 'im. 'At's why Dunn lured Thompson inta the middle o' the murder. 'At's why Rodrigo in 'is cloak an 'ood played 'is ghostly game."

"But how can you be so sure he didn't commit suicide?" Dickens asked. "Perhaps he felt how close your investigation was getting to him, perhaps he despaired that he could escape justice for poisoning those two young women."

" 'Ee didn't poison those wimmin," Field insisted patiently, "an' 'ee didn't commit suicide."

"How . . . how can you be so sure?" Dickens persisted.

" 'Is eyes."

We all stared at Field, no one, not even Rogers, able to interpret that cryptic declaration. I, and the others, all looked down at the corpse. There seemed nothing unusual about its eyes. They were the wide-open, empty eyes of a dead man.

"An' 'is neck, an' thet note, an' this 'ole muddle o' a room."

"Please, I am at sea in all this," Dickens pleaded for explanation for all of us, even Rogers, who was equally adrift.

" 'Is eyes were wide open when I cut 'im down," Field explained patiently. "I've seen more than fifty 'angin's an' their eyes always roll all the way back in their 'eads when they choke. They don't bulge out an' stare at yew like this 'un does."

"He's right." Rogers leapt at this opportunity to toady. "Hafter the hangin's, the hundertakers has ta roll the hanged man's heyes hout with his finger. Hi've seen hem do hit."

"This 'un wos dead afore 'ee wos 'ung." Field took up the narrative again. " 'Is neck proves it."

We all bent to inspect the hanged man's neck, but I saw nothing out of the ordinary. No one else seemed to either. Like supplicants to some riddling Sphinx, we all turned back to Inspector Field.

"The rope burn"—he directed our attention with his commanding forefinger—" 'tis too narrow an' reg'lar. There's no wide rubbin' o' the sort yew git when a dyin' man struggles an' kicks on the end o' the rope.

"Hit's has hif he didn't fight hat hall." The light dawned in

216

Rogers's voice as if he were emerging from the Dark Ages. "Has hif he niver danced Jack Ketch's jig."

It certainly could have been more sensitively put, but Rogers's vulgar version struck a vivid image in the air and expressed what all the rest of us were thinking.

"An' then, lastly, there's the note," Field dangled his final lure of evidence before us.

"And what, pray tell," Dickens's voice dripped with sarcasm, "is wrong with the note? It certainly seems clear enough."

"Look 'ow 'tis written," Field prompted Dickens, who read the note through once more.

"I am sorry," Dickens did not pronounce those words as an apology, "but I do not see anything out of the ordinary in this note. He says he killed Palmer's wife. He admits to a Sodomite love for Palmer. He declares that he can not continue to live. That is all that it says."

" 'At's wot it says all right." Field chuckled. "But 'tis not wot it says but 'ow it says it which is important. Yew, a great writer, ought ta know that." Field could not resist ending with a friendly taunt.

Dickens threw up his hands in frustration: "What? I cannot see it, I'm sorry. What?"

"Look 'ow 'tis written." Field had become the patient teacher. "Is 'at the style o' a foreigner? Would the man yew interviewed at Bart's write such a note? The last sentence"— WITHOUT HIM I CAN NOT LIVE; we all looked at it over Roger's shoulder—"is inverted as a foreigner speakin' in an' unfamiliar tongue might, but the second sentence"—He mourns her death, and rejects my love, we all read it again—"words like *mourns* an' *rejects*, an' punchchooated jus' so, an' not inverted a'tall. Would a foreigner write like that?"

"You are absolutely right." Dickens's head was nodding up and down like one of the swinging ducks in Captain Hawkins's Shooting Gallery. " 'Tis all too neat, is it not?"

"An' wouldn't 'ee write 'is suicide note in Portuguee if Portuguee is the langwidge 'ee speaks?" Inspector Field was

217

but warming to his task. "An' why would 'ee print it in big letters like that, an' not in 'is own 'and. A'cause, like that 'tis in nobody's 'and. Those printed letters are unidentifiable. A suicidal man doesn't care if 'is 'andwritin' is recognised. 'Ee don't care about nothink, an' 'ee an't thinkin' straight either. This bloody note is jus' too bloody sane an' correct."

"So . . ." Dickens was thinking this all through as he went, "so what do you think really happened here, Field?"

"I'm not sure I know," Field admitted right away, but Dickens had offered Field the detective the opportunity to once again become Field the playwright, composer of bloody revenge tragedies in the Ford and Webster way,* and Field was not at all inclined to turn down that offer. "I think Palmer drugged 'im, then poisoned 'im, then 'ung 'im ta make it look like a suicide."

"It does look like, his face I mean, like that curious 'curare' death rictus which the others had," I interjected as they stalked the text of that corpse, that room.

"Yes, that is exactly wot bothers me the most." Field stared down at the stone face of the dead man. "If 'ee's a suicide, then all the Medusa Murders falls right inta line. But if 'ee's not a suicide, if 'ee's been poisoned too, then the book is still open on all o' this."

"But you are certain that this is not a suicide, are you not?" Dickens was puzzled, since Field had just offered four different arguments against suicide.

"Oh yes," Field assured us, "I bleeve this is murder . . . an' yew bleeve all my reasonin's on it, don'tchew?"

"Why, of course, why shouldn't we?" I was becoming more and more puzzled by the insecure turn our conversation was taking.

"Because it is all circumstantial, all too speculative upon Inspector Field's part," Dickens spoke slowly as if he had just

*John Ford is the author of *'Tis Pity She's a Whore* (1629) and John Webster wrote *The Duchess of Malfi* (1613).

218

realised the import of Field's dilemma. "This suicide ties everything up all clean and neat, does it not?"

" 'At's right!" Field tapped the desk against which he sat lightly with his demonstrative forefinger. "Yew *would* wear well in my line, Dickens!"

"What is so clean and neat?" I must admit that I was utterly confused. "Why do you still talk of this as suicide if you have ruled it out?"

"Because we cannot prove to a court, Wilkie, that it is not suicide," Dickens spoke like a great teacher's apt pupil instructing the class dunce. "Because Doctor Vasconcellas's death seemingly solves all."

"Don'tchew see, Mister Collins"—Field looked around in a kind of mild despair—"all the proof for solvin' yer Medusa Murders is right 'ere in this room, 'as been dropped right into our laps by this suicide. Evrythin' 'as been neatly tied up in a bow for us like the last chapter o' one o' Mister Dickens's three-decker novels. Only thing is, in the detectin' line, that an't the way it normal 'appens."

"He is right, Wilkie." Dickens had quickly picked up the resignation in Inspector Field's voice. "Suddenly, just with this suicide of Doctor Vasconcellas, all the questions seem answered, all the mysteries seem solved."

"Except you two do not believe any of it." I was beginning to understand.

"Except 'oo gits the money o' it all?" Field's voice was hard as saber steel.

"And who gets off free as the American colonies?" Dickens formed a chorus with Field.

"Palmer does," I answered their chorus of questions as if I had just been delivered the news by an angel.

"Aye, Palmer does," Field's voice had gone grim again. "Damn, 'ee's guilty an' we 'ave no way in Gawd's world o' provin' it."

THE FIRE-WOMAN

February 2, 1852—evening

As the snow melted and the faked suicide of Doctor Rodrigo Vasconcellas the Sodomite sank in, and was widely speculated upon in the most outlandish ways in the Grub Street broadsides, the whole case of the Medusa Murders seemed to hang fire. Two, three, four days passed. I made my daily pilgrimage to the *Household Words* office, but Dickens was possessed of no new intelligence on the case. Beyond that, however, he seemed uncharacteristically calm about it, not the least bit impatient or concerned that Field was not more aggressively pursuing it. It struck me as curious at the time, but I thought little about it. He would work calmly away for hours upon his new novel or the editing of the magazine, not jumping up to pace the room, not frantic for Field's summons, not the obsessive Dickens I had come to expect as this case had strengthened its hold upon him. Actually, I found not having to deal with his restless agitation rather restful and welcome. What I am sure of now, looking back, is that Dickens's calm in those intervening days was counterfeited, all for my consumption. I am certain that he was in conspiracy with Field on another aspect of the case that they did not wish me privy to. It comes clear to me now that Field did not want my interference in his next dangerous gambit, and thus had instructed Dickens to keep me in the dark.

All those around me were drifting out of character, it seemed. Irish Meg was also acting strange. As I look back upon it now, my reaction was predictably comic and irrational, reflective of all of my insecurities of that confusing time. Meg certainly was as ardent as always in her sexual attentions to me, as saucy as ever in her struttings in her secret things before me, yet she was also somewhat preoccupied. It was as if she was not telling me something, holding something back, afraid to tell me something, instructed not to tell me something, or just plain lying to me. In the grips of my sexual insecurity and possessiveness, I convinced myself that she had involved herself with another man. *She has grown impatient with all the interruptions and my absences on the case,* I feared, *and she has ventured out once again into the streets to seduce another. I have been detectiving too much with Dickens and Field,* I speculated.

She had, indeed, been acting strangely, but I, too, needed to get a grip upon my own runaway imagination. *Surely I am exaggerating all of this,* I told myself, and on the spot resolved to talk to Meg about our domestic life at the very first opportunity. But then, on the fifth day after Doctor Vasconcellas's supposed suicide, I returned to the flat in the evening . . . and she was gone.

I panicked. It was not a seemly thing to do, but I utterly broke down. I was sure she had left, ever a whore, run off with some whoremonger. I was, I realised, hopelessly in love with her, addicted to her.

Tossing all discretion to the winds, stammering like a love-sick schoolboy, I ran straight back to Dickens, begged his help, pleaded for him to intercede with Inspector Field on my behalf to find her.

Dickens took it with such a preternatural calm that I should have been suspicious. If I had not been so muddled and upset, I surely would have thought his reaction strange. But it utterly escaped me as I struggled in the throes of my anxiety. Dickens could not imagine where she had gone, he assured me. "We must get Field to find her," I implored. Finally he acquiesced, and the two of us set off for Bow Street.

It was as if Field knew that we were coming to see him that night. He was waiting in the outer room of the station house. He did not usher us directly into the bullpen as was his usual courtesy. Equally strange was his attentiveness to me. He hardly noticed Dickens's presence when we arrived. It was "Mister Collins, 'ow good ta see yew," and Rogers, not sullen at all as was his usual attitude, helped me out of my greatcoat and hung it on a peg. I was, however, too distracted to notice these solicitous departures from their usual habit of ignoring my presence. From the moment we entered the station house and I spied Field, I was upon him with my fears for Irish Meg's disappearance. With a knowing glance Dickens's way, he brought me up short.

"She 'as not disappeared, Mister Collins." His crook'd forefinger scratched at the side of his eye preparatory to his hand moving, quite fatherly, around my shoulder. "She's a good lass, that Meggy, she is," he confided. "Now yew wouldn't mind 'er comin' back on duty for Inspector Field, would yew now?"

I did not know how to answer. I was too tossed by the frantic workings of my own mind to really understand what he was saying. I looked to Dickens for help. None was forthcoming. He merely grinned, somewhat sheepishly, and shrugged. I looked back to Field who was smiling as solicitously as a coffin merchant. Rogers stood beside him, smug as a cat who had just dined on a pigeon. It was a strange, passive kind of torture they were inflicting upon me.

They were waiting for my answer. But what was the question? Something about Meggy working for Field.

I certainly did not know how to answer. What I did know

223

was that I could never presume to answer for Irish Meg. Stupidly, I stared at the lot of them, uncomprehending.

It became awkward after a moment.

"Why don'tchew come in," Field ushered me toward the bullpen. "I wants yew ta meet some'un." He opened the door and stepped aside, motioning politely for me to enter before him. I was looking back over my shoulder at the assembled company as I passed through the door, thus I did not see her immediately. They were all acting so strange, so smug. It puzzled me. But their behaviour was nothing compared to the shock I experienced when I turned my head back before me as I walked into the room.

The fire was blazing in the hearth as always. The easy chairs were pulled up to the heat as always. The gin bottle sat on the small table as always. Rude snoring sounds came from the holding cages as always. But in the midst of all that everyday reality stood this apparition, this goddess of beauty and wealth. She stood before the hearth, the firelight flickering behind her, in a rich blue day gown with a white lace bodice that reached up like a churchman's collar to encircle her neck. Her rich dark hair was coiffed in a mob of wild ringlets, which cascaded around her face, caught the orange glow, and blazed out as the light from the fire behind burned through it. A diamond pendant shone against the white skin of her throat. Her dark eyes flashed above the slashes of pink that were her cheekbones and the fiery circle of red that was her mouth. It was, of course, Irish Meg, my fire-woman, standing there, once again, before that very Bow Street blaze where I had first laid eyes upon her. My heart leapt in relief, in surprise, in love, in an irrational jumble of emotions quite beyond any talent I might possess to describe.

"Meggy!" I cried out, and ran into her arms.

"Oh Wilkie, I loves yew." She crushed me in her desperate embrace. "But I 'ad ta git out o' those rooms. I owes Fieldsy this much, don't I? Pleese let me do this."

Still I was confused. She looked once again like the fine lady that Dickens had, as a joke, dressed her up as for the Queen's

224

performance of *Not So Bad As We Seem** the previous April. Holding her closely, I caught a stiff movement off over her shoulder. Tally Ho Thompson, dressed as the Irish gentleman on horseback whom I had seen through Field's monocular five days before, was rising from one of the overstuffed wing chairs.

I stepped one step back from her embrace, resting my hands on the white lace of her shoulders. The firelight played in her dark Medusa curls. The fire of her power over me burned in her eyes. She was my *belle dame sans merci* and I her hapless, hopeless knight, utterly confused by this violent collision between love and independence within the charmed circle of our arms.

"Meggy, what are you doing here?" I stammered. "Dressed like, like . . . this. My God, you are so beautiful." I pulled her back into the protection of my arms as if I could hide her beauty from all the others bent to prey upon it.

"Fieldsy said yew'd niver let me do it, Wilkie. 'Ee said I couldn't tell yew 'til 'twas all done."

"He swore me to that same secrecy," Dickens interceded on her behalf like some Lincoln's Inn solicitor.

"Do what? Tell me what?" I felt as if they were spinning me in some dizzying game of blindman's buff.

"I'm ta be an Irish hairuss," Meg stepped back and curtsied, quite proud of herself. "Miss Megan Theresa Gilbride come up ta see London."

"An I'm 'er neer-do-well rake o' a brother 'Arry"—Thompson stepped up beside her and bent in an actor's bow—"rider o' fast 'orses an' fixed on gamblin' away 'is 'ole in'eritance. I ben schoolin' Meggy on the brogues the actors at Covent Garden spout."

*Collins' first memoir (or secret journal) ends with this scene of Dickens' amateur performance of Bulwer-Lytton's play before the Queen. As a joke on Collins, Dickens had dressed Irish Meg, Scarlet Bess, and Tally Ho Thompson up as gentlefolk and seated them in the midst of the Queen and her court.

"What?" I looked from one to the other of them as if they were mad.

"They are our bait"—Field spun me around once more—"our last chance ta bring Palmer out. There is no real plan. Thompson 'as set up a race with 'im, will gamble with 'im. Meggy will try ta seduce 'im, weaken 'im with liquor. All in 'opes 'ee will say or do somethin', anythin' which will give us a leg up on this case."

"Bait? Seduce?" I was burbling like a village idiot.

"You see, Wilkie"—Dickens tried to pacify me—"we knew you would not take it well." He was actually making a small joke of it. The others grinned tentatively, waiting for my reaction.

"Not take it well," I huffed. "How dare you? She could be killed. Meggy"—I took her hand, begging now—"this is not a game. This could be dangerous."

"Tally 'O will be there. Yew will be close by." She was determined to go through with it; I could tell by the set of her voice. "I've 'andled men in rougher 'ouses than some posh ridin' club in 'Ampstead." She laughed weakly, turning to the others for support.

"She will niver be out o' Thompson's sight." Field tried to calm me with his organisation. "Yew an' Dickens will be right on the premises yerselfes the day o' the race."

"Good God! He's killed two women already." It was a last spasm of resistance on my part. They outnumbered me. Meggy wanted to do it, to prove something—God knows what!—to herself, perhaps to me, that I didn't own her, that I couldn't keep her closed up in my Soho rooms with no employment other than our domestic entertainments. As I look back upon it now, that was the sum of it for her. She was proclaiming one of Burton's territorial imperatives, a woman letting her man know what her boundaries (and his) were. But, at the time, all I could see was the danger of it; all I could feel was the fear that I might lose her. She was an addiction I clung to like an opium smoker to his pipe.

"It's jus' for one night." Field knew already that he had

won. Now he was only palliating me. "I wants ta see if our Doctor Palmer is on the lookout for new money in the way o' a wife."

"Tally 'O's an actor now. Yew two go onstage in Mister Dickens's plays." Meg was beaming at the fun of it. "Now's my chance ta be an actress too."

"The play's the thing, eh mate?" Thompson clapped me on the shoulder and I recoiled from his presumptuous familiarity. "We thought o' my Bess, but she don't keep 'er 'ead the way Meggy does, an't the actress Meggy is, don't play the rich bitch near as well."

Meggy beamed at his compliments, looked at me doelike then mischievous. *Give it up, luv. Let me 'ave me fun,* she was telling me with her eyes and the coy pursing of her mouth. She knew I would do whatever she asked. I do not know why they all even bothered. Wilkie Collins, convenient doormat, ever ready to follow his masters and do their mad, heedless bidding. I vowed that someday I would rebel against my role as pawn in the risky gambits of Dickens and Field, but, alas, this was clearly not that day.

"All is in readiness, Wilkie." Dickens, in his enthusiasm for their outlandish plan, had nonchalantly cast aside the main issue, that of Irish Meg's participation. "I have imposed upon young Jekyll to invite us to view the match race. Spectators can double back upon the course in their carriages."

"An' I 'ave reserved rooms for meself, me sister, an' me 'orse at the 'Ounds Club the night afore the race." Thompson was veritably brimming with the whimsy of it. " 'At's when we makes our run at Palmer."

"An' Rogers an' I shall stay close, we will," Field assured me.

They were all mad. It was a contagion that Thompson spread like some plague carrier spitting death across Europe. My consternation, my skepticism, must have shown in my face because they all looked at me as if I were a ghost at the banquet table, putting a damper on their fun.

"I admit," Field went on the defensive, tried to answer the

skepticism he had read in my mien, "that I 'old little 'ope that Palmer will break down an' confess or lead us ta the poison or 'and over any new evidence on which we can bring 'im ta justice. But we 'ave no witnesses"—this was, indeed, an argument of desperation—"an' I am determined ta follow through, ta try ta entrap 'im, ta lead 'im ta contemplate yet another murder for gain. If 'ee is greedy, we can git 'im."

It was a long speech for Field, the apologia of a man brought to the end of his tether. Ridiculous as it may seem, I felt sorry for him.

"I'm ridin' this road ta its end," Thompson unexpectedly declared—serious, for God's sake!—his jaw set, his heedless jokester's grin nowhere to be found, "a'cause she wos a good lass." None of us had ever experienced this grim, vengeful version of Tally Ho Thompson before.

"What?" I was startled by Thompson's intensity.

"Who?" Meggy's hands went to her hips like a governess about to punish her charge.

"Just what do you mean by that?" Dickens was bursting with curiosity.

"She wos a good lass." Thompson shrugged. "Palmer's wife."

"Wot do yew know about Palmer's wife?" Field glared at him. "Yew said yew only took 'er ridin' once or twice."

Dickens looked at me, raising his eyebrows and rolling his eyes in one of those "well that's odd" looks. It was me who had, for the sheer contrariness of it, speculated that there was more to Thompson's involvement with the late Missus Palmer than merely the horse riding.

Thompson closed up like a Portsmouth clam, but Inspector Field was having none of that.

"Jus' wot are yew sayin', Thompson?" Field had that murderous look of the night streets upon him again. *This is no longer a game,* that look announced. Field did not like his familiars withholding anything from their master. Suddenly that powerful right hand leapt out and clasped the lapel of Thompson's foppish red riding coat. "Tell it, all o' it, yew 'ear, or I'll clap yew back inta Newgate so fast the streets won't even know yer gone."

"She wos a good lass. I liked 'er." Thompson hesitated.

Field let go of the front of Thompson's coat, but, with a scratch of his crook'd forefinger to the side of his eye, ordered our somewhat rattled highwayman to "go on with it, the 'ole tale."

Thompson stretched his hesitation with a quick guilty glance at Meg.

Field was exhibiting miraculous patience. I expected him, at any moment, to lunge for his knobbed stick and begin beating the confession out of Thompson.

Myself, Meg, Dickens, that stupid Rogers, we all stared wide-eyed at Tally Ho Thompson, waiting like greedy gossips in the tea-tent on Market Day.

The veins in Field's neck began to bulge and I think Thompson realised that he had no choice but to confess.

"She said 'er 'usband 'ated 'er. Said 'ee didn't even live with 'er, loved 'is 'orses more," Thompson began in apologia. "I felt sorry for the lass. We 'ad this one time together, 'at wos all."

"Yew slept with 'er!" Irish Meg was all shocked propriety and matronly rage. It was really quite comical, considering.

"Yew mussn't tell Bess." Now Thompson was the desperate man pleading for understanding. "I felt sorry for 'er. 'Er 'ole family wos in the country an' they thought Palmer a good match despite the stiff dowry. Business people at Henley they are. An' 'ee beat 'er, she said that. She wanted some'un jus' ta prove she wos alive. We went ta a 'otel on 'Eyde Park. I'd niver been ta 'er 'ouse," he said that last as if he thought that Field might still suspect him of murdering her. "I only slept with 'er that once. 'At's why I niver went back ta ride with 'er. 'Twas not the play kept me away. Yew see . . . I luvs Bess, in my way."

Tally Ho Thompson was, indeed, a marvel. For all of his talent, his looseness, his maddening heedless view of the world and life as some comical careening game, there was this powerful instinctive rightness about him. Dickens and I have

229

more than once laughed as we referred to our highwayman, actor, womaniser, thief of a friend as one of the truly "honest" men of our acquaintance, a sort of Robin Hood "honesty" that always seems to do the right thing no matter how at odds with conventional thinking it may be.

A DEVIL'S WAGER

February 3, 1852—night

"All our interviews tells us 'ee luvs ta gamble an' 'ee 'ates ta lose." Field was referring to Palmer on the eve of that desperate endgame by which he hoped to trap his prey. It occurred to me that he might, as well, have been describing himself. Inspector Field, through the many years I have observed him ply the detective's art, has always been a stolid man who refused to give up. Even though all of his witnesses to murder were dead, even though all of the evidence of the case pointed to Rodrigo the Spaniard, Field remained determined to pursue Palmer, to expose the poisonous truth. No wonder Dickens was so relentlessly drawn to the man. William Field was a veritable avenging angel who, indeed, loved to gamble and hated to lose, and he was down to the turning of his final cards, his stake riding upon my Meggy and Tally Ho Thompson.

They had taken up their residence that afternoon as brother and sister, rich young Irish gentry, in adjoining rooms at the Hampstead Hounds Club. While Thompson

231

had busied himself seeing to the accommodations of his horse and the preparations for the match race the next day, Meg had prepared herself for the seductive drama of the evening. Though I was not present, both Thompson and Meggy told their versions of their little play to Inspector Field within my and Dickens's hearing. Thus, I am satisfied that, curious as you, dear reader, will find it to be, it actually did happen in precisely this way.

They all sat down to dine in the private salon of the club just after eight. Palmer knew Thompson as Harold Aloysius Gilbride of the County Cork Gilbrides and called him affectionately, as one always treats one's pigeons, "young Harry." My Meggy was introduced that evening as Harry's sister, Megan Theresa Gilbride. Thompson, to all evidence, convincingly passed them off as an extremely rich Irish brother and sister off together on the first leg of their Grand Tour.* Being the heir to one of the largest farms and finest, though modest, racing stables in Ireland, young Harry Gilbride never travelled anywhere without his racer, Magillicuddy, a sleek bay who, he consistently bragged, "niver balks an' kin outrun the divvil on summer's 'ottest day." Guiliano, the Italian tout, was also in attendance, but certainly not earning any retainer upon which Palmer obviously kept him. Cut from whole cloth out of Inspector Field's fictive imagination, the Gilbride-Farms-and-Stables fiction, which a truly knowledgeable trackman would surely have questioned, was swallowed whole by Guiliano. Two other men joined them, card players, horse gamblers, a young Lord Billy Buckler and an aging roue Mister Robert Patten of Fleet Street. Five men and my Meggy dining in that private salon in that men's hunting club out

---

*The "Grand Tour" was a coming-of-age tradition of the Victorian era. Young, rich gentlemen, and some heiresses, regularly took a year-long tour of Europe during which they experienced firsthand all of the great art, historical sites, architectural wonders, and cultural entertainments as well as drinking, gambling, and whoring their way through the Continent's brothels and casinos. For an Irish heir and heiress, London would naturally be the first stop on the Grand Tour.

there on that blasted heath—and Dickens and Field raised their eyebrows at my lack of enthusiasm for their little play!

When Meggy described the way she dressed for her role and how she chose to play it, it convinced me all the more that I never should have allowed her to be cast in Field's heedless little drama. "The gown wos shiny brown satin cut verry low 'round me bubs, but with these wonderful little puff sleeves," Meggy gushed like a schoolgirl. "An' dimond earrings an' a pendant 'round me neck, only pastework I knows, but Lord did they sparkle."

"We decided ta play the scene incestlike," Thompson took up the story as I shot a stiletto look at Meggy.

"Oh it wos so nasty the way I 'ung on me deer brother," Meggy said as she laughed. I know she was just saying it to taunt me and make me jealous, to titillate the whole company listening to their tale there in the bullpen after it was all over.

"After the supper wos cleared off, we set in at cards," Thompson went on, "an' Meggy sat on the arm o' me chair an' played with me 'air an' ran 'er 'and o'er me neck, pettin' me like a 'ousecat."

At that, I shot another angry glance at Irish Meg. She raised her eyebrows and moistened her lips with her tongue, mocking me.

"All o' it wos done for Palmer's sake," Meg cut in upon Thompson's too-elegant narrative. " 'Ee wos drinkin' away with 'is racetrack friends an' losin' money ta Tally 'O on nearly evry 'and. It wos only a matter o' time 'til 'ee started lookin' ta me for a toss."

"It wos when we were pretendin' ta be drunk an' she put 'er tongue in me ear as I wos playin' a 'and that she really got 'is attention." Thompson was getting a bit carried away, for my blood, in his enthusiasm for the artistry of their performance. In fact, I sorely longed to strangle him, and then poison Field with the cheap gin we were drinking.

"The gyme wos dwindlin' down. A couple o' the players gone off ta bed drunk—" Meggy took up the narrative— "when Doctor Palmer turns ta the sex part."

" 'Yew an yer sister seems quite close,' 'ee says ta me,"
Thompson mimicked him. "Feigning drunk, I tips ol' Palmer
a wink an' runs me 'and up me lovin' sister's arm. 'Closer'n
any brother an' sister ever been,' I laughs an' tips 'im another
dirty wink."

"Besides the hundred pounds we have placed on the race,"
Palmer, though tipsy, said quite seriously, "would you be
interested in a gentleman's side wager?"

"Wot sort o' side wager?" Thompson was curious.

"Because I must ride my best against you, I will retire and
sleep soundly this night," Palmer began, "but tomorrow
night will be an altogether different matter."

I've got 'im! Meg thought as she subdued her elation.

"So?" Thompson coaxed.

"My horse if I lose"—Palmer smiled evilly at them both—
"against a full night abed if I win."

"Yew wants me ta bet me sister against yer 'orse?" Thompson feigned offense.

"No, not at all"—Palmer glanced in amusement from
Thompson to Meggy and back—"it is you I want in bed,
young Harry, not her. She may watch if she wishes, but it is
you I hope to win. Are you prepared to make that wager?"

"Prepared!" After, retelling the story to all of us in the
bullpen, Thompson actually jumped up and paced nervously
before the hearth. "I wish I coulda seen the look on me own
face when 'ee proposed that little bet. I looked at Meg an' she
looked like she'd jus' been jilted by the Prince o' Wales."

"I wos surprised, thet's all," Irish Meg defended herself.

"Surprised," Thompson teased her, "yew were madder 'n a
scorned tart."

"I wos a scorned tart, yew jack-a-muffin." Meg laughed.
"Yew should o' seen the look on yer pip. 'Ee looked like"—
Meg turned grinning to the rest of us—"an insulted virgin,
'ee did; like 'ee wos searchin' the room for a chastity belt ta
lock 'imself into."

Even Thompson had to laugh at that characterisation of his
own recoil at Palmer's proposition.

"Meg saved the day on that jolter," Thompson went on with his narrative. "I didn't know wot ta say. Meg's right. I wos shocked. Right off she starts laughin' at the two o' us, tauntin' me. 'Wot's the matter, sweet brother?' she jibes me. 'Yew'd not balk at puttin' me up against 'is 'orse. Are we afraid ta wager our own arse?' At that, both Palmer an' Meggy 'ad a good roar at my expense."

"Finally Tally 'O chimes in," Meg took up the story. " 'Yer serious,' 'ee says ta Palmer. 'Never more,' Palmer says back, caught up in the hilarity o' it. 'Done then!' says Tally 'O. 'Yer the one ta be done in more ways than one,' says Palmer as 'ee trundles 'imself off ta bed."

"An' 'at's it." Thompson shrugged, indicating the end of their story. "Palmer's a boy-boy jus' like Dickie Dunn an' our dead Spaniard. That oughta be worth sumpin'."

" 'Ee's more than that." Irish Meg was no longer laughing at the oddness of their story. " 'Ee's a woman 'ater, 'ee is. Yew could see it in 'is eyes when 'ee looked at me there in that card room. 'Ee wouldn't think twice about killin' 'is wife. 'Ee 'ates wimmin."

"I've seen 'im come in off the 'eath after a ride." Thompson, too, had become reflective. " 'Ee'd ridden 'is 'orse shameful. The animal wos all foamed, its sides bloody with spurrin' welts, wobbly on its legs from the whippin'. 'Ee's the kind 'oo rides a 'orse 'til it drops, then jus' climbs on another an' rides it ta death too."

"Mebbe 'at's 'ow 'ee treats 'is wives," Inspector Field murmured.

"It is akin to everything else these days." It was Dickens's turn to add his somber comment upon the fallen human condition. "One cannot tell what is real or true just by looking at it. There are hidden secret things"—my eyes flashed to Meg's and she caught me in my guilty look—"beneath all of the appearances that we all put up."

" 'Ow bloody true 'at is." Meg gave her crooked little grin.

Not one of us disagreed with her. To do so would have been as hypocritical as casting the first stone.

TALLY HO!

February 4, 1852—morning

T he day of the match race broke sunny and chill. Nothing, however, could have been colder than Inspector Field's resolve to confront Doctor William Palmer with the four murders that had fueled this investigation.

"He is counting upon Palmer losing control." Dickens, ever analytic and motive-conscious, appraised Field's plan as we rode in Sleepy Rob's cab toward our rendezvous on Hampstead Heath. "His only hope is to drive Palmer into some incriminating act or some imprudent admission," Dickens argued. I could not help but think that it was a somewhat hollow hope.

Field and Rogers, busy with their spyglass, were waiting for us in the black Bow Street post chaise in the meadow of Jack Straw's Castle at the top of the heath. Greeting us enthusiastically when we reined in, Field was uncharacteristically expansive and metaphoric. "Today we write the final chapter of this novel of murder, ring down the final curtain on our little play," he said. Clearly, he had been spending far too much time with Dickens.

Through the spyglass, we observed that preparations for the race were already afoot on the grounds of the Hampstead Hounds Club. At half after ten, resplendent in his red riding coat, Tally Ho Thompson marched out to commune with his horse. Minutes later, appearing no worse for wear from his card-playing and imbibing of port the night before, Palmer appeared, gotten up in an all-black riding habit and black boots to match. His dress formed a fitting ensemble to the unbroken glower of his dark black eyebrows. He and Thompson greeted one another cordially enough and proceeded together into the stables. When my turn with the glass came round, I quickly scanned the porches, fenced rings, and walkways of the club for any glimpse of Irish Meg, but was disappointed. As the sun moved toward eleven of the clock, she had not yet put in an appearance out of doors. Needless to say, her whereabouts were to me the most worrisome aspect of what Field and Dickens called their "little play."

Dickens had made arrangements to meet Doctor Jekyll at the club at eleven. That young worthy's arrival in a hansom proved the next noteworthy event to be observed through the glass.

"It is time. We must go," Dickens announced to Field. "Jekyll is on the premises."

"Rogers an' I will follow yew down." Field startled Dickens with this announcement.

"Surely you are not going to confront the man in his own club before the race, before Thompson reveals his true identity?" Dickens was visibly thrown by Field's revision of their play. "I thought you were going to observe the race from a point of vantage on the course and then move in when Thompson confronts Palmer with the murders."

"Plans change." Field seemed quite cavalier about it.

"Hour presence will put hadded pressure hupon him," Rogers explained the new plan's rationale as if *he* had devised it and we were two dim dolts deserving of his patronisation.

Dickens did not challenge Field. I could tell, however, that he was not particularly comfortable with this new turn of the

238

screw. "Sometimes too much pressure upon a guilty or criminal mind produces an utterly unpredictable reaction," Dickens, talking more to himself than to me, muttered in Sleepy Rob's cab as we trundled down the hill toward the racing club. Field had agreed to stay back a few minutes to allow Dickens and I time to make our excuses for our being there to Palmer. All felt it best that we establish a nonthreatening presence before Field challenged him with the arrival of the Metropolitan Protectives upon the scene.

When Dickens and I disembarked from our cab and rounded the corner of the club building on the walkway to the stable yard, I saw Palmer glance toward us then snap his head upward on alert as recognition flooded in. It was immediately evident that he was unhappy with Dickens's presence, but he said not a word as Jekyll and Dickens greeted one another. Smiling idiotically, Dickens offered some inanity about "what a superior winter's day for a horserace, is it not?"

"Indeed it is," Jekyll answered, turning with a smile from Dickens to the group composed of Palmer, Thompson, and Irish Meg (to my great relief!), and two men in coarse tweed coats who looked to be stablemen cashiered to double as race officials.

Palmer simply glowered at Jekyll's cheerfulness and turned back to his conversation with the others. He offered not so much as a rudimentary polite acknowledgement of Dickens and I. What Dickens did next, I am absolutely certain he did out of pure spite for Palmer's snub.

"Ah," Dickens said in a voice rather louder than it needed to be, "here is Inspector Field of the Metropolitan Protectives come to observe the race with us. Where did you say would be our most profitable point of vantage, Jekyll?" For one who but moments before had expressed nervousness concerning Field's decision to intrude precipitously upon the scenario, he certainly had changed his tune.

Dickens's clearly enunciated comment snapped Palmer's head around once again. The good doctor's hooded eyes beneath that black brow watched the sharp-hatted, heavysticked, bullnecked detective stride up the walk with his hunting hound Rogers at heel.

Dickens shook hands fawningly with Inspector Field and, conveniently forgetting the personal snub of only a few moments before, turned with great relish to introduce Field to Doctor Palmer: "Inspector Field . . . Doctor Palmer. The doctor is one of the contestants in this race that I have told you about."

Palmer stepped forward and extended his hand, which was uncommon steady, Field noted later, for a man who had murdered four people. "I have heard your name." Palmer seemed under complete control. "You are pursuing my wife's murderer, I believe. I wish you luck."

Field bowed silently.

I did not know whether to take Palmer's words as a mere statement of recognition or as a challenge.

"This is Harry Gilbride, my opponent in the race," Palmer, out of politeness, introduced Tally Ho Thompson.

"Yew look passin' familiar, yew do." Field, with a twinkle in his eye, shook hands with the young gentleman.

"I fear I have not yet made the acquaintance o' the English police"—young Harry laughed—"only the Irish constables in County Cork."

"We must see to the horses," Palmer growled and stalked abruptly off to the barn. Young Harry of Ireland followed, cheerily tossing a wink to Field as he went.

All of the preparations for the race were complete. The course would begin and end in the stable yard of the Hounds Club. The two riders would take off down a chute formed by the white fences of the club which fed into the forest bridlepath. After a rather short curving run of two turns through the trees, they would emerge upon the open heath, and race straightaway to the base of Downshire Hill where they would circle the Druid's Oak and race back to their starting point. As Guiliano the tout described the course to us spectators, the grooms led out the horses, already saddled, from the barn. The two principals, talking, walked behind their mounts. All

240

seemed quite congenial; amateur sport contested among gentlemen.

Palmer's horse was a strapping black, rippling power through its shoulders. Tally Ho Thompson's mount was a sinewy bay with flaring nostrils. It looked the epitome of run. We found out later that this horse, bearing the pseudonym Macgillicuddy, was really Allie's Skin (remember that Tally Ho Thompson's Christian name was, indeed, Aloysius— something he shall never be allowed to forget), and had been Thompson's mount when he was haunting the night roads round Shooter's Hill. Allie's Skin had been maintained by that worthy in the stables at the Spaniard's Inn ever since he had left the profession to take up acting in the city. Thompson may have given up being a highwayman for a while (actually well over two years), but he had never given up his horse.

The horses were led out of the barn snorting and skittish, as if they knew full well what they were in for. The big black pawed the dirt angrily while the bay tossed its head like a child eager to play. In the chill winter air, their breaths exhaled in short, smoky plumes as if they were steam engines stoking up for their mad dash into the English countryside.

All of the spectators gathered in the club's yard were either mounting up on their own horses or climbing into their carriages to take up points of vantage along the course in order to better view the race. My Meggy was of a party in a large open carriage. Said party was made up of a number of male members of the club who, I learned later, were also the cardplayers of the evening before. Young Jekyll, on horseback, directed Dickens and I in Sleepy Rob's cab, followed by Field and Rogers in the black post chaise, to a position atop a small hillock at about the midway point of the course overlooking the first straightaway (which, after the turn around the Druid's Oak, would be the home stretch). From that point of vantage, we could watch as the riders emerged from their gallop through the trees to ride full out down the heath and back.

A pistol crack!

241

From our hilltop perch we knew the race was on. Long moments passed as we strained to catch a glimpse of the riders through the trees. Then, suddenly, the two horses, neck and neck, their riders poised forward, knees up in the high stirrups, heads buried in the rushing manes, burst out of the skeletal grey forest and thundered onto the heath.

Palmer, on the surging black, held the slightest of leads, a stride at most. He flourished his whip to the back in his right hand and flogged his horse's flank with a mad intensity. Tally Ho Thompson, hand riding his mount, glided easily across the hard ground just off the black's shoulder. He carried no whip and seemed to talk to his horse as they went. For some reason, I knew—felt, I guess—that Thompson was holding the bay in, keeping the race close, riding comfortably at Palmer's breakneck pace. I found out later that, indeed, the reason for Thompson riding so close for so long at Palmer's pace was so that he could talk to him, badger him I should say, during their gallop. He kept the bay in close on his prey so that he could easily exchange words.

Thompson revealed his identity and openly accused Palmer of poisoning his wife and did it while they were still racing through the trees. As they burst out of the trees, Thompson was describing how he had slept with Palmer's dead wife and how, when naked in bed, she had repeatedly denounced the doctor to him as a faithless husband and a compulsive gambling man. Many of the ensuing events of this chase over the heath I witnessed for myself, for we were always close at hand. For some of the more intimate details, however, I am forced to rely upon the somewhat questionable account of Tally Ho Thompson. For example, as they rushed breakneck through that wood, was Thompson really taunting Palmer with his cuckolding? Thompson laughs and claims he did. Whatever the truth, whatever Thompson did, indeed, say, he turned the good doctor into a frothing madman.

Bursting out of the wood and coursing down the heath toward us, Palmer ceased beating his horse's flank with the whip and took a vicious cut at Thompson. He raked Thomp-

242

son across the cheek just below the eye and sent that worthy sidesprawling out over his horse's haunch. Miraculously, Thompson managed to stay on and right himself in the stirrups as his horse, sensing his rider's distress, yawed away from the fierce black. That intuitive bit of communication between horse and rider allowed Thompson to regain his seat.

"Drive after 'em, Serjeant!" Inspector Field, witnessing Palmer's sudden attack upon our man, shouted the order to Rogers.

Rogers, however, was not quite ready to the task. He was in the process of making water behind the post chaise's rear wheel when the race had commenced and, though rushing to finish, was not quite buttoned up when Field's order came.

"After them, Rob," Dickens ordered at the same moment, "he needs our help." Much to my personal astonishment and, I am sure, to the others as well, Sleepy Rob, who seemed to be perpetually dozing in the box, reacted much more alertly than that supercilious martinet, Rogers. As the two riders streaked across the heath, kicking up dirt and loose stones at every plunge, riding the whirlwind, Sleepy Rob whipped his horse into motion and sent our cab careening down the hill in close pursuit. Rogers was just pulling himself back up into the box of the post chaise as we clattered by.

Aright in the saddle once again, Tally Ho Thompson gave his bounding bay its head and urged it back into the pursuit. That racer caught Palmer's black beast with barely an effort. Thompson's horse was a runner all right; what a pity this was no longer a race!

The two riders came abreast of us spectators at the moment we rumbled down the hill toward the bridlepath. They thundered by in a blur like the Brighton train. Sleepy Rob whipped us in close behind them, but they, just as quickly, at full gallop, pulled away. From behind, I watched the riders rushing side by side. I could see, or perhaps I even imagined that I could hear, Thompson screaming at the enraged doctor. The two horses, whether at the physical command and control of their riders or not I cannot say, suddenly lugged

243

together, bumping in the rutted, weather-pocked path, almost unseating both riders. In fact, all control seemed slipping away.

Palmer recovered with malignant intent. Realising that Thompson was once again within reach, he struck out fiercely with his riding crop.

For this blow, however, Thompson was prepared. He parried it with his upraised forearm and ducked under Palmer's down-slashing return. Not waiting for Palmer to strike out again, Tally Ho turned the obedient bay sharply in to bump the black. At the precise moment of contact, Thompson launched himself out of the stirrups and onto Palmer's back. The momentum of this leap carried both men off of the rushing horse's back and landed them atop one another in the brown scrub of the winter heath.

By this time, we had fallen back behind the riders at least ten coach lengths, but I could still see the astonishing physical exchanges of these two men even as they were racing along on horseback. I was having trouble staying upright next to Dickens in Rob's cab as we careened down that rutted path in the wake of the racing horses.

When we rumbled up to them, Thompson and Palmer were grappling on the ground. With a lunge, Palmer rolled away from his antagonist and was reaching inside his riding coat as he came up onto his feet. When his hand emerged from beneath that black waistcoat, it held a miniature twin-barreled pistol. I saw it all unfold from the window of our cab as if time had slowed and the whole scene were a painted tableau. The squat little gun came out in Palmer's hand and was murderously leveled at Thompson, who was scrambling up off the ground. It was then that a most extraordinary thing happened, a surprise for which none of us was prepared.

There was a mad, utterly inhuman hate twisting in Palmer's face as he prepared to pull the triggers of his ugly little gun and blow twin holes in Tally Ho Thompson. He looked like Satan brought to earth. Sleepy Rob must have seen that hateful look; perhaps it frightened him into action; who knows?

244

Nonetheless, he moved more quickly than he had ever moved before, awoke from his sleep of ages. Jumping to his feet in the box, he twirled his cabman's whip once around his head in a wide arc in the air and lashed out at Palmer's outstretched arm where that small pistol sat like a venomous toad ready to spew forth its bile. Deftly the long lash of his whip snaked 'round Palmer's wrist and snapped back hard. Palmer's outstretched hand flew wildly up and both barrels discharged harmlessly into the air in twin puffs of grey smoke.

Thompson's eyes had gone wide at the sight of the gun. Momentarily, he had turned to stone with his hands out in a pacifying gesture as he stared into those twin barrels. But once this aid struck in from that unexpected source and Palmer was disarmed, Thompson did not hesitate. He charged toward the doctor, driven by rage at the lethal threat that the gun had presented.

Palmer, however, recovered sufficiently to evade Thompson's blind, headlong charge with an adept sidestep. Then, choosing flight as the better part of valour, he turned tail and ran for his black horse, which was grazing unconcernedly just up the rutted path.

Thompson took after him, but was not quick enough. Before he could be stopped, Palmer had leapt into the stirrups and was putting his spurs to his mount.

It was precisely at this moment that the Bow Street post chaise stormed up and reined in.

" 'Alt for the Protectives!" Field shouted from the carriage, but Palmer paid him no heed.

Wrenching the black beast's head around and spurring him hard, Palmer rode straight at the onrushing Thompson, tried to ride right over him, flailed at him once more with his whip, succeeded in bumping Thompson hard with his horse's haunch as he coursed by.

Thompson's agility saved his life. He was, however, neither quick enough nor agile enough to totally avoid Palmer's murderous charge. He was bowled over, knocked sideways onto his back on the frozen ground. Though but a glancing blow

245

from the rump of the charging horse, it felled Thompson utterly, leaving him dazed and incapacitated in the frosted grass.

Seeing Thompson go down, Palmer reined in hard, yanking back so brutally on that black beast's head that the terrified thing reared straight up upon its hind legs. Palmer sat the rearing horse like a wide-eyed devil and, when the black returned all four legs to earth, turned him full around to make another run at the downed Thompson.

Hesitating not an instant, Dickens leapt out of our cab and ran willy-nilly in front of the wheeling horse, Daniel right into the den. Screeching and waving his arms, he taunted the black-browed devil: "You killed her for the money, did you not Palmer? You killed them all, did you not?"

As I look back upon it now, it was an ingenious attempt upon Dickens's part. That was the question Inspector Field needed answered. Dickens confronted the man with that crucial question at precisely the moment of the man's ultimate derangement. Though they were behind me in the post chaise, and I did not, in the fury of the moment, look to see what they were doing, I am sure that Field and Rogers were straining to hear Palmer's reply, hoping for some ill-considered confession.

"Damn you all!" Palmer cursed as the black once again reared menacingly above Dickens's head. "Why do you plague me, damn you?"

Dickens stared up at him, waiting.

Thompson lay groaning on the ground.

Field, Rogers, and I strained to hear their angry exchange.

Again, the moment seemed to stop and the actors became tableau.

Palmer scowled down from under his black brow. The black horse, its nostrils flared, pawed hard at the grass. Dickens stared up at the man on the horse as if resigned to whatever fate that heedless horseman held in store for him.

Suddenly, with a harsh growl, "aarghht," half-curse, half-bark, Palmer wheeled his horse once again and rode off breakneck down the heath.

Thompson was hurt and confused. I remember jumping down from Rob's cab and running to Thompson's side where he sat holding his shoulder, unable to rise. We found out later that his collarbone was broken on the right side.

"I mus' be gettin' soft," Thompson said, pain in his face, as I came up to him. "Can't take a bloody fall off a 'orse no more."

"You didn't fall off." It was no time to debate him on details, but I did nonetheless. "His horse ran you down."

" 'At's good then." Thompson flashed his maddening grin and fainted dead away.

"Wot did 'ee sigh? Wot'd 'ee sigh?" Field ran up shouting. For the life of me, I do not know if he was asking me what Thompson had said or the swooning Thompson what Palmer had said when accused of the murders. I think Field was desperate, for he had not envisioned his little horserace scenario getting so out of hand.

Where is Charles? I thought. *Why did he not rush to Thompson's aid and arrive here before me?* I swivelled my head to find him and, to my astonishment, caught a glimpse of his grey coat flapping over those long legs as he ran up the rut away from us.

Thompson's bay horse was drinking calmly from a small ditch up the path and Dickens was dashing straight for it. Charles certainly was athletic and always kept himself quite trim, but, at that time in our acquaintance, I had no evidence whatsoever that he had ever sat upon a horse in his life. Therefore, I was utterly astonished to see him pull himself onto Thompson's mount and ride off toward the Druid's Oak in pursuit of Palmer.*

*According to Peter Aycroyd in his biography *Dickens* (1991), Charles Dickens early in his career (1839) would do "his writing in the mornings, his riding in the afternoons, alone or with Forster" (p. 270). Thus, he was no stranger to horseback.

247

"Hi didna know hee could ride," Rogers verbalised what we all were thinking as we stared off in astonishment after Dickens. On horseback, in pursuit, "the Inimitable" was galloping off into the highroad toward London.

AFTER THE FOX

February 4, 1852—afternoon

Dickens, by some miracle managing to stay aboard Thompson's horse at a full gallop, disappeared over the crest of Downshire Hill. With the same tenacity he tapped when writing his three-decker novels, he had ridden off unhesitating in pursuit of a conclusion.

It took long moments for our ragged company on the heath to gather its collective wits. Perhaps none of us possessed the inventiveness and imaginative drive that had mounted Dickens on that horse and so precipitously sent him off in search of his ending. Irish Meg rushed up and was designated nurse to Tally Ho Thompson by Field's sharp order. Sleepy Rob and his cab were left at Meggy's disposal for the transport of our injured friend to hospital. Indeed, Meg laughed later about Thompson's insistence that they stop for a drink at the Spaniard's Inn before proceeding into Hampstead proper to find a bone-setter. (Meg speculated, just between us, that Thompson's bravado was but a ploy to gain sympathy and attendant mothering from Scarlet Bess, who was quartered there.) Our fallen comrade attended to, Field and I clambered into the black police post chaise and, with Rogers flogging the horse from the box, we set off in pursuit of Palmer and that miraculous neophyte equestrian, Dickens.

Because of the large wheels on our coach, we were forced to stick to the road, such as it was, with its deep wagon ruts and muddy holes. We were forced to take the long way round the Druid's Oak in order to enter the highroad at the base of Downshire Hill. Because Dickens and his quarry were well out of sight by the time we joined the chase in earnest, what follows is not a firsthand account of events, as the bulk of this memoir has been. What follows is Dickens's account, much of it in his own words (always more elegant than my own) narrated afterward in the Lord Gordon Arms, of his single-minded pursuit of our flushed poisoner.

"I rather enjoyed the horse-riding," Dickens laughed with Thompson then. "Took to it rather well, I think."

"Sirtennly quick, I'd sigh," Thompson joked. "Satan's suspenders! Yew jus' climbed on an' rode off like some buckskin postman in the American Wild West."*

"I had no idea at the time why he rode off like that," Dickens admitted, "but he seemed worth pursuing, for whatever reason."

At that, Inspector Field gave Dickens one of his rare smiles. "I've always said yer instincts as a detective wos sharp"—he raised his crook'd forefinger to the side of his eye—"but yew were as mad as 'im ta ride off like 'at on a strange 'orse."

"For what good it did"—Dickens shrugged—"you are certainly right."

As Dickens told it, he had all he could do to keep Palmer in sight and hold on to Thompson's horse. The chase thundered down the highroad to Highgate Hill, then up and over into Kentish Town.

*Thompson's reference is to the Pony Express riders of the American frontier who, by 1852, had been widely celebrated in the penny dreadful press.

"It was there, on Highgate Hill, that I began to gain on him," Dickens took up the story. "His black horse, carrying at least a stone more than mine, began to tire, I think. The persons in the carriages we passed on the highroad must have thought us two wild Indians. Two well-dressed gentlemen chasing after each other on lathered horses."

"As we crested Highgate Hill, Palmer realised it was I and that I was after him. I think it angered him all the more. Or perhaps his horse badly needed a blow. I know not why he stopped, but in the center of the hovels of Kentish Town he reined in. He turned his horse to face me head-on as I galloped up. As for me, I was struggling to keep my seat on Thompson's bounding devil.

"He was standing in the stirrups astride the highroad glaring murderously with his whiphand ready to strike when I rode up. But I was not able to stop the horse. I rode right by him and he watched me go with a look of astonishment upon his face. I must confess, it took twenty more strides before I got the animal under control."

At this point in Dickens's tavern narrative, the whole company, led by Tally Ho Thompson, burst out in uncontrollable laughter.

" 'Damn you, you bloody fool!' Palmer screamed as my horse bolted and jumped backward and forth as I tried to control it with the reins."

" 'Ee is a puller," Thompson lent factual support to Dickens's narrative.

"At that," Dickens went on, "Palmer spurred his horse straight toward me and, screaming *'Why do you plague me, you bleeding sod? You cannot even ride that horse!'* or something like, took a murderous swipe at me with his whip.

"I felt as if I had been cast unarmed into the midst of some latter-day medieval joust. I was utterly helpless before his rush. Thank God for the bay! Your horse is, I think, more intelligent than you and I together Thompson."

That aside occasioned another volley of laughter from the assembled company as Dickens warmed to the absurdities of

251

his story. I marvelled at how, in his inimitable style, he had transformed this life-threatening encounter into a comical narrative.

"As he bore down upon me, to strike me from the saddle, your horse, at precisely the right moment, shied away, almost tossing me into the roadway, but saving me from the blow of the upraised whip."

Dickens took a needed draught from his pint, the showman, I am sure, building the suspense of his narrative, as we all waited eagerly for him to continue.

"Even as he overshot me and misfired with that slash of his whip, the devil was pulling hard on his reins. He wheeled the black around and I was sure he was preparing for yet another charge. He glared and cursed, but suddenly he seemed to alter his murderous intention. His horse was pawing the dirt some five or ten strides from a narrow indentation in the ground, which cut across the roadway like the bed of a shallow stream. Palmer was looking to his left in the direction of a growing sound, a low growl or whine like that of some mammoth beast charging down upon us. The earth began to tremble. The poor patchwork hovels began to rattle on both sides. Palmer shot one last hateful look at me, wheeled his horse away, and put the spurs to the black beast."

Dickens's comical style had given way to the virtuosity of his representation of pure horror. The whole company hung upon his every word and gesture. It was the murder of Nancy, the wild and twisted death of Quilp, bearing down upon us like a juggernaut.

"The ground shuddered and bucked. A huge fiery devil, spewing forth smoke and fire, spitting hot cinders in its wake like poison darts, bore down upon us.

"He spurred his horse and rode straight into its growing roar. A rush of fiery air blew off the rushing dragon's smoking flanks. At the edge of its narrow sunken path, Palmer dug in his knees and spurred the black into a desperate jump over that narrow iron road. And then he and the great black horse

252

were gone. That iron monster rushed by burying all existence in its sound and fury."

Dickens had us all, he knew. With a maddening pursing of his lips, he fell silent. He reached for his pint, took a slow sip, then glanced 'round mischievously at the whole company, as if to say, *My little story has captured your attention, has it?*

"It was the morning mail to Scotland," Dickens, after working us all up into this horrific suspense, spoke as calmly as a midwife. "He jumped the track and got away. At first, I thought he had ridden the horse right into the path of the onrushing train, but when it had passed by, horse and rider were nowhere to be found. As for me, I was flat on my back in the mud of the road with hot cinders raining down upon me. Your bay may be sharp, Thompson, but the steam engine's rush and roar were too much for him. He tossed me like a skimmity witch.*

When we—Rogers, Field, and I—in the police carriage came upon Dickens, he was sitting dazed in the mud of the rail crossing with the haughty bay calmly grazing at his side and the urchins of the Kentish Town hovels timidly venturing out to peruse the oddity of this long-legged, unhorsed, quixotic gentleman brought to ground in their midst.

---

*In the eighteenth and early nineteenth centuries when the inhabitants of an English village wished to humiliate one of its women caught in adultery they would organize a "skimmity ride" in which a rag effigy of the offender would be tossed on a blanket while being paraded down the village streets.

THE MURDER HOUSE

February 4, 1852—evening

"Where 'as 'ee gone?" Inspector Field was, once again, communing with himself. "Why is 'ee runnin' away?" Though Dickens, Irish Meg, and I were there, Field gave no indication that the questions were addressed to us.

With Serjeant Rogers on the box, we were all in the black Bow Street post chaise proceeding down the Hampstead highroad toward London. After helping Dickens up out of the mud where Thompson's red horse had unceremoniously deposited him, and after dusting him off and otherwise restoring him with some brandy that Field kept handy in the police coach for just such emergencies, we felt obliged to return the bay to its owner at the Spaniard's Inn and to ascertain the extent of that worthy's injuries.

Among assorted bruises and whip welts, Tally Ho Thompson had sustained a broken collarbone, which a country sawbones had so securely trussed up that Thompson could barely raise his right arm. Due to this unfortunate incapacitation,

255

Scarlet Bess seemed compelled to wait hand and foot upon her highwayman beau. One might have supposed that Thompson might grow grim from the pain of his broken bone, or frustrated from the failure of his ploy to draw out Palmer's guilt, or embarrassed at having been unhorsed, but it was quite the opposite. When we peeked in upon his convalescence in an upstairs bedroom, he greeted us with a wink and, feigning great pain, implored Bess to provide us all with a tumbler of hot gin. She dutifully sprang to Thompson's request as that worthy favored us with yet another wry wink. Having thus ascertained that Thompson was in good hands and having warmed his heart and our own with that aforementioned tippler of hot gin, the rest of us set off for London.

It was nearly five of the clock, and, spread out before us, a cold white winter sun was readying itself to set over the dome of St. Paul's as we crested Holborn Hill and rolled down into the smoke of the city. Much to our perplexed amusement, Inspector Field was still muttering to himself. Bent forward on the edge of the black leather carriage bench, his forearms on his knees and his forefingers to his temples in a pose of intense concentration worthy of a sculptor's art, his eyes boring holes in the horse-blanketed floor, our detective genius was, in unintelligible whispers, still puzzling out his next move.

" 'At's *it!*" he suddenly exclaimed, tapping his forefinger hard upon the leather of the seat between Dickens and himself. Meggy and I, occupying the opposite bench facing him, jumped at his sudden animation.

"What is 'it'?" Dickens maintained enough composure in the face of Field's violent declaration to pose the obvious question.

" 'At is why 'ee ran." Field's head came up, his eyes wild with the possibility. "There is still somethin' left, some last loose end 'ee 'asn't tied up."

"What?" Dickens pressed.

"I don't know. Somethin' incriminatin'. Letters? A diary?

256

The poison, per'aps! It could be anythin', but wotever 'tis, 'ee knows it could 'ang 'im."

"His house," we could barely hear Dickens say it. "The murder house in Cadogan Place," he said it softly, speculating even as he spoke, like Field before, speaking more to himself than to his auditors. "You remember what Thompson said? 'There is a secret in that house that we haven't found yet.' All along what Thompson said has been sitting in my mind waiting to be remembered. Palmer's house, that is where I would look."

Field levelled his gaze upon Dickens for a long moment. It was a taking-your-measure look, a just-how-serious-you-truly-are look. Field must have found what he was looking for in Dickens's open gaze, for he again tapped his decisive forefinger on the stiff leather seat and, shouting up to Serjeant Rogers on the box, ordered: "To the murder 'ouse, Rogers. At a fast trot now."

Serjeant Rogers drew us up, turned us around, and with a shout down of "Done, sir!" sent us hurtling off through the gathering dusk toward Knightsbridge.

The house was dark when we pulled quietly up on the narrow green in front.

"He is in there," Dickens whispered, purely upon instinct (but Field had always averred that Dickens had excellent and uncanny instincts). Creeping around the house in Inspector Field's wake, the five of us strung out in a line like an exploring expedition into the dark continent. We found Palmer's black horse eating oats in a small stable in the mews to the rear.

" 'Ee 'as been 'ere an' gone or 'ee is still in 'ere." Field clapped Dickens upon the back in reverence to both of their "instincts."

"Too bad Thompson is not here," Dickens whispered. "He would have us in this house in a breath."

Inspector Field looked at Dickens as if insulted. "No need for Thompson," Field growled. "I've kept the key we took off 'im the night o' the murders."

257

He ordered Rogers to stay with Meggy by the black horse. Rogers drew in a quick breath and we could see his disappointment. "Remember the Ashbee affair," Field cautioned him. "Don't come rushin' ta our rescue no matter wot yew 'ear. Yer job is ta cut off 'is escape if 'ee gits by us." Then Field grinned: "Chance ta use yer fishnet agin, this is."

Rogers, of course, acquiesced to his superior's plan and Irish Meg offered not a word of protest about being left behind. To be honest, I think she thought we were all deranged at best.

When you are breaking into a house where a murderer may be waiting, you long to be as invisible and as silent as a curious ghost. Field let us in with the key at the garden door. The high house was utterly dark and we stood still inside the door for long moments, in the kitchen, listening.

Nothing. Not a sound. Not the creak of a floorboard or the tick of a clock. Not a man crying or the scuttle of a rat. Only a trace of a sharp acrid smell in the air as if that weak scent were something—a gas? a fire's fume?—seeping up out of a grave or a cellar.

"Smell 'at?" Field whispered. " 'Ee's 'ere an' 'ee's burnin' summan."

Neither Dickens nor I answered. I was fighting to accustom my eyes to the utter darkness of the house. Since its mistress's murder, it had been closed up, the windows shuttered, the furniture sheeted, the gas cocks all closed off. We listened another long moment. Field was getting his bearings, plotting his course. That smell had a chemical tint to it, the smell of the jugs in an undertaker's embalming room.

When you are an amateur housebreaker standing in the dark of a strange kitchen of a house where murders have been done, a pressure starts to build within your chest, a heat begins to gather behind your eyes, a fear begins to dash frantically about in your mind. It is the feeling of a man lost in a labyrinth, his air giving out, the darkness impenetrable, and the sense that other animals are prowling those same confused corridors. With every sound, every smell, every

258

breath of musty air, my chest was tightening, my fearful imagination starting to pulse. Needless to say, I was most uncomfortable waiting there in the dark of our good doctor's kitchen. I had no sense whatsoever of where this whole heedless adventure was going. It all seemed like a novel willfully resisting resolution, refusing to offer that orderly ending of the sort for which Dickens was so famous. When Field lit his ever-present bull's-eye, the sudden light in that black pit of threat startled me almost out of my wits.

"Step lightly," Field whispered as he moved across the kitchen. We followed like the other two blind mice in the tow of their leader with his cane. Field's cane of light, moving first from side to side on the floors and then up the walls and 'round the furniture arrangements of the rooms, led us slowly through doorways, down corridors, up stairways and into each room on the three ascending storeys of that narrow house. All was quiet, empty. Undisturbed dust had collected on the window sills and any other unsheeted surface.

As we moved through that murder house, that smell—or combination of smells, rather—became more prominent. No one seemed to be there, yet that sweet, acrid, burning musk was rising through that house as if someone, only moments before, had released it from its jar or set it afire in its iron barrel.

" 'Ee's 'ere," Field repeated himself. "Yew kin smell 'im."

I almost laughed aloud at Field's way of putting it. It was a strange chemical smell that we had encountered in that dark, but it couldn't be Palmer we were smelling. Or could it? There had been strange tales from America of the spontaneous combustion of human beings in *The Times* of late. Or perhaps he had doused himself with some chemical and set himself afire in some secret subterranean area of that house. Evidently we were all thinking the same things as we descended the stairway, and blindly followed the tapping beam of Field's bull's-eye back into the kitchen where our crack of Palmer's house had commenced.

259

"There must be a secret cellar," Dickens voiced our shared suspicion.

" 'Ee's down there doin' sumpin'." Field was grim, losing his patience, cultivating his mood for breaking down doors or striking out with his murderous knobbed stick. "We must git ta 'im. 'Is own evil is all we've got left."

"A stairway down, it must be here someplace." Dickens seemed the only one capable of retaining his composure. Field was so angry and frustrated that I would not have been alarmed to see smoke coming out of his ears. I was as terrified as a schoolboy in the dark. Dickens, however, was already searching the kitchen for a hidden stair or a trapdoor. "Field, I need that light"—he shook the Inspector out of his steaming reverie, and we joined him in his search for Palmer's secret stairway.

If he is down there, somewhere, beneath this house, I thought, the pressure beginning to pulse once again through all of my terrified person, *surely, by now, he knows we are here, has heard us whispering or marked our footfalls, and is lying in wait for us to descend into his trap.*

There was no secret stairwell in the kitchen or the front parlour. At the end of a short corridor was a rather spacious room, which served, it seemed, as a combination library, for its walls were lined with glass-fronted cabinets filled with books, and as a music room, for its center was dominated by a small, upright spinet. Ironically, upon the piano sat a hand-painted miniature of Doctor William Palmer and his young wife, she now almost two fortnights dead. Under the small Persian rug upon which the spinet bench sat, we found the trapdoor. It pulled up to reveal a narrow stairway down into the depths beneath the house.

There was a weak, flickering light, as might be given off from a small lantern or from a fire dying in a hearth. That weak light was dancing seductively in that cellar at the bottom of that concealed stair. Our three heads hung over that hole in the floor, staring down both fearful and curious. At length, however, the increased intensity of that sweet, acrid smell drove us back. My eyes were actually smarting from the burn of it.

"Now I kin place it," Field whispered, "the smell. It's opium, but somethin' else as well."

"Is he down there, do you think?" Dickens had become a damnable genius for verbalising that which was plaguing my mind.

"Only one way ta find out." Field resigned us to our fate as, with his heavy knobbed stick in one hand and his bull's-eye in the other, he stepped through that trapdoor onto those stairs and led us down into that flickering dark.

The cellar was divided into two low rooms, each equally perverse in its own way. The smaller of the two rooms, into which the narrow wooden stairway delivered us, was some sort of obscene museum or torture chamber or stage for flagellant scenarios. Gathered in a tight knot at the foot of the stair, we gaped as Field shined his bull's-eye over the dirt and stone walls of this dungeon. On those walls were hung all manner of primitive weapons—South American blowpipes and hatchets, African spears, arrows, and slings—and medieval implements of torture—whips, chains, leather masks, gloves, iron manacles—and grotesque instruments for sexual perversion—huge indiarubber dildos, benches for sexual bondage. As the light crept over this eccentric collection, we catalogued it in stunned disbelief. That first room was a combination primitive armory, medieval torture chamber, and perverse sexual theatre of the sort that Lord Henry Ashbee and his colleagues of the Dionysian Circle might employ.*

As Field's timid light passed over those obscene walls, other senses awakened to the death lurking in that cellar. The heavy damp mustiness of the air diluted that sweet, acrid opium smell. The silver webs of spiders heavy with mummified sacks of death were strung up in corners, while torn cobwebs hung

---

*In Collins' first secret journal, the Dionysian Circle was a defloration society of rich and noble rakes who kidnapped and menaced Dickens' fifteen-year-old actress-lover, Ellen Ternan.

from the ceiling rafters to brush across our faces and stick in our hair as we traversed the room.

The faint flickering light was coming from the far room through a low doorway upon which no door was hung. Even before we stooped through that low hole in the dividing wall we could see that the second room was a scientist's laboratory. All the accoutrements—bottles of vile-looking liquids, edifices of glass tubing, dishes, jars, containers of odd shapes and sizes—of the experimenter in chemical concoctions were collected on two narrow tables lining the two walls visible through that low doorway. This laboratory room was also hung heavy in smoke, which gave the low light a deceptive golden hue, a romantic mellowness that belied the perverse squalor of those two cellar rooms.

We passed through the low entranceway, and then all three of us stopped short in shock.

I remember it as clearly as if it were only yesterday. My eyes ricocheted between two stunning features of that dim underground den. On the far wall of that cellar, on the rough mantle of the hearth in which a fire was guttering out, stood a large ornamental clock with its hands stopped straight up at midnight. Below and to the left of that stopped clock, the wide-open yet empty eyes of Doctor William Palmer stared up at us.

It was a room in which everything seemed to have stopped, like the lives of those two murdered women with their faces frozen in a scream. At first, I (and the others, I am sure) thought that Palmer was dead. He was not moving. His eyes were open and vacant and staring. But it was only the opium. He was lying propped up on a pallet on the floor, one opium pipe cradled in the crook of his arm as tenderly as a babe, two others discarded on the ground next to his place of rest. Sitting as still as a buddha with his eyes wide and empty staring up and his skin as yellow as parchment in the waning firelight, he looked as if he were a character in a tableau in a wax museum. But he was not dead. When we entered through that low doorway, the movement caught his eye and he turned his head ever so slowly toward us. His mouth twisted slower still into a jagged smirk of glazed satisfaction. His eyes looked straight at us, then through us, as if he took us for something quite else, devils perhaps, stumbling out of some dark cavern to carry him off, or Sodomite revelers, descended into these secret rooms to join him in his pipes and in some unspeakable orgy of the flesh. He looked straight at us, but what he saw in his opium dream would only be the wildest speculation upon my part.

He began to laugh grotesquely, then abruptly stopped. He drew deeply upon his opium pipe, but it was empty, burned away. All he puffed was insubstantial air. It troubled him, and he sighed pitifully.

Field moved hungrily to an open drain in the middle of that laboratory room's wooden floor. We followed. Water, an open sewer, could be heard moving sluggishly beneath that hole in the floor. Field went down upon one knee at the vent hole. He extracted a long shard of glass, as from a chemist's jar, from a gap in the floorboard where the vent hole cut through.

" 'Ee 'as thrown sumpin' out, broken a jar into this 'ole, I'll wager." Field carefully placed that shard of glass into a paper envelope and deposited it in one of the inner pockets of his greatcoat.

When we turned back to Palmer, he was staring up at us with a stupefied grin upon his drugged face.

Field stood over him. For a brief moment, as the doctor looked up at him with that death's-head grin and Field glared down at him in anger and frustration, I felt that we might have to restrain our policeman friend from beating this drug-glazed object of his professional hate to death with the knob of his murderous stick.

But Field did not raise his stick to Palmer. He began to speak to him in a harsh, quiet, barely controlled voice.

"Yew killed 'em all, didn't yew . . . ?"

"Yew murdered yer wife for the money an' the others ta cover up the deed . . ."

That glossy-eyed cadaver stared up at Inspector Field in wonderment.

"Yew poisoned those two young women, din't yew . . . ?"

Suddenly Palmer blinked. He shook his head as if trying to right himself, to snatch his muddled brain back from the grasp of the opium.

"Yew killed yer own wife. . . ." There was a cold anger in Field's voice as he confronted this suddenly shaking object of his disgust.*

Palmer was struggling to his feet, but he only made it to his knees. With both hands he reached up to Field, imploring, bereft, begging for something, yet still not able to speak, still a captive of the opium. For a long moment, his hands outstretched in a gesture of supplication, he held Field's eye.

Abruptly, with a snap forward and back of his head upon his neck, Palmer seemed to right himself, reenter the reality of that cellar beneath his house, his private laboratory and opium den.

"I loved her, you fool!" he growled at Field like a vicious cornered animal as he struggled to his feet. "I loved her"—he shook his head sadly, as if he were going to cry—"and she slept with other men . . . that Thompson fellow, my Rodrigo. He killed her, you fool. Rodrigo killed her because she still loved me. Rodrigo killed her . . . Rodrigo . . . Rodrigo . . ." and his voice trailed off as he slowly sank back down upon his pallet and floated back off into his opium dream.

His head lolled, but his eyes popped back open and that sly, demented grin crept back across his face. He began to croon in a strange sort of Oriental singsong. He strung together mad phrases which seemed to be some sort of disconnected explanation and apologia for not being a better host:

*In Collins' first memoir, in a private moment, Irish Meg confessed to Wilkie that Inspector Field's wife had died of consumption in 1849, only one year before the events of that memoir, and that Field had, a number of times, hired her for sexual solace.

264

I must flee to my pipes, you see, you see?
Flee, you see. Pipes, you see.
When the rage must bite and the world must fight,
When the horses race, when I hate my face,
The pipes stop time and set me free,
You see?
I flee.
We all flee, you see?
You, me, she.
To our pipes, you see.

Then he stopped his mad song and for one terrible moment he became once again lucid. He stared straight up at Field and, in a voice of pure hate, level and vicious, stated the one truth that Field did not wish to face: "You plague me with her death, but no one will ever believe you."

It was a bravura performance, one of the most innovative and eccentric bereaved husband acts ever gotten up. It was worthy of the stage at Covent Garden or any other theatre in the West End. He protested his innocence with a mad, disconnected intensity. He had clearly smoked those three pipes of opium. Its seductive musk still hung in the air. Yet, his characterisation of a man in mourning for his murdered love was disciplined, unfaltering, confident, and flawless, worthy of a Garrick or a Macready. We all bore witness to his performance, an audience of three in his cellar theatre, but none of us believed it.

"Yew killed 'em all!" Field repeated in that tight voice of controlled hate.

But Palmer just stared up at him with that mad, cadaverous, blank-eyed stare. No, none of us believed Palmer's act, his protestations of innocence, but there simply was nothing we could do. There were no clues or proofs left for us to find, no new paths toward understanding for us to take. Yet, in concert with Inspector Field, we all knew that Palmer had killed them all. That murky firelit cellar room went silent as Field glared down at Palmer in professional hate and Palmer replied with the empty smirk of the village idiot.

265

With a sudden violent pivot on the toes of his boots, Inspector Field, without so much as a look back at that drugged lump on the floor, stalked out. Dickens followed, imploring in desperation, "Surely there is something more we can do." But this was not one of his novels. He could not invent the evidence against Palmer out of the fertile play of his imagination. He could not create fresh characters to testify against Palmer, or bring already dead characters back to accuse him. Fact had proven itself much less manageable than fiction.

As they left that laboratory room debating, I straggled after them. As Dickens and Field began to mount the narrow steps up out of that dungeon of bizarre weapons and dildos, I reached the empty doorway that separated the two cellar rooms and paused for a quick, last glance back at Doctor Palmer. Slumped on his pallet on the floor, ringed by his empty opium pipes, his eyes came up and, for a brief moment, met mine.

He winked.

Whether in madness or in mockery, I do not know, but he winked. It was certainly nothing that could be used at the Queen's Bench. I did not even know how to interpret its meaning (if, indeed, it had any meaning). Why then did my mere reception of that wink make me feel like a co-conspirator, as if I had poisoned those women myself, as if I had turned so many lives to stone?

We left Palmer there, chanting his opium songs, floating in his grand illusions, twirling out his great expectations.

"BLEEK 'OUSE INDEED!"

March 15, 1852—early evening

Bitter March evening. Wind cutting like a saber off the Thames. No sun seen for at least a week past. Implacable damp. Mildew creeping out of every mews, staining every cobblestone on every street in that pestilent city.

Fog smothering all and every. Fog rolling off the river in a smoky flood. Fog obscuring everything farther than ten meters from any ill-advised traveller's frost-pinched nose. Streetlamps adorned with misty haloes; their weak gaslight filtered through a coarse, yellow-grey, smoke-streaked blanket of fog.

An evening as cruel and discouraging as this must, naturally, be the one upon which Dickens would insist that I dine in with him and then walk out into that slashing wind and stifling fog. It was an established ritual with Dickens. Upon the evening, no matter what the weather, that the first little green numbers of his newest novel hit the streets, Dickens had to walk out (this time with me in tow) to spy upon his sales. We had grown comfortable in the role of spies, and this was a somewhat easier assignment than those which in the near past Inspector Field had bestowed upon us. We were spying upon a small street kiosk of the circular yellow sort out of which a large potbellied seller of ballads and broadsheets with a voice that could lead lost ships to port was hawking the first number of *Bleak House* to the surprisingly steady flow of customers who had braced the wicked elements of the evening to satisfy their hunger for the newest Dickens offering. Indeed, the little green numbers were leaving that street stand faster than lawyers abandoning destitute clients. Business, in other words, was quite as brisk as the evening weather. Dickens was exhilarated. I think that Charles constantly needed the reconfirmation that his audience still loved and needed, not so much him, but the stories of his imagination. He loved to watch the ordinary people, his people, the ones he really lived his life for, flock to buy his words, affirm his view of their world. "It has always seemed miraculous to me, Wilkie," he once confided, "that I write a chapter one day and it appears in print the next, or we meet a chap in the street of an evening and he is a full-blown character in one of my novels a fortnight later."

We were standing in the shadow of a wall of a formidable stone building, a bank, I believe, in the Strand with the fog swirling around us when Field suddenly materialised, like some menacing truth, out of the vapour. More than a month had passed since that frustrating day and night in pursuit of Doctor William Palmer's secret life. For Dickens and I, that had been the closing of the case which I had so whimsically, at its very inception, dubbed the Medusa Murders. For Inspector Field, however, as we would certainly learn in the course of our twenty-year association with that gentleman, no case was ever closed until he, and he alone, was satisfied that justice had been done. That, unarguably, was certainly *not* the reality of this case of the Medusa Murders. Oh, there had been an inquest, an investigation, even a court hearing upon the case to see if it should actually go to the dock. That hearing had taken place this very day.

As we loitered there watching those little green leaflets of

Dickens's words being plucked from that commercial tree and carried off into the fog, Field cut his way out of that stifling grey blanket with befitting sharpness.

"Aha! A private surveillance, eh?" Field greeted us with a deep bellow. "Workin' a case without yer detective colleague, are yew?" he joked. "Yer man Wills told me yew might be 'ere," he explained, coming to a halt before us.

"Not at all." Dickens laughed and shook Field's hand heartily, happy to see him. "Just checking sales, that is all."

"Sales o' wot?" In the excitement of real murders and living characters by the coach-load, it had evidently slipped the detective's mind that his colleague, Charles Dickens, still occasionally indulged himself in fictions and associations with the characters of his imagination.

"The first number of *Bleak House,* my new novel." Dickens beamed. Little stirred him more than turning one of his offspring loose upon the London streets.

"Wot manner o' title is *Bleek 'Ouse?*" Field followed the pointing of Dickens's finger to the busy broadsheet kiosk. "Sounds a bit grim for an entertainment, yew asks me."

"But no one asked you, my friend," Dickens jibed right back.

"Well, they ought ta 'ave. *Bleek 'Ouse* indeed! Sounds like some Rats' Castle claptrap, or a prison story, or a depressin' mad'ouse tale."

"In a way"—Dickens smiled—"it is all of those, except all of England is the Rats' Castle, the prison, the madhouse."

"But what sends you out looking for us on a horrible night like this?" I interrupted their literary conversation, for my teeth were chattering like castinets.

"We lost Palmer at hearin' today." Field's mood went from joking to somber in the flick of a racehorse's tail. " 'Ee got Jaggers o' the Temple ta speak for 'im. Niver even 'ad a show 'is face at Queen's Bench. Now thet 'ee's gathered 'is lawyers 'round, we're sunk."

"That is absurd!" Dickens bristled. "The man is a murderer."

269

"Not in the eyes o' the magistrates." Field seemed resigned to this defeat. "Jaggers 'ung it all on the Spaniard."

"Rodrigo!" That was but my own tiny squeak of surprise.

"None other." Field nodded.

"For God's sake!" Dickens took up my indignation. "Rodrigo may have had nothing to do with it at all. Palmer could have imitated his voice, hung him, and faked the suicide. Lured him in and trapped him the way he did Thompson."

"Palmer's a slippery 'un 'ee is, but ta the judges all o' thet is jus' fiction." Field shrugged.

"Just fiction!" Now Dickens was thoroughly indignant.

"Our only 'ope"—Field was calm, preternaturally composed, considering the magnitude of the defeat he had suffered this day—"wos ta so anger an' bestir Palmer as ta make 'im give hisself away, drop some incriminations our way, or confess, or summat, then yew two could 'ave testerfied. It would o' made all our other little bits o' evidence stand up." Field paused. His crook'd forefinger scratched regretfully at the side of his right eye. "But 'ee would not do it."

"What about Tally Ho Thompson?" I persisted in overlooking the obvious and posing the transparently naive question.

"Wot about 'im?" Field gave a weary little grin. "Lawyer Jaggers o' the Temple 'ud grind 'im up an' bake 'im in a pie."

"What?" I said, aghast.

"How?" Dickens was exasperated.

"Yer an ex-'eyewayman, a thief. Yew were robbin' Doctor Palmer's 'ouse when the bodies were found. Yew 'ad a'ready drawn a sword against Dick Dunn afore 'ee wos murdered. Yew'd slept with Palmer's wife afore 'er death. 'Oo's goin' ta tyke the word o' the likes o' yew. 'At's wot Jaggers 'ud sigh o' Thompson. Thompson 'ud be lucky the judges didn't take 'im up for the murders on the spot 'isself."

"It does seem better to leave Thompson well out of this," Dickens acquiesced. "But is there nothing to be done? There is evidence to present, is there not?"

"The piece o' glass from the sewer in 'is basement floor

didn't tell us wot 'ee threw out. The broken jar could o' 'eld curare poison or cheap gin. Mebbe 'ee didn't even pour anythin' down that 'ole in 'is floor thet night, but I'll wager 'ee did. I wager 'at's why 'ee ran back there like thet, ta destroy thet poison."

"His gambling debts? The insurance scheme?" Dickens was grasping at straws.

" 'Ee killed 'er." Field was quiet as he spoke, yet grim and determined. "I knows thet. Yew two knows thet. Look for the one 'oo profits from 'er death an' thet is yer murderer."

"But arguing that is not enough"—Dickens was struggling toward the state of resignation which Field seemed already to have reached—"is that it?"

"Jaggers argues thet Thompson kills 'er while robbin' the 'ouse, or thet Rodrigo kills 'er a'cause 'ee loves 'er 'usband. Witnesses confused. Judges confused. Too menny murderers. No one kin see for the confusion. Case is tossed in confusion. The Queen's Bench makes for a very confusin' place."

"England's bleakest house!" Dickens said it softly, almost a whisper, as if affirming its truth to himself, utterly unaware that we were still participating in this befogged street-corner conversation.

Field looked at me and I at him, both momentarily puzzled by Dickens's sudden departure into self-absorbtion.

Dickens recovered himself almost immediately. "This is not at all a satisfactory ending to your case, is it?" His voice was more consoling than inquiring as he addressed Inspector Field.

"Life's a mess an' don't end like novels do." Field shrugged once again.

There seemed little more for us to say to one another. We stood there against that blank stone wall as an awkward silence, like the fog, settled between us.

"The gentle art of poisoning is not hitherto a highly developed form of insurance fraud," Dickens groped for some words to cheer Field up, "but I will wager it shall be in the future."

Field's eyes shot up, stared levelly first into Dickens's eyes and then into mine. " 'Ee will try it agin'." Field tapped his stick decisively upon the bricks of the walkway. "Mayhaps some other poor girl will die. They acquires a taste for murder, they do. S'like an addiction. Palmer got away with murder, 'ee did, but 'ee will try it agin'," and a fierce determination edged Field's voice. "An' I'll be there when 'ee does."

With one final sharp tap of his stick to the stones, he stomped off into the fog.*

*As all readers of this second of Wilkie Collins' recently discovered commonplace books have no doubt noticed, there is a striking coincidence in that one of Inspector Field's prime suspects herein, Doctor William Palmer, and this editor's name, working 140 years later, are one and the same. Notwithstanding romantic arguments on the mysterious operations of that force known as destiny, the facts of history tend to override the whimsy of fate. I consulted the noted Scottish genealogist, Mr. Alistair McKenzie, Ph.D., who, he assured me, is himself a descendant of the legendary Alistair McKenzie noted as the principle inventor and practitioner of the great international game of golf. After some research, for which I am somewhat grateful, Mr. McKenzie assured me that my own family is descended from a clan of ancient horse thieves and footpads who specialized in preying upon pilgrims en route to Canterbury, while the notorious Dr. William Palmer of Collins' memoir is descended from the Staffordshire Palmers, a respectable farming family of that district. But the coincidences do not stop with those identical names. While editing this second commonplace book in the summer of 1991 at the University of North Anglia, I took a weekend holiday to London. Caught in a sudden downpour on a Sunday afternoon in Regents Park, I took refuge in Madame Tussaud's Waxworks right outside the York Gate on Marylebone Road. While browsing there waiting for the rain to stop, I wandered into the Gallery of Murderers where who should confront me, brandishing a dripping vial of poison in his right hand, but the one and the same Doctor William Palmer. The legend on the wall next to his wax effigy trumpeted that he was reputed to be England's most notorious poisoner, responsible for the deaths of six known victims over a period of seven years. Whether or not the Medusa Murders victims were included in this accounting was not stated. What caught my eye, however, was the history of his final murder for which he was brought to trial in 1855, convicted, and sent to the gallows on June 14, 1856. The arresting officer on the case was none other than Inspector William Field of the Metropolitan Protectives. My curiosity about Doctor William Palmer, my unwelcome and notorious namesake, whetted by that chance bit of research in Madame Tussaud's, I consulted more conventional research sources and found an article titled "The Decameron of Murderers" in Dickens's own news periodical *All The Year Round* on the very date of Palmer's hanging, June 14, 1856, which recounts the lengthy trial of Doctor Palmer. Though the article is unsigned, it could only have been written by either Dickens or Collins because it alludes to the mysterious deaths of Palmer's first wife and maid, which were not the crimes for which Palmer was tried and found guilty. Who knows? Perhaps Field, Dickens, and Collins pursued Palmer all those years until they finally brought him to justice. In fact, the testimony of Inspector Field at Palmer's trial as described in the *All The Year Round* article intimates that, in the four years following the events of this second Collins journal, Palmer became for William Field the identical sort of nemesis and obsession that another notorious doctor would become for another great English detective in the later years of the century. Perhaps one of Collins' later journals will recount further confrontations with Doctor Palmer, but that is the stuff of another case and would be getting too far ahead of ourselves and the editing of the remaining secret Victorian journals of Wilkie Collins that have thus far been discovered.

273